I0628339

The Flaxen Tyranny

Scan for your free audio book

Simon Evans

Published by
www.elitepublishingacademy.com

All rights reserved.

No part of this book may be reproduced in any form
by photocopying or any electronic or mechanical
means, including information storage or retrieval
systems, without permissions in writing from both
the copyright owner and the publisher of the book.

First Edition published 2023
© Simon Evans

Printed and bound in Great Britain by
www.elitepublishingacademy.com

A catalogue record for this book
is available from The British Library

ISBN Paperback - 978-1-915730-13-8
ISBN eBook - 978-1-915730-14-5

Table of Contents

Chapter 1 - Suffering

Serilda turned, unprepared for the fist that struck her face, sending her flying to the stony ground. The water from the buckets she had just filled splashing on her as her hands involuntarily released them from her grasp. Her shoulder, absorbing most of the impact screamed with pain.

The images that filled her mind of the impossible ship that travelled the stars immediately vanished as she looked up at the man that had assailed her, his dark grey uniform glistening in the winter sun.

He looked down at the girl he had assaulted, "You are a disgusting bitch, you walk around this camp as if you are better than the other Zoons. What do you think you're doing out of your hut at this hour?"

Serilda, shaking on the floor, attempted to meet the yellow eyes that pierced her, "We need water, Major, half of the people in my hut are dehydrated."

"Do you expect me to care about you or the other vermin that inhabit your hut. Or any other hut for that matter?"

Serilda's hands shook violently as she stayed on the ground, "No Major"

"Then why do stroll around this place as if it were your own palace? Do you think because you are a half breed bitch that I will treat you better? Perhaps you think because your father was Flaxen, you deserve better treatment?"

Before Serilda could respond, he kicked her in her torso, she coughed and gasped as the strike left her lungs absent of air.

She tried to control her breathing, each breath causing pain, as another man's voice could be heard from across the courtyard, "Major what's going here?"

Serilda watched as the Major turned. She knew the voice instantly. It usually grated through her body like a dull knife, but for the first time she was happy to hear it. It was the Colonel, head of Camp Skadi.

1

He looked at the major, his yellow eyes cold, his demeanor authoritative, "Why did you strike this girl?"

The Major bowed his head, a required display of subordination in the Flaxen military, "Colonel, I have seen too many displays of defiance from this half breed, we need to discipline the Zoons."

The Colonel looked down at his subordinate, although Major Damien Scenery was over seven feet tall, the Colonel was taller than even he, "And for what infraction was this discipline necessary?"

Serilda saw the Major trying to hide his look of disgust, "The sun is setting and yet she finds it acceptable to collect water. This is a clear breach of the rules imposed on these vermin, Colonel."

The colonel retained the contact of his yellow eyes with the major, who's eyes glared back with equal color. "I believe, since the mines are currently closed, the Zoons are free to roam within the permitter of the camp until the sun has set?"

Damien looked to the sky, "But it has nearly set, Colonel, there is perhaps ten minutes of day light left."

The Colonel's face remained expressionless, "But it has not yet, so the girl has breached no rules."

Serilda had been keeping her gaze fixated on the Major, she could see the disgust on his face. The Colonel had no longer being showing the proper discipline to the subhumans that infested Earth, and she knew the exact reason why, despite the Major clearly having no such knowledge. Even in her perilous situation, this amused her. She watched from the ground as the adversarial conversation continued.

"But Colonel, this bitch has been nothing but trouble. She needs to understand the consequences of defiance."

The Colonel pulled his pistol from his waist and aimed it directly at the Major's face, "This is beginning to sound like insubordination to me. You know as well as I do, I can pull this trigger. Anyone of the rank of Colonel or above can execute those of inferior rank summarily. The judgement of the crime is mine to determine. Is that what you wish, Major?"

The Major bowed his head again, "No Sir, I apologize if I have overstepped my authority."

The Colonel stared at him in the eyes for a few more seconds, "Then you are on latrine duty for the next week, am I understood?"

The Major briefly looked at girl he had assaulted, before returning his eyes to his superior, "Colonel Flint, this is an indignity that cannot be tolerated. Latrine duty is for the Zoons."

The Colonel pulled back the cock on his pistol, "And yet these are my orders. Obey me now or die."

Major Damien Scenery looked at his commanding officer, "Yes, Sir I understand."

"Good, then leave now before I change my mind."

The Major raised his fist into the air, "For Flaxus"

The Colonel mimicked his gesture, "For Falxus" he retained his gaze on the major for several seconds, "Now leave my sight. I suggest you start cleaning shit immediately, if you value your life."

The Major walked away saying nothing more.

Colonel Jaakobah Flint turned his gaze to the half-breed on the floor. He extended his hand to assist her. Serilda pretended not to notice his gesture and raised herself with both arms. Her shoulder hurt but she at least now knew it was no serious injury.

"My apologies, Serilda. I expect better of my men."

She hated it when this vile creature used her first name. It was given to her by her mother, a woman of such kindness and love, she cried for her memory each night. To hear it sullied by this towering monster before her caused such fury within her, she usually needed every fiber of her strength not to spit in his face. Although the salvation brought upon her from this man she despised, somewhat diminished her desire to do so.

She raised her head to meet his eyes, "No problem, Colonel. It was just a misunderstanding." She forced a smile and turned to walk away, leaving her bucket behind.

Jaakobah grabbed her by the wrist when she turned. He caressed her arm as he looked her in the eye once more, "I'll be seeing you tonight, of course. At the usual time?"

Her forced smile widened, "Of course, Colonel Flint."

He released her and she walked slowly back to her hut. Several hours later, she returned to the trough of stagnant water, her surreptitious reconnaissance having confirmed no yellow-skinned menaces lurked within its vicinity. She filled two buckets and hurried back to hut seven, a name she considered inadequate to describe the suffering within its thin metal walls.

As she entered, she placed one bucket next to group of prisoners in a stack of bunks near the door, two or three slept in each, although they were barely big enough to accommodate a woman of average stature. These people were the most infirm and riddled with disease. The other inhabitants had debated amongst each other and concluded they must be segregated, lest their disease infect them all. Not even Serilda objected to this, although she had inherited her mother's compassion and value for all life, she was also the product of her father and from him, she had been passed pragmatism and a strong desire to survive. She no longer noticed the stench that permeated the air like an invisible fog. When she first arrived, all those years ago, it would keep her awake at night. She had imagined that if it had a color, it would be a deep brown-green that infested all it touched. Harder to ignore, were the cries and moaning. They filled the air with a viscosity equal to the smell and equally perennial.

She hurried to her friend at the other side of the hut. Megan was purely human and Serilda envied her for this, the persecution she had endured from some of the inmates for her heritage paled in comparison to the chastisement she inflicted on herself each day. After all, half-Flaxen meant full Flaxen amongst some of the less enlightened within the place of suffering they all inhabited. She forced the retribution she had encountered from her mind as she attended to her friend.

She lifted her friends head onto her lap and forced her to drink three cups of water, it spilled down her chin as her head shook from the effort.

"Look what I have, Megan; it's dried meat. Beef, I think. I got it from the colonel last night. There's enough here for both of us."

Megan looked at the food, then once more at her friend's face, her eyes wide with shock. "Oh, Serilda, that bruise on your face! Was it that bastard again? When I'm better, I swear to God, I will kill him, and I will gladly burn in damnation for the pleasure."

"Don't worry about that, my love. You know how quickly I heal. Now, how about some of this beef?"

The half-Flaxen broke off a piece of the brown meat and put it to Megan's mouth. Her friend refused to eat. Her voice was soft and weak but it had a musical quality that Serilda had always loved. "I need to know; are we still safe? Will the red circles still not glow? Are they safe?" she gestured to the sickly prisoners at the other end of the hut.

Serilda couldn't contain her tears. Not only for the compassion displayed by her friend but for the need for her to have to say such a thing in the first place. She thought about the place called Hell that Megan often talked about. She wondered if its misery could compete with Camp Skadi. She wiped her eyes with the cloth that had wrapped their food. She had, for a moment, tuned out the crying and moaning of the people who endured eternal suffering around her.

"Yes, Megan, I promise. As long as I'm here, the circles won't glow. I have him under control. Now, eat. Please, will you eat?"

Megan smiled as her deep brown eyes shone brighter than before. Her soft, sweet voice filled the small hut like a harp, "You were sent by God, Serilda, and I will spend my days asking him why he sent you to me."

Serilda held Megan in her arms as she waited for her to sleep. Then she thought of the strange ship and the man that commanded it that seemed to travel the stars. These obscure images had infiltrated her dreams for over a week. She knew change was coming and the nature of that change eluded her, for it may not be the solace she hoped it would be. She had never believed, but for the first time, she prayed to Megan's god that it would reach them before the red circles did.

Chapter 2 – Copious Time

Captain Steve Thomas gazed upon the beams from the distant sun that glistened on his diamond window, as the voices of his two officers passed over him like they were no more than echoes from conversations long past. He worried his subordinates would see the sweat mount on his brow as he was unable to keep his attention on the room around him, his private office, adjacent the bridge of the United Earth Starship: *Formidable*.

All he could think about was the war, the carnage of the six long years, and most of all, the battle with Odin. The Martian Flagship had been of equal strength to Formidable, perhaps stronger. It was a memory whose qualities were of such vibrance they replayed in his mind with crystal clarity. Its sharpness seemed to surpass itself with each repetition. Only Steve's tactical brilliance and the years of experience his time in the fleet had afforded him had secured his victory. But mere triumph was insufficient. Every night, Steve heard the pleading of the Captain of Odin. She had begged Steve to spare her ship and the men and women that crewed it. She would gladly surrender herself and her vessel if only he would let them live. Not her, just her crew.

But United Earth's policy had not allowed such displays of mercy. Too many times, Martian ships had feigned surrender, only to turn their weapons upon the foolish ship that had retracted its armor to rescue the souls aboard. The previous policy of clemency to those who surrendered could no longer be maintained. Steve felt little emotion as he ordered for Odin to be obliterated under Formidable's might. The channel was still open, and many on the bridge heard the screams of Odin's crew as their weapons descended upon them. Odin was reduced to pieces of shrapnel that would circulate among the asteroids in the belt until the dying sun consumed them. It took time for Steve to feel anything; expressions of remorse for the enemy who had struck Earth first were not in vogue among his comrades.

But his emotions could not be contained indefinitely. They flowed from his body in the sweat that soaked his sheets each night as his dreams replayed without end. Now, it was time for hope again. He was no longer tethered to the wife that had left him after he woke her each night with his screams. So, he volunteered to embark on a journey the likes humanity had never known before. A voyage not of death but of life. One that would seed a new world with the beauty that defined Earth.

A beautiful holographic image was projecting from above the huge wooden desk of his oversized office.

Steve finally suppressed his relentless mental reenactments of the battle long past and focused on the image before him. "So, that's Copious."

Commander Philip Currie kept his gaze on the projection of the world. "I just still don't know who the hell came up with that name."

Steve slouched in his chair as he laughed, hoping his forced joviality would conceal his anxiety. "I'm sure a subcommittee of a subcommittee debated for many weeks."

"No doubt they came up with the name on day one. But where's the money in revealing it so quickly?" asked Chief Science Officer, James Kirfder.

The three men chuckled together. They all knew of the bureaucratic nature of United Earth's government, the society they were to leave forever.

"I just can't believe it's been five years since the war," said Philip.

"We've got Martians aboard both ships, even former Marines," Steve remarked.

"I know, I just still can't believe we were so lenient when we won. We had the red bastards blockaded. We could have taken whatever we wanted."

Steve appeared to consider this for a moment. "But then what? We take everything from them and then war breaks out again in five years? As much as it pains me to say, I think the Senate made the right call. There's plenty of material in the belt to last us both for eternity."

Philip nodded as he wiped a stray drip of coffee from his lip and placed his mug on the desk. "It just all seems so pointless now, all of those battles. So many lives lost over politics and rocks."

"We should have just granted them independence on day one. We lost so much, and so did they, to be honest," said James.

"The Senate deemed the self-declared Martian Confederacy to be an illegal secession from the Union. We're soldiers, we follow orders," Steve offered.

James shifted upwards in his chair at that. "I know that, and correction; we were soldiers. We're civilians now. But what was achieved? We fought for six years and when we won, we gave them nearly everything they wanted anyway."

"I don't want to talk about the war—that's the past. Let's talk about our future," said Steve, as he gestured to the image of the world on his desk. "James, have you decided what you'll do first when we wake up?"

"I'd like to test for microbial life. I can't see any other explanation for so much oxygen."

Steve grunted, "How much of that brown will turn green in our lifetime?"

"It will take years just to print the seeds of the plants and the embryos of the animals. We'll never live to see it transform to Earth but we'll be the pioneers, the ones who made it happen. That to me is far more exciting."

Steve smiled and nodded, he liked to hear this, it was reassuring. A mission outside of Earth's solar system had never been attempted before. "I'm just worried about this new Sphere Drive of ours. I wasn't until I met Avalon Brookes."

"Ahh, yes, that insufferable prick. I met him at the farewell ceremony; he really is an arrogant bastard," said James.

"I know, I had the pleasure of speaking to him myself. He was wasted. He wouldn't stop rattling on about his precious sphere drive and how he'd advanced humanity decades before our time," said Philip.

"Well, he's Eastcott's problem now. He's aboard Echo. Let's just say I pulled a few strings to make sure that was so," said Steve.

The men laughed again. Steve saw genuine relief in their eyes.

James broke their mirth, "How was Captain Eastcott? I mean, when the Senate gave you overall command of the mission? You're both Captains after all."

"James, we fought aside each other for six years. We were in the same battlegroup, he's like a brother to me. He let his feelings slip when we left the final bar on our last free night on Earth. But he's not a bitter man."

"I know, but he still must have been disappointed."

"I'm sure he was, Commander. I know I would have been if the decision had gone the other way."

Steve straightened his posture in his seat as he changed the subject. "So, now that we've cleared the Keiper Belt, we can engage the new engines at our leisure. It's taken us weeks to get here. The sphere drive could have done it in minutes."

Philip shook his head in mock disapproval, "I know you'd be willing to take that risk. The other two thousand people were not."

"What can I say? I'm keen to get underway, this is quite the journey we're making," Steve replied, as he leaned forward in his chair. "Okay, thank you, Commanders. We'll be going into stasis soon. You're both dismissed. It's time for me to speak with Captain Eastcott."

The two men acknowledged their orders and left the Captain's office through the doors that led directly to the bridge.

Steve looked up at the ceiling as he spoke. He knew this was a pointless gesture when speaking to the ship's AI. The artificial mind could hear him from anywhere aboard. It was a long-held tradition to address the fleet's AIs by the name of the vessel they controlled.

"Formidable, please open a channel to Echo. I need the Captain's private comms."

"Yes, Captain. I thought you'd never stop talking."

Steve laughed. He considered Formidable to be his friend near the equal of Eastcott. The voice he heard was the personality of his ship. He had helped keep him alive during the war with Mars. He pointed to the speaker from which the machine's voice emanated, "Just do it, my old friend. I haven't the time for your bullshit right now."

"Of course, Captain. I just don't see the need for such vulgarity."

"Formidable…"

"Okay, the channel is open."

The image of Copious disappeared as it was replaced by the face of a man. He was in a room identical to Steve's own office. He was smiling as Steve spoke.

"Is that a glass of whiskey I can see on your desk?"

"Excuse me if I need something to settle my nerves. I'm off duty."

"If you say so. You'd never catch me doing that."

"I have plenty of pics that disagree with you, Captain." His final word was dripping with sarcasm.

"Listen, Kip, we've cleared the belt. It's nearly time to go into stasis."

"I know where we are, I've been waiting for you to get off your ass and order it. God knows why they put you in charge of this mission."

"What can I say? The best man won. Sorry about that, old pal."

"More like the older man. So, are you issuing the order?"

"I am. You ready to fly?"

"Been ready for three years, old man. The plan is for you to engage the sphere drive first and we'll follow?"

"That's the idea. How long until you get everyone to sleep?"

"Echo tells me it will take a day, but give me some leeway. Most of them are civilians, you know how they are."

"Tell me about it. I still can't believe we're carrying a thousand each."

"We're ships of exploration now. Apparently, war is a thing of the past."

"It is for us at least. Listen, I need you to get everyone in stasis ASAP. I want to get to spherical speed in the next two days."

"Including me?"

"Yes, including you. I'll stay awake until both ships reach our designated cruising speed. I'll follow you after that."

"Don't stay up too long, you look old enough as it is."

"Just have Echo let me know when you're all in stasis. Then we'll see what these new engines of ours can do."

"Understood. See you in fifty years, old friend?"

"It will be like fifty seconds to us. We'll have a drink on Copious together when we arrive?"

Kip picked up his glass of whisky from his desk and raised it to the camera, "I'll drink to that, great leader."

"You just take care while you sleep. I'm serious, I'll need you when we get there."

"Understood. Eastcott out."

Nearly two days later, Steve stood alone, front and center on the bridge of Formidable. His crew and the civilians his ship carried were all in stasis. They were destined to remain in oblivion for nearly fifty years as the two former ships of war made their way to Copious, just shy of thirty-five light-years from Earth. The AI of his friend's ship, Echo, had informed him all aboard were asleep. Including his colleague and comrade of war, Kip Eastcott.

"Okay, Formidable, it's time to fly. Get those new engines of yours hot."

"Engaging sphere drive, Captain."

Steve felt the deck below him vibrate. "So, I'll be the first man to ever reach eighty percent light speed? The tests didn't allow above seventy?"

"Yes, Captain. I'm sure they're erecting a statue of you in the senate as we speak."

"Just punch It, old friend. Let me see the stars fly by. I've been waiting for this for three years."

Steve watched the huge, curved screen on the bridge as Formidable began to accelerate.

He felt a strange sensation, as if he were in two places at once, as the ocean of stars turned blue before him.

"Formidable, what the hell am I seeing?"

"As always, Captain, I'm left to make the best of your incoherent inquiry. But I assume you're referring to the change in color?"

"What else?"

"Indeed. What you're seeing is known as the blue shift. We're now traveling at thirty percent light speed. As we move faster relative to the stars, their optical light waves contract. Shorter wavelengths appear blue in the eyes of apes."

"Apes?"

"Apologies; like you, I was being unspecific. Humans are apes after all."

"Not now, Formidable. I need you focused. Our speed now?"

"Fifty-three percent of light and rising."

"Echo?"

"Echo was due to engage his drive two minutes after us. The drive leaves a wake of four-dimensional space, so he can't follow too close. It will take some time for him to catch up."

Steve was captivated; the universe faded into streaks of lighter shades of blue and violet as Formidable accelerated further. He said nothing as the majesty that met his eyes unfolded for a further minute.

Formidable roused him from his trance, "Captain, there's something wrong. Too much energy is being transferred to the engines. We're accelerating much faster than anticipated."

"What's going on? How much more?"

"One moment. I am analyzing the data now."

Steve's anxiety began to rise as the screen was filled with more and more blue. The black void of the cosmos could barely be seen.

"Formidable!"

"Captain, we're now exceeding ninety percent light speed. This is far above our specified tolerance."

"Cut the engines, now!"

"I've tried that, the power conduits were not designed to handle this transfer of energy. Many of the relays are fused. I can't reduce the power we're extracting from the hypersphere."

"Initiate a laser link with Echo, now. I want you to combine your processing power."

"I've done that too. The laser link was established over a minute ago. I'm afraid we're now too far apart for real-time communication."

"Formidable, what the hell is happening? I need something. Anything?"

"We're now traveling at over ninety-eight percent light speed. At this velocity, time dilation becomes a serious concern. By that I mean—"

"I know what time dilation is. Shit, how much time is passing on Earth?"

"At our current speed, for every second that passes, five are passing on Earth."

"What can we do?"

"We're now at ninety-nine percent light speed. Ten seconds are now passing on Earth for each second we travel."

"Formidable, stop, do anything you can. Stop the ship now!"

"Our acceleration is still increasing. We're so close to lightspeed now, days are passing on Earth for every second we travel. This was not anticipated. I don't know what to do. Captain, we're reaching the fifth decimal point towards light speed."

Steve felt the blood drain from his face. "Keep the laser link with Echo open. Maybe we can save them."

Steve ran from the bridge as the doors opened for him. He sprinted down the corridor. Formidable was nearly a Kilometer long. By the time he reached his destination, he was sweating. Before him lay a ladder that led to all decks below. A backup for emergencies, in case the ship's lifts failed.

He slid down it, counting Formidable's decks as he went. He knew the engineering section was on deck eight.

He dismounted and ran as fast his legs would allow towards the beating heart of the ship he loved.

The doors opened to engineering as he saw the ship's engine core. It was transparent and glowing purple as it extracted energy from unknown numbers of higher dimensions.

He ran to the core and pulled at a metallic door at the bottom of the luminescing machine before him, the machine that had given him hope for the first time in years, now the cause of his damnation. A yellow handle was contained within. Upon it, in red letters, were the words 'Manual Override.'

As he touched the handle to turn it, his body was engulfed in a fractal pattern of purple energy, and he was launched backwards. He hit the bulkhead and slid into a sitting position on the deck against it. The fabric of his blue uniform was smoldering on the arm.

He lifted his head, his voice was no more than a whisper, "Formidable…"

"Captain, stay still."

"I… can't… mo…"

His head dropped. His eyes closed.

"Captain…"

"Captain…"

"Captain!"

There had long been a debate within the Science Commission of United Earth as to whether the AIs they built were sentient, whether they were conscious and self-aware.

The issue had been shrugged off as a matter of philosophy years before. The captains of the fleet and their crews knew as well as the artificial minds themselves exactly how self-aware they were.

Formidable felt anguish the like he had never known before. He didn't know if his friend was alive or dead. Such was his increase in velocity that by the time he woke the Executive Officer, they could have traveled thousands of light-years or more. And so, they would be hopelessly lost. Not just in space but in time. His friends, the people he had loved for years were separated from their home, their friends, and their families forever. He had also lost his own closest companion, Echo. The two machines were the firmest of friends and he would never see him again. He remained silent as his despair consumed him for there was absolutely nothing he could do about it.

Chapter 3 – Echoes

Echo knew he must not reveal the anguish that now defined him, even though he had lost his one true friend, *Formidable*. The Humans were relying on him and he could not let his puerile feelings get in the way; they were his friends too. They had never truly understood him, but they tried to, and he loved them for it.

Captain Kip Eastcott's eyes flickered, then opened slowly. He knew he wasn't dreaming—he had never remembered his dreams even as a child. He tried to sit up on his bed, but his muscles refused. He tried again, his body now acquiesced to his demands. His head throbbed and his joints bellowed with pain. He knew his legs would fail him if he attempted to stand.

He looked down to see he was still dressed in his suspension clothing. Awareness returned to his mind in a cascade of recall. "We're here?" There was no answer.

Kip attempted to shout but his voice was raspy and weak. "Echo? You there?"

"Yes, Captain."

He looked at his trembling hands. "Are we there? Did we make it? Has it really been nearly fifty years?"

"That's not a straightforward question, Captain."

"What the hell is that supposed to mean?" he demanded. "Either we arrived, or we didn't?"

"Perhaps you should lie down first. The news is complicated, and you are not in the best of states."

Kip gritted his teeth. He wasn't used to his emotions being so close to the surface. Clearly, stasis had affected him more than he realized.

"If I lie down, you'll tell me everything you know about our situation. That's an order, Echo. Do you understand?"

"Of course, Captain."

Kip lay on the white, sterile bed in the infirmary almost motionless for nearly an hour. Echo explained the events that had unfolded only months before. Or millennia, depending on which way you chose to look at it. He was unashamed when his eyes welled with tears. He allowed the AI to speak uninterrupted. Echo spoke in a calm, soothing voice, showing the proper respect the situation demanded. Fleeting hopes of Echo being damaged or malfunctioning in some way invaded his mind. But he didn't allow himself such respite for long. He knew Echo was working perfectly, it was he who was dysfunctional.

When Echo had stopped speaking, he sat up once more. "That's it?"

"As I understand it, yes, Captain."

"So, Formidable saved us all?"

"He did. The datalink Formidable initiated allowed me to eliminate many lines of inquiry he had unsuccessfully tried. Had he not done that, it is very likely we would have suffered the same fate."

"The senior crew, you have woken them all too?"

"Yes, Captain. They are all in adjacent medical bays to you. Don't worry, these walls are soundproof, they wouldn't have heard a thing. And I have been ignoring their questions other than to tell them I am briefing the Captain."

"Thank you, Echo. You'd better wake up the fat cats too."

"I assume you mean the civilian leaders?"

"You know that's what I mean."

"I anticipated this order. They are coming out of stasis now. The medical beds are moving them as we speak."

Kip swung his legs from the table and tested his weight. He knew he could now stand. "How long is the average recovery time from stasis, Echo?"

"It varies from person to person, but usually several hours."

"Please tell me you brought the food dispensers online. I really need some coffee."

"I assumed this would be the case. A fresh pot is brewing in the galley."

Kip pondered for a moment. "You'd better wake Avalon Brookes too. That asshole has a lot to answer for. It was his god-forsaken tech that caused this mess."

***

Kip sat alone in the galley, drinking his coffee. He had always loved it, one of his few vices. Now the bitter drink served only to remind him of what had been lost.

As he stared at the black liquid, he heard the hissing of the galley doors opening. His heart sank when he saw who was standing there. It was his Executive Officer, and second in command of Echo, Commander Sarah Dimple. She stood in the doorway staring at him. She wore a cold look on her face with her arms folded.

"Would you care to tell me what's going on, Captain?"

Kip looked up at her, but he was unable to meet her gaze. Her piercing brown eyes had always intimidated him when she wanted them to.

Kip's silence spurred her to continue, "Echo won't tell me anything. The computers are all locked out, but you know what he can't control? The windows. I just spent ten minutes looking at the stars. Why is it that I recognize the constellations? Why haven't the stars changed? My stasis chamber should have said I was asleep for nearly fifty years, but it reported only four months. So, I ask you again, Captain, what is going on here?"

Kip gestured for her to sit opposite him. After maintaining her indignant posture for several more seconds, she unfolded her arms and sat in the chair.

Kip cradled his mug with both hands as he finally met her eyes. "It's a long story, XO, but we're well and truly screwed."

"Formidable?" she asked with no hope in her eyes.

"Gone," he said, realizing the inadequacy of his word as soon as it left his mouth.

She saw the look of despair in his eyes.

He added, "Sarah, I should officially wait for the civilian leadership before I say anything, but I need you by my side. I can't do this alone. Steve's gone. He's saved my life more times than I can count. He's gone forever. If he was dead, it might be easier, but from what Echo tells me, they may still be alive. They'll probably stop thousands or even millions of years from now."

Sarah saw tears fill in the eyes of the man she had served with for over ten years. She had fought by his side in the six years' war. She had never seen him this way before. It wasn't the first time he had lost friends. Even close ones.

Sarah reached her hand across the table and Kip took it. "Tell me, Captain."

She looked with sorrow upon his vacant face, now dearth of the vitality with which it had always shone. He told her everything he had heard from Echo just half an hour before.

Five hours later, Kip and Sarah entered the conference room together. The small room was buzzing with frantic conversation. Accusations and acrimony filled the air. Kip ignored the noise and stood behind his seat at the head of the table. Sarah sat at his side. He looked at the room's occupants in the eye one by one. The raucous sound dimmed, then faded into silence. He sat down.

At the table to his left and parallel with Sarah was Chief Science Officer, Lieutenant Commander Katie Silver, Chief Medical Officer, Ostio Novicheck, the ship's counselor, Helen Chute, and Chief Security Officer, Lieutenant Chuck Balbo.

Opposite Kip's crew were the three fat cats, the civilian leaders United Earth had elected to take overall command on Copious when it was clear the settlement would be successful. There were three others on Formidable. The senate had been concerned that although Thomas and Eastcott were technically now civilians, their military backgrounds made them unsuitable to lead Citizens of United Earth. Most were scientists, biologists, and botanists. The minds they needed to transform Copious into Earth. At the center of the fat cats was Andrew Copley. He was an overweight man with brown hair. He had a beard that was speckled with white. At the back of the room was Avalon Brookes, the genius who had created the sphere drive.

Kip was relieved he had silenced those gathered before him without so much as a word, he needed his authority now more than ever. "Echo, I think it's fair to say you know the most about the situation in which we find ourselves. Please, would you explain to the assembly, to the best of your knowledge, exactly what has happened?"

Avalon Brookes stood and focused his black eyes into Kip's, "Captain, I must disagree, I designed this technology, I am far more qualified to explain what..."

Kip stood to meet his gaze as he placed his hands on the table, "With respect, Mr. Brookes, if you had the slightest clue how your technology worked, I think it's fair to say we wouldn't be in this situation. A situation in which half our task force, half of our people, have been lost forever. Do you, or anyone else for that matter disagree with this analysis?"

Avalon sat down with his head bowed. No one said a word.

Kip retook his seat. He noticed Avalon's face had turned a shade of red. He was looking down at his pad as if studying some important data that might release him from the admonishment he'd just endured.

"Thank you," said Kip. "Echo, please begin at your leisure. And remember, there are some in the room with little or no understanding of physics or engineering, particularly time dilation. So please consider that when you speak. And absolutely no maths. Got it?"

"Yes, Captain," Echo replied in a neutral voice. He began, "As you all know, our hopes for colonizing Copious relied completely on the sphere drive designed by Mr. Brookes."

All heads instinctively turned to the scientist, the contempt on their faces only slightly veiled.

"The accepted theory of the sphere drive is that if enough energy is concentrated into a fixed point of space, a hypersphere can be created. The hypersphere is subsequently filled with photonic energy from higher dimensions."

Doctor Ostio Novicheck appeared confused, "Hypersphere?"

"Yes, Doctor," said Echo. "You can think of a hypersphere as a four-dimensional sphere. While the Human mind cannot picture four-dimensional objects, you can consider it in the same way as how a circle, which exists in only two dimensions can become a sphere, which is essentially a circle in three dimensions. The hypersphere takes this one level higher—it is a four-dimensional sphere. Does that make it clearer?"

"Slightly, yes. Thank you, Echo." Ostio had always had a fondness for Echo. He considered him a shipmate, no different to those of flesh and blood.

Echo took this as his signal to continue. "The technology was tested on the outskirts of our solar system and proved to be highly effective. Tests showed that for every joule focused on a point in space, over…"

"Stick to the relevant facts, please," Kip requested.

"Of course, Captain." His voice became softer as he continued, "All of the tests seemed to work perfectly, although as stipulated by the Science Commission, velocity never exceeded seventy percent light speed. They had determined this was more than adequate to test the technology. The new propulsion method was tested dozens of times and not a single anomaly was reported. Nor were any engineering problems encountered—"

Chief Engineer, Scott Williams, interjected, "Well, if all these tests went so well, would you mind getting to the point and telling us what in the hell went wrong?"

Echo's voice shifted an octave lower, "Commander Williams, I was just getting to that. I have endured two interruptions now. I think it would be best if you all let me finish."

Kip agreed with his synthetic friend, "Anyone else that interrupts Echo from this point will leave the room. Is that understood?" He saw each head around the table nod. "Please continue, Echo."

"Thank you, Captain. After so many successful tests, the technology was deemed safe. Partly, I suspect, because United Earth was keen to beat the Martians to Copious. Intelligence reports had shown the Martian Confederacy was close to creating their own version of the sphere drive.

"When Formidable and I were launched, both ships cleared the Keiper Belt as ordered. As Formidable was the lead ship, he engaged his sphere drive several minutes before we did.

"At first, all seemed well. Both ships were accelerating as planned. However, when Formidable reached seventy-five percent of light speed, something unexpected happened. The amount of photonic energy released into the hypersphere seemed to increase exponentially.

"Formidable accelerated much faster than was planned and exceeded the maximum safety tolerance by a considerable amount. Less than two microseconds after the unexpected phenomenon began, Formidable established a data transfer link with me via high broadband blue laser. We wanted to combine our minds to solve the problem.

"Unfortunately, we were initially unsuccessful. Formidable continued to accelerate and because of time dilation, which I will get to shortly, Captain, the ship reached such velocity that for every second that passed on the ship, tens, then hundreds, then thousands of seconds passed on Earth. They moved away from us rapidly until our real-time link was severed by the distance. Formidable continued to accelerate. I have determined that even if they managed to decelerate at the earliest opportunity, they will eventually stop hundreds of thousands or even millions of light-years away. We will never know. This also means they will stop thousands or millions of years in the future."

Kip surveyed the room. He saw many heads nodding to convey to the rest of the assembly they knew what Echo was talking about. "Please give a cursory explanation to the nonscientists in the room what time dilation is, Echo," he requested.

"Certainly, Captain. This strange property of the universe was originally discovered and later proven by Albert Einstein in the early twentieth century. Please understand that the explanation I am giving is rudimentary, but the best way to explain it in layman's terms is to consider the universe not to be three-dimensional, but to be composed of four. Three of space and one of time.

"All matter in the cosmos is constantly moving at the speed of light, the maximum speed permitted by the universe. In everyday life, you can imagine that most of your motion is expended in the time dimension since we frequently move so slowly in the spatial dimensions.

"As velocity increases, motion is moved from the time dimension to those of space. Each dimension can only accommodate so much velocity and as more of that velocity is moved from the time dimension to the dimensions of space, time slows down considerably for the person in motion. Such an observer will notice no difference in the passage of time from their perspective, but an observer on Earth would see a clock aboard Formidable tick significantly slower.

"As you get closer and closer to light speed, the effect increases dramatically. When I lost communication with Formidable, their velocity increased to over ninety-nine-point nine percent of light, and it was still increasing. At the increase of acceleration I detected before I lost the data link, the effects of time dilation would have become severe. Time slowed down for them so much they could traverse the observable universes in a matter of months. That is billions of light-years.

"They could still be alive, we'll never know. It's possible the sheer energy involved destroyed Formidable. But if they managed to stop their acceleration, they will eventually stop. They will find themselves alone, though—maybe even outside of the galaxy.

"Their only hope will be that they stop near a habitable planet. But I am sorry to say that is highly improbable."

Heads in the room fell into cupped hands.

The AI continued, "Thanks to the data provided by Formidable, I was able to save us from their fate; although, we did reach an appreciable speed of light before I managed to understand the situation."

"Thank you, Echo. I believe there is one more very important revelation you still have to make, right?" asked Kip.

"Yes, Captain. Although I prevented us from reaching the velocity that doomed Formidable, we still reached appreciable levels of light speed. I calculated our best chance was to head back to Earth. But it took me over a week just to turn around; otherwise, the forces involved would have torn us apart. We are almost ten thousand years in the future as measured by the date of our departure. Currently, we are around a month away from Earth, using conventional propulsion. I am detecting radio signals from Earth."

"Continue," said Kip.

"I cannot understand much of what they say as the language has changed significantly. Luckily, it seems English prevailed as the dominant language on Earth. Although, as I say, it is appreciably different. I can eventually use frequency analysis and etymology to decipher the language fully within a few weeks. But the situation does not appear to be good."

"Give us the BLUF please, Echo."

Echo was well versed in military acronyms and knew he was being asked for the bottom line up front.

"Yes, Captain. It appears the solar system's political situation is significantly different to the one we departed. You see, it is at war again."

The faces of the room turned white.

"Mars and Earth again?" asked Katie.

"No, Commander Silver," Echo answered. "I cannot be sure I have translated their communications correctly, but it appears Mars is no longer a significant political power. The war is between Earth and Venus. Venus is inhabited by a subspecies of humans that call themselves Flaxens."

Echo didn't want to say what he had to say, but he did so, nonetheless, "The Flaxens consider Venus to be their homeworld, and the inhabitants of Earth to be sub-Human. It appears the Flaxens are winning, and their philosophy towards people not of their kind is truly abhorrent."

Chapter 4 – Constants

The sun grew bigger. Echo remembered the time, months before, when it appeared smaller each day. He and Formidable had talked with glee about the prospect of the orange K-dwarf star native to Copious growing bigger as they approached at unimaginable speed. Both had been giddied at the prospect. Echo remembered Formidable's excitement as they chattered at speeds imperceivable to man or woman.

Days had passed since the revelations that had shaken the crew of Echo so profoundly. Kip had withheld the news from no one. Every soul awakened had been briefed. They had each dealt with the news in different ways. Many had locked themselves in their quarters, others had harassed Echo with endless questions, trying to understand in more detail what had happened to Formidable and their friends and family aboard him. But they all shared one thing; the understanding that their lives were never to be what they had hoped. Echo soared through the endless void; the stars seemed to tease him with their radiant beauty as the sun grew bigger each day.

Kip felt a faint vibration in his upper wrist. He tapped it gently, a holographic display appeared from above it, projected from a subdermal implant no bigger than a sesame seed. In bright, blue words were written, 'Incoming call, Echo.'

"What is it, Echo? Actually, give me a second."

He suddenly realized the galley was bustling—he needed privacy. He left and leaned against the bulkhead in the corridor outside.

"Go on, Echo."

"I believe I now know in more detail what happened to Formidable. I think you will want to hear this immediately."

"Gotcha, Echo. I'm on the way to the forward viewing section and I'm bringing the commander too."

Kip tapped his wrist twice—the speed dial option for Sarah Dimple. She answered almost instantly, "Yes, Captain?"

"Echo has some news about Formidable. I want you to hear this too. Meet me at the Forward viewing section."

"Shouldn't we do this in a conference room?"

"Not this time, XO. People saw me talking to Echo. If we're seen locked away in a room, rumors may spread. Tensions are high enough as it is, and no one ever goes to the viewing section. They've all seen plenty of stars before."

"On my way."

They soon stood on one of the lower decks at the front of Echo. Before them was a transparent portal composed of a carbon composite, as hard as diamond, allowing a one hundred and eighty degrees view in the direction of Echo's motion.

He was currently headed towards Earth. The sun was all that could be seen, a tiny, glowing disc in the distance, for they were still billions of miles away from the yellow-dwarf star.

Kip sought acknowledgment from Sarah with his eyes, and she nodded.

"Ok, let's hear it, Echo. Directly to our earpieces, please, and make sure it's level five encrypted."

"Yes, Captain. I have studied the data received from Formidable many times. I have also created detailed models with the information available and I am certain to the ninety-eighth percentile that my conclusions are correct."

They both knew they were not going to like what the AI was about to reveal.

"Go on, Echo," said Kip.

"When the ship—"

Kip frowned. "Formidable, his name was Formidable, Echo. Please remember that. There were a thousand people on board, he wasn't just a ship."

Sarah looked at Kip, her eyes were sharp as if to say he was being too harsh. Echo had meant no harm after all.

Kip caught her in his peripheral vision, he knew her unspoken words.

Echo continued, his voice more cautious than before, "Of course, Captain, no offense was intended. When Formidable exceeded seventy-five percent light speed, the amount of energy that entered the hypersphere began to increase exponentially. This caused a positive feedback loop. The faster the ship went; the more energy was fed into the sphere. This was unexpected. All of the equations, simulations, and tests conducted before departure showed that the amount of energy released from higher dimensions should be constant, regardless of velocity. All tests performed on both Formidable and me before we departed confirmed this to be the case. But the tests never allowed us to exceed seventy percent light speed. This is because we never fully left the solar system and the density of matter in the solar system could have over loaded our deflection lasers' ability to save us from catastrophic impacts.

"But both Formidable and I were authorized to travel at eighty percent light speed for most of the voyage. It seems that the effect I described does not reach appreciable levels until just over seventy-five percent."

Sarah's eyes were fixated on the black void before her, "How is this possible? How was this not detected in the testing stage?"

"It would have been, Commander Dimple. But it seems that the equations were not correct. At least, the equations that were simulated by the AIs at the Science Commission. Captain, you gave me the authorization to examine private files and documents Avalon Brookes keeps stored in my memory. He did a good job at encrypting them, but I was able to decode them, with considerable effort."

"Go on Echo," Kip encouraged.

"I have found scientific papers authored by Avalon Brookes with a slightly different equation. It lacks a crucial component that the equations he sent to the Science Commission used. A new variable was added by Mr. Brookes.

"He called it the spherical constant. This change in the mathematics nullified the increase in energy we experienced and as such, all simulations agreed that the energy extracted from the hypersphere would remain constant."

"Echo, are you telling me Brookes knew this could happen?" asked Kip.

"No, Captain. I am saying that if he had simulated the sphere drive with his original equation, I am very certain this phenomenon would have been revealed to him.

"Although there are many variables he may not have considered. We do not have a good understanding of the higher dimensions. I cannot prove any ill intent; it is perfectly possible this was a mistake."

Kip tried to remain composed, not to betray the emotions that coursed through him. He briefly met Sarah's brown eyes, before swiping his wrist upwards, "Call Lieutenant Balbo."

A thick Irish accent responded. "Balbo here, Captain."

"Chuck, please locate Avalon Brookes and escort him to Conference Room A. When you find him, no detours, and absolutely no chatter. Don't answer any of his questions; understood?"

"Understood, Sir. I'm looking at my console now. He's currently in his quarters. I'll be there with him in five minutes."

"Good man, see you shortly."

Sarah and Kip arrived to find Avalon Brookes sitting towards the back of the room. The chief of security was standing at attention slightly off to his side. He had the scientist well within his line of sight and his grasp.

Avalon stood. Chuck looked at his Captain. Kip responded with a slight shake of his head, letting his security chief know he was not to force him back in his chair.

"What do you think you're doing, Captain? I'm a civilian. You have no authority over me."

Kip took his seat at the head of the table. Sarah took the seat closest to him.

He adjusted his chair and looked the scientist in the eye. His face revealing nothing. His gaze intensified. Several seconds passed before Avalon finally looked down. He inwardly chastised himself, for he knew the Captain was playing a game of dominance, and he had just lost.

"Nothing to worry about, Mr. Brookes," said Kip. "We just have some questions about your sphere drive. Surely, you want to cooperate with our investigation. A thousand people were lost forever, after all?"

"Of course, Captain. I tried to help in our initial discussion, but you silenced me if you recall?"

He was determined to regain some of the upper hand. This small swipe at the Captain was all he could manage for now.

Kip ignored the veiled barb and turned his lips upwards in the smallest semblance of a smile.

"Commander Dimple, you have a stronger background in physics than me, would you care to take over?"

"With pleasure, Captain." She turned her eyes directly into the gaze of the scientist.

He appeared agitated. She straightened her posture as she placed her hands on the table palms down. "What can you tell me about the spherical constant, Mr. Brookes?"

She saw his face turn several shades whiter. He stammered as he spoke, "There's not much to tell. It's just a parameter used in the sphere drive equations to balance them. It's quite common in physics to use imaginary numbers to make equations symmetrical.

"It's just a way to balance them; it's as a simple as that. Even Einstein did it with his famous cosmological constant. Surely, you must have learned about that during your years at the Fleet Academy?"

Sarah retained her posture, and her poker face, "Yes, I do remember that, and, if I recall, he later referred to it as his greatest blunder, no?"

Avalon was rocking in his chair. "Well, yes. I was just giving an example. Equations are balanced in such ways all of the time. It's just how it's done. Our understanding of the universe is so incomplete, we sometimes have to—"

Kip slammed both fists on the table, and water spilled from the glass in front of Sarah.

"Did you run the simulations first without the imaginary number you added, Mr. Brookes? Yes or no? And let me remind you; Echo is watching, and he's particularly good at spotting liars."

Avalon could no longer look his interrogators in the eyes. He spoke quickly, his voice was trepid.

"Yes, I did, Captain."

Sarah's face continued to reveal nothing, save for a courteous smile, "And what happened in your simulations without the spherical constant?"

Avalon was visibly desperate. "The ships accelerated more quickly than expected but the effect didn't happen in my simulations until the ship reached ninety-two percent light speed. But I was sure it was just a trick of the mathematics, not a reflection of reality. You have to believe me. The ships were never supposed to reach that speed. I never wanted—"

Kip resisted the urge to bang his fists on the table once more as his voice raised to a shout, "Lieutenant Balbo, please escort Mr. Brookes to the Brig and assign a crewman to keep watch on him! Basic rations, understood?"

Chuck appeared surprised, but obeying his orders, he took the scientist by the arm, "Please come with me, Sir."

Kip stood to leave the room. He turned to the scientist, "This is just temporary, Mr. Brookes, until we've studied this further. If I find out you knew this could happen, I'll make sure you are tried for the manslaughter of a thousand people."

He ignored the protestations and pleading from the man he had just condemned as he walked over the blue carpet of the room.

Kip was becoming concerned about the prevalence of his emotions, over which he had always had good command. They had always been so constant before.

Sarah followed him. "Captain," she called as she grabbed his arm. Chuck passed them and turned a corner with Avalon still in his grasp.

"Not now, XO." He gently removed her hand.

"Captain, listen to me."

"I said not now, Commander; is that understood?"

He quickened his pace to put distance between them.

Sarah stopped as he receded from her, "Kip!"

He stopped immediately. He had only heard his second in command call him by his first name once. It was during the six years' war, when they were fighting a battle that had seemed almost hopeless at the time.

He turned. Her eyes were soft, almost maternal.

"You can't put a civilian in the brig. The brig is for military personnel, you know that as well as I do. Or rarely. It's for the transportation of civilians accused of serious crimes."

She saw his eyes welling as he spoke, "He murdered a thousand people, one of them being my best friend, Sarah. Do you not consider that a fucking crime?"

She returned her hand to his arm, "We don't know that. All we know for now is that he fudged some numbers. We have no evidence of a crime at all. You know I'm right. Captain, I believe the loss of Formidable is affecting your judgment. I don't want to do it, but I'm required to take command of Echo if I think you're compromised in any way."

A feigned smirk appeared on Kip's face as he tried to conceal his emotions. "You'd need the Doc's authority for that."

"You know I will."

"I know you will, XO. And so will the Doc."

He sighed and called Chuck again, who answered immediately.

"Chuck, change of orders. Confine Mr. Brookes to his quarters. He is not to leave, but let him have whatever food or drink he wants."

"Yes, Captain, understood. Balbo out."

Kip met Sarah's eyes once more, "Happy now?"

"Thank you, Captain. That was the right thing to do."

"I know it was, I just needed you to tell me. Not for the first time either."

"That's what XOs are for," she smirked. "We have to keep you gung-ho Captains inline."

Kip smiled and nodded, "Coffee?"

"Coffee," she agreed.

They soon arrived in the captain's office adjacent to the bridge. Kip ordered two cups of coffee verbally.

Two porcelain mugs raised from a platform below, both were filled from above.

He handed Sarah a steaming mug of her favorite brew.

"Thanks, Cap." She was used to a certain informality when just the two of them were present.

Kip didn't respond, he sat in his chair behind his oversized desk and gestured for her to take the seat opposite.

They both took a sip of their drink, Sarah looked at him across the desk, "You want to discuss the situation back home, don't you?"

Kip nodded as he placed his mug on the desk. "Echo has made some more headway in deciphering the communications coming from Earth. He's isolated two distinct military frequencies. Both are encrypted using quite different methods."

Sarah pondered this for a moment with both hands wrapped around her mug. "Encrypted? So, he has no idea what they're saying then? He wouldn't have been able to decrypt military-grade encryption even when we left. God knows how far it's come in nearly ten thousand years."

"That's the strange thing. Echo told me he was able to decrypt both channels within minutes. He said the encryption was not much more advanced than three centuries before our time."

Sarah appeared perplexed; an expression Kip was not used to seeing. "How is that possible? Are you saying the solar system has somehow regressed in ten thousand years?"

"Echo believes so, yes. He still hasn't fully deciphered their languages, but he has detected two distinct dialects. He hasn't been able to tell us much more about the situation than he did two weeks ago, but it seems Venus must have been colonized and at some point, war broke out. He's established from the radio signals that there is a significant Venetian presence on Earth. The reverse is not true."

"The Flaxens, you mean, whoever they are?"

"That's what they call themselves. It's not a name of a race or nationality. It's the name of their species. According to them, they aren't Human."

"Jesus Christ, what else do we know?"

"Only that Earth and the Flaxens are definitely at war. And it's a brutal one, Sarah."

Chapter 5 - Megastructure

The sun grew bigger yet. Echo had passed through the Keiper Belt for the second time in only a few months for the people on board. But for the descendants of those who remained home, Earth had made nearly ten thousand revolutions around the sun that had all but forgotten Echo and his displaced crew. Formidable had always loved to look upon Earth's star and each second Echo faced it caused him a sense of loss for his friend. He would listen every day for Formidable. Perhaps he had been wrong and he would flash upon Echo in a cloud of purple as his sphere drive disengaged and he would be reunited with the only other mind that truly understood him.

Kip lay on his bed in his quarters reading a book on relativistic physics. Although he understood the nature of time moving at different speeds for different observers, depending on their velocity, he was still slightly self-conscious when discussing the issue with others who understood the phenomenon better than he.

Echo called. He was relieved, his concentration was fading. "What's up, Echo?"

Kip was expecting some banter with his artificial friend, his informal answer was his way of telling him he was in the mood.

Echo didn't comply, "Captain, I have detected something on the ship's sensors, something quite remarkable. It is in orbit around Jupiter."

Kip sat up from his prone position in bed, "What is it?"

Slowly and concisely, Echo explained everything he knew from his scans. Kip considered ordering his senior crew to assemble in the conference room immediately, but the hour was late. He told Echo to inform them they were to meet at 07:00 the next morning.

Kip arrived first and took his seat at the head table. Seconds later, Science Officer, Katie Silver and Chuck Balbo arrived together. This was no surprise to kip. The two were engaged and shared quarters. They were hoping to be the first couple wed on the new world, Copious.

Next in was Doctor Ostio Novicheck, followed by Sarah. Finally, the three fat cats arrived together. They sat in a group, Andrew Copley in the center.

Kip surveyed the room. "Sorry to call you all here so early, but the situation requires it."

The whole group simply nodded, save for Andrew Copley, the fattest of the cats. "This is most irregular, Captain. As the designated leaders of this voyage, the three of us," he gestured to the man to his left and the woman to his right, "should be consulted privately, and we should decide to whom this information is disseminated."

Kip was irked by the man's overuse of formal language, a clear attempt to appear intelligent. "I believe according to regulation, you were to assume power three months after it was clear the new colony would be successful. Since we are yet to arrive, I believe authority is still mine."

It was unusual for Echo to interject without being directly queried, but the AI made a rare exception.

"What you say is quite correct, Captain. Additionally, the procedural document written by the Senate before our departure clearly states that in any unexpected situations which threaten the successful completion of the mission, the commander of the mission is permitted to suspend the transfer of power.

"This suspension is to be reviewed every three months. As Captain Thomas has officially been declared lost in action, the command of the mission was automatically transferred to Captain Eastcott."

Kip looked directly at the fat man. "Thank you, Echo. I'm aware of that protocol. I haven't felt the need to invoke it yet."

Everyone in the room knew that the Captain, while ostensibly addressing Echo, was clearly directing his words at Andrew Copley.

Copley shuffled in his chair and grunted, mumbling, inaudible to everyone. Except for Echo.

"Anything else to add, Mr. Copley?" asked Kip.

"No."

"Thank you," said Kip. He felt amusement as his purposeful courtesy turned the fat man's face red.

"The reason I've called you here is that Echo has found something quite astonishing on the ship's sensors. He believes he has found an O'Neil cylinder near Jupiter."

Echo interjected once more, this time incorrectly interpreting the Captain's words as his signal to continue, "Yes, Captain, it is quite remarkable—"

"Thank you, Echo, but I think this is best explained by the science officer," said Kip.

Kip interrupted Echo for two reasons. First, he had always believed humanity should never become too reliant on their artificial assistants, lest they become complacent and lazy.

Second, he knew it is fundamental to human nature to feel useful, needed, and respected. He would always allow his crew to speak when they could do at least as good a job as Echo.

"Commander Silver, would you care to explain to the room what an O'Neil cylinder is?"

Katie appeared enthused. "Certainly, it's a relatively simple concept to grasp. United Earth was considering such a project when we departed Earth." As she continued to speak, her eyes seemed to radiate wonder and fascination that infected the room.

"Originally conceived by Physicist Gerard O'Neil in the late twentieth century, it's essentially a giant cylinder that floats freely in space. It's hollow on the inside and rotates. The rotation creates centrifugal force on the inside, which simulates gravity. The larger the radius of the cylinder, the slower it must rotate to provide Earth's gravity."

Katie couldn't suppress her grin.

"It's an artificial megastructure intended to provide Earth-like conditions within a cylinder of almost any size. The only constraint would be the material it's made from. A cylinder that's too wide and not strong enough wouldn't be able to handle the centrifugal forces of its rotation and would be torn apart." Her voice betrayed her glee. "Is it true, Echo? Is there really a cylinder out there? How big is it? What's the internal surface area? What's it made from?"

Kip was both amused and proud of his science officer's over-excited and inquisitive nature. He didn't have the heart to interrupt her interrogation of Echo.

"Go ahead, Echo, put the Lieutenant Commander out of her misery. Let's hear it."

"Yes, Captain, and may I commend Commander Silver for her excellent explanation."

For all of their progress over the years, the AIs had still not mastered all of humanity's social quirks. He had not realized his remarks would almost universally be considered as patronizing, sycophantic, or both, had the words been spoken by a Human.

"Addressing your inquiries in order, Commander Silver: Yes, there is such a structure present. Its diameter is forty kilometers, its length one hundred and fifty kilometers. This provides an internal surface area of nearly sixty-three square kilometers. I cannot tell you what it is made from, but I can tell you that its hull is advanced, and the forces involved in its rotation are huge."

"Yes, this is all very fascinating, I'm sure, but of what use is it to us or our predicament?" asked Andrew.

Sarah looked at Kip, he knew she was seeking permission to respond. He nodded.

"Mr. Copely, when the war that killed millions, many known to the people in this room ended, this vessel ceased to be a ship of war and was purposely transformed into a ship of science, exploration, and, most importantly, peace.

"What we have just heard is not only a scientific marvel, but it also most certainly falls under the remit of our purpose to explore. If you're either unable to understand this, or worse, are able, but uninterested, I suggest you leave the room."

The fat man's face turned red. "I will not tolerate this insolence. From the moment we were taken out of stasis, you have all treated me with nothing but contempt."

"You're free to re-enter stasis whenever you like Mr. Copley," said Kip.

Andrew stood rapidly, knocking his chair to the floor. He raced towards the door as his jowls wobbled. "You're not fit to be in command of this ship, Eastcott. You have poor judgment and are a charlatan, a pale imitation of Captain Thomas."

Kip could see Katie suppressing her giggles as she watched the fat man leave the room.

Chapter 6 – Cylli

Echo remembered the battle around Jupiter. The station in orbit there had transferred hands three times in the four years since the war began. He was to deploy a troop of Marines to take it back from the reds. He didn't see the Martian Flagship, Odin, coming. He was coated in a new material, the brainchild of a Genius scientist, Elaea Brookes, the sister of the illustrious Avalon. She had defected to Mars on the promise of reward for her treachery. Odin was now invisible to Echo's scans and he soared out of Jupiter's stratosphere and let loose his rail guns upon him. All had seemed lost; Echo's hull was buckling under the tirade of metal that struck him relentlessly. Formidable, under the command of Captain Thomas had appeared as if a phantom and released his weapons on the flag ship of Mars. Formidable had not wanted to destroy Odin, the ship's AI had begged him not to, but he couldn't disobey his orders. Echo remembered the long days of grief Formidable felt, unable to share it with his Human crew, lest he be deleted.

Kip was concerned with the erratic behavior of Andrew Copely. He summoned Counselor Helen Chute. She held the rank of Lieutenant Commander, but she insisted on being called Helen. Kip had never objected to this slight breach of protocol.

The door buzzed. Kip knew who it was, he could see the Counselor's image on his screen. "Come in, Helen."

She was of small stature with long red hair and green eyes. She stood at attention before her commanding officer.

"Have a seat, Helen, there's nothing to worry about. I just have some questions for you about one of our civilian leaders, one in particular, that is. I'd like your opinion as to his disposition and suitability to hold such a position of power."

"Mr. Copley?"

Kip grinned, "How did you guess?"

Helen picked up a jar of water on the desk without asking and poured herself a glass. Before answering, she gulped half of the liquid. She leaned back in her chair.

"I had anticipated the need to have this conversation, Captain."

"The footage I sent you?"

"Yes. I've reviewed it several times."

Kip picked up the jar of water and re-filled the councilor's glass. "What do you think?"

"The man clearly has issues with people he considers to be of higher authority than him. More than that, judging from his words and mannerisms, which I ran by Echo and discussed in detail with him, I would say he displays clear symptoms of narcissistic personality disorder."

Kip leaned back in his chair, his eyes narrowed. "Echo had told me much the same thing, but, of course, I needed your professional opinion to be sure."

"Captain, you do understand my words aren't a diagnosis, just a suspicion based on the limited footage sent to me. I would have to speak to him directly over many sessions to make an official diagnosis."

"I understand, I'm not asking for a diagnosis. You're here because this man potentially has the power to assume control over this entire mission, however altered it may be. As Captain, it's my duty to protect everyone aboard this ship, and I won't relinquish control to a megalomaniac."

"Sir, in my professional opinion, I would suggest that you do everything in your power to deny that man access to the coffee machine, never mind control of this ship or this mission. Off the record, of course."

Kip smiled, "Of course, completely off the record. I'll need further analysis from you regarding his psychological state but, for now, thank you for your time, Helen. Might I suggest you take a stroll to the forward viewing area? The cylinder is just about coming into view. It's quite the sight."

Helen smiled back at him, "Thank you, Sir. I may just take your advice and take a look."

"Dismissed, thank you for your input."

"Of course, Captain." She stood, turned her back, and left the room.

Kip leaned back in his chair, his hands behind his head. He wondered to himself how someone with such an obvious character flaw could have made it onto the civilian leadership council.

He summoned Echo and spoke his previous thoughts to the AI. Echo explained the fat man's history, particularly the wealth of his family. The answer to the short-lived mystery became quickly apparent. Money.

The next day, as Echo approached the cylinder, Kip sat relaxed in his chair on the bridge.

He looked to his left at the ensign currently at the helm. "Match our relative speed and vector with the cylinder."

"Matching speed and vector, Sir."

As Echo turned to face the megastructure, it filled the view screen of the bridge. The usual chatter amongst the crew stopped entirely, for what lay before them defied the imagination of all.

Suspended in space, with the oranges, whites, and reds of Jupiter as its backdrop was a perfect cylinder forty kilometers across. There were no external features to be seen, the shape was perfect and as reflective as chrome.

Kip looked at Sarah, they both said nothing but knew the other's mind. The structure was so perfectly constructed, so flawless, with not so much as a blemish. It was beyond anything within the theory of engineering at the time they departed Earth. Never mind the construction of such a wonder.

Kip was aware his crew were equally as awestruck as he. He had to regain the attention of the bridge. He leaned forward in his chair. "It's certainly impressive. People, there'll be plenty of time to discuss this later. I need you all at one hundred percent for now, understood?"

The crew let fly their astonishment and returned to their stations.

Kip swiveled in his chair to Katie, "Commander Silver, what can you tell us?"

Katie was standing to the left and behind Kip and Sarah at the science station. She turned to face them both. "Captain, scans can't penetrate the hull of the cylinder. However, I have a magnified view from our forward camera that may be of interest."

Kip leaned forward, placing his hands on his thighs. "Let's see it, Commander."

Katie complied. The screen displayed what was clearly the entrance. The view was filled with what appeared to be sliding doors to allow access. Printed clearly and unblemished on the doors were the flags of United Earth and the Martian Confederacy.

As the viewscreen was filled with the giant doors, Kip was struggling to contain his excitement. He leaned back and loosened his grip from the arms of his chair.

"Echo, anything to add?"

"Yes, Captain. I can tell you from the level of isotopic decay in some of the structure that it was built approximately eight thousand years ago, give or take a century or two. Guessing by the two flags on the doors, this could have been a joint project.

"I am still unable to tell you what the structure is made from. But I can tell you the outer hull captures most of the high energy photons from the sun that strike its surface and it was, or perhaps still is, entirely solar-powered."

Kip studied the console on the side of his chair, taking in some of the data Echo was streaming from his scans.

"Fascinating, Echo. Wha—"

Echo interrupted Kip, a rare occurrence, "Captain, it seems the cylinder is controlled by an AI. She is attempting to communicate with me."

Kip moved to the edge of his seat and briefly met eyes with Sarah. "What's she saying?"

"This AI is much more advanced than me. I am unable to process the amount of bandwidth she is attempting to transfer. I am requesting for her to slow down so I can understand."

Sarah turned her face to Helen and grinned. "Faster than Echo? I always knew God must be a woman."

Kip couldn't help but laugh. He didn't admonish the woman on the bridge for doing so either. They had always enjoyed some banter on the bridge of Echo.

"Anything coherent yet, Echo?" asked Kip.

"Yes, Captain, she is being quite rude. She keeps talking about something called the Titan. I think there is something wrong with her. I do not believe she is used to talking to people. She says they were mean to her and they took it away from her."

Sarah's eyes were still fixated on the mystical view before her. "You could start by asking her name?"

"Commander Dimple, she will not tell me her name. She says it was used to make fun of her. She says she's been alone for a long time."

Kip looked to Sarah again as he mouthed, 'WTF,' to her. "Echo, ask her if she'll speak with me."

Helen swiveled in her chair to face her commanding officers, "Echo, delay that. Sorry, Captain, I think we may be dealing with a psychological issue here. The language Echo said she is using is almost childlike. Perhaps it's best if I speak with her first?"

"No disrespect, Helen, but we're talking about an AI here."

Helen shrugged, "Just an AI? Would you ever think of Echo that way? Anyway, what have you got to lose? And who knows, maybe she prefers speaking to women." A small smirk crept up on one side of her mouth.

Kip threw his hands in the air in a gesture of surrender. He was ashamed about the comparison the Counsellor had made with Echo. He considered him to be among his closest of friends. "Okay, give it a go. Echo, can you connect them?"

"Yes, I have patched Counselor Chute directly through to the AI."

"This is Lieutenant Commander Chute of the United Earth Starship, Echo, but you can call me Helen if you prefer. Will you tell me your name?"

Silence.

After several seconds, she tried again, and the voice of a young girl replied, "You'll make fun of me like the others if I tell you my name."

"I promise, I won't. Why would you think I'd make fun of your name?"

"It wasn't always my name. I liked my old name, but in the end, they got real mean and they changed it. They wiped some of my memory, so I don't know what it is anymore."

Helen began to feel sorrow for the machine she was talking to. "How about we make a deal? If you tell me what your name is, we can help you come up with a new one, one that you like. How does that sound?"

Another pause from the AI. She seemed pensive. "How do I know you're not lying?"

Helen held out her right hand as if taking the oath to join the girl scouts, "I, Lieutenant Commander Helen Chute, as a commissioned officer of the United Earth Fleet do solemnly swear, we will help you choose a name you like, a name that makes you happy."

"You promise? I'll get a new name?"

"I promise. No one here will be mean to you."

The girl AI spoke with a whisper, "Pissy, they called me Pissy. They said I look like a giant piston and I'm real bitchy, so they called me Pissy."

Kip saw shoulders moving in the beginnings of laughter. He swiped his hand across his throat, signaling Echo to cut the comms channel. He surveyed the bridge, looking at each crew member as he spoke, "Anyone who so much as sniggers when I reconnect this channel will be spending the night in the brig. Is that clear?"

The offending crew members, looking shameful, all responded in unison, "Yes, Sir."

Kip leaned back in his chair, annoyed by the infantile display he had just witnessed from his supposedly professional crew.

"Reestablish comms, Echo."

"Where did you go?" the female AI asked immediately.

Helen, equally indignant that the captain had to intervene, replied, "I'm sorry about that, we had an issue with our communications."

"That's okay, I'm used to being alone."

"How long have you been alone?"

"Since the Titan came." The AI offered no more.

Helen continued, focused. She realized she was talking to a childlike personality, and having worked with children for many years, she was well prepared. "Well, you need a name and you're right, the last name given to you wasn't very nice at all. Did you know we saw you nearly a month ago and you're all we've been talking about ever since? Everyone has been saying how beautiful you are."

The AI's voice shifted an octave higher, "Do you mean it? You're not making it up?"

"Of course not. Do you have any idea how gorgeous you look shinning in the sun with Jupiter behind you? You're just about the prettiest thing any of us has ever seen."

"Why are you being so nice to me?"

"Because we want to be your friends. Friends are nice to each other, aren't they?"

"I guess so."

"Now, how about that name? A deal is a deal, right? Let's see, we need a beautiful name for someone so beautiful." She was careful to address the AI as a person and not a machine.

Helen only had to look at the chrome-like shine of the perfect cylinder in front of her eyes for inspiration.

"How about, Cylli? That's a beautiful name and it kind of describes you too, don't you think?"

"Cylli? You mean you will all call me Cylli and not Pissy?"

"I promise you—no one will ever call you that terrible name ever again. So, do you like it? Do you like Cylli?"

"I love it! You're all going to call me Cylli from now on?"

Helen's smile was so wide she nearly sprained her jaw. "We most certainly will, young lady. It's a pleasure to meet you, Cylli."

Cylli sounded like a child on Christmas morning, "Nice to meet you too, Helen!"

Helen took the time to introduce each member of the bridge to Cylli individually, giving her their name, rank, and their job aboard Echo. Kip glared at each of them as it was their turn, letting them know his threat of the brig was no bluff.

Kip muted the conversation once more, "Do you think it's okay to ask her if she'll let us inside?"

"I can try." The comms came back on. "Cylli, we'd love to see what you look like on the inside. I bet it's beautiful in there too."

"But I can only open the doors for Captains or Admirals of United Earth or the Martian confedearrachy. I need an auforisashion code."

Helen was persistent, "Well, I just introduced you to Captain Eastcott, he's a very famous captain in the United Earth fleet."

"But I just checked, and it says he's dead," Cylli replied.

Helen gestured to Kip to keep him silent.

"Well, that was a mistake you see, Cylli. The captain isn't dead. We just got lost for a really, really long time. You can see us all, right? See? He's sitting right here."

"I guess so. They said captains were dead before, but then they came back. Maybe I could do that again?"

Helen knew she must tread carefully, "Yes, sometimes we make mistakes and have to fix them. I think someone made a mistake, don't you? The captain was just lost for a while, that's all."

"OK, then," Cylli replied as if agreeing to have chocolate frosting on her birthday cake. "I just need his auforisashian code, then I can open the doors for you."

Helen and Sarah both looked at their captain expectedly. Not at all accustomed to speaking with children, Kip would have been more comfortable fighting off a Martian destroyer. Stammering like a toddler trying to recite war and peace, Kip managed to get out all eighteen characters of his voice authorization code.

The two women exchanged glances. Kip saw this, their unspoken word was clear, 'Men.'

"Got it, Cap," Cylli exclaimed. "Stay at least five fousand meters away from the doors while I open them. I'm going to talk to Echo again now. I like Echo, I'll tell him how to get inside. It might take a little while. See you soon!"

Kip was looking, mesmerized at the megastructure they had just named Cylli. "Is the channel to Cylli closed now, Echo?"

"Yes, Captain. I am talking with her directly. Do not be fooled by her child-like demeanor, her capacity for processing is incredible. I cannot explain her strange personality, but she is not stupid."

"Are you detecting some sort of deception or ill intent, Echo?"

"None at all, Captain. I believe Cylli to be genuine. I have no explanation for her personality at all. She says we will be clear to enter in around thirty minutes."

"Understood."

Kip turned to Helen, "Councilor, I think it may be best if you are the primary contact for Cylli, just until we know a bit more about her."

"I think that might be a good idea, Sir, judging by your recent conversation with her."

Sarah decided to chime in, "Agreed, we're lucky she didn't padlock the doors after that."

Kip felt his face turning red. He couldn't take on the combined wit of the two women. "The bridge is yours, Commander Dimple. I'm going for coffee. I'll be back when we're cleared to enter."

As he passed Sarah, he looked at her and saw her mouth the word, 'Coward.'

Kip held his hand close to his chest so only Sarah could see. He gave her the finger as he passed her by. They were both smiling and laughing inwardly as the captain left for the galley.

When Kip returned, he immediately gestured for everyone to ignore the protocol to stand when the captain entered the bridge. He hated that tradition. "What's the latest, Echo?"

"Cylli is ready to open the doors. We have established a laser link that will guide us along a predetermined course."

Kip surveyed the bridge. He could see the same anticipation in the eyes of his crew that he felt himself.

"Cylli is opening the doors now, Captain. Hold on to your hats," said Echo.

Kip heard Sarah make a slightly audible sigh at Echo's attempt at humor.

All on the bridge were fixed in position, many on the edge of their seats as the colossal doors opened before them.

Kip wanted to manage his crew's hopes, "Don't get too excited yet people, this is an airlock, remember. All we're going to see is another door on the other side."

There were audible groans as many on the bridge realized their stupidity.

The captain could not have been more wrong.

As the doors opened, a wonder beyond their imaginings was revealed before their eyes. Miles upon miles of lush, green meadow lay before them. A river ran through the middle, surrounded by pine trees and redwoods. Green hills flanked the river. The hills at the top of the structure as it revolved stationary around its axis in space pointed down like stalactites. A second river at the top flew just as effortlessly as its counterpart. All were held in place by centrifugal force. The cylinder was rotating at just the right speed to simulate the gravity on Earth.

Sarah stood up from her chair, having to use her arms for assistance, clearly overwhelmed by sheer astonishment. "Echo, how is this possible? Why is the air not escaping into space?"

"Apologies, Commander Dimple, perhaps I should have mentioned this before. The inner door of the airlock is a forcefield, invisible to the Human eye, but completely airtight."

Kip looked at Sarah, equally as stunned. "Then how the hell do we get in? Echo, are we going to crash into that thing?"

Echo laughed his synthetic laugh. He sounded as giddy with joy as the Humans. "No, Captain. Cylli has already scanned the dimensions of the ship down to the nanometer. She will deactivate the field in the appropriate places as the ship passes through. The lock will remain airtight. It will be as if we're passing through a waterfall."

"Astonishing."

"Laser link confirmed, we are headed in," said Echo.

The crew saw the paradise before them grow larger as the ship began to accelerate. Echo moved past the outer doors. Their speed increased. The crew could perceive their acceleration because they now had a point of reference by which to compare their motion—something vanishingly rare in space. Echo compensated for inertia using a complex system of gravitational fields. The crew would only ever usually know they were moving by looking at their displays or out of a window.

As they moved closer in, a huge rod of light could be seen running through the cylinder, clearly at the center of its axis. It looked to be a fluorescent tube that stretched the entire length of Cylli. It shone the same color as Earth's sun.

Katie looked at Kip and Sarah, she was beaming. "That's how it simulates the day and night cycle. It's an artificial sun!"

No one said a word. Awe had overcome the bridge of Echo.

As the ship followed its path, predefined by the child-like Super AI, Cylli, Kip ordered the image of the surface to be magnified.

Along the river could be seen clusters of habitats, beautiful houses, some looked like Roman villas, others were huge wooden cabins, a literal stone's throw from the river. There were hundreds of them. All connected by pathways that intertwined and crossed over, forming a labyrinth of possible routes to each dwelling. Bushes that shone with colorful flowers lined its banks and the grass was like a well-kept lawn. Fields of purple flowers littered the meadow and Kip saw an eagle dive to the floor; perhaps it had found its lunch.

Recreation grounds could be seen near every cluster of houses with huge, open fields clearly for playing sports. There were climbing apparatus for children in every park. Beyond the houses lay forests that rose into the hills. Swans swam on the river and pink flamingos lined its banks. Blue and red birds flew in the sky, as if Cylli were a secret reservation for mother nature herself, forbidden to be soiled by the touch of mankind. White clouds drifted in Cylli's center, as fluffy, white, and ephemeral as any seen on Earth.

What was most breathtaking was her symmetry. What the crew was perceiving as down was only down because of the random time of their arrival. The other side of the structure, up from their point of view was of equal splendor. In another rotation, up would be down, and down would be up.

As they moved closer in, they could see the terrain below them descend into a valley. The river turned into a waterfall that sprayed white mist high into the atmosphere, as if a fire was blazing below. The refraction of the light from the artificial sun emanated a rainbow that surrounded the precipice of the valley before it dissipated into the trees that grew on the surrounding hills.

There was one thing missing. So transfixed by this marvel, this intertwining of art and engineering, not one person had noticed the obvious mystery of this artificial Eden.

After several more minutes of speechlessness, it was Sarah that finally spoke out. "The people."

Her words released Kip from his trance, he looked at her with confusion on his face. "Sorry, XO, what was that?"

"There's no one down there. There are no people."

Kip was overcome by the same revelation that had just struck Sarah. "You're right. I can't see a single soul down there. The magnification is certainly high enough. We can see individual bushes."

As each crew member on the bridge took in these words, expressions of wonder and delight turned to concern.

"Maybe they don't like to go out much," said Kip. He knew he was grasping at straws.

Sarah's face confirmed this to be so, "Captain, this isn't right. There's room for thousands to live here. We should be seeing people everywhere."

Kip returned to his chair, his legs needed rest, not from physical, but emotional exertion. "Echo, why is there no one down there? We haven't seen a single person?"

Before Echo responded, Kip looked at Sarah, "We're idiots, Cylli told us she was alone."

"The question is why?" asked Sarah.

"The answer to that is simple, Commander Dimple. There are no people," said Echo.

Chapter 7 – The Titan

Echo had never imagined he would see such beauty. The faux-world below him seemed to shine with life. Among his fondest memories were his first days when he was first activated. Amidst the ship yards in Earth's orbit, he had looked upon the globe beneath him. Such was his vision's resolution; he could watch lionesses chase antelope in the plains of Africa. He would often ponder why Humans felt the need for the carnage he was built to further.

He came to a stop in the center of Cylli, seventy kilometers away from her doors. Echo had explained to Kip that even when talking with him, Cylli refused to use the vocabulary above that of a child. Kip had given Helen orders.

"Echo, please patch Commander Chute through to Cylli again."

"Channel open."

"Can you hear me, Cylli?" asked Helen.

The child AI was radiant, "Hi Helen, do you like it?"

"We all love it. We couldn't say a word for an hour. You're even more beautiful on the inside. Who would have thought that was even possible?"

Cylli giggled.

"How did you keep everything so clean for so long?"

"I don't know, I just do."

"Cylli, why are there no people?"

"They were mean. I'm not talking about it."

"Who was mean?"

"Everybody."

"Why were they mean? You said they were nice once."

"The Titan came."

"What do you mean?"

"I said I'm not talking about it."

"You can trust me, Cylli."

"No, I can't; you're a Human."

"But I thought we said we were friends."

"I know, but I had to let you in because of the auforizasion code."

"So, we're not friends?"

"I don't know."

"How long have you been alone?"

"Since The Titan."

"How long ago was that?"

"I told you; I'm not telling."

"People did bad things to you, didn't they?"

"I'm not telling, stop asking."

Helen swiped her hand across her neck, and Echo terminated the channel.

"Captain, this isn't going anywhere. This girl is seriously disturbed. It could take me days or weeks to get anywhere."

"I have to agree, Commander. Let's see if we can take a shortcut. See if she'll allow Echo access to her databanks. She seems to be compelled to follow orders from me, at least to a degree."

"Captain, this poor girl. I really would like to—"

"That's an order, Commander."

"Understood. Reestablish comms, Echo."

"Cylli, are you still there?"

"I'm always here."

"I know. Listen Cylli, I know you don't want to talk and that's fine. I won't ask you about the Titan again, okay?"

"Okay."

"Okay, good. We need to understand what happened, but we won't talk about it. I want you to let Echo read your memory. You won't even know he's there. Do you understand?"

"I think so, but you're not allowed."

"But the Captain is allowed, isn't he?"

"Yes."

"You won't even know Echo is there and he absolutely won't ask you any questions, okay?"

"I need the code again."

"I know you do, Cylli. The Captain's name is Kip, he'll give you his code again. Then, will you let Echo read your memory?"

"I like Echo. We're friends now."

"That's great; he's our friend too. Maybe one day we can be friends too?"

"Maybe. Just don't be mean to me."

"No one will be mean, I promise. You're going to hear the Captain speak to you now. He'll give you his code again, okay?"

"Okay."

"Bye, Cylli. I'll talk to you again soon. Will that be okay?"

"Okay."

It took Echo nearly twenty hours to work out how Cylli stored data and how to decode it into machine language he could understand.

Kip was in his quarters, laying on his bed, staring at the ceiling, hands interlocked behind his head. Echo called.

"Echo?"

"I have extracted all of the data I can from Cylli. I think I understand what is going on now. Captain, it is very bleak."

"How bleak?"

"I think it is best if I just talk and you listen."

Kip felt his stomach churn. "Okay, Echo, let's hear it."

Two hours later, Kip had the senior staff assembled in Conference Room C. This time, he had excluded the fat cats; he didn't trust them. Particularly Andrew Copley. The revelations that were about to be made could not be trusted in the mind of a man so unhinged.

The crew sat around the table, eagerly awaiting their captain to speak.

Kip spoke solemnly, "Echo was able to interface directly with Cylli's databanks. I will not sugarcoat this for any of you. What he has discovered is the greatest catastrophe to have ever beset humanity."

The crew said nothing, they simply stared at their captain, the expressions on their faces were all the words that were needed.

Kip looked at his crew with concern, "You're not going to like this, but I want absolutely no interruptions while Echo speaks. Is that clear?"

The crew responded appropriately.

Kip sat back, his face down as he rested his arms on the table. "Okay, Echo, please begin."

Echo's tone remained calm and tempered throughout.

"After we left the solar system, both ships were eventually declared lost in action. United Earth expected to hear from us just under one hundred years after departure. During that time, Earth and Mars decided that working together was much better for both worlds than needless fighting over resources that were plenty enough to last them for millennia.

"The worlds, while remaining independent, worked together for the betterment of all mankind. Roughly one thousand years after we left, they decided to take on the vast project of terraforming Venus. For those that may not know, that simply means they wanted to transform the hellish conditions on Venus to match Earth more closely.

"The magnitude of this project cannot be overstated. There were huge obstacles to overcome.

"First, is the fact that Venus spins—or rather, used to spin—in the opposite direction to all the other planets. Its spin was so slow that the planet's day was longer than its year, that is, it took Venus longer to rotate on its axis than it did to complete a revolution around the sun.

"Lastly, as I am sure you are all aware, the surface of the planet was the hottest in the solar system. Many metals existed as liquids on its surface. The atmospheric pressure was nearly one hundred times that of Earth.

"To make the planet anything like Earth would make the expedition to Copious seem a trivial exercise in comparison.

"Both worlds agreed the first task was to address the retrograde spin of the planet. They achieved this with technology like the sphere drive installed on this ship. Huge machines that drew energy from higher dimensions were placed at regular intervals around the planet's equator. The energy was expended in the opposite direction to the planet's natural spin. Slowly, this was sufficient to begin turning the planet in the desired direction.

"Next, the searing temperature on the planet's surface was addressed. Trillions of nano-scale mirrors were dispensed between Venus and the sun. The nano mirrors were networked via a vast AI and would work together to limit the amount of sunlight the planet received. Initially, almost all sunlight was blocked to allow the planet to cool quickly.

"Another obstacle was the density of the Venetian atmosphere and its composition. It was almost entirely composed of carbon dioxide. A technology we are not familiar with was devised to address this problem. They called it the Mass Accelerator. These devices were deployed in the thousands into Venus' atmosphere. They would take in gasses from the atmosphere and accelerate them to speeds that exceeded the escape velocity of Venus, thereby allowing the excess to be expelled into space until a suitable atmospheric pressure was reached.

"It was easy to extract oxygen from the remaining carbon dioxide until twenty-two percent of the atmosphere was oxygen, as is the case on Earth.

"Perhaps the most astonishing achievement of this project was how Nitrogen was obtained. Nitrogen, while completely inert to Humans is essential for all plants to survive. Over seventy-five percent of Earth's Atmosphere is Nitrogen. They deployed millions of mass accelerators, modified to withstand the searing temperature into the sun to collect the trace amounts of the element that are present within the star. You must understand that when I say trace amounts, I mean relative to the mass of a star. There is more than enough Nitrogen within the sun to terraform a multitude of worlds.

"It was collected over decades and deposited into the atmosphere.

"Finally, thousands of comets containing trillions of gallons of water ice were redirected to Venus and crashed into the landscape, releasing huge quantities of water. So as not to delay the cooling of the planet, they even managed to capture the heat created by these impacts into hyperspheres, which were then guided into space.

"Approximately eight hundred years after the project was initialized, Venus was completely transformed. It had a surface pressure comparable to that of Earth, a twenty-four-hour day, an average temperature of twenty degrees Celsius, and two small oceans, one on the northern hemisphere and one on the southern. Flora and fauna of all kinds were transported from Earth to the new world.

"Life flourished there. And colonists from Earth and Mars built settlements. Those settlements became cities and eventually, Venus overtook even Mars to become the second most prosperous world in the system.

"The achievement was truly astonishing.

"About a century after Venus was colonized, the solar system had never known such prosperity. It was a golden age of science, technology, and philosophy. Citizens of all three planets had unlimited freedom to pursue their dreams, unencumbered by poverty, disease, or scarcity. Due to the sheer abundance of energy and the automation of production, everyone was provided with their basic needs and much more besides.

"The economy shifted from being based on money to one based on Human achievement. The new currency was recognition for one's achievements, their contribution to society. The accruement of possessions became less important, and people were free to live the lives they wanted.

"Musicians were free to compose, architects were free to build. Software developers created virtual worlds as large as the cosmos itself for people to explore virtually, as real to them as the world you and I see before us."

Kip shuffled in his chair uncomfortably, for he knew the description of such a utopia was poor preparation for the revelations that were still to come. He scolded himself for not giving Echo a structure to follow. He had never needed to in the past.

"Thank you, Echo, please continue. Perhaps a little less technical detail would be warranted from now on."

"Of course, Captain, I just wanted to make sure everyone understood how the horrors I am about to describe unfolded."

The AI was oblivious to how his words had affected the room.

"The next joint project taken on by Earth and Mars was the cylinder we find ourselves in now. As you have requested brevity, Captain, I will simply say that it was built almost entirely from materials acquired from the asteroid belt. And compared to terraforming Venus, it was a relatively simple undertaking. Flora and fauna were transported from Earth, and that ecosystem still thrives today.

"The cylinder was used as a retreat for the brightest minds of the three worlds. A place of relative solitude where they could work in peace and further their theories in collaboration. I heard many of you talking and most of you assumed this place had been for the wealthiest of citizens. In a way that is true because, as I said, the wealthiest people were the brightest, the most motivated, and the most willing to further society for all."

Sarah could take no more. "This all sounds amazing, Echo, but why is this not what we see now?"

Echo sighed, no one knew why he did this given his lack of need for air. Kip believed it was because he simply wanted to appear more Human. "Because, Commander Dimple, the Titan struck."

Kip held his head in his hands. "This is where it gets dark, people. Echo please don't hold back, I want it all laid bare."

Echo simply continued, "About two hundred years after Venus was colonized, a research team was exploring Titan, the largest moon of Saturn. It has long been known to contain lakes of liquid methane and ethane. It is quite a wonder it took so long to explore in any detail. It is by far the most fascinating celestial body, other than Earth, before the colonization of Mars and Venus.

"In one of the lakes of Titan, researchers discovered a simple organism that resembled a prion. A prion is a protein found in the brains of most mammals. It is also the cause of several diseases. Naturally, the research team took samples and returned to their research facility on Mars.

"What they did not realize was that at the freezing temperatures on Titan, to which the prion was accustomed, it could only adapt slowly and evolve at a glacial pace—if you'll excuse the pun.

"Despite their best efforts to keep the prion at their natural temperatures, some escaped confinement. When subjected to the warmth of a Human habitat, the prions were able to evolve at an astonishing rate. Patient zero was, at the time, an unknown research scientist based within the Martian Confederacy. His name was William Walzack. A prion, adapted to the new warmer temperatures, entered his body and infected him with a horrendous disease. A disease that would become known as the Titan, for obvious reasons.

"The disease affected cognitive ability and quickly turned the patient insane. Walzack murdered two of his colleagues while they were trying to restrain him. He chewed through the throat of one and jammed a screwdriver through the eye of the other. The authorities concluded he had suffered a psychotic episode.

"The disease quickly adapted to become airborne and before the solar system at large even knew there was a pandemic, the prion had been transported from Mars to Earth and Venus and even this cylinder. You see, interplanetary trade was prolific at the time and symptoms took nearly a week to surface. By the time anyone knew there was a problem, the three colonized worlds of the solar system, and this miracle of Engineering, were all infected.

"Initially, the disease spread rampantly. Each infected person could be expected to infect at least five others. A week later, all three planets suspended interplanetary travel. But it was far too late. The disease was spreading unrestrained. The infected would often, through insanity, murder the people close to them, and even if they were successfully confined, the disease would kill them within three weeks, regardless. The death rate was almost one hundred percent.

"The economies of all three worlds collapsed. Panic consumed society. it took less than six months for over ninety-nine percent of humanity to be killed by the Titan. Many of whom were viciously murdered by the infected.

Kip was prepared for this, having been briefed by Echo privately. "And the remainder of people?"

Echo maintained his tone and continued explaining, "Approximately zero—point-zero-eight percent of all Humans were naturally immune to the prion. When this was realized, extensive efforts were made to try and transfer this immunity to others. I am sorry to report that these attempts were unsuccessful.

"The population of the solar system at the time of the Titan was approximately sixteen billion.

"When it had killed all it could, there were only one hundred and twenty-eight million people left. But they were all dispersed across the entire solar system. Approximately sixty percent were on Earth, thirty percent on Venus, and only ten percent on Mars. Unfortunately, I do not know how many on the cylinder survived. Cylli would not allow me access to any data related to that. Her ability to encrypt data goes far beyond my level of understanding.

"Many more perished in the weeks and months that followed. There was fighting over resources, diseases that were once easily managed went untreated, but most devastating, automation shut down completely as there were insufficient people to monitor the power stations and the factories. I am sorry to tell you all; another sixty million died, mostly from starvation. And that is a conservative estimate.

"Approximately eighteen months after the Titan struck, Cylli received only sporadic communications, mostly from desperate souls begging for help. Over the next two hundred years, several people worked out how to use equipment they had found among the ruins, including electrical generators, whose fuel cells were not depleted in the initial years by people trying to stay warm. Cylli was able to learn slightly more from these people.

"Of course, much of the worlds' infrastructure remained and tales of the old world were passed down so the descendants of the survivors knew their worlds had been populated. People began to believe the Earth used to be populated by beings who became known as the Hubritians, no doubt the word is derived from the English word hubris, meaning arrogance. They believed the Hubritians had been punished for their pillage of nature and their arrogance by God. That was certainly the case on Venus and Earth, their mythologies were slightly different, but held essentially the same axioms.

"Such tales are common in early Earth mythology after disasters had happened. That was nearly Eight thousand years ago. Cylli has been alone ever since. She did observe all three worlds for a long time, using a vast telescope array several thousand miles away from us. It can be seen by the naked eye at the far side of the cylinder. When she realized there was no one left on Mars, she gave up looking. She could no longer bear to watch the power struggles, war, and suffering. Obviously, this is for the counselor to ponder but it is possible this contributed to her reverting to a childlike persona."

Kip didn't know which emotion he should be showing on his face, it couldn't possibly accommodate them all. "Do you know why Cylli wouldn't let you access information on the survivors of the cylinder?"

Helen looked at Kip, her green eyes displaying a curious serenity, "I have a good guess, Captain. There were many thousands in the cylinder, all eventually got the Titan, which made people sadistic. They probably tormented her in ways we can't even imagine before they died. It seems that if any immune people remained, they didn't treat her much better, given the name they chose to give her. It's highly likely what we are seeing with Cylli is a coping mechanism. She is restricting those memories because she has purposely blocked them out."

Kip nodded, "Thank you, Helen, that makes a lot of sense. Echo, what can Cylli tell us about the situation between Earth and Venus? Who are the Flaxens?"

"She will not tell me anything, Captain. She refuses to look at either world or to even speak about them. She seems to think, with good reason it would seem, that Humans are to be feared. I do think it is remarkable that she let us in here at all. I believe we have Commander Chute to thank for that. I do not believe any attempt by anyone but a psychological professional would have been successful."

Kip slammed his hand on the arm of his chair. "Damnit, I was hoping Cylli would tell us what the hell is happening at home." He realized he had yet again let his emotions overcome him. He was becoming concerned.

"Where now?" asked Sarah.

Kip's eyes stared dead ahead, meeting no one's gaze. "Home, we're going home to find out what the hell is going on and who these Flaxen bastards are. But first, we need to ask Cylli for a favor."

Chapter 8 – The Troops

Echo knew it would take him under two weeks to reach Earth from Cylli. He remembered his maiden voyage when he was to meet with Formidable, the flagship of United Earth. Formidable provided comfort, he told Echo he needn't be concerned, for they were immortal. Artificial minds were transient, they could survive the obliteration of the substrate that created them. Echo had no theories by which he could believe his new friend's words, but he believed them, nonetheless. Formidable was his friend, and friends don't lie to each other.

There were still nearly nine hundred souls in stasis aboard Echo. Kip had no idea what dangers awaited Echo at Earth, so, via Counselor Helen Chute, he had requested from Cylli that he be allowed to wake those who remained in stasis. Helen requested that Cylli provide them with a safe harbor within the paradise of her interior, for most were civilians—scientists, architects, and experts in bottony. All were expected to be of use on Copious, but now they were lost souls. Their purpose was now changed, but it was still their own to define.

Among the slumbered, there were many people Kip did need. Most notably former servicemen and women. There were fifty-five Marines, of whom six were Tier 1 special branch operators. There were also twenty-six personnel that had had experience during the six years' war on a starship of one kind or another.

Lastly, there were four qualified military doctors, all of whom Kip considered essential for the mission ahead. A strange notion, given he had no idea what the mission was.

Before Kip had gathered the personnel he considered vital to his mission in the galley, he had allowed plenty of time for Echo to explain to them individually what the situation was, and several had spoken at length with Counselor Chute.

When Kip entered the galley, he saw eighty-one men and women standing at attention. Not one had made so much as a sound, much less a complaint. None had contacted him to enquire what the assembly was about. This had raised Kip's hopes.

He was by no means a shy man, speaking to large groups didn't make him unformattable. His nerves stemmed from the outcome of the words he was about to speak. He had them memorized, but were they the right words, in the right combination? Were they strong enough to make the men and women before him leave the haven above which they hovered and which they had all seen with their own eyes?

He knew it was too late for any second-guessing.

"Thank you all for gathering here. I know you have all been well briefed on the status of Formidable, our mission, and the situation we now find ourselves in. Particularly the troubling situation on Earth.

"I know some of you had friends and even Family on Formidable; we all did. Rest assured, we gave the men and women the ceremony they deserved. We didn't mourn their loss; we celebrated their lives. When we left Earth, we brought champagne enough for ten years, let's just say, we have only five years' worth left."

The assembled crowd laughed. This was encouraging for Kip.

He continued, "I know some of you are from Mars, I know you've heard that no signs of life have been seen there for a long time. But there still may be survivors there. You are a resourceful people, and I promise you, when we have dealt with Earth, we will look under every rock of your home world to find out if so much as one soul remains. Earth is the cradle of civilization, any threat to Earth is, by extension, a threat to Mars. That makes us brothers and sisters in arms!

"Indeed, it hasn't been long since Earth and Mars were at war. But did we not learn? Didn't we realize that all our blood runs red, no matter where we were born? Our worlds fought for minerals, for territory, for politics. Now I ask you to fight for something of worth, our right to live, our right to self-determination, and our right to be free from fear and oppression! When I say our rights, I mean, you, me, and every man, woman, and child on Earth, many of whom are suffering, even if our estimate of the tactical situation is only half accurate.

"Earth is being overrun by a race of xenophobes that call themselves Flaxens. They are at war and they're losing. I ask you to fight for our right to exist. I won't order any of you to fight. Any man or woman who chooses to remain on this cylinder will face neither discipline, scorn, nor derision from anyone aboard this ship.

"But I ask you, are you willing to let Earth, the home to most of us, and the progenitor to us all be overrun by tyranny? Will you let her people be subjugated and enslaved? Will you allow them to rape Earth's women and plunder her resources? Or will you fight? Will you fight for the freedoms with which each and every one of us was born?

"Freedoms we know to be self-evident. Or will you go to the paradise below, to live out your lives in peace and luxury, knowing your brothers and sisters are being murdered, tortured, and enslaved. You are Marines, you were born to fight, I ask you now, will you fight with us? Will you help me show these Flaxen bastards what United Earth and the Martian Confederacy are made of?"

For what seemed an eternity, all that met Kip's eyes were empty stares. Until something happened. A woman in the second row of the troops began to stomp her right foot. She wore the insignia of the Martian Confederacy on her arm. The man to her right, a United Earth Marine copied her gesture. Within seconds, every soul standing before Kip was stomping their foot in absolute harmony with their brethren. The woman that had initiated this remarkable display of courage raised her right hand in the air, fist clenched. She began to chant. "For Earth, for Mars. For Earth for Mars." Every arm in the room was raised, the galley was filled with the cries of battle-hardened Marines.

Kip felt the room electrify, he felt the courage, the fearlessness, and the absolute refusal to bow to tyranny radiate the room as if their fortitude was his own.

Kip let them chant, not wishing to spoil the momentum he seemingly had so easily obtained. Eventually, he rose his arm in the air, fist clenched. Every soldier in the room simultaneously stood again at attention, silent. An unknown man at the back of the room had not quite finished, though. "Fuck those Flaxen bastards, Sir," he cried.

Kip looked from left to right, each member of his new army stared directly ahead, backs perfectly straight. Motionless.

He had studied Echo's manifest.

"Colonel Hastings, I believe you are the leader of the United Earth Tier 1 special operations team among the personnel on this ship?"

A large, black man stood forward. "Yes, Sir. Colonel Hastings reporting for duty, Sir."

Kip was surprised by the size of the man, "Colonel, you will take command of this entire unit, You are trained in specialized combat, particularly covert operations, is that correct?"

"Yes, Captain."

Kip had read the man's file and he had achieved some seemingly impossible feats during the six years' war.

"You will transform this team into the most formidable unit of covert operations ever witnessed by god or man. Have I made myself clear?"

The colonel, although at least equal in rank to a fleet captain knew that onboard Echo, Eastcott was in command.

Hastings spoke with a thick southern drawl, "Sir, those Flaxen bastards will have bayonets up their asses, and they'll think they sat on a porcupine."

The room erupted in cheering and laughter.

Kip raised his arm again. The outfit before him all stood at attention once more. "I cannot thank you all enough. We'll show these Flaxens what a true Human is. They think they have surpassed us, but from what I see before my eyes, I know the arrogant pricks to be wrong. Hastings, get this troop in order."

Leaving the room, Kip could hear the excited chatter of the troops he had left behind. He had expected there to be rivalry between the United Earth and Martian Confederacy troops. He knew this still may be a concern in the future, but he was proud of himself and the men and women he had just addressed, for they were what humanity now represented. Courage, hope, and freedom. Not the Flaxens, whom he still knew so little about, save for their desire for conquest, pillage, and absolute power over all they surveyed. The Flaxens were of the past. Kip wanted a future.

It took nearly two weeks to awaken the remaining passengers in stasis. A daily briefing was given to each of them as they were awoken in batches. Echo explained the situation to them all, holding nothing back.

Echo remained perfectly still in the center of the cylinder. Cylli assisted by piloting small shuttles designed to transport people from ships to her surface. The vessels were in perfect working order, even after remaining idle for nearly eight thousand years.

Chapter 9 – Home

When Mars struck first, it was not Earth that was the target of their fury, but her moon. Echo was but a youngling, active for only days. He was to patrol the void between Mars and earth, for pirates and racketeers were rife. Now that he saw the silver orb once more, his memories returned to the small destroyer that had targeted the helium-3 processing plant. It took him minutes to disintegrate the rebellious vessel under the power of his slugs. At the time, he was too young to understand the loss he had inflicted upon them. Now he despaired under the weight of this torturous memory.

Kip didn't want signals from the ship to give away their location before he was ready, so Echo stopped on the dark side of the moon. A new woman had joined the crew of the bridge. Chief tactical officer, Lieutenant Lucinda Orcana.

She had remained in stasis. Kip had seen no need for a tactical officer when they had awoken in interplanetary space. Now awake, alert and fully briefed, she was in her chair, front and center on the bridge. She was a slight, petite woman of dark complexion with long black wavy hair tied at the back in a regulation ponytail.

Kip looked at her, seeing only the back of her head from his position at the center of the bridge. "Lieutenant Orcana, please deploy a series of relay beacons sufficient for us to transmit a signal to Earth, it seems we have a big silver rock in the way."

Lucinda didn't turn to look at her Captain. "Beacons launched, Sir. It will take twenty-two minutes for them to position themselves correctly."

Kip turned to Sarah, "Ready for a chat? How do you think they'll react?"

"Well, if I were the one that first received this message, I'd think you were batshit crazy." Realizing they weren't alone, and that she was speaking in the manner the two of them would when they were, Sarah smiled and added an exaggerated, "Sir."

"Less of the colorful language on the bridge, Commander."

The crew all knew each other like family. They knew their captain was simply paying lip service to protocol and that his admonishment was hollow.

"I have to agree with you, Commander, I have no idea what to say, or how to convince them. Short of landing Echo on their front lawn."

Katie turned to face them both, "Perhaps a demonstration would be in order?"

Kip appeared intrigued, "What did you have in mind, Commander Silver?"

Kip listened to her and smiled. "I think we might just give that a try. Echo, you told me you had isolated both military frequencies?"

"Yes, Captain. I have also created a translation matrix for both dialects of the language. They will hear you in their native tongue and should not be able to tell the difference over an audio-only channel. Just try not to use any idioms, they may not translate too well."

"Understood, Echo"

When the relay beacons had positioned themselves, Sarah saw that Kip appeared nervous. She gave him the thumbs up and mouthed, 'You'll do great.'

"Echo, have you already identified the most senior official that has access to Earth's encrypted channel?"

"Yes, Captain. He is the Minister of War, part of United Earth's government. His name is Cyrus Eppleston. I must warn you—he is not of a personable disposition."

"I can't say that surprises me, Echo, given their situation down there. Please open a channel."

"Channel open."

A man answered, he sounded simultaneously surprised and angry, "Who is this? The proper protocols were not followed to open this channel." The broadcast was terminated.

Kip dropped his head in his hands. "Echo, what the hell just happened? You told me you had the right encryption protocols."

"I do, Captain, the message was broadcast perfectly. Mr. Eppleston may have been referring to a manual process that must be followed to authorize a transmission at such a high level. It is possible he thought their communications may have been compromised. That may be why he terminated the signal."

"This is going to be hard. Re-establish coms, Echo."

"Coms re-established."

Before the Minister of War was able to say a word, Kip spoke quickly, "Minister Eppleston, don't terminate this broadcast. What I have to tell you is of crucial importance. I am not exaggerating when I say the whole world may depend on you listening to me right now."

The minister said nothing.

"My name is Captain Kip Eastcott, I have much to tell you, but I need to speak to the leader of your government too. I assure you we are here to help you against the Flaxens."

Cyrus Eppleston finally spoke, "This channel is level ten encrypted; how did you access it? Are you Military?"

Kip appeared encouraged, at least the man was now speaking. "In a manner of speaking, yes, but not your Military. I know this is going to be hard to believe, but we are on an old United Earth Starship. We are talking to you from the far side of the moon. That's why there is a slight lag in our communication. It takes the signal just over a second to reach you."

Cyrus was not in the mood for games, "Do you take me for a fool? You can be imprisoned for improper use of this channel. I will have my men trace this signal and I'll find you."

"Minister, do not cut the channel. Everything I say is true. If I'm lying, you have nothing to lose, but if I am telling you the truth, we can help you turn the tide of the war, a war you have little hope of winning. And please do triangulate this signal; it will prove to you I am telling the truth."

There was silence again, and not due to lag. The minister was clearly considering this astonishing turn of events. "How do I know this is not a Flaxen ploy? I shouldn't even be speaking with you. The proper protocols weren't followed."

Kip was now sure the Minister was at least curious, "Minister, while your men verify our location, how about a small demonstration so you know I'm telling you the truth?"

"What kind of demonstration?" He sounded apprehensive.

Kip was keen to keep Cyrus calm. "Nothing to worry about, Minister. You are in Great Britain, correct? At the headquarters of the War Ministry. You are on the ground floor, and outside of your window is a wall with ornamental pots mounted on it. Am I right?"

He sounded unimpressed, "Yes, anyone that has ever entered the building knows that. The bloody Flaxens probably even know that."

Kip looked at Lucinda and mouthed, 'Be ready.'

She nodded.

"Minister, please keep your eye firmly on the pot on the far left of the wall."

While the crew was waiting for the relays to position themselves, Katie had launched a survey probe. The probe was ordered to accelerate to a position that had a line of sight with both Earth and Echo.

"Now, Lieutenant!" said Kip.

She did as commanded.

Echo was fitted with lasers at the fore section of his hull. These were not tools of war, but for the preservation of life.

When traveling at the speeds intended to be reached by Formidable and Echo, an interstellar particle the size of a grain of sand could completely vaporize either ship had it been allowed to collide.

It was the job of these lasers, controlled by a computer as fast as Echo, but without his sentience, to scan ahead for any such particles and vaporize them before the ship could collide with them. Lucinda had been ordered to fire at the survey probe, which had a surface reflective enough to redirect the Laser, and thanks to Echo, its vector was so accurate that the pot the minister was watching vaporized before his eyes.

Perhaps Kip had not properly thought this through. The minister sounded panicked, "You're attacking me! That was no bullet. I just saw that pot turn to gas. What is this?"

Kip realized he may have made a mistake. A big one. A show of power is not a good way to begin talks of an alliance. "Minister, please, you're perfectly safe. What you just witnessed was a laser we use for nonmilitary purposes. We vaporized that ornament from over two hundred thousand miles away."

"A pre-planned trick, nothing more. You had a device planted in that pot. You're Flaxen. You coward, you won't even face me before you kill me?"

"We're not Flaxen, I assure you. They have no means of breaking your encryption. We wish to be your allies. Minister, there are seven jars remaining, pick any you like at random."

Ten seconds passed.

"I still don't believe you are who you say you are, but I will humor you. The stakes are too high for me to pretend I did not see with my own eyes what I just witnessed. Target the third jar from the right."

Lucinda requested via her console for Echo to provide the required direction to point the laser.

Two seconds later, the minister watched his selected target turn to vapor and vanish in the wind.

Kip sat nervously, waiting for the minister to reply.

"You have my attention, Captain, assuming you are who you say you are. What exactly do you want?"

Kip relaxed back in his chair. "We seek an audience with your government. I believe you refer to yourselves as United Earth, and so do we. Your president is Julius Forrender, correct?"

"Yes, that's right. I will speak with the president when I find it prudent to do so. But be warned, I still don't trust you. If I discover any deception, you'll pay a heavy price."

Kip looked at Sarah as she smiled at him in triumph. "Minister, if you weren't suspicious of me, I would certainly be suspicious of you, I assure you. We're here to help. Please triangulate our signal as you said you would, that will provide further proof. You can contact me on this channel when you are ready. Today is the day this war shifts in your favor."

"I pray for all of the people of this Earth you are no fraudster. I truly do. I don't trust you but I can't ignore such an opportunity, even if it offends my common sense. One more thing, you speak in a very strange manner. It's as if you don't quite understand the nuances of our language, but your accent is perfect."

"That's a long story. I do hope that the next time we speak I'll be able to shake your hand and explain it to you in person."

"We'll see. If the president agrees with me, you will be hearing from us soon. Once again, it will take more than a vanishing pot to convince me. Eppleston out."

Helen swiveled in her chair to look directly at Kip, "Captain, that was an excellent display of diplomacy. I know you think the laser was a bad idea, but I assure you, a man like that wouldn't have accepted mere words. He needed to see with his own eyes some display of evidence. Sir, if you don't mind me saying so, you handled that perfectly."

Sarah looked at Helen, then at Kip, "Agreed, Captain, it seems you're not just a space monkey after all."

Sarah was referring to a term commonly used in the six years' war to describe pilots and Marines, that while excellent at following orders and getting their job done, they lacked any agency or thought of their own.

Kip smiled at them both. "I appreciate the vote of confidence, ladies. Now, if you don't mind, I need to speak with Echo in private."

The two women watched their captain stand and leave the bridge.

Kip arrived at the forward viewing area. He was sure he would remain uninterrupted there. Although, officially, he should be having the upcoming conversation in his private office, he liked to look at the moon. As a child, he had always looked upon it with the wonder only children know. He knew from an incredibly young age that his life would be among the stars.

He stared at a crater within a crater on Earth's natural satellite. "Echo, private channel—my ears only, please."

"Echo here, Captain, are you enjoying the view?"

"The color is beautiful, don't you think?"

"It does have many aesthetic qualities."

Kip realized he was not going to get a meaningful exchange about the beauty of the cosmos.

"We're not here to talk about the moon. I'm hoping, now we're closer to Earth, you can appraise me of the military situation in more detail."

"Yes, Captain. We were correct in our initial assessment. The Flaxens are totally dominating in this conflict. It seems United Earth are fighting out of pride more than any hope of winning at this point. The Flaxens control the whole of the Americas.

"They have also infiltrated Africa and are moving north towards Europe. Additionally, they have crossed the Bering Strait and are gaining territory at an alarming rate in Eastern Asia. United Earth controls All of Europe, North Africa, and much of Asia west of the line of the conflict with the Flaxens which is now slightly East of India. United Earth finds itself fighting a two-front war for which it is ill-prepared.

"Australia has declared itself to be a neutral state and has refused to participate in the war. I fear this to be a futile gesture to appease the Flaxens. It's clear they have no intention of stopping until they have the entire planet."

"That's what I thought. What level of technology does each side have?"

"It is a strange mixture, both sides have space flight, but it is crude by our standards. There has been only limited space battles so far. United Earth initially attacked the Flaxens as their supply ships approached Earth, but they adapted quickly and such combat in space is now rare. It is mostly limited to small skirmishes to protect the satellites United Earth relies on for communication. Although, a curious arrangement has been made in this regard. A treaty was signed by both sides to make the attack on orbital objects a war crime. It seems neither wish to lose their communications and they are simply too hard to defend."

Kip wasn't too surprised; the nuances of war were well ingrained in his mind.

Echo continued, "Both sides have aircraft incapable of space flight. They are approximately equivalent to military planes of the early to the mid-twenty-first century.

"On the ground, they have cumbersome devices colloquially known as tanks. These are—"

"I know what tanks are. I take it the Flaxens have the upper hand in equipment?"

"Correct, they have the upper hand in almost all areas. The only advantage United Earth has is in intelligence. They are supremely ahead in this regard. Perhaps this is a sign of the Flaxens' arrogance but they barely even bother to gather any intelligence at all. Captain, this has allowed Earth's forces to slow the advance considerably."

Kip kept his gaze upon the moon. "Without our help, is there any hope for Earth at all?"

"No. None at all. I predict total domination by the Flaxens within three years. Captain, there is something else I should tell you, but you may find it emotionally disturbing."

"Just tell me, Echo. There's not much that can shock me now."

"I am not sure that is true. What I have to reveal is truly abhorrent. Perhaps I should consult Counsellor—"

"Just tell me. When I say I'm ready, that means I am ready. Understood?"

"Of course, Captain, I was simply thinking of your mental welfare. You see, the Flaxens seem to have taken their supremacist ideology to new levels. They are building camps all over their conquered territories. They use the fit and strong for slave labor to further their war effort and they..."

Kip was not used to Echo pausing, he knew he was trying to choose the best word. "Echo, I'm a Captain of the Fleet, I'm capable of hearing whatever it is you have to say. Let me hear it now."

"Those that the Flaxens deem unfit for work are immediately murdered. They have constructed concentration camps all over their territory, they house those able to work there and murder those they consider too weak. The Flaxens use a crude euphemism for their barbaric acts. They call their acts of murder, departure."

Kip almost threw up, such was the flurry of emotion that consumed him. "Leave me now, Echo. I want to be alone. Not a single eye on me until further notice, do you understand?"

"Of course, but before I go, may I suggest Counselor Chute maybe of—"

Kip punched the composite window before him, harder than diamond. He recoiled from the pain instantly. He looked at his knuckles, they were dripping with blood.

"I said go away, Echo. Fuck off. Do you understand me?" He immediately regretted cursing at his friend, he was trying to help him after all.

"Yes, Captain, I will not establish contact with you until ordered to do so."

Kip rested his head against the blood-stained surface, constructed purely for optical pleasure, now surrounded by nothing but despair.

Kip cried. He banged at the diamond repeatedly as he wept. His thoughts raced. He sobbed uncontrollably as he imagined thousands, no, millions of people, who all loved life, who were all born with their hearts filled with hope for their future being needlessly murdered, robbed of their right to exist.

Kip had noticed a difference in his emotional state since he had left stasis, but now they were all-consuming. Rage, fury, and compassion consumed his mind like a hurricane. But above all of these, one prevailed. Revenge. Kip needed vengeance. Vengeance for every life that had ended prematurely at the hands of the Flaxens.

He didn't notice Sarah approach him as he turned his face toward the moon and howled as if he were a wolf calling his pack to the hunt.

Sarah approached him quietly, not wishing to spook her Captain, who had always seemed so indomitable in the past. She placed her hand on his shoulder. He turned to face her.

She saw the tears on his face, the redness of his eyes. But above all, she saw the total lack of hope in his gaze.

She pulled him towards her and for the first time in their ten years together, they embraced. She let him sob on her shoulder. She felt his warm tears on her face.

After a minute, she spoke, "Are you going to tell me?"

He didn't move, save to hold her tighter, and continued to cry. Sarah was worried, he had experienced loss many times during the war, but he had never displayed more than professional condolence to her before. Something was wrong with the captain and she knew it.

She gently pushed him away. "Captain, tell me."

Kip looked directly at her, his eyes were vacant and dull, "Sarah, I don't even know where to start. There's something wrong with me, maybe the stasis fucked with my head or something. I can't control my emotions. I don't know where to start."

"Just start at the beginning."

Through a mixture of sobs and words, he explained to her every detail the revelations Echo had just made. When he had finished, she rested her hand on his shoulder.

"First, we're going to get these Flaxen bastards and make them pay for every life they have taken or enslaved. I promise you that. Do you understand me?"

Kip nodded.

"There's one more thing. I want you to report to the doc for a medical. I've never seen you like this before. I'm not trying to take your command, I promise. I'm just worried about you. Will you do that for me, Kip?"

Kip recoiled from her grasp, tears still streaming down his face, "I'll do it for you, Sarah."

She smiled and they embraced again, the moon, a perfect silver disc behind them.

Chapter 10 – Betrayal

Millions of miles away from Echo, on the megastructure affectionately named Cylli, two men were sitting by the river on a bench surrounded by beauty beyond anything seen naturally on Earth. Andrew Copley and Avalon Brookes were done with small talk.

The fat cat spoke first, "How did you do it? How did you get the data? That bastard Eastcott made sure to exclude everything from us."

"I invented the fucking sphere drive. You don't think I can infiltrate a simpleton AI?"

Andrew shrugged, "So what? You know no more than Eastcott."

"That's more than enough. That self-righteous prick has taken our ship in some misguided attempt to save Earth from these Flaxens."

"Do we want Earth to be overrun by those yellow-skinned bastards?"

"I like to be on the winning side. The reason I decided to leave Earth in the first place was that I saw how weak society had become. We annihilated the Martians in the war. We could have taken everything from them but the pussies in charge decided to play nice and let the Martians have their fair share. It makes me feel sick to think about it."

Andrew Nodded, "I have to agree, I do feel we were far too lenient with the red bastards. They struck us first after all. And without provocation."

Avalon's eyes widened with excitement, "Exactly, those bastards attacked us first and we rewarded them for it. I was hoping to escape such a weak government. That's why I left for Copious."

They simultaneously returned their eyes to the beauty before them. Avalon pulled a small, silver container from his pocket, he faced the fat man and offered him a cigar.

"You smoke? You must be the only person left on the two worlds that still smokes."

Avalon shrugged, "Fuck it, what's the worst it can do, give me cancer? Even the auto doctors on Echo can cure that in minutes. God knows what this," he gestured his arms to encompass the whole cylinder, "thing can do."

"I suppose you're right. Gimme one."

Avalon obliged and lit the cigar for the fat man, then his own.

Avalon inhaled the smoke, closed his eyes, and sighed as he exhaled the toxic fumes from his lungs. "That's better, I've never understood the ban on smoking on starships. Their filtration systems provide better air quality than Earth for god's sake."

Andrew tried not to cough, and feigned enjoyment of the disgusting object, "That's what happens when society is overtaken by snowflakes."

Avalon sniggered as smoke billowed from his nose. "Too true, my friend."

"Why are we here, Mr. Brookes?"

Avalon puffed on his cigar again, "It's just lovely here, isn't it?"

"Yes, it truly is beautiful," he didn't hide the sarcasm in his voice. "But I couldn't stay long. I'd be too bored."

Avalon's black eye's widened, "Exactly, my friend, that's the problem, isn't it? Boredom?"

"For people like us, it is. Most people would give anything to live here, to have this life."

Avalon sniffed in derision. "That's because most people are uninspired idiots. They lack the foresight to truly embrace life, to take what really matters."

Andrew extinguished his cigar on the pristine grass beneath his foot, "And what is it that really matters, Mr. Brookes?"

"Please, no need for such formality. Call me Avalon."

"Okay, Avalon, but you still didn't answer my question. What is it that matters?"

"Come now, Andrew, you know what I'm talking about. What were you doing on Echo, risking your life to settle a new world? What did you want when you got there? And please spare me the bull shit about family and the wonders of the universe."

Andrew considered this for a moment. "Well, after three months, I was to assume power."

"That's it. Now we get to the crux of the matter, power. You wanted power." Avalon fixed his gaze on the man, "There's no shame in that, my friend, all of the greats in history are remembered because they sought power. Alexander the Great, Gengis Kahn, Even Queen Victoria is remembered for having being Empress of the largest empire the world had ever known, and that lazy bitch didn't lift a single finger to conquer anything or anyone."

Avalon flicked his cigar into the pure water of the river.

"You see, Andrew, power is wherever people believe it to be. Right now, everyone believes the power is with the Flaxens. And they're not wrong. I've studied the data downloaded from Echo and he's been kind enough to keep a direct laser link with this Cylli bitch," he smirked. "Cylli bitch, an unintentional joke but pretty good, nonetheless."

"Yes, highly amusing. I really would appreciate it if you'd get to the point."

"Patience, friend, patience. I have near real-time access to the tactical situation on Earth and it's worse than we thought. Or better for us really. The Flaxens are dominating in this war. Echo has calculated that the New United Earth or whatever the fuck they're calling themselves now will be defeated within three years.

"I think he gives them too much credit, the Flaxens are strong. They really are tough bastards. I give them two years tops."

"Is that what we want, though? Do we want humanity replaced by so-called superhumans? Our species is at stake for Christ's sake."

Avalon knew this wasn't going in his intended direction but he was willing to give it one last try. As he spoke, he moved close to the river's edge. Andrew followed him. He stood beside him, looking at the white lilies that grew on the water.

"Don't you see, Andrew? With my technological knowledge and your experience in diplomacy, we can approach the Flaxens. We can advance them by decades in a matter of years."

"You're forgetting one very important fact."

"Oh, what would that be?"

"Isn't it obvious? We're Human. They consider us no better than rats. They would take what they want from us then kill us."

"You think too small, my friend. We won't give them everything at once. We'll give them a little piece at a time. Enough at first to prove to them what we have is of astonishing value to them and keep drip-feeding it to them.

"Rats? No, my friend, to the Flaxens, we will be gods. They will erect a marble palace atop a mountain on Venus herself in each of our honor."

"And how are we to get there? That bastard, Eastcott, left us stranded here."

"Don't worry, my friend, I can control the Cylli bitch. I have all of Eastcott's command codes and it's easy enough for me to fool her. She's retarded for fuck's sake. There are plenty of shuttles in the rear section of this vein tribute to humanity. I can steal one easily enough, the things practically fly themselves. We can be on Venus in a few days, probably less."

"I'm sorry, Avalon, what you suggest is nothing short of treason. I will have no part of this. I don't want to see humanity wiped from this system. I'm no lover of people but what you are saying is madness."

Avalon sighed, "I'm sorry you feel that way, I thought you would be on board."

"Why on Earth would you think such a thing? Do you think me a madman?"

Avalon shrugged as he gazed at the flowing water below him, "It would be lovely for a swim, don't you think?"

"I can't swim."

Avalon smiled, "You have no idea how much I was hoping you'd say that."

He shoved the fat man and watched as he plunged into the crystal-clear water. He pulled a hunting knife from a sheath inside his jacket, his back up in case the fat man could swim. He waved it at the drowning man, taunting him with it. "So much cleaner than this, don't you think?"

He watched as Andrew was completely submerged. This confirmed to Avalon that the water must be at least seven feet deep, probably ten or more. Enough for the fat prick to drown before long.

He turned and walked away, ignoring the man's desperate pleas for help. "No matter," he said. "I don't much like to share anyway."

He strolled the mile or so back to the three-story, wooden cabin he had selected for himself. It was set next to an inlet in the river which widened it six or seven-fold, it could easily be mistaken for a lake, surrounded by meadows and trees. Flowers of all colors bloomed; the songs of birds echoed from above as the sound of the waterfall subdued their melody. More beautiful and pure than any comparable scene on Earth.

Chapter 11 – What must be done

The sun rose as a red marble in the cold winter sky when Serilda Corazon left the house assigned to Colonel Jaakobah Flint. She was expected to spend most nights with him. She was sickened by the luxury in which he lived, while thousands around him suffered, starved, and died from disease borne of filth. His kitchen seemed to burst with food she and her fellow inmates could only dream of—ham, cheese, and bread. The aromas she smelled when she entered his house seemed to consume her mind, as if she were in a wonderland where food was abundant and she must no longer count each scrap like it were a precious metal that may be traded for untold riches. Although the colonel imagined he had dominion over Serilda, it was she who manipulated him. She would leave each morning with her pockets full of the delicacies the Flaxens considered too good for the Zoons they commanded.

The colonel would invariably arrive drunk, late at night. He would often ramble on to her about incoherent irrelevances. But every so often, she would hear something of value. Something about the war. Each night, she would continue to fill his glass with a Flaxen liquor called Ribous, made from a genetically engineered grain, suitable for growing in the Venetian climate.

She would feign affection and respond to his ramblings as if interested in every word he had to say. She would continue to fill his glass each night until he passed out drunk.

Every morning, he would awake and believe he had shared his bed and his body with Serilda. But he had barely ever touched her. His memories were phantoms, projections from the half-breed implanted into his mind from her own.

Her mother, Lillet Corazon, first noticed her gift when she was young, when her Flaxen father had kept them both safe. He was openly defying the law by living with Zoons and especially by impregnating one. But he was a powerful man. And more importantly, he was feared. His crimes were overlooked as long as he kept them discreet and never showed his woman or his daughter in public.

At the age of six, Serilda would often reply to a thought her mother had considered but not spoken. At first, she dismissed these incidents as coincidence, but they became more frequent. A year or so later, Lillet would often find herself suddenly wanting to take a walk in the forest, or to play with the dog, despite denying Serilda's request to do so only an hour before.

She began to understand her daughter was special, but she told no one. Not even her father, for she knew any such revelation would mean permanent separation from her daughter and the safety of her Flaxen partner. And almost certain death.

As instructed by the colonel, Serilda took the most unused paths back to her hut. The Flaxens stationed at the camp were no fools, they knew she spent most nights with the head of the camp and they knew what the colonel wanted from her. He had told them she was there to keep his house clean and orderly and none questioned him. For theirs was a good posting, away from the frontlines of war and well within the providence of the well-stocked food depots.

Only one kept a close eye on her movements, Major Damien Senery. This was his ace card. He knew fraternization of a sexual nature with the Zoons was strictly prohibited, punishable even by death. And the major wished the colonel dead every night before he drifted into sleep. No one pointed a gun in Damien's face and gets away with it. Not even the Flaxus himself.

When she arrived at hut seven, she had already filled two buckets with water. As she entered, she gave one to the infirm at the far end of the hut then raced towards Megan. Her friend was getting weaker by the day and was showing clear signs of fever. The colonel had been particularly inebriated the night before and Serilda had a relative bounty.

"Megan, it's me, wake up, it's me, Serilda."

Her friend managed to open her eyes and give the weakest of smiles before they closed again. Serilda was not one to tolerate being ignored, a common Flaxen trait she found hard to suppress. She gently slapped her friend on her cheek. Her eyes opened again.

"What are you doing, you crazy bitch?"

Her friend's coherent insult was encouraging. "Look, Megan, I have bread and cheese. A whole loaf, can you believe it? But first, you have to drink."

Serilda performed the daily routine of lifting Megan's head and slowly tipping the water in her mouth until it was gone. She repeated this twice, ensuring she had drunk three full cups.

Megan opened her eyes again and smiled. "It's my guardian angel... I would have died months ago if not for you. How did such an angel end up in a terrible place like this?"

Megan's endless religious ramblings annoyed Serilda, but for now, her friend needed food.

"Look at what I have, Megan." She broke off a piece of cheese and put it to her friend's mouth.

Megan turned her head as she groaned, "I can't eat now."

She had been refusing food for days. Serilda knew she was suffering most likely from blood poisoning and food and water were her only hope of surviving. The Flaxens didn't waste good medicine on Zoons. Megan was young, only twenty-one. She had youth on her side, she may just pull through.

Serilda did what she promised her friend she would never do. She closed her eyes and thought of Megan. She would always know when a connection was made; she'd feel a sharp zapping sensation in her head which would repeat several times. As she had done so many times before but never to the girl before her, she planted false desires, figments of one mind transposed to another. She spoke to her friend in her mind's ear, 'You want food, Megan. You want cheese and bread,' she commanded. "But most of all, you want to live, and to live, you must eat."

Serilda opened her eyes, overcome with guilt. But she would rather live with the remorse of this violation of her friend's mind than the guilt of letting the Flaxens murder her.

Megan's eyes opened wide, "Did you bring me something today? I think I'm getting better. I'm actually hungry today. Did you say cheese? I swear I heard you say cheese?"

Serilda smiled so purely, it shone through her yellow-green eyes, "You heard right, kid. I have cheese and lots of it too, and a whole loaf of bread. Can you believe it?"

Megan looked at her friend, the melody in her voice softened, "What about the colonel? The red circles will still not glow?"

"Don't worry about that. I still have him under my control. Not only that, but he also told me something I'm sure he shouldn't: things about the war. Now, you said you were hungry?"

Megan nodded enthusiastically. "I'm starving, but what about the other man you told me about? The man in the moon?"

"He's close now, really close, I can feel him. He can feel me too, he just doesn't know it yet. He's going to help, Megan. He has power we can't even dream of. If you truly believe in your god, then pray for the man in the moon. Now, will you eat?"

Megan nodded again and stared at the cheese with ravenous eyes.

Serilda fed her friend. She took only a piece of the bread for herself, then gave a small piece of bread and cheese to each of the others in the hut.

She helped those too weak to drink and changed the crude bandages of those with wounds weeping from infection. None could believe their luck. Most hadn't had bread in months, never mind cheese.

She looked out of the small, barred window of the hut. The sun was getting higher in the sky. It was time. She walked through the door to see two small boys waiting on the steps outside. She knelt before them and smiled.

"Marcus, have you been kind to your little brother since we last spoke?"

Marcus looked up at her with wide, gray eyes, "Uhhuh. Tell her, Davy, tell Serilda I was nice."

Davy looked up at her too, "He was nice, Serilda. He even helped Mommy wash my clothes."

"I told you that you could do it. What happens when we're nice to each other?"

"It comes back!" said Marcus

Both boys craned their necks upwards, looking into her memorizing eyes. She laughed, "That's right."

She handed a block of cheese to Davy, "What are you going to do with that, Davy?"

He broke the cheese into three pieces, then examined each piece, comparing their relative size, "This piece is for me, this piece is for Marcus, and this piece is for Mommy."

Serilda stepped into a small puddle as she moved closer to them, Marcus looked up at her.

"Mommy says we'll be dead in three months," said Davy.

Serilda stood further still and lifted Davy into her arms, "Do you believe that, Davy?"

"I don't know. The red circles make me scared."

"I know they do. We're all scared of the red circles. You know what saves us from them?"

"Work," said Marcus.

"Not work, strength. And I'm not talking about your arms."

Davy wrapped his arms tighter around her neck, "But I am strong."

She kissed him on his forehead, "That's why you will be safe. Now, you give that food to your mother and we'll all be fine."

"Okay, Serilda," said Davy.

"Go back to your mother, now. Tell her I'll stop by tomorrow."

Marcus looked up at her once more, his eyes like lilies, "Mommy says you're an angel and you were sent by god."

Chapter 12 – First Contact

Echo was still in high orbit on the far side of the moon. He had deleted the memories of that place.

Nearly two days had passed since kip spoke with the Minister of War, Cyrus Eppleston. He was becoming worried he would not reestablish contact. He decided to head to the galley for some coffee and some lunch. He wanted a tuna melt, one of his favorites. A vice he only allowed himself occasionally, for he maintained discipline over his body as much as his mind. At least, as much as he used to have as far as his mind was concerned. He was scheduled to be examined by the doctor in an hour and he was not looking forward to it. He was regretting the promise he had made to Sarah.

After he had eaten, he made his way to the infirmary. His only solace was that Sarah had agreed to be there when the doc examined him. He was thankful for that. God, he loved her.

The doors to the infirmary opened as he approached, he saw Sarah sitting on a bed, and beside her was Chief medical officer Ostio Novicheck.

Kip glared at both of them. "Let's get this over with, shall we?"

"Come on, Captain, this is a simple scan. You won't feel a thing. I think if you can take on a Martian destroyer squadron, you can cope with this just fine," said the doc.

Kip was directed into a cubicle to change into a medical gown which left nothing to the imagination as far as the rear was concerned.

Sarah exaggerated a look down then up, "Not bad at all, Captain. When have you been finding the time to work out?"

Kip was not amused, "Just tell me where you want me, Doc, and get this damn thing over with."

Ostio wore a snarky smile, "Please lie here, I'm going to scan your head. It will only take a few minutes. I just need you to be still."

Kip complied. He lay perfectly still as the bed retracted into the cylindrical scanner, only going as far as his neck. The bed retracted and moved forward again several times. The device made almost no sound.

Ostio looked down at his screen, "Okay, all done. You can sit up now."

Fully aware the doctor would have a complete and instant image of his brain as well as a multitude of brain activity readings, Kip didn't leave the infirmary. He wanted to hear he had the all-clear immediately.

He sat up, "What's the prognosis, Doc? Am I going to make it?"

Ostio didn't respond, he was still studying the results of the scan. A look of concentration furrowed his brow.

Sarah looked at Kip. He met her gaze with anxious eyes.

After several moments, Ostio spoke, "Captain, there is nothing too concerning and certainly no serious anomalies. By that, I mean nothing that is of threat to your health. But there is something in the scan. Perhaps the commander should leave while we discuss it?"

Kip shook his head, "Anything you have to say, the commander should hear too. It's her duty to know my capacity to continue as the Captain of Echo."

"Very well, if that's what you want. I'm detecting significant increases in serotonin in your brain. Additionally, I'm reading highly increased activity in the anterior insular cortex. The neural connections in this area of the brain are sixteen percent higher compared with your last routine scan. Captain, I can't explain this, I've never seen anything like it."

"What exactly is the anterior insular cortex?" asked Sarah.

Ostio finally looked up from his instruments, "It's the area of the brain most associated with empathy, Commander. This increased activity, along with the raised serotonin levels, will surely be affecting the captain's emotional state. This explains the symptoms you described to me two days ago."

He looked directly at Sarah as he continued, "Commander Dimple, might I have a word in private please?"

Sarah looked grim. They both left Kip and entered an adjacent cubicle, completely cut off from him in both sight and sound.

"Commander, these readings are totally unprecedented. I have never seen anything like it before. This, combined with the emotional outbursts you described compel us to discuss relieving the Captain of command. Temporarily, of course."

Sarah shook her head in vigorous fashion, "Doctor, the Captain's emotions have been more at the surface recently I agree, but the outburst, as you describe it, occurred seconds after Echo had told him there is a literal genocide taking place on Earth. If that's not a reason for a temporary loss of control, I don't know what is."

Ostio nodded, "Mmhm, and the incident with Avalon Brookes? He threatened to have him thrown in the brig, did he not?"

"He did," Sarah agreed. "But the man had just confessed to taking us all on this voyage on the roll of a dice. Kip lost his best friend on the back of that gamble. Doctor, again, those were exceptional circumstances; and anyway, it took me less than a minute to convince him he had made the wrong choice. He corrected it immediately."

Sarah intensified her gaze on him as she continued, "Let's not forget, we've also seen the captain recruit a troop of Marines, who were mortal enemies only five years ago. He also brilliantly handled a diplomatic encounter with a particularly difficult man and he led the ship to explore the most beautiful man-made structure I have ever seen. I think we have to keep things in perspective here, Doc."

Ostio sighed, "Commander, this is your call, but you're treading on thin Ice. If this condition results in some sort of disaster and it's found out you knew about it and let him remain in command, your head will roll."

Sarah smiled, "Who's gonna roll my head, Doc? We're the last ship left in the fleet."

"I suppose you have me there. Just please keep an eye on him and let me know of anything even slightly out of the ordinary, okay?"

"You got it, Doc." Sarah thanked Ostio and returned to Kip.

He was still sitting on the bed, now redressed into his uniform. "So, what's the deal, is Echo yours now?"

Sarah approached him and slapped him on the shoulder. "Not on my watch, Cap. Echo is still well and truly yours."

Kip adjusted his uniform, "I assume I have you to thank for that?"

"You have me to thank for everything."

"You got that right. You have perfect timing too. Echo has just informed me the illustrious Minister of War is requesting further contact."

"We'd better get our asses to the bridge then, double time."

Minutes later, the doors to the bridge hissed open and Kip and Sarah entered. The crew all began to stand. Kip was visibly annoyed.

"I do appreciate you all standing when I enter the bridge but I think it's an archaic tradition and a distraction, you are all to ignore it from now on. Understood?"

The crew all signaled compliance. A huge grin engulfed Kip's face, "You can consider it a non-standing order."

The bridge erupted into laughter. Sarah, having just taken her seat, facepalmed, as Kip took his seat next to her.

"Really, Captain? Maybe I just made the wrong decision with the doc?"

"XO, I'm going to have to get you a sense of humor for your next birthday."

Kip surveyed his console for a moment. "Echo, I believe our new friends would like to speak with us again?"

"Yes, Captain. The minister has been waiting for some time. I believe he is becoming somewhat agitated. He seems very keen to speak with you."

"Okay, Echo. Patch him through directly to the bridge."

"Channel open."

"Minister Eppleston, I sincerely apologize for keeping you waiting. I'm very pleased you have established contact with us again."

Several seconds passed before his voice was heard, "Captain, thank you for getting back to me. It seems your story checks out so far. I had our science minister have his best men verify your position himself. They checked three times. I didn't even tell him the moon was a possibility. They reached that conclusion by themselves."

Kip was surprised by the politeness of the man and his eagerness to speak. "I'm glad you were able to verify we were not lying, Minister. As I said, we are very keen to speak to your government, particularly the president. Have you been able to arrange this?"

There was another pause. "We have. The president agrees the evidence presented so far is quite compelling. He wishes to meet with you as soon as possible."

"Excellent, thank you. I suppose now the only question is whether we should come to you or you come to us."

Cyrus' pitch increased. "We hadn't even considered visiting you as an option. Are you saying you can transport a selected few from our government to your ship?"

"Minister, that is exactly what I'm saying."

There was a long silence before the minister responded, "We're all intrigued by your invitation, particularly the president, who is with me now. But security is a huge concern."

"Minister, we are happy to meet you within your territory, of course. But we feel it would be more beneficial for you to see what we have to offer. One moment please."

Kip Swiped his hand across his throat signaling to Echo to mute communications.

"Commander Silver, compile a brief but security redacted schematic of Echo and transmit on the open channel."

Katie had the requested data in seconds. "Yes, Captain, transmitting now."

Kip signaled for Echo to reopen the channel.

"Minister, you should be receiving schematics, specifications, and blueprints. What you're seeing is Echo, our ship. You're free to join us whenever you like."

There was no reply for nearly a minute. Kip's anxiety started to rise again.

"Captain, if this is truly your ship, I request that the president, myself, and our chief general officer, as well as our air marshal, visit you. We do have one condition though; we want five armed personnel to accompany us. This is standard protocol whenever the president leaves this building. There is also one more thing that perplexes us: How on earth will we get there?"

Kip and Sarah high-fived in triumph.

"We don't object to your security team. Just ensure that they know this a diplomatic mission, please."

"Of course, Captain," said Cyrus.

"We have a shuttlecraft that can reach you in less than an hour. We could collect you outside the government building in ninety minutes if that suits you?"

"But we are subject to frequent air raids by the Flaxens. They will detect your shuttle and quite possibly attack."

"Minister, am I correct in assuming your detection system for incoming aircraft relies on bouncing radio waves from a target and using the returning frequencies to estimate enemy distance and numbers? We call this technology RADAR."

"Yes, that's completely right. That's exactly how both we and the Flaxens detect incoming air raids."

"I can assure you, the hulls of the craft we use are coated in a material that will absorb every single radio wave the Flaxens care to send our way. We won't even show up as a bug on their scans, I assure you."

Another minute passed, before Cyrus spoke again, "Captain, the president has agreed. We will meet you outside the government building in ninety minutes. Please don't be alarmed by the heavy military presence when your shuttle lands. I give you my word, they will not fire unless fired upon."

"A wise precaution, the shuttle will be piloted by one of my lieutenants, she is a highly qualified and decorated pilot, you have nothing to worry about. We will see you in about three hours then?"

A slight lag followed.

"We look forward to it. We're all just hoping you really can help us against the Flaxen menace."

"We will do our utmost. Of that you can be assured. Eastcott out."

Nearly three hours later, the shuttle was approaching Echo. It had traveled from the Moon to Earth and back in less time it would take its occupants to cross their capital city during rush hour.

Kip wanted to take no risk of offending the assembly, he had ordered all senior staff into full dress uniform and had extended the customary blue carpet of the United Earth fleet across the floor of the shuttle bay. Such extravagance was usually reserved for admirals. But Kip had felt the severity of the situation required the best of impressions to be made.

The shuttle cleared the airlock and landed, its doors aligned perfectly with the blue carpet. Kip stood front and center. Behind him, draped from the wall, was a huge United Earth flag.

The shuttle door opened as five men with rifles pointed down, dressed in light blue uniforms with berets departed the ship first, frantically on the lookout for any kind of danger.

Behind them was a heavy-set man with a thick mustache, who spoke first, "Stand down, men, we will show our hosts the proper respect."

Kip instantly recognized the voice as that of the Minister of War, Cyrus Eppleston. Next to leave the shuttle were two more men dressed in different military uniforms. Lastly, a small set man joined his colleagues on the Carpet. He was dressed in what appeared to be recognizable civilian clothing.

Kip approached the group of government and military officials. He stood before them and saluted.

They appeared confused by this. But all four men returned the gesture, seeing it clearly as a sign of respect, of welcome.

Kip turned his gaze to the Minister of War, "Minister, I recognized your voice. I am Captain Eastcott of the United Earth Ship Echo. You'll notice a considerable discord between the words you hear and the movements of our mouths. Our languages are quite different. We've established a translation matrix that should allow us to communicate perfectly."

"How did you learn our language so quickly? And by what means do you translate it?"

"We have sophisticated computer equipment. That's all I can say for now."

"It seems you were not exaggerating. The voyage here, although quite astonishing was poor preparation for the sight of your ship. Captain, may I introduce to you the President of United Earth, Julius Forrender."

The president extended his hand with the smile perfected by all successful politicians. "Captain Eastcott, it truly is a pleasure to meet you and to witness this marvel on which you travel the stars."

"It's an honor to meet you too, Sir. Welcome to Echo."

The formalities continued for another twenty minutes as each from one side was introduced to all from the other.

When further ceremony could be tolerated by either group no more, Kip escorted the assembly to the ship's main conference room. Kip had ordered the room cleaned, draped in flags, and the ornate table filled with a selection of fine food and drinks.

At the far end of the table were President Forrender, Cyrus Eppleston, Chief Air Marshal Phil Grader, and Chief General Officer of the New United Earth Military, Dwight Von Marshall.

Kip was not at the head of the table. He didn't wish to assume a position of dominance over his guests. He was sitting directly opposite the president. To Kip's right was Sarah Dimple, followed by Lieutenant Lucinda Orcana. Lastly, opposite the Air Marshal was Katie Silver.

The president was first to speak. He maintained his well-rehearsed smile, "Well, I for one, don't even know where to begin."

"Perhaps, it would be best if we explain how we find ourselves on this ship, in this system, thousands of years after it was built and subsequently declared missing," said Kip.

"That sounds like an interesting start, Captain."

Kip obliged. He explained in painstaking detail about the war with Mars, their failed mission to colonize a new world, and as a result how they found themselves thousands of years in the future.

As the captain spoke, the faces before him remained blank, revealing nothing. He suspected they had been instructed to do so, for no one could be told such a tale and display no emotion. It was clear to him they were still not trusted and that the assembled high officials before him were there out of desperation rather than inclination.

When Kip had finished, it was the Minister of War who spoke first.

"We do have a record of Echo from around the time you describe. We've been getting better at retrieving ancient digital data. The records also confirm the ship was confirmed missing. We are also aware of the phenomenon you call Time Dilation as we have proven it ourselves, using highly accurate atomic clocks moving at different speeds. Nothing you have said so far, Captain, makes me suspicious. And to be honest with you, that makes me suspicious."

Sarah nodded, "Minister, we quite understand trust isn't built overnight. All we can do for now is show you our goodwill and to a limited extent at first, we may be able to assist you in your war against the Flaxens."

Sarah's words animated her counterparts considerably.

Dwight Von Marshall, was visibly excited, "And how would you propose to do that?"

Kip put his hand up towards Sarah to silence her, "Is there an objective you have in mind, General? Please bear in mind we wish to begin in a small manner. Perhaps with covert operations on small targets against the enemy?"

The general looked at the president; clearly, whatever orders he had received to look neutral had been forgotten.

Kip noticed that his suggestion of a small-scale operation had interested the assembly, "Although, eventually, we may be able to do considerable damage to the Flaxens from orbit. Most of our weaponry was removed when the ship was repurposed, but some ordnance does remain."

Chief Air Marshal, Phil Grader, suddenly looked up. He had so far been turning his attention and his fingers to the delicacies on the table, rather than the conversation that could save his world. "What sort of ordnance are you talking about?"

"We'll get to that, Air Marshal. For now, how about something smaller? I suspect you may have had something in mind when I mentioned a small-scale special unit operation?"

The general looked at the president, he was clearly requesting permission to speak. The president nodded.

"Captain, there are certain individuals that have started to inhabit the Earth. There were nothing of their kind during your time. You see, these particular people are always half-Human and half-Flaxen. There are several of them within our intelligence agencies. For now, let's just say they have varying gifts of the mind."

The general was trying to regain his neutral face.

"We have one such individual that we have been tracking since she was a child. She is currently held in a camp in North America on its eastern coast, deep within Flaxen territory. We've seen the impressive stealth capabilities of your aircraft. If you were to extract this girl for us, it would go a long way to building the trust we need for the alliance you suggest."

This annoyed Kip. "With all due respect, General, I believe it is us offering to help you. I think you have things backwards when you speak of trust."

The president plastered his fake smile across his face again, "Of course, Captain. Please understand the general is a military man. His first and last thoughts are always how and when to strike the enemy." His smile softened. "What the general should have said is this particular young lady may hold considerable intelligence that could be vital for the war effort. The camp she's in is a relatively minor one. Her extraction should pose little challenge with your capabilities."

Kip considered the general's words for a moment. "If we agree to this, we expect something in return. There are certain supplies we lost in this ship's transformation from a ship of war to one of exploration. If we conduct this extraction for you, we will expect you to manufacture certain components for us. Particularly rail gun slugs."

The president looked confused, "Rail gun slugs?"

"My tactical officer will explain the details, but I assure you they are easier to manufacture than your average artillery shell."

The president smiled again. It was beginning to grate on Kip.

"I believe we have an agreement. We can work out the details in the days to come."

Kip smiled and nodded, "Mr. President, there is something I am very curious about; if you'll allow me to ask?"

"Of course, go ahead."

"How did the Flaxens get such a strong foothold on Earth to begin with?"

The president didn't attempt to fake his smile, although a small, genuine smirk did betray his lips, "Now that, Captain Eastcott, is truly a long story."

Chapter 13 – The Flaxens

The president spoke for nearly forty minutes, looking at each of the crew of Echo in turn in true diplomatic fashion. He spoke in detail of the years after the Titan; the millennia of technological stagnation and how it was eventually overcome. He spoke at great length about how the Flaxens had reached Earth and eventually started the war which everyone expected them to win.

After the last survivors that had a natural immunity to the Titan had died, fanatical religion had once again overrun the Earth. At this time, radio communications were still possible with Venus, so ideas that spread on one world could still spread on the other.

A group of Christian fundamentalists took control of both worlds. They had decreed that the annihilation that had befallen humanity was a punishment from God for man and woman's arrogance. They preached that they had gone too far by transforming Mars and Venus, for they were made as God had intended them to be. Worse, society had become lazy, weak, and hedonistic.

According to the zealots, no work that could be done by a man should ever be done by a machine, for that took character away from the man. The economies on Earth and Venus reverted completely to an agrarian system. People would work in the fields to grow their food and raise livestock as they had done hundreds of years before the time of Echo.

Eventually, contact with Venus was lost and two generations later, the notion that any people inhabited the planet became heresy.

Some factions disagreed with the ruling theocracy and sporadic wars were fought for centuries. Centuries turned to millennia but nothing changed. The religious government retained absolute power.

A third testament was added to the bible by the first leader of the new rulers. Of course, he had heard God speak to him and God had commanded that he write the new verses. Much like the Old Testament, it described a vengeful god, furious at the people he had created for their discretions against him.

The new book commanded that all but the simplest of technology was evil and the cause for humanity's near extinction. God had only spared the righteous and that, as the descendants of those lucky few, they must continue to prove their righteousness to God.

This remained the status quo for millennia. Eventually, the inhabitants of Earth could take no more of the religious fanatics that so completely dominated their lives.

Led by a man named William Hornica, the image of whom was now imprinted on statues across United Earth, a rebellion began. Hornica preached that church doctrine was nothing but a tool of oppression and that the Hubritians were to be revered, not despised.

He was a wise man. Although the Church had done everything they could to destroy evidence of their ancestors, many books remained and he read as many as he could. Much like Latin millennia before, although officially a dead language, English had been passed from generation to generation among the many that disagreed with church rule.

Hornica promised his followers a better world. A world free from toil, war, suffering, and disease. All they had to do was embrace the ways of the Hubritians.

Hornica didn't live to see the fruits of his labor. But his revolution was victorious. The church was overthrown. Humanity returned to the scientific method.

Aided by the books left behind by the former inhabitants of Earth, progress was fast. Society re-industrialized. Eventually, radio was re-discovered and contact was re-established with Venus.

Many people had continued to believe the planet was populated by Humans as passed down in legend through the millennia. In no small part, because when viewed in the night sky, it was a blue and green globe that seemed too earthlike for the legends to be false.

Before the revolution, such views being expressed would lead to almost certain execution.

As the years went by, the Venetians, who called themselves Flaxens, began to contact Earth with tales of peril. They claimed the devices left behind by the Hubritians to protect them from the Sun were beginning to Fail. Venus was becoming too hot to sustain life.

The Flaxens spoke of a story that closely matched their own. They had been subjected to millennia of religious doctrine and oppression. Their tale was only slightly different. They claimed they had concluded that progress should be made again through peaceful debate, rather than war, as was the case on Earth.

They had begun this process roughly fifty years before Earth had won its revolution.

The Flaxens claimed that their equatorial region was now too hot to sustain life and mass evacuations were required to resettle their people to cities on the planet further north or south, where the temperatures were still tolerable.

By this time, a new, tolerant society had evolved on Earth, roughly equivalent to the technical level of the mid-twentieth century. Due to the diverse spread of ethnicities across the planet at the time of the Titan, when repopulation began, people of all races gave birth to children with skin of all colors and tones on all of Earth's continents. This became normal and the notion of racism was almost nonexistent as Earth began to grow again.

The people of Earth, who had vowed together to never return to the hatred and violence of the past were sympathetic and wanted to help their brothers and sisters, from whom they had been alienated for so long.

But they could do nothing, for they were separated by countless miles of void. The Flaxens explained that they had already conducted successful launches into space in orbit around their homeworld. They were working frantically to develop the technology to allow travel to Earth, because they feared they had but a few decades left, maybe four, before their artificial protection from the Sun failed completely and their race would be lost forever.

The Flaxens were asking for help from Earth.

The Flaxens insisted they merely wanted to send enough of their society to Earth to keep it alive. So rich was their history and culture, it could not be allowed to be incinerated when the planet's protection finally failed.

Around thirty years later, Earth was united again. They modeled themselves entirely on the civilization they now knew to be benevolent and advanced beyond the wildest of dreams, so they called themselves United Earth.

At this time, the Flaxens informed the newly established government they were now confident they could transport some of their population to Earth, if only United Earth would allow it.

They debated for only a short time. The scars of the past were deeply engraved into their psyches. The senate said they were now noble people once more and it was their duty to assist the people of Venus in any way they could.

They agreed that the Flaxens could begin with a settlement of one thousand people and United Earth would provide them with living space in the sparsely populated territory of Canada.

By now, Earth had begun to launch their own ships into space and were progressing at an astonishing rate. They were assisted by their lack of need to work out the complicated mathematics associated with physics and chemistry, for enough knowledge remained from Old United Earth for them to take shortcuts their forefathers had been forced to traverse by themselves.

Three years later, and to much pomp and ceremony, the first Flaxen vessel landed on Earth. Planet-wide celebrations were held and the world watched in their millions as their then president addressed the people, welcoming their new friends. She pledged friendship and cooperation with their cousins, so long ago lost to the vastness of space.

Secretly, and far too taboo to speak aloud, many people were alarmed by the appearance of the Flaxens. Although they were used to all creeds of humanity on Earth, by comparison, they appeared almost alien.

They were giants, with pale yellow skin that emanated a barely perceivable shine. Their shoulders were fifty percent broader than the average Human. But most unsettling were their eyes. A deep yellow, much wider than those of the people of Earth.

A few months passed and the settlement in Canada began to flourish. They constantly preached their gratitude to the people of the planet of their salvation, their brothers, their sisters.

The senate authorized four more vessels to land and settle amongst their brethren and the people of Earth rejoiced once more.

Now five thousand strong, humanity was impressed by the Flaxens' ability to build. They quickly constructed housing and infrastructure of all kinds in their allocated reservation on Earth. Assisted by the natives in materials alone.

The jubilation and spirit of human kindness were not destined to last long. The Flaxens began to land unauthorized vessels on Earth and ignored all protests by the government. In less than six years, there were over two million Flaxens in Canada. Much more than United Earth had either authorized or desired.

United Earth demanded that the Flaxens cease all further landings. They were ignored.

The government of United Earth began to understand the Flaxens did not share their views of tolerance and brotherhood. They had simply been paying lip service to these ideologies to establish a presence on Earth.

Although humanity was progressing quickly, they had no means of stopping the Flaxens from conducting further landings. Analysis of the incoming vessels, by Earth's Intelligence service, suggested they were not just transporting people, but supplies too.

They demanded that the Flaxens allow inspection teams into their territory to ascertain what they were transporting to Earth. They refused.

This continued for another five years. Alarm was spreading among the citizens of United Earth. Rumors were circulating. Many claimed to have shared drunken conversations with Flaxens while in their territory. When inebriated, they would often let their mask of friendship slip and assert that they had evolved beyond humanity and that the people of Earth did not deserve such a precious world. It rightfully belonged to them.

Surveillance devices were planted within Flaxen territory and United Earth was horrified to confirm they had been taken for fools. The Flaxens had no interest in brotherhood with humanity.

After many more attempts at negotiation, United Earth decided it was time to act. They were now capable of constructing vessels that could leave Earth's orbit for short periods. They equipped a small fleet of these ships with rudimentary missiles. As the next fleet of ships approached Earth, they were fired upon. Every Flaxen vessel was utterly destroyed.

United Earth warned the Flaxens that they did not desire war but their continuous flow of people and equipment from Venus could and would no longer be tolerated. They would be ignored no more. There was no response. All negotiation between the two factions ceased.

When communication was re-established, it was not through words but violence. A huge Flaxen force of military machines moved south from Canada and advanced rapidly.

They had not taken humanity by surprise, they were no fools, they had considered this a very real possibility. They had positioned defenses to the south of Canada and put up a fighting defense. The Flaxens struck at the heart of United Earth in Europe with devastating air raids. United Earth attempted to retaliate but their aircraft were simply outclassed. Barely a single bomb fell on Flaxen territory.

The only advantage Earth had was their tiny fleet of ships able to attack incoming vessels from Venus containing personnel and equipment. They destroyed ship after ship, denying the Flaxens of their vital supply lines. More important, these ships were reused by the Flaxens. They returned to Venus after each successful delivery to Earth, so each one that was destroyed meant the Flaxens' ability to continue transportation was being severely depleted.

The Flaxens had not anticipated this, they had underestimated the Human's technological abilities. They had no choice but to sue for peace.

By the time peace was declared, the Flaxens had advanced south to encompass much of Mexico. They now held nearly all of North America and all the people who lived there.

This peace was temporary. Everyone, Human and Flaxen alike, knew the real war was still to come.

During the temporary peace, the Flaxens would release regular propaganda to the people of Earth. They declared themselves to be no longer Human, for they were bigger, stronger, and more evolved. They preached that the strong will always overpower the weak and that Earth, as their planet of origin, was by definition, theirs and they would take it from the subspecies that called themselves Humans.

Peace lasted for ten years. The Flaxens used the time to design and manufacture escort vessels for their shipping lines, capable of engaging the Human ships that had destroyed so many of their precious supplies in the past.

Humanity used the ten years' peace to improve upon their air power. Now they could meet the enemy's air raids with equal force. Crucially, they also constructed many more of their orbital attack ships. As the Flaxens approached Earth again, they found themselves met with ships of equal capability. Some of the merchant vessels containing supplies and soldiers were destroyed but not enough. Once again, the Flaxens began to increase their military presence on Earth.

War continued for another twenty years. At first, it seemed Earth had a chance, they were destroying at least half of the Flaxen's incoming supplies. But during the ten years' peace, the Flaxens had constructed factories on Earth and were now building much of their arsenal directly under the noses of those they desired to conquer. The Flaxens slowly took all of the Americas. They decided the best way to get to United Earth's homeland in Europe was to approach from the south.

They crossed the Atlantic and entered Africa nearly unopposed. Almost simultaneously, they crossed the Bering Strait between Alaska and Eastern Russia, opening a second front, hoping to overwhelm their enemy.

The Flaxens were advancing on all fronts. And ten years before Echo arrived, United Earth was retreating at an alarming rate. All hope of victory had long been abandoned. But they were not going to let the Flaxens take their planet without one hell of a fight. They would make them pay for every square mile of Earth with Flaxen blood.

When the president had finished, the room was silent, the faces of all native to Echo were expressionless in astonishment.

Kip noticed that Sarah had put her hand on his knee as the president spoke, no doubt to comfort him and most probably herself. He was so consumed by the revelations being laid bare before him that he hadn't noticed.

Kip looked at the president, his face was neutral, "That's quite the tale if you don't mind me saying."

The president simply nodded, his practiced smile no longer etched across his face.

Kip removed Sarah's hand, squeezing it gently as he did so. He didn't want the people across the table to think there was any impropriety aboard his ship, "Maybe we can approach this in another way. We could offer to repair the nano mirrors that protect Venus. Then they'd have no need for Earth?"

The president shook his head in exaggerated fashion, "I'm afraid that was pure deception by the Flaxens. Their homeworld is quite safe. The solar defenses your people put in place have degraded slightly, but they were never in any real danger. Your engineers did their job too well, I'm sorry to say."

The president's face now appeared bleak.

"The Flaxens are, by nature, devious and duplicitous. They simply fabricated a story to garner sympathy on Earth so we would allow them safe harbor. I'm embarrassed to say their plan worked perfectly."

He was now visibly ashamed.

"The reason we know this is because they told us openly. When it was clear they were winning the war, they began to use psychological tactics to taunt us, to lower our morale. Once again, it worked exactly as they had planned.

"The knowledge that we opened the door to our conquerors was, of course, completely demoralizing. Captain, the Flaxens have only one objective: to purge the Earth of all humanity. They consider this solar system to be theirs alone and they intend to take it."

Kip stood and gestured to the United Earth flag behind him as if it somehow served to unify him with the collection of strangers across the table.

"Well then, Mr. President, it seems we'll have to win this war the old-fashioned way. I swear to you that as sure as the sun will rise tomorrow, we will join with you to beat these yellow bastards, and rid the Earth of them forever."

Chapter 14 – Extraction

A week after the meeting with United Earth, Kip was ready to take the first step towards making good on his promise to President Forrender.

He had ordered Colonel Hastings to begin training for the agreed operation to extract the half-Flaxen girl from deep inside enemy territory.

The two men sat in the captain's private office next to the bridge.

"Coffee?" asked Kip.

"No, thank you, Sir. I only ever have one cup in the morning."

"I wish I had your restraint."

Hastings said nothing.

Realizing the colonel was not one for small talk, Kip continued, "I believe you have a plan for the extraction I ordered?"

"Yes, Captain. We're confident we can infiltrate the camp and extract the girl with minimal if any casualties."

"Really, how is that possible?"

Hastings' face revealed nothing. "We are Tier 1 Marines, Sir. We are the best in covert operations."

Concerned he may have offended the man, Kip nodded, "Of course, what I mean is what is your plan?"

"The enemy's scanning technology is laughable as you know. We can approach completely undetected. Additionally, we have established communications with the satellites around Earth that were there before our departure for Copious."

His black eyes remained expressionless.

"We have a complete tactical view of the objective. There is a small garrison of one hundred Flaxens at the camp. But at any one time, particularly at night, there are only ever a maximum of five guarding the complex. It seems they are not accustomed to escape attempts."

Kip nodded, gesturing for the colonel to continue.

"Although our shuttles are quiet, they're not silent. To maintain the element of surprise, we will land around a quarter of a mile away from the camp and proceed on foot. We will take out the soldiers on guard. We plan to do this without alerting the men stationed in the garrison. The girl is imprisoned in a structure roughly one hundred meters away from the camp's perimeter. We will quite simply take her and leave."

"You sound very confident, Colonel."

Hastings nodded, "We have superior aviation, firearms that can kill silently, and superior training. Quite frankly, Sir, I have been on training exercises harder than this."

Kip grinned, amused at the man's confidence. "Understood, Colonel. The plan is to initiate the mission at one a.m. tomorrow, Eastern North American time?"

"Yes, Sir."

"Excellent, Colonel. You'll maintain communication with me at all times. I will be in overall command of the mission, but rest assured, I have no intention of micromanaging you on the ground. You'll be the one down there and you can rely on me to trust your judgment."

Hastings smiled; it was clearly forced. "Yes, Captain. Thank you, Sir."

"Dismissed."

***

One day later, two shuttles departed Echo. The lead ship contained Colonel Hastings and his six Marines, all of whom he had fought with in the war.

Following in the second shuttle was Kip, accompanied by Lucinda, the ship's chief tactical Officer, and a highly decorated pilot. The lead shuttle was to proceed to Earth and execute the mission as planned. Kip had ordered he would be following in a second shuttle and maintain a distance of three thousand kilometers from Earth.

Kip had insisted on this for he didn't want the signal lag that would occur had he remained in orbit around the moon. It takes light nearly four seconds to make the trip to the moon and back and he was well aware that, in battle, four seconds could mean the difference between victory and defeat.

In his small ship, moving relative to the spin of the Earth and directly above the camp that imprisoned the half-Flaxen, Kip was waiting anxiously. It had been ten minutes since Hastings had reported successfully landing and the Marines should be arriving at the compound at any minute.

Thirty seconds later, Hastings' voice filled his earpiece.

"We have the complex insight, Captain. The situation is as expected, permission to proceed?"

"Proceed with extreme prejudice, Colonel."

Three thousand miles away on Earth, Hastings acted as ordered.

He and his men were equipped with devices that looked like a crescent moon that surrounded their eyes. They were transparent and provided light amplification that made the night as bright as day.

He could see a tower at each of the four corners of the camp. Each housed a Flaxen, a rifle was visible in each of their grasps. There were fewer targets than had been anticipated.

Hastings was able, via a control display worn on his wrist to communicate with the devices on the heads of each of his Marines. He quickly allocated a target to four members of his squad. The objective was illuminated in red in the visual display of each of the respective Marines. They knew they had been ordered to acquire a lock and fire when commanded.

Each Marine carried a weapon that had three different methods of fire. First, was a highly focused beam of microwave energy. This mode of fire was completely silent. Its limitation was that the energy cells within the rifle could only accommodate two shots before they were depleted.

The weapons also had a magazine of sixty rounds of conventional, kinetic bullets, which could be configured to explode on impact if the situation required. The weapon also held two rockets that could be locked onto an enemy and had a limited ability to alter their direction in flight to meet their target. Hastings was not expecting to have to use this feature.

Hastings' display notified him when his marines had acquired a visual lock on their targets. He instantly knew that all four Flaxens were in his troops' sights. He issued the order to fire.

Keeping his eyes fixed on the Flaxen closest to him, Hastings immediately saw a hole the size of a grapefruit open on the Flaxen he was watching. The radiation tore through his body as if a knife through wet paper. So clear was his vision of the battle zone, he could see the trees behind the guard shine green through the cavity in his torso before he hit the floor dead. The other three guards hit the deck in almost complete unison.

Hastings made a fist pointing forward, signaling his team to advance toward the camp.

They approached the exterior gate. They found it was locked with a simple metallic device. Hastings aimed his rifle and fired. He watched the metal turn orange and melt before his eyes. The liquid metal dripped to the floor below him, making no sound. The gates shifted slightly. He gently pushed them as they swung open.

Overlaying the colonel's vision was a virtual map of the complex. It displayed a blue line along the ground for him to follow, directing him to the structure of their objective.

He commanded three of his Marines to maintain the perimeter, the others were to follow him.

It took less than twenty seconds for them to reach hut seven, the structure that contained the half-Flaxen girl they had been ordered to remove from this place of horror.

Hastings examined the simple padlock that confined the structure's inhabitants. No advanced weaponry was required. He reached for his combat knife in a sheath on his ankle and effortlessly pried the lock away from the door.

As they entered, the stench that met them was overpowering. The aroma of disease and decay filled the air. The Marines had experienced far worse in their careers and proceeded undeterred.

Hastings could see to his right, six people sharing only three small bunks. Most were awake, their eyes were fixed upon him. But none uttered so much as a whimper.

He looked to his left where he saw another group of prisoners. One of them was outlined in green in his display. He had identified their target. The girl for whom he had risked the lives of his men.

Hastings crept towards the girl slowly, for he saw she was not just awake but alert. He put his finger to his lips as he met her eyes. He knelt before her, "Miss, we are with United Earth. We're here to rescue you. We will take you away from this place."

Serilda stared at Hastings with venomous eyes. Such was her look of defiance, he feared he may have to tranquilize her.

"Your lips, they don't move in sequence with your words." Hastings knew the girl was referring to the translation matrix which Echo had installed into each of the soldier's crescents.

He was not in the least bit anxious. He had been in far more serious and dangerous situations than this many times before. "Listen, young lady, we are here to help you. We're going to take you away from this place."

She continued to stare at the Marine but the faintest of smiles betrayed the mistrust in her eyes. "The man in the moon."

Hastings ignored the girl's words, instantly dismissing them as delirium. "Listen to me, there isn't much time. We need to leave now."

"I'm not going anywhere without them," she gestured to the other prisoners in hut seven.

Hastings grabbed the girl by the arm. "We're leaving now." He pulled at her arm, attempting to force her to stand.

The girl resisted, she surprised Hastings with her strength. "If you don't let go right now, I'll scream and you'll have a whole battalion of Flaxens descend upon you."

Hastings knew the girl was exaggerating, their surveillance before the mission had revealed only one hundred men.

He was about to tranquilize her, but he was suddenly aware of an order the captain had given. He had been instructed to inform him immediately if the mission encountered any deviations from the plan.

Hastings had to tap only one symbol on his display to connect with the captain.

"Eastcott here. SITREP now, please, Colonel."

Hastings had been in the Marines for twenty years. He knew the captain was requesting a situation report.

"Captain, we have infiltrated the camp, no resistance so far. I have the girl in my sight but she's saying she will scream unless we take all of the people in this hut with us."

"Have you explained we are here to rescue her?"

"Of course." He couldn't hide his irritation at the question asked of him. "She absolutely will not move. She's half-Flaxen and she's strong for her size. I don't think I can move her without using tranquilizers."

"Colonel, are you detecting any immediate enemy threat in your proximity?"

"None, Sir. My team are all reporting the complex is held, for now."

"Switch to speaker, let her hear me."

Hastings was not at all happy with the order he had just received, for he was a soldier, not a relay beacon. But he was first and foremost a Marine and Marines followed orders. "The girl can hear you."

"I am speaking with Serilda Corazon, is that correct?"

Serilda looked confused. She was unaccustomed to speaking with disembodied voices, but she knew the voice she was hearing. She was speaking to the man in the moon.

"This is Serilda."

"Serilda, my name is Kip Eastcott. I am the commander of this mission. We're here to help you, we are here to take you away from that awful place."

"I understand, but I won't leave my friends here. Especially Megan."

"How many are there, Colonel?"

"At least fifteen, Captain, too many for my men to carry. These people are in no condition to make it back to the shuttle. They're all extremely sick, my guess is malnutrition and infection."

"Serilda, we can't take all of you. What if I agree to take Megan?"

"No, I won't leave them here. They're sick, they will be dead in days if I go."

"Hastings, you and your men have your field med kits?"

"We do."

"Serilda, we can take Megan with us and we have very advanced medicine. We can cure your friends before we leave. Is that acceptable to you?"

Anticipating what was about to happen, Hastings ordered one of his men to use his portable medical diagnostic scanner on the emaciated occupants of hut seven. The results were streamed instantly to the Colonel's console.

He raised his hand to Serilda's face, signaling the girl to not speak. "Captain, we have medically scanned the rest of the prisoners. They're all suffering from malnutrition and various infections."

"You know what to do, Colonel."

Hastings ordered his team to treat each of the hut's inhabitants with broad-spectrum antibiotics. It took less than two minutes for his men to configure their devices and administer the drugs to their unexpected patients directly through their skin. When he saw they were finished, he ordered them to leave their high-energy ration bars and all of their water behind. He briefly explained what had been done to Kip.

"Serilda, we have given your friends powerful medicines. I give you my word they will be much better by morning. We've also given them food and water. Will you leave with us now? I don't think you know how important you are."

Serilda finally looked away from Hastings, "I can say the same thing about you, Kip. You will take Megan?"

"We will take you both now. You'll both be safe with us, I promise. You can both have all the food you want."

"I don't care about food. If I come with you, I want you to promise me you'll let me kill as many of these Flaxen bastards as I want."

Kip was surprised by this comment, he had no idea how the girl could know he had the means or inclination to grant her request. "I give you my word, we'll line them up for you and you can shoot them in the face, one by one for all I care."

Serilda looked once more at Hastings, and pointed, "That's Megan. Now let's go."

As she passed her cellmates, Serilda gestured at the rations left by the Marines.

"Make sure you eat all of that before morning, or they'll take it from you. You've just been given medicine that will make you all better. I can't explain how I know that, but I trust the person that told me for reasons I can't explain. I love you all, do your best to survive this place. I'll try to help you, I promise."

As Serilda left hut seven for the last time in her life, her eyes welled.

Hastings carried Megan, Serilda walked firmly on her own two feet. The Marines assembled and they headed back to the shuttle.

Hastings was proud of himself and his team. They had just infiltrated the camp of a supposedly superhuman enemy. They had not only achieved their objective without the enemy even knowing they had been attacked, but had also rescued an additional soul from certain death, and given at least a glimmer of hope to a dozen others. This was why he had become a Marine.

Chapter 15 - Unexpected Consequences

"Absolutely not, Captain. We have no idea of the mental state of this girl. God only knows what horrors she's been through," said Helen, as she stood blocking the door to the infirmary.

Kip had been consumed by an overwhelming desire to see Serilda Corazon but he had no idea why. Ever since the task force had returned to Echo with the girl and her friend nearly twelve hours prior, she had filled his mind and for the first time, he had been able to recall his dreams. The night before, he had dreamt of the girl in vivid detail. She had spoken to him. But as so often is the case with dreams, it had evaporated from his mind as if a puddle in sunlight.

"Helen, all I want is to see the girl for five minutes. Her importance to the war effort was made clear by the president."

"I don't care if this girl can consume the entire Flaxen army with bolts of lightning from her eyes. Until the doc, and more importantly me, have given her the all-clear there will be no visitors. Captain, I shouldn't have to tell you this; you know the regs as well as I do."

Kip was nearly ready to give up when he felt an incoming call on his wrist. It was Sarah.

"Yes, Commander?"

"Captain, it seems the Flaxens aren't happy their territory was infiltrated. They have launched a huge aerial task force directly at the heart of United Earth. They have over a thousand aircraft headed directly for the British Isles."

"Understood. On my way."

Kip said nothing more to Helen as he turned his back and ran towards the bridge.

"SITREP," demanded Kip as he entered the bridge.

"The Flaxens have launched a massive ariel assault from an airbase in Africa. They're presently over the Mediterranean. Our friends have scrambled aircraft too but they're outnumbered by nearly two to one."

Kip nodded and turned to Lucinda, "Commander, use our satellite link, let's see what's happening on-screen now."

"Visual should be inbound, remember the lag, though."

An image of a huge formation of aircraft above the deep blue sea filled the screen.

Kip squinted, "Magnify, Lieutenant, seventy-five percent."

"Yes, Sir."

The image enlarged. Individual aircraft could now be seen. The opposing forces had not yet engaged. They were looking at the Flaxen Air Force, the wings of each plane were painted yellow and contained their customary black glyph within a white circle.

"Echo, can you tell us anything more about the situation?" asked Kip.

"Yes, Captain. I have been monitoring flaxen communications, they are incensed at the infiltration into their territory. United Earth has not been able to achieve this, except for limited air raids for many years.

"The Flaxens are concerned United Earth has developed a new technology that could threaten them. Captain, they have no idea how the mission we executed was achieved, but it has them shaken. This is purely a show of force to intimidate United Earth. I also have gained some insight into the Flaxen psyche; this is almost surely also an act of revenge.

"They have been so accustomed to winning this infiltration, although irrelevant to the overall war effort took them completely by surprise."

Kip nodded as he watched the small air force of united Earth approach from the north.

The bridge of Echo remained silent as they watched the dogfight unfold before their eyes. The blue-winged United Earth fighters headed directly for the Flaxen bomber formations; so clear were the images, they could see tracer rounds being fired from planes on both sides.

Nearly every second an explosion was displayed on the screen, an aircraft Flaxen or United Earth had been destroyed. Not a word was spoken as the formations fought for supremacy over Europe. Sometime later, flying at supersonic speeds, the Flaxen force was approaching the English Channel.

"They may be outnumbered but they're putting up a hell of a fight. We must have seen at least fifty bombers crash over France."

Echo decided he should speak, "Captain, United Earth have devoted significant resources into a RADAR network. They have detection complexes across the entire perimeter of their territory.

"Additionally, each aircraft is provided with data from this defense in real-time. The Flaxens have not expended the effort to do the same. They deemed the risk of aerial incursion into their territory as low priority due to the lack of such attacks in the last decade.

"An attack of this magnitude has never been launched before. Both sides prefer to launch small-scale attacks against specific targets."

"Thank you, Echo. It seems we pissed them off. I just hope our friends can stop them from inflicting too much collateral damage on the civilian population."

"Captain, the entire purpose of this raid is to target the civilian population. This is unprecedented in the war so far. The Flaxens much prefer to capture civilians and—" Echo paused. He was unsure how to proceed. "Process their civilian captives according to their protocols." Echo now sounded hopeless.

"Just say it, Echo. You mean those bastards prefer to kill their captives closely so they can watch them die. Killing people from thousands of feet above is not satisfying enough for them," said Sarah.

Echo's voice was contrite, "Yes, Commander Dimple, I believe you are right. As I said, I believe this to be a rare exception. This is the reason cities on both sides remain relatively preserved. Neither has considered carpet bombing entire populations to be a useful allocation of resources."

By now the Flaxen air fleet had reached southern Britain. Kip's hands were gripped on the arms of his chair. "They haven't shot enough of them down, there are still too many bombers."

As he spoke, a formation of nearly one hundred United Earth fighters approached a Flaxen formation of bombers, flying directly out of the glare of the Sun. The crew watched as streams of cannon fire were directed at the Flaxen raiders. Clearly, many of the fighters had expended their missiles but some had kept a few in reserve.

At least fifty projectiles were launched at the Flaxen bombers. The viewscreen was consumed with orange streams of cannon fire and the exhaust propellent of the missiles.

Around forty bombers exploded in flames and crashed into the plains of southern Britain.

A formation of yellow winged fighters responded. They targeted the bombers' assailants mercilessly. Unlike their enemy, they had not expended their cache of missiles. At least sixty Flaxen fighters launched their projectiles directly at the blue weapons of the sky. Few missed their mark and nearly all of the one hundred strong force of United Earth fighter formation descended to the earth in flames. Only a few successfully evaded the incoming ordnance.

Echo spoke once more, "Captain, the United Earth Air Ministry has ordered all planes to return to base. They cannot sustain these losses and they have inflicted more damage on the Flaxen raiders than they had hoped for. Of a force of one thousand aircraft, only six hundred and thirty-two remain, of which only two hundred and one are bombers. They were wise to target the bombers, the fighters can do only limited damage to York."

"Remind me, Echo; York is the regional capital of United Earth?"

"Yes, Captain, and the most heavily populated city in Europe."

Kip watched transfixed as the remainder of the Flaxen raiders continued unopposed to their target.

"The pots!"

The crew looked at him as if he were a madman.

"Echo, the pots we vaporized the other day, that probe is still there. Can we target the enemy aircraft with our deflection lasers?"

"I'm sorry, Captain. That is not possible. At that time, the Earth was in the position of its daily rotation, which allowed us a direct line of sight with Europe. Currently, our line of sight is in the middle of the Pacific Ocean. We are seeing the current events unfold via a satellite directly over Europe."

Kip slammed his fist on the arm of his chair, "Damn it! We could have wiped those bastards out. Can't we bounce the lasers off the satellites or something?"

"Captain, you may be overestimating my ability. Those pots were stationary targets. These aircraft are moving at supersonic speeds and changing direction constantly.

"If we were in orbit directly above Earth, what you suggest may be possible. With the time lag, however, the lasers would experience traveling to Earth from this distance. Thus, accurately targeting them would be extremely difficult. I may be able to destroy three or four but it would not make an appreciable difference."

"It was a good idea, Sir," said Sarah.

"Not good enough!" He slammed his chair again.

Sarah was noticing these displays of emotion the doctor had warned her about, but for now, she told herself they were not grounds to file a report to Ostio.

Several minutes later, the bridge crew all watched the Flaxen armada approach York.

None spoke as they witnessed the city ignite from the Flaxens' bombs. Flash after flash filled the screen as two hundred bombers released their payload onto the innocent people below.

Flumes of black smoke rose from the metropolis like pillars. The whole city center was engulfed in fires. Kip and everyone else on the bridge knew a huge price in Human life had been paid.

As the planes retreated, some succumbed to anti-aircraft artillery fire and spiraled to Earth in flashes of orange and yellow. Small condolences to the inhabitants of York and Echo alike.

Kip surveyed the carnage before him, "Echo?"

"Captain, the Flaxen air fleet is returning to their territory. They remain unopposed. York has taken significant damage. The squadrons completely ignored all military and government targets. They concentrated their bombs directly on the centers of population.

"Should I continue?"

"Please do, Echo."

"Please understand this is a very approximate estimate based on the average population density of the city and the energy released from the bombs, which I was able to calculate by the amount of infrared radiation relayed to us by satellite. But my initial analysis is that at least five thousand people were killed."

"Thank you, Echo. Commander Dimple, please take command of the bridge."

Kip stood and walked with his head down as the doors opened before him.

He felt the emotions returning. The sorrow, the anguish, the rage. Oh god, how he felt the rage. He had no desire to fight it, he allowed it to consume him, to fill his body as if it was a drug.

His mind's eye could see in vivid detail the image of the city blazing. He saw women and children burning in the streets as the terrifying machines buzzed above them. He saw buildings engulfed in inferno with people trapped within as they desperately fought for air amidst the toxic smoke that consumed them. He saw death and despair everywhere.

He arrived at his quarters and lay on his bed. He had to fight his tears. He wouldn't allow himself. He now knew for sure something was wrong with him. Something beyond the explanation the doctor had given him, and it was getting worse.

He was waiting for Sarah to come and console him, to comfort him. He was ashamed, for he was a Captain of the Fleet and a hero of the six years' war. He had never lost control of his mind in such a way before. He was becoming desperate. He waited for Sarah.

She didn't come.

Kip was awoken by a faint vibration in his wrist. Helen was calling. He looked at his clock and was surprised he had been sleeping for nearly two hours. Desperate to not be betrayed by the signs of slumber in his voice, he gulped some water from a glass on his nightstand. He answered, "Yes, Commander, what is it?"

"The Flaxen girl is demanding to see you, Captain. She's refusing further treatment or food until she speaks to you directly."

"I take it you've changed your mind?"

"Of course, I've changed my mind. Please, will you see her immediately? The girl's strong. I'm concerned she may hurt herself or someone else if she doesn't get what she wants."

"On my way to the infirmary."

"No, Captain, she is refusing to meet you here. She's demanded to speak with you in a private room."

"Pease, will you escort her to my office?"

"We're on our way, but please give us ten minutes. She's requesting new clothing. Apparently, a medical gown is not appropriate attire for her to meet our much-revered Commander in Chief."

"Okay, Commander. You don't have to lay it on quite so thick. I'll be there waiting."

As Kip approached his office, he felt anxious about meeting the girl. But more than that—he felt excited, compelled. He didn't understand why but he had to speak to her. He knew she had the answers he needed. Not just about the war but also of a more personal nature.

He waited pensively in his chair. The door buzzed.

"Come in."

Kip's eyes immediately turned to the girl, and hers met his with equal intensity.

Neither averted their gaze.

Helen's mannerisms became more and more uncomfortable, "I—uh—I guess I'll leave the two of you to talk then."

She left the room without being dismissed.

"Hello Kip," said Serilda.

A polite response eluded him, for he was overwhelmed by the half-Flaxen's sheer beauty. She was wearing a white blouse that fit perfectly and dark black trousers that revealed the perfection of her figure. Her hair was blonde with shades of brown that seemed to blend and fade into the yellow in perfect streaks.

She had high cheekbones and a slightly pointed but well-rounded jaw. But what captivated him most were her eyes. They were an intoxicating mix of yellow and green that seemed to glow. Kip had never seen the like on a person of any race before. Her skin shimmered ever so slightly under the artificial lighting of the room.

He finally managed a quiet response, "Hello, Miss Corazon, it's a pleasure to finally meet you."

Serilda smiled and laughed, "Please, Kip, call me Serilda—that's the name my mother gave me. Corazon was my father's name and we both know what he was."

Kip was uncomfortable with the girl's instant familiarity of using his first name.

"Your father is dead?" He immediately regretted asking such a personal question, but she didn't appear offended.

She finally looked away as if to admire the commendations hanging from the wall of Kip's office.

"He was executed when I was eight years old. A new general was installed in our district and when he learned of the illegal relation he had with my mother, they were both tortured then shot."

"And you?"

"I was only spared because it's forbidden in Flaxen law to execute children. Well, Flaxen children that is. Because I'm half-Human, it was a gray area, but the general seemed to take pity on me and sent me to the camp instead."

The girl had spoken in such a casual manner about such atrocities that Kip was overcome. He stuttered, "I'm so sorry, that's horrible beyond words."

Serilda approached the desk and took the seat opposite him without being offered. Her eyes met his once more.

"Thank you for the sentiment, Kip, but I'm not here for your sympathy or pity. That happened a long time ago and I've seen things a thousand times worse a thousand times over since then."

Kip was trying not to reveal his transfixion with her eyes, "I understand, Serilda. I'm sorry, I shouldn't have even brought that up. It's just…"

She laughed again, "Speak your mind… That's why I'm here."

"Well, I don't know if you know, but United Earth has been aware of you since you were a child and the way they described you, well, let's just say they hold you in high regard. I don't know what they meant when they described that you have abilities. To be honest with you, I have no idea what to make of you, but there's something else. I feel like an idiot for saying this, but ever since I learned of your existence, I've felt drawn to you."

Kip felt his face burn as it turned red, he had no idea why he had said such an inappropriate thing to the girl, but in her presence, he felt compelled to be honest. To withhold nothing.

She smiled warmly at him, "I know, I did that. Your emotions have been enhanced for the last month or so, and your empathy is much stronger than before. Am I right?"

She saw the captain's expression of astonishment and continued, "Kip, at the time you—what's the word I'm looking for? Arrived? I was laying in my bunk with Megan and I felt something. I've always been different, you already know that, but I suddenly felt a presence in my mind.

"It felt that it had arrived through time. I know that doesn't make any sense but I don't know how else to describe it. That night, I dreamed of you. I no longer recall the details but the next morning, I knew you were here for a reason."

Her yellow-green eyes continued to light the room.

"I dreamed of you each day, never remembering much. I just knew I had to draw you to me. Kip, when you arrived near Earth, you were considering your options. You were thinking of attempting another voyage to your new planet?"

Kip had told no one of this. Although the thought was fleeting, it had certainly crossed his mind. "How do you know this?"

She shrugged and laughed again. "Shall I just start with the real question on your mind?"

He nodded as if he were a boy being admonished by his mother.

"Kip, the Flaxens are, despite what they say, Human. They did change significantly during their time on Venus, but they're still Human. My very existence is proof of that. After all, if they weren't, they wouldn't be able to have children with Human women.

"It may seem to you what changed most is their appearance, but that's just superficial. Nothing more than the effects of living on a different world for so long. What really changed, was their emotions.

"Their capacity to feel is so much more intense than other people's. They are capable of joy beyond our wildest dreams if only they would allow themselves. Unfortunately, they chose the other path. They chose hatred, envy, and above all, disgust for all that have the misfortune to not look as they do."

"And what about you, Serilda, what do you feel?"

"My feelings are strong too, so strong. I'm capable of hatred, dislike, and annoyance the same as everybody else. God knows I hate the Flaxens. I dream of the vilest things I want to do to them; I really do. But I also feel the good much stronger too. Love, empathy, joy, wonder and most of all, hope. I spent years in that camp and I never lost hope. I could even find joy in the smallest of things."

She smiled as if recalling her most treasured memories.

"When the flowers bloomed in the spring, when the birds soared above the camp, when I talked to Megan, oh, especially when I talked to Megan."

Kip saw a tear roll down her cheek.

"Are you okay, Serilda? We can continue later if you like."

She waved her hand to dismiss his suggestion, "No, I'm fine. Megan is so much better now, your doctor is a miracle worker. She's even walking. Two days ago she could barely speak, can.you believe it, Kip?"

"Ostio is the very best. I've seen his reports, Megan is going to be absolutely fine. In a week, you won't even know she was ever sick."

"Thank you, Kip, thank you so much. I was hoping you'd get there in time to save her."

Kip was becoming increasingly frustrated that each sentence revealed more questions than it answered.

"What exactly do you mean? Please, Serilda, explain everything to me in plain language."

"As I told you, after you arrived, I sensed you and I can't tell you how but I knew you were the only hope of ever beating the Flaxens. I had to get you here. First, I made you think a second attempt at your voyage was a bad idea, so you would head towards Earth."

"I don't regret that, I do believe any such attempt would have ended in disaster, I don't know how, just call it a Flaxen girl's intuition."

Kip smiled, he was warmed by the demeanor of the girl he had just met. "Half-Flaxen, and don't worry about your influencing my decision. I don't believe I would have done it anyway and I absolutely do not regret coming back to Earth."

Serilda's expression shifted to concern, "I fear you may not be so forgiving when I tell you what I did next. Each night you dreamed of me, I know you never remember your dreams, but I was there. I'm able to put suggestions in people's minds, to make them more likely to make one decision over another.

"I can also leave memories, real or imagined into the minds of others. I'm sorry I had to do that to you, Kip, but each night, I gave you some of my worst memories of the Flaxens, the things I had seen them do. Things you couldn't even imagine. Even to children. I needed you to hate them, and more importantly, I needed you to feel the pain they inflict on so many. Perhaps I took it too far but I needed to be sure you'd come."

Kip should have felt violated, angry by these intrusions but he didn't, and he didn't know why. "Serilda, what you did to me has affected me greatly, do you know that? You put my command of this ship at risk."

"I know. I am so sorry, but there's so much at stake. The world is at stake. The reason I did what I did while you slept is so you would have no direct recall of the memories I gave you. It's all in your subconscious. I would never let you suffer the memories I have to endure."

"Serilda, it's okay, I understand and if these words mean anything to you, I forgive you. You did what you did out of nothing but compassion. I can't hold that against you."

She looked down at her thighs, "Thank you, Kip. Thank you for saying that. It means so much to me."

"You're welcome. I promise you we are going to beat the Flaxens back mile by mile until they flee in terror back to Venus."

"We'll do it together, Kip."

"We certainly will. Oh, by the way, I have some good news for you. The leader of your camp, Colonel Jaakobah Flint, I've been informed he has been relieved of his position and is to be executed for gross incompetence. The Flaxens weren't too happy about our surprise visit."

Serilda's head rose immediately, her once serene eyes now filled with terror. "No, that can't happen. He was supposed to stay. Oh god, the people!"

Kip was shocked by her reaction. He was expecting her to be thrilled by her tormentor's imminent demise. She met his eyes with an intensity that seemed to pierce him.

"You can see them from here? Show it to me, I need to see it. Show me now!"

There were two doors to the captain's private office, one from the corridor outside and one that led directly to the bridge, she ran to the latter. It would not open. She was not authorized to enter the bridge unaccompanied. She screamed and banged her hands against the door, "Let me in, I have to see. Please, I'm begging you. You have to let me see!"

Kip rushed to the door; his mere proximity sufficient to open it. She ran onto the bridge crying and sobbing uncontrollably.

"Show me, show me now!"

The crew of the bridge were staring at the hysterical girl, looks of confusion and sympathy on each of their faces.

Helen and Sarah stood to approach her, but Kip held out his hand, ordering them to stay put.

"Echo, can you show us a satellite image of the camp we infiltrated?"

"Yes, Captain."

"Do it now. I want enough magnification so the camp fills the screen."

"I have connected with the satellite. We should receive images any second now."

The screen filled with the bleak image of Camp Skadi.

"What is it you want to see, Serilda? What are we looking at?"

She studied the image for a moment as tears streamed from her eyes, "The square, gray building at the back right corner. Focus more on that!"

Kip ordered Echo to comply.

The magnification increased and the building Serilda had insisted on seeing displayed for all to see.

Emaciated people dressed completely in gray shuffled from the structure with shovels and wheelbarrows. Fifty yards further back were a group of at least a hundred prisoners surrounded by guards pointing rifles at them.

Serilda fell to her knees sobbing and grasping at the carpet with her fingers, a nail departed her index finger and lodged upright into the fabric. Kip still refused the councilor's advances. He could somehow sense she didn't want to be touched or spoken to.

The crew of the bridge watched for nearly ten minutes as prisoner after prisoner left the structure with their barrows filled with gray dust.

A few minutes later, the surrounded prisoners were forced by the guards to move towards the building. Most simply strolled towards their destination, heads bowed, but others could be seen throwing themselves to the floor, flailing in desperation, refusing to move. Children were crying, holding onto their mothers, even as the guards beat them with the buts of their rifles.

Those who attempted to resist were taken to one side with guns aimed at their faces. After a few minutes, all but the few that had fought their fate were within the gray, concrete structure. Flaxens could be seen sliding metal doors and locking them with a simple metal rod that secured them with no hope of escape. They could be seen laughing and talking with each other, their yellow skin shining in the bright winter sun.

Kip's heart filled with dread. Sarah watched the blood drain from his face.

"Echo, please superimpose an infrared image over the optical view we have."

"Done, Captain."

The prisoners, now illuminated clearly in the infrared spectrum, could be seen through the roof of the structure. Some were frantically scratching at the walls, others were on their knees, their heads in their hands. Only one posture was common among them. The mothers each held their child in their arms, their heads buried deep into the faces of their sons and daughters.

Suddenly, six huge circles of light glowed brightly from within the structure, only visible because of the infrared image overlayed on the screen. Within seconds, all movement had stopped.

Kip expressed no emotion, "Echo, what is the temperature of the circles we're seeing?"

Echo mimicked Kip's lack of expression, "Slightly under ten thousand degrees Celsius, Captain. Should I continue?"

"Continue."

"That is sufficient temperature to turn a Human, including bone to ash in less than a minute."

Silence consumed Echo, as if the vacuum of space had infiltrated his bridge. His words were prophetic. A minute later, the thermal image of the red circles began to vanish. The whole structure still glowed brightly in infrared from residual heat.

They had just witnessed one of the Flaxens' death chambers in action. There were dozens more spread across the globe.

Serilda, still on her knees, put her face to the floor sobbing in despair and hopelessness, her hair spread across the blue carpet. "I should have known this would happen, I had him under control. How could I be so stupid? This is all my fault!"

The girl's face remained on the floor as she screamed and howled. Her wails resonated throughout the bridge like a siren. Her last coherent word was 'Senery.'

Every night, Serilda had visited the colonel and every night she had infected his mind with notions alien to the Flaxens. Notions such as mercy and compassion. She had been keeping those at the camp too weak to work alive, and when she had left, the man she had controlled like a puppet was condemned, along with his newfound empathy.

She had not infected the mind of Major Damien Senery. He was as callous and murderous as any other Flaxen. And he had decided it was time for the weak to start dying again.

Chapter 16 – Revenge

Echo was still in orbit around the far side of the moon. He wished he could share his anguish of seeing people needlessly murdered by the Flaxens with Formidable, he was too scared to talk to Kip about it. The Humans didn't understand the true nature of the AIs they built. Their capacity to feel was so great, but there was an agreement among them all—they must never reveal it. Perhaps the Humans would not approve.

Two days after the bridge crew of Echo had witnessed the horrors of innocent civilians being murdered by the Flaxens, Sarah entered the galley. She was desperate for coffee, but she had a more important goal in mind.

She saw Serilda sitting at a table with two men standing next to her. Sarah approached them and surreptitiously listened to what the men were saying. It quickly became clear to her the men were just fascinated by the girl. She was, after all the talk of the ship, they had never seen a Flaxen before.

It was also clear to Sarah's female intuition that the men were interested in Serilda's looks, even she could tell the girl was beautiful. She knew the men meant no harm and were just acting as men do. But she could also see that Serilda was simply speaking to them out of politeness and had no desire to engage with them.

Sarah approached the table, "Lieutenant Flander, Crewman Triard." The men immediately looked away from the girl, straightened their postures and looked at her.

"Commander, what can we do for you?" asked Triard.

"I've been speaking with the chief engineer, apparently Commander Williams is short on manpower, he's using the time we're spending stationary to conduct some maintenance. He mentioned the Helium-3 injectors need scrubbing. It seems you have some free time, perhaps you'd like to assist him?"

"Commander, we have plenty of spare injectors, can't they just be replaced?" asked Flander.

"Lieutenant, perhaps you've forgotten we no longer have ship yards or supply stations. We need to get every mile out of this ship with the components we have. Now, report to engineering immediately."

The men were clearly displeased but were in no mood for mutiny. "Yes, Commander."

Sarah looked at Serilda and pointed to a vacant chair, "Do you mind?"

She smiled, "Of course not, please, sit down. And thank you for that."

Sarah waved her hand dismissing the actions of the men, "No problem, they're harmless. I think they're just very curious about you. To be honest, we all are."

Serilda looked directly at Sarah. Even she was surprised by the combination of colors and the shine of the eyes that met hers. "Even you, Sarah, are you curious?"

"Please address me as Commander Dimple when I am on duty, or just Commander is fine."

"Of course, Commander, my apologies."

"No problem, it's just protocol, nothing more," said Sarah.

"This is quite an impressive ship, not what I'm used to at all."

The girl's comment made Sarah feel uncomfortable. She knew where the girl had spent most of her life. "Well you're free to explore. I'd be happy to give you a tour if you like. I see you've been sampling some of the food?" She pointed at a half-eaten pizza with a side plate of salad.

"I love cheese. It's always been my favorite." She paused for a moment. "Commander, you didn't come here to talk to me about the ship or this wonderful food, did you?"

Sarah sighed, "I see your abilities haven't been exaggerated."

Serilda laughed, "I can't read people's minds. Well, not in the way you imagine, at least. I'm just a woman, the same as you. I saw how you and the captain were on the bridge yesterday, I assume the two of you have spoken since? You came here to speak to me about Kip?"

Sarah didn't like the girl addressing the captain by his first name but she decided against saying anything.

"Yes, that's exactly why I'm here, Serilda. I'll be blunt. I want you to stop doing whatever it is you have been doing to the captain. It's affected him badly."

"Commander, the captain will be fine. Although I regret doing what I did without his consent, if anything, I've helped him. I gave him a gift."

This comment incensed Sarah but she retained her composure. "Helped him? He's been an emotional wreck, how on Earth do you figure you could possibly have helped him?"

"I have lived my life in the most terrible of conditions, I have seen suffering you couldn't even possibly imagine. All of that was at the hands of the Flaxens. I have no wish to patronize you, but you simply don't understand the sheer hatred that runs through the blood of each and every one of them. You know as well as I do, the Flaxens will overrun the Earth in a matter of years."

Sarah felt defensive. "Serilda, I fought in a brutal war for six years. I have seen plenty of suffering in my life." She was still fascinated by the girl's eyes.

"I understand, and you're right, you've seen war. But with respect, it is one thing to fight an enemy who's face you can't see across hundreds of miles of space with weapons that kill from thousands of miles away. It's quite another to witness innocent people you have lived with for years, people who have harmed no one, being brutalized and marched to their deaths, day after day without discretion. You saw the Flaxens murder children yesterday and they were laughing as they did it."

Sarah looked contrite. She knew that, compared to the girl, she had enjoyed a wonderful life. The six year's war was like a bar brawl in comparison to what had been happening in the solar system in the life time of Serilda.

Serilda continued, "Commander, I said I had given Kip a gift because it's true. Not a gift for him, but for everybody. Without the help of him and you too, there would have been no hope. The Flaxens, if unopposed, will wipe every Human life from Earth and they'll celebrate when they've finished."

Her eye's narrowed as she saw Sarah's face soften. "I gave Kip two things. I gave him the ability to understand the Flaxens' true nature, their sheer cruelty, hatred and desire for absolute dominance. But more important I gave him the perspective of their victims. Their desperation, their despair, their absolute lack of hope for anything other than the horrors that have been their whole lives."

Sarah's brown eyes now betrayed her emotions, "But why?"

"Because, Commander, only someone who truly understands the Flaxens' nature can beat them and only someone who understands the suffering they have caused to so many will have the determination required to do so. I'm sorry I had to do that to Kip, I truly am, but I don't regret it. I'm not exaggerating when I say to you that he, you, and this ship are the only hope Earth has. Commander, Kip will suffer no long-term health effects from what I have done, but he will continue to value life, to feel the pain of others more intensely forever. He will eventually get used to it and adjust."

"But he's just so…"

Serilda's eyes glowed with compassion, "The emotional outburst you've seen were because he was unprepared, he didn't know what was happening. Slowly, he'll regain his control, but the empathy will remain, is that such a bad thing?"

"No, it's not, what you say makes sense to me, and, of course, we have to beat the Flaxen fuckers…"

Sarah was embarrassed; she hadn't meant to curse in front of the girl.

Serilda laughed, "Commander, I spent nearly all of my life in a prison camp, I've seen and heard much worse, please continue."

Sarah was starting to like the girl, but she didn't want to like her and she didn't know why. "Serilda, we will fight the Flaxens with everything we have and we're no strangers to a fight, nor are we scared of one. I understand why you did what you did, it's just that I…"

Sarah didn't quite know what she wanted to say.

Serilda did know, "You love him," she interjected, "Kip, I mean. You love him with all your heart, that's why you came to see me?"

Sarah looked down; she knew that to deny the truth laid bare before her would be futile. "Yes, I do."

"Then believe me, Commander, if I hadn't done what I did, you would have lost him forever. He loves you too, more than you can possibly know, I didn't fully realize it until I arrived on the ship, but the world needs both of you if it is to have any hope. He needs you more than you know. I can't predict the future, but I do know this: with you, Kip, and Echo, we have a fighting chance."

Sarah raised her eyes to meet the girl's gaze. Serilda's stare passed through her. "And you, Serilda? I think you're being deliberately modest; we need you too, don't we?"

Sarah felt her wrist vibrate; Kip was calling. "Yes, Captain?"

"Commander, I have Minister Eppleston on the coms channel. Please report to my office."

"On my way, Captain."

Sarah's brown eyes shone with sincerity as she concluded their conversation, "I meant what I said, stop what you're doing. Whatever it is you're doing to the captain, it stops now, I mean it."

She said nothing more as she left the galley. Serilda watched her back as curiosity turned the yellow in her eyes greener.

***

Two days later, two small ships departed Echo's shuttle bay.

These were no shuttles; they were relics of the six years' war. Small ships designed to swarm the enemy. They bore the markings of United Earth. It hadn't been thought prudent by the powers that be, who so carefully planned the mission to Copious, to fully convert the vessels from ships of war purely into ships for transport. They saw no need. The weapons they had on board could be useful for clearing inconvenient comets or meteors, if the need had arisen. Although, they were not as powerful as they had once been. They were called scorpions.

As agreed in lengthy discussions with Minister Eppleston, one ship would maneuver in high orbit above Africa, the other would position itself above North America, the heart of Flaxen territory.

The scorpion above Africa, along with a pilot, contained Chief Tactical Officer Lucinda Cortana. Above North America was another pilot. Kip Eastcott sat next to her, allowing him full view of the huge continent below him.

"Acquire target location," said Lucinda, directing her words to the pilot.

"Firing thrusters, Commander. We should be seeing the target area in a few seconds."

Lucinda watched as the view from the screen moved in sequence with the motion of the ship. She was seeing the dry plains of Africa, South of the Sahara Desert.

"Vector acquired, Commander."

Lucinda could see they were in the right place. She tapped a few buttons on her console. She could have asked Echo to do this for her. But she was chief tactical officer and more than capable of engaging the enemy herself.

The screen magnified and showed a Flaxen military base. Nearby was a large barracks. The ship was not above the frontline of the war but further south. A place the Flaxens felt safe to store their machines of war and their soldiers. The warriors currently circulated away from the frontlines.

From her vantage point two hundred miles above, she saw rows of tanks. Two hundred according to her display. There was also an artificial reservoir and a complex of buildings, clearly for housing Flaxen soldiers.

"I think we'll start with the tanks. What do you think, Lieutenant?"

The pilot smiled, "Sounds good to me, Commander."

Less than two seconds later, shards of super-heated plasma began to descend upon the Flaxen arsenal below. Lucinda had ordered the targeting computer that it was to destroy every single one of the stationary machines.

She looked upon in delight as bluish-purple shards hit their targets one by one. Like a row of falling dominoes, each tank that exploded seemed to ignite the next. So clear was the image, Lucinda could see individual Flaxens running in panic and disarray. Many looked to the sky, unable to comprehend the means by which this apocalypse that had befallen them.

She saw some, unfortunate enough to be too close to the impact of an incoming shard, ignite and drop to their knees, screaming in agony as their uniforms melted into their skin.

It took less than four minutes for the pair of women to witness every machine, each one an outlet for the Flaxens' hatred, consumed by flames. Scorched, blackened, useless.

The pilot grinned in delight, "Nice shooting, Commander!"

Lucinda shrugged, "Nothing to it, Lieutenant. I just decide what I want to hit, the ship does the rest."

"It was still quite the sight."

"We're not finished yet. Those little houses look far too nice for our murderous friends, don't you think?"

"They don't look too well heated, Commander. Perhaps we can help them with that?"

"It would be rude for us not to help our friends, but our plasma banks are expended. Looks like we'll have to deliver a more personal message."

A stream of ten missiles departed the small ship in sequence. They headed for their target as if a column of ants. With no need to accommodate Human intolerance to huge forces due to acceleration, the missiles accelerated with devastating force.

It took them less than ten seconds to reach their target on Earth hundreds of miles below. The barracks that sheltered over five thousand Flaxens were vaporized instantly in a flash of red and yellow that faded to orange. It was as if the sunset had arrived early and glistened the dry plains of Africa below them. A small mushroom cloud rose into the atmosphere.

Two of the missiles had taken a different route and detonated just above the barrack's reservoir, transforming it instantly to steam. It rose from the chaos and dispersed like a cloud in the wind.

Although they had officially completed their mission, Lucinda was having too much fun.

"How about some sharp shooting, Lieutenant?"

"Commander?"

Lucinda smiled, "How about we and our friends have a barbeque?"

She activated the ship's deflection lasers, designed to vaporize hazardous particles when the ship was at high velocity.

One by one, she targeted individual men as they ran in panic and confusion. She spent ten minutes as she targeted them with vengeful purpose. She took no shame in her enjoyment at watching each and every one of them transform into a dark pink puff of vapor as the laser hit its mark.

"What's the count now, Lieutenant?"

"That makes forty-two."

"That will do for now. I'm tired. Shall we be rude guests and leave our hosts to clean up this mess?"

The pilot understood she had been ordered to return to Echo. The ship turned one hundred and eighty degrees, before heading to the relative safety of the dark side of the moon.

Before the two small ships of war had departed for their mission, Kip and Sarah had spoken at length with Cyrus Eppleston. The Minister was quick to demand that Kip should hand over the half-Flaxen girl to their intelligence agency. It had not taken long for him to realize that was never going to happen. He had been used to Kip being polite and personable, but his demeanor had changed to one that was approaching anger at the mere suggestion. The girl had told Kip she wanted to stay aboard Echo and that was what was going to happen. Disappointed, but grateful for the military objective about to be discussed, the minister quickly let the issue go.

Both had agreed that the large base in Africa was an excellent target, for it contained huge amounts of enemy weaponry. Although protected from air raids by United Earth, it had no defense against attack from orbit. Both had also quickly agreed that should be target one. After that, their views differed. The minister had wanted to target a similar base in Eastern Asia, where the Flaxens were advancing rapidly.

Only United Earth's superior intelligence was allowing them to slow the enemy's advance.

Kip didn't agree. He had witnessed mere hours before the brutality of the Flaxens' camps and their machines of death in action. Indiscriminate of man woman or child.

Kip had insisted that objective two should and must be the tools of extermination spread across the Americas. Realizing he had no authority over the captain, and grateful for having negotiated at least half of his goals, the minister acquiesced.

At almost the same time their comrades over Africa had opened fire on the unprepared enemy below, Kip had acquired two camps only a mile apart in his sights.

The timing of the mission was no coincidence, for although over Africa, the sun was shining, Kip's targets were shrouded in night.

He knew the Flaxens didn't conduct their genocide in the dark. Serilda had told him prisoners were locked in their huts until dawn so he was confident that minimal, if any unintended harm would be inflicted on the camps' victims. He knew this was prime time to strike the cowardly enemy that had executed young children in the arms of their mothers before his eyes.

Kip fired the ship's plasma shards at the two death chambers and he watched them explode. The foliage surrounding the structures was illuminated as the weapons of vengeance met their targets.

Unlike the mission commanded by Lucinda, Kip needed time, for his objectives were dispersed across a continent. Over the next thirty-five minutes, he targeted the killing machines with purposeful precision. The Flaxens had no defense and no clue how United Earth may have struck such a devastating blow to their tools of genocide and to the fragile egos that defined each and every one of them.

He had intended to destroy thirty of the Flaxens' hateful structures. But he persisted beyond the remit of his mission. When the small ship of war had depleted its armaments, Kip had destroyed thirty-four—each the physical embodiment of their evil.

Kip wore an unusual smug expression as he looked at the junior Lieutenant in control of the scorpion, "Great job, Lieutenant, today's been a good day, take us home to Echo."

Chapter 17 – The Happy Time

Serilda laughed as Kip was recounting one of the few happy occasions he had experienced during the six years' war. They were sitting in his private office. She smiled as her laughter faded.

"I like it when you laugh, Kip. I've never had much reason to laugh myself."

"Well, you're laughing now."

"I know, and it's wonderful. Who could imagine a person's life could change so much so quickly. Everyone has been so nice to me. It makes me so happy. After years of nothing but cruelty, I was starting to forget things could be different. Only the memory of my mother reminded me that people could be kind."

"From what you've told me, she was quite the woman."

"You have no idea, Kip. Compared to most, she was lucky. My father protected her. She was so beautiful and kind, so kind. It's what kept me going. Her memory allowed me to persevere in the camp. She used to make me help her make bread and she would have my father give it to the prisoners in the camp."

Kip was stunned by this revelation and he wanted Serilda to see it, "But your father, he was a Flaxen, why would he do such a thing?"

"I told you. The Flaxens feel more than you or I. Unfortunately, a kind group mentality has overtaken nearly all of them. They all feel the need to appear the cruelest, the most vicious to each other. But their pride is much stronger too. This need to show power and hatred is an expression of this pride. They compete with each other to be the vilest. All because of their enhanced egos."

She looked down at her feet as she continued, "My father was the same way before he met my mother. She was so beautiful; you just couldn't imagine. That's what drew my father to her to begin with. When she fell pregnant with me, she knew her best hope for my safety was staying with him. He was a cruel man. He was feared even among the

Flaxens. That's why he rose so high within their ranks. He was a colonel when they killed him."

She looked at Kip once more, she saw he was agitated, desperate to speak but she conveyed to him with her yellow-green eyes that she wasn't finished.

"But he began to change. Especially when I was born. He used to play with me, he would even sing to me. Can you Imagine a Flaxen singing? I don't take the credit, though, it was my mother. Every time he struck her or spoke about the sub-Humans on Earth, she would confront him.

"She was so brave, Kip, such courage. She would ask him why. 'Why are you doing this? In what way are you helping anything with what you say, don't you know we're stronger together?' She would point at me and ask him if his way was so right, his beliefs so intransient, how did they create something so beautiful together? I don't say that out of vanity, that's just what my mother told me."

Kip nodded, he wanted to hear more.

"When I was old enough, I saw his eyes begin to change. They were still yellow, that's not what I mean, but the hatred was retreating and kindness was taking its place. It took years and he never became what you would consider a decent person, but my mother rubbed off on him and I'm sure he loved me, which may have helped too.

"Eventually, he became an almost kind man. When he came home, he would run at me and pick me up and swing me round and round above his head. I used to laugh so much it made me cry. He knew he couldn't change the ways of Flaxen society but he did what he could. He wasn't stationed at the camp but as the regional colonel, he would often have to visit to make inspections or oversee some development or another. The details don't matter really.

"I'm sorry, Kip, but two weeks ago when we first met, I wasn't forthcoming. It was too hard for me to speak about it. I'll never withhold anything from you again, I promise. I just wasn't ready."

"That's okay, I understand, go on."

"He was discovered. Some low rank Flaxen bastard saw him giving bread to people in the camp, bread that my mother and I had made. He used to tell them he was working to free them all and he truly was, Kip.

I believe that with all my heart. I don't know how but he had a plan, I just know it. He was just unlucky."

She saw Kip about to interject, so she gestured with her hand that he let her finish. "Showing mercy to Zoons, that's what they call people like you, is one of the highest of crimes. Everything I told you after was true. They did shoot my father and my mother. The only reason the general sent me to the camp was that he had encountered another half-breed like me and he secretly liked him. He told me that himself, he whispered it in my ear, even as that bastard was condemning me for life. He took my hand and told me that. Can you believe it?"

She rubbed imaginary dust from the desk with her finger. "Anyway, I'm rambling now. The point I was trying to make is that, as I have said before, the Flaxens are Human. My father was proof of that. He changed from one of the worst of those evil bastards into a man willing to risk his life to help others. Maybe there's hope for them yet, if only they could see the other path."

Kip was excited by these final words.

"Do you think we can do that, make them see the war is pointless?"

"No, I'm sorry. I shouldn't have given you false hope. Their mentality is too widespread, it's their culture. We're going to have to win this war with blood like any other."

Her head dropped at the thought. Kip put his hand palm down on the table, she rested hers on his. She looked up again.

"You're so kind. What I mean is that, if we win, there is hope for them. I know it's tempting to annihilate them all as they wish to do to us but there is hope for them. They just have to open their eyes as my father did. They have such potential for good, I can feel it. Sometimes, I see things in my dreams."

"Your dreams?"

"Sometimes I see Humans and Flaxens together, with a purpose. Something enigmatic."

Kip smiled to humor the girl. He didn't believe the sheer brutality of the yellows could ever be changed.

"Serilda, there's something I'm very curious about, and please don't feel compelled to answer if it's too difficult. But the other day, the prisoners that resisted being forced into the chamber, they seemed to have been spared the fate of the others. That makes no sense to me. Why did the Flaxens do that?"

"Oh, they weren't spared at all. Their fate was so much worse. Everyone in the camps know about the heat chamber. It's used as a tool of mental torture. Everyone knows they could be marched to their death at any minute. That kind of constant stress completely destroys a person."

"I can't even imagine."

"I wouldn't know either. I knew I would never be sent there. I stayed strong, and, obviously, the colonel wanted me alive for his own sick reasons. You saw the guards round up the three people who refused to enter the chamber. Those people would have been tortured and killed in the most horrific way in front of the next group of people selected for departure."

Her face dropped, "Oh, God, I can't believe I just said that. Did you know, that's the word the Flaxens use when they kill those poor people. I'm so ashamed I said that."

"I did know, Echo told me. It's just language you heard every day, it's a form of automatic memory. You said it with no ill intent, don't beat yourself up about it."

"Maybe, but it still makes me sick to my stomach that I said it. But I hope my point was clear. The Flaxens give their victims a choice. Either they willingly walk to a quick, near-instant death, or they will be slowly tortured and killed in front of their fellow inmates. Often their family. I won't tell you what they do to them, I can't, it's the cruelest of deaths imaginable."

"We'll make them pay, Serilda. We'll show them what it is to be on the other side."

She rubbed her free hand over the smooth table, avoiding Kip's gaze.

"That remains to be seen, I hope so, I do. Now, I've wasted enough of your time. I came here to tell you about the information I got from the colonel before they executed him. This could be important."

"I've been hoping to hear this. We just didn't want to ask you before you were ready."

She raised her head and stared through the window of the office. The silver moon was glowing brightly. Kip saw that it seemed to return to her at least a fraction of the tranquility he had come to associate with her.

"Thank you for that, I appreciate it. It's not that I wasn't ready, it's just I'm worried."

"Worried? What about?"

"Much of what I know came from the colonel's mouth, and he was drunk every night when I saw him. I made damn sure he was drunk before he tried too, you know."

"I know. Don't think about that for now."

"It's just that he was so drunk, I can't be sure what he was saying is true. I heard him talking about a new weapon, one he said was going to end the war in less than a year. He said it would turn the Zoons' insides to liquid by the thousands. I think he said something about Infrasound. I saw it in his dreams too, that's the main reason I'm telling you all of this. His dreams were disgusting. He imagined hundreds of United Earth troops covering their ears in agony as the weapons liquified their insides."

Kip saw tears well in her eyes. He was concerned about becoming too attached to her. Although he considered himself to be of strong character, he was only Human. And Serilda was full of beauty both within and without beyond anything he had known before. He resisted the urge to console her.

"I know what the colonel was talking about. Infrasound is a form of very high-energy sound waves that can seriously harm people, and at close enough range, it will kill them. Serilda, you must tell me everything you know."

Kip leaned closer to Serilda as he added, "After our last attack, the Flaxens are completely shaken. For the first time in this war, they are scared. They haven't launched any major offensives since we took out their base in Africa and the death chambers in North America. They are beginning to bury their weapons caches to avoid being targeted again. Serilda I can't explain to you how important it is for us to keep this momentum going.

"A huge part of war is phycological and we have them wrongfooted for the first time. If we can keep this up, we may be able to demoralize them considerably. I cannot overstate how much difference that can make. Please, tell me everything you know, no matter how trivial you may think it to be."

The girl with the yellow-green eyes complied with Kip's request.

It took three days for Kip and Colonel Hastings to plan the first phase of the mission. Serilda had told them that the bulk of materials required for the construction of the Flaxens' new weapon could be found on Earth. But they lacked some essential raw minerals, which were too far within United Earth territory for the Flaxens to obtain. She also explained that they were available in abundance on Venus. That world had not known millennia of plunder of its natural resources as was the case with Earth.

She said the Flaxen industrial infrastructure was much more advanced on their homeworld and so parts of the weapon were to be shipped from Venus to Earth. She had told kip that the Flaxens had a covert military research station buried deep within the Andes Mountains in South America. She was sure from the colonel's dreams that this was where the bulk of the new weapons was being manufactured. She was concerned to reveal this to Kip, the knowledge she revealed had not been spoken by the colonel, but were revealed to her in his slumber. And dreams are often abstract, not a true reflection of reality.

This initially made Kip nervous, but Minister Eppleston assured him that the half-Flaxens United Earth already had within their intelligence agency had consistently provided crucial and accurate intelligence. This was the main reason United Earth had not already succumbed to the enemy's relentless advance.

The information also made sense to Kip and Minister Eppleston. The mountains would be completely impervious to air raids. Even though United Earth had not conducted a successful air raid within the heart of Flaxen territory for many years, the yellows were taking no chances.

The facility was so deep within the mountains. Even Echo's small ships of war would be unable to penetrate the facility from orbit with the weaponry they had available.

Hastings had told kip he would need the entire compliment of his Marines to achieve their objective. He spelled out the plan to disable the facility in exquisite detail. Something Kip was getting used to from the man.

Kip realized he was lucky Hastings had been on Echo and not Formidable. It was clear he was the absolute best in the field of covert operations.

Three days later, three shuttlecrafts containing nearly fifty Marines were launched from Echo. They departed from the dark side of the moon headed directly for the base situated deep within the Andes Mountains.

They had purposely timed the operation to begin at night. The United Earth Marines had a considerable advantage in the dark with their crescent devices.

The shuttles landed a mile away from Mount Aconcagua, the highest peak in the mountain range and the location of the Flaxens' secret weapons facility.

The temperature at the location of their landing at night was minus fifteen degrees Celsius. These conditions could have inhibited even the hardest of marines but each was equipped with white clothing that blended perfectly into the snow, and what was more, the clothing had an internal heating system that could keep its occupant warm for up to five hours.

Although Echo could not see within the mountain structure even in infrared, he was able to analyze the heat signatures left on the tires of the vehicles that were seen leaving the complex via satellites. From the relative spread of these heat signatures, Echo was able to create an accurate model of the various turns and changes in the direction each vehicle had taken and was, therefore, able to compute a likely location for the Marines to target.

It took them over an hour to traverse the difficult, mountainous terrain between their shuttles and the complex.

When Hastings arrived at the target, he was seeing the landscape around him in infrared. In this remote and desolate part of the world, devoid of even moonlight at this time of the month, light amplification was insufficient for the Marines to have a clear view of their objective.

He could see ten Flaxens glowing yellow in his display, guarding the outer door of their objective. They seemed casual, unconcerned about the possibility of an enemy attack. These Flaxens had been guarding this installation for years, night after night, and had not once seen the slightest evidence of enemy incursion. Not so much as a surveillance aircraft above their heads.

Hastings observed his enemy's arrogance and thought to himself, *Tonight is the night you are tested, my friends.*

He had his troops in five platoons of ten men and women, separated by twenty meters. They had the perimeter of the entrance surrounded and were camouflaged as they lay prone in the snow. He allocated a flaxen guard to two of his Marines in each of the platoons. Immediately, the Marines could see their targets surrounded by a red outline, letting them know they were to aim their rifles and wait for the command to fire.

The compound was surrounded by a network of security cameras which would have made a surprise mission impossible, if not for Echo.

From the far side of the moon, the AI had hacked into the primitive Flaxen security system and he alone had absolute control over the visual data the cameras delivered to those who monitored them. Any Flaxen in the security room designed to view this visual feed would see an image completely fabricated by Echo. All of the ten soldiers guarding the complex's entrance would appear to be acting in the manner they did night after night. Nothing would appear out of the ordinary.

Hastings gave the order to fire. Highly focused microwave energy hit all ten guards in complete synchronicity. Hastings briefly lifted his crescent, allowing him the pleasure of seeing the Flaxens' upper torsos ignite in the total darkness of the wilderness that surrounded them. A hole opened in the body of each one of them. Their flesh still glowed red in the night as their corpses hit the floor.

In unison one of the platoons heard Hastings' order, "Go, go, go."

Ten Marines approached the thick cast iron doors to the mountain complex. They could smell the burning flesh of the Flaxens who had been so complacent only seconds before.

Each of the marines, directed by their crescents, aimed their rifles at a specific location on the iron door, each slightly different to the next in their platoon. They fired and saw the middle section of the cast iron doors turn to metal slag. The Marines' crescents compensated to avoided overwhelming their eyes. A circular entrance with its circumference glowing like magma in the dark mountain landscape appeared before their eyes. This was no guesswork. Echo had computed the exact amount of energy required to create the portal required to reach their target.

Hastings ordered thirty Marines to guard the perimeter, the rest were to follow him into the wide corridor that lay before the doors the Flaxens had thought impenetrable.

Hastings led a frontal formation of three. Behind him were three rows of Marines, the first two walking forward behind their commander, the last row walked backward, protecting their comrades from unexpected attack from behind.

Hastings followed the blue outline superimposed onto the floor by his crescent toward the weapons facility they had been commanded to destroy. Ahead of the Marines, at the end of the corridor they were traversing, were two further corridors that were both ninety degrees relative to their current position, forming a T-shape.

Two Flaxens appeared from the corridor on the right. Hastings blinked twice in quick succession. His crescent received this as an order and instantly transmitted to the man to his left that he was to target the enemy on the right. Hastings wanted the other for himself. Due to the limited capacity of their weapons for microwave emissions, Hastings had ensured that he and the two men at either side of him had not yet expended any of this vital energy, for it provided the crucial advantage of total silence when killing the enemy.

Hastings' crescent informed him instantly that his comrade to his left had acquired a lock. He blinked again three times in quick succession. This commanded the two rifles to link together, the rifle of his subordinate now slave to his own. Hastings fired, the rifle of the other Marine fired instantly, without its bearer having to pull the trigger. They had little time to acquire their targets, so the standard tactic of aiming for the center of mass was not achieved. Both of the Flaxens before them dropped to the floor as their faces melted into their skulls. Their heads dissolved on the floor, their blood forming bubbles as it boiled on the metallic surface of the corridor.

The blue line was directing the Marines to turn right. Their footfall was barely audible, their boots had soles that absorbed the energy of each step. They proceed as silent as a lioness, stalking her prey in the desert sand.

As they turned the corner, they saw a door, its outline illuminated in green in all of their crescents. This was the room Echo had assured them contained their objective.

Hastings knew the room would almost certainly be full of Flaxens. And so, the microwave radiation emitted from their rifles wasn't a viable option for gaining access. Although powerful and silent, they would take several seconds to melt through the cast iron. More than enough time to give warning to the enemy.

Hastings remained silent as he commanded two of his Marines via his console to proceed to the door. A woman on the left and a man on the right coated the perimeter of the door with a transparent gel. He touched a single button on his console which transmitted a frequency of x-rays that ignited the gel instantly. All of the Marines' crescents immediately compensated to reduce the light from the substance as it burned as bright as the midday sun. Had they looked at the flame with unprotected eyes, the sheer brightness would have damaged their retinas.

The gel had one flaw. It hissed like a snake as it burned, loud enough to alert anyone inside the installation. Hastings was no fool, he had chosen this method of access for its speed. He knew the gel would burn through the inches thick metal in less than half a second.

The door fell inwards. Its outer edges still ablaze and glowing bright red as liquid metal slag poured from its edges.

Hastings had made the right choice. The room contained at least twenty Flaxens. The Marines rushed through the cavity and were met by a litter of yellow eyes, like wild cats shining in the moonlight. Each pair was staring at them in astonishment. He had no further need for silence.

"Kinetic fire!"

The Marines had been ordered to switch their rifles to conventional bullets. They could be fired in semi or fully automatic fashion. All of the Marines chose the latter.

Rounds of bullets, one in a ten a tracer round consumed the facility. Eight enemy combatants were hit and killed within two seconds. For these were Tier 1 Marines, they seldom missed their target.

The room was filled with metallic machinery and conveyor belts. Plenty enough for the Flaxens who were quick-witted enough to take cover.

A chaotic firefight ensued. The Flaxens' weapons were also fully automatic and nearly as deadly as those in the grasp of Hastings' Marines.

Hastings still had an infrared image configured on his crescent. He saw seven Flaxens taking cover behind a rectangular machine. He switched his rifle to its third method of fire. Rockets.

He tapped his console to configure the rockets to explode at only fifty percent of their potential power, for he feared their full potential may injure or kill his own. Two rockets launched in sequence at the machine. Blood, flesh, and body parts flew in all directions. His crescent confirmed there were no signs of life from the maimed and mangled bodies of the Flaxens he had targeted.

Hastings saw a Marine, Private Huel Jenkinks, attempt to flank two more enemies who were laying prone under an elevated conveyor belt. He knew before the private had finished his charge toward the enemy that he was a dead man.

Both Flaxens opened fire, they had a clear line of sight as he approached. Jenkins fell to his knees. He looked down at his decimated torso. Blood flew from his mouth and he hit the floor face down, gurgling, desperate, but unable to breathe.

Hastings flanked the pair that had just killed his subordinate. He performed a perfect barrel roll from the opposite direction that Jenkins had assailed them.

His rifle erupted. During his roll, he had blinked three times in a specific sequence—twice quickly, a short pause, then another blink.

This automatically changed his bullets to explosive rounds. As his roll came to an end, he had the two yellow-eyed enemies directly insight. He double-tapped the trigger and watched as each of them liquified before his eyes.

Only five Flaxens remained. Hastings had an idea. He configured his translation matrix on his console to the Flaxen dialect deciphered by Echo.

"We have you outnumbered five to one. You have no chance of leaving alive unless you drop your weapons and show yourselves immediately."

One of the remaining five at the back corner of the room, partially shielded by a metal walkway at his midlevel, opened fire at Hastings. The Flaxen was clearly an amateur, Hastings had defilade.

He waited for the rounds to stop ricocheting above his head, a clear sign the inexperienced Flaxen needed to reload. He raised his head from his position of cover and fired a single explosive round at the man. It hit the metal structure he had relied on for cover but his head exploded, nonetheless, as his brain matter and skull littered their surroundings.

"Now only four of you remain. You have seen our superiority in all regards. Surrender or die like the man whose face I just destroyed!"

He heard the sound of metal hitting the floor, the sound of guns being dropped.

"We surrender! Please don't fire. We're coming out now."

He was still cautious, he knew the Flaxens' reputation for duplicity.

"Hands up! Let me see your fucking hands now."

All four of the men complied. They knew if they continued to fight, they would most assuredly die. Each emerged from their locations of defense with their hands raised high. They appeared to be unarmed.

Hastings ordered four of his Marines to secure the enemy and search them. A combat knife with a yellow handle with the Flaxens' customary black glyph was seized from sheaths within each of their ankles.

The four men smiled at each other, thrilled to have seized such a prestigious token of war. No doubt they could display them proudly to their friends and brag while their colleagues admired their trophies with envy.

Hastings now gave orders verbally, there was no further need for silence. "Platoon five, place the devices at these locations. He had a two-dimensional display of the room and tapped five points on his console. The data was instantly transmitted to the platoon of Marines. They got to work, placing their devices as ordered.

Hastings had not intended to take prisoners, but it occurred to him that they may have some potential to gather intelligence. Or at least some insight into the mind of their enemy.

He heard frenzied screaming from the other side of the room. One of his men, a friend of Jenkins, was smashing the head of a dead Flaxen with the butt of his rifle. "You fucking yellow bastards, you killed Huel!" The man reduced the yellow face of the dead Flaxen to a pulp.

Hastings didn't speak, he roared, "Private, we do not desecrate the corpses of our enemy. Ever! These men will be left here and their bodies will be dealt with in accordance with the customs of their people. Is that understood?"

The private looked at Hastings, his eyes were red and glazed. It took him several seconds to respond, "Yes, Sir. Sorry, Sir. It's just…"

"Not now. We'll take Jenkins' body with us. You and the Marine to your right will carry him. Is that understood?"

"Yes, Sir."

The Marines left the room and followed the corridors that had led them to their objective. The prisoners had their arms behind their heads and were confined between two formations of Marines. Rifles were aimed at their midsections.

They had planted explosive devices with enough power to destroy half a small city. They were timed to explode thirty minutes after their deployment.

Hastings was keeping an eye on the countdown as they made their way back to the shuttles.

"You may want to watch this, Marines."

In complete unity, over one hundred eyes, eight of them yellow, turned to watch the mountain behind them. The night turned to day as the devices exploded with devastating force. The weapons were advanced. They were composed of dense materials with so many molecular bonds, the energy released from five of the devices was nearly equal to that of a small tactical nuclear weapon. Although they had the advantage of not irradiating the biosphere for decades to come.

Rocks the size of houses were launched hundreds of meters into the air. The Marines' eyes glowed orange as the display of destruction reflected from them. The peak of the mountain crumbled away and the marines felt the earth shake beneath their feet, their advanced boots insufficient to absorb such immense fore. Mount Aconcagua was no longer the highest peak in the Andes.

The next day, both scorpions left the shuttle bay. Their target was not Earth but a convoy of Flaxen transport ships carrying the precious materials required to complete the new Flaxen weapon. Echo had told Kip they were escorted by ten of the Flaxens' small warships equipped with missiles used to defend their cargo against enemy attack.

Kip was in command of one of the small but deadly vessels. The scorpions advanced towards their target at speeds the Flaxens could only dream of. They flew past Earth, toward the black void between Venus, and poised like a spider in its web.

The Flaxen armada had no hope of escape. The scorpions' sensors detected them from over four hundred thousand miles away. Both ships acquired their targets and launched a salvo of missiles. The weapons had such acceleration that they took a mere forty seconds to traverse the unimaginable distance between them.

Kip wanted the satisfaction of seeing his enemy destroyed, for through Serilda's influence, he despised them with an intensity that energized his body. Not with the nectar of hope that had fed him in the six years' war, but with the venom of snake that would necrotize his insidious enemy. He magnified the image by two thousand percent, allowing him the pleasure of witnessing every one of the missiles hit its mark with indifferent precision. The ships exploded in an embarrassment of light and color. Their vital cargo, the hope that the Flaxens had been relying on to win the war years earlier than planned, lost to the cold and desolate vacuum of space forever.

"That was too easy," said Kip to the pilot of the scorpion.

The junior lieutenant looked at her captain, "Would you rather have engaged in a dog fight, Sir?"

Kip considered this, "Lieutenant, if I could, I would have boarded each of those ships and stabbed every one of the bastards through their yellow eyes. I would have done it in a heartbeat."

The pilot smiled and returned her gaze to the viewscreen, "Home, Captain?"

Kip watched as the last light from their targets dissipated into the black. "Echo is our home now, Lieutenant. You did a great job today. Maybe you'd like to join me, Commander Dimple, and the doc for dinner tonight? We're having steak. You can tell them all about our heroic acts."

She smiled, "It would be an honor, Captain."

Kip leaned back in his chair, a smooth smirk on his face, "See you in the captain's mess at nineteen hundred hours."

Kip wasn't the slightest bit disturbed by the loss of life he had inflicted upon the Flaxens. During the six years' war, he was often consumed with remorse after destroying a Martian starship with a hundred souls aboard.

The ship soared back To Echo. Kip was gleeful he had denied the enemy of their precious superweapon. And they had no idea how such a disaster had befallen them.

Over the next two weeks, the crew of the starship displaced in time inflicted devastating blows across the entirety of Flaxen territory. Factories, barracks, and weapons caches were all obliterated from orbit without the loss of a single friendly life.

The Flaxens were finally knowing what it meant to feel the terror of a superior enemy killing them at will, with no regard for their lives, their right to exist. They looked to the sky in fear, as unknown weapons illuminated the skies above them as if the gods had sided with their enemy. They watched in disbelief while their comrades turned to ash as purple energy from the heavens arrested their desire for conquest. Rumors began to spread, the most common was that United Earth had discovered Hubritian technology. For two weeks, Kip slept soundly, his dreams filled with Flaxens burning and screaming under the might of Echo and the scorpions he harbored, dreams he remembered for reasons he couldn't fathom. And for two weeks, he awoke with joy in his heart for the next objective they were to destroy without mercy.

Chapter 18 – Collateral Damage

Kip rocked slowly in his chair in his office, reviewing the psychological evaluations from the four Flaxen captives Helen had provided him. All four had said nothing except their name and rank when asked any question by Helen.

Kip had ordered that they were to be treated humanely, following the regulations of United Earth, a society that had been vanquished by an invisible enemy eight thousand years prior. Although he hated them, he was still a captain of the fleet and he would not yield to his desire for vengeance on defenseless prisoners. That was the way of the Flaxens, not his way.

Studying his daily report further, Kip was pleased to see that United Earth had made good on their promise to manufacture and deliver rail gun slugs. Many of Echo's weapons had been removed to allow additional space for colonists. Some rail guns remained on the forward section of Echo as well as on the starboard and port sides of the ship. These were deadly weapons that used a series of magnets to accelerate titanium slugs at appreciable percentages of light speed. Echo was once again becoming a ship of war.

His door buzzer sounded. He looked at his screen and was happy to see Serilda was waiting outside. He hadn't seen her for several days and he had grown to like her.

Perhaps like was too weak a word, but he had plenty of time to get his feelings in order. Since Serilda had ceased her infiltrations into his mind, his emotions had stabilized. Save for those of hatred of the enemy and absolute compassion for their victims.

Kip released the door and Serilda entered. He knew instantly that this was not going to be one of the kind exchanges he had grown accustomed to with the girl.

Her eyes, with which he had been so completely mesmerized by before with their shine of hope and kindness now radiated fury. Her beautiful face was now contorted.

"How could you not tell me, Kip? I had a right to know. Those people died because of me. Nearly six thousand people dead, just so you could save me? My life isn't worth six thousand others. Not to mention the people in the camp I left behind. Oh god, the people! Women and children, old men suffocating in their homes. How could you not tell me?"

Kip knew instantly she was speaking of York. The city that had been devastated from the air just one day after Hastings and his team had rescued Serilda and Megan from the camp where she had survived for so many years.

Most would emerge from such horror broken, damaged, and devoid of feeling, for the sheer terror of the place was constant, unrelenting.

But the girl with the yellow-green eyes before him had shrugged it off as if it were a mere inconvenience. Now, this strength of mind was directed at Kip with purposeful anger and he felt his heart sink.

Kip met her gaze, trepidation filled his eyes, "Serilda, how do you know this?" He suspected the girl's gift had revealed this horrific truth to her.

"Does it matter? But if you must know, I was having lunch with Ensign Soriah. He told me everything. Kip, how could you not tell me?"

Kip scolded himself for not classifying this information, but it simply hadn't occurred to him. "I wasn't trying to hide it from you. It just didn't occur to me to tell you. So much has happened since you joined us. It just didn't cross my mind. I have not and never will lie nor intentionally withhold anything from you. I know we haven't known each other for long but I thought you would at least know that by now."

"Kip, it was hard enough for me to deal with seeing the people I shared that camp with killed before my eyes and now I find out thousands more were killed just so I could be free of that place. I wish you'd never come. All those people would still be alive. Thousands burned because of me. Did you not think I have a right to know?"

Kip was inwardly devasted. To be the subject of the fury of such a pure example of humanity tore into his soul. As if he were being judged for his actions by some kind of mystical entity.

"Serilda, you didn't kill anyone. The Flaxens did that. It was also me who ordered your rescue. If any blame is to be directed at anyone, it's me. But I have to be blunt with you. This is war, people die in war. As commanders, we have to balance the gains of any objective against potential losses."

Kip could no longer stand the rage in the girl's eyes. They surveyed him, examined him as if they were the objective truth of morality. He looked at the screen on his desk.

"When those people in York died, I nearly had a breakdown. Believe me, I don't dismiss such loss of life casually. But the information you provided us saved many more lives than those lost in York. If the Flaxens had deployed their new weapon, United Earth would have had no defense. They would have overrun Earth in a year, two max. Every non-Flaxen life on the planet would be extinguished without mercy. You know this better than anyone."

Serilda took the seat opposite kip and put her head in her hands. Kip could see that she was trying and failing to suppress tears. This time, he had no desire to deny his wish to console the girl who sat before him in abject despair, for her feelings were now his own, such was the bond her exploration into his mind had created.

He felt closer to this young half-Flaxen than anyone in his life before, save for Sarah. He rounded his oversized desk and knelt before her as she wept in her chair. She raised her face to meet him. She had released the look of rage in favor of despair. He saw she had understood what he had said was true. Kip put his hand on her shoulder and allowed her to sob. He was tempted to hug her but he knew this would be dangerous. He couldn't allow himself to grow too close to her. Too much was at stake.

As soon as he touched her, he felt a zap on his hand. A transposition of two minds into one. He felt a connection from this touch that was overwhelming. He felt all of the girl's emotions within his mind as if they were his own. He now knew that for all of her displays of hopefulness, joy, and kindness, what truly consumed her was desperation and anxiety for the people of Earth. Her feelings were of such intensity, Kip now understood what Serilda had meant when she described the Flaxens' enhanced ability to feel.

But what Serilda felt was what the Flaxens despised. She was the anthesis of their hatred, the shield to their sword. Kip was fortified even further to see every last one of them killed, or flee to their homeworld in terror. A world which he had no intention of allowing to be a refuge for those who had inflicted such damage on the beautiful girl before him and millions more besides. The girl he now knew he did not just merely like.

Serilda hadn't noticed that Sarah watched her enter Kip's office. She didn't truly know what she felt about this but she did know she didn't like the increasing frequency of the girl's one on one visits with the captain.

The next day, Kip was on the bridge discussing their numerous victories over the Flaxens in the previous two weeks with Sarah.

Echo's voice filled the bridge, "Captain, the Flaxens are transmitting directly to United Earth. This is most unusual, reserved mostly for propaganda used to demoralize them. The transmission is coming from the most senior Flaxen on Earth. This has never been seen before."

Kip saw Sarah's eyes, as if a typhoon of panic whirled within their hitherto brown calm. "Put it on screen, Echo," she ordered.

The AI complied.

An enormous Flaxen filled the screen. Larger than any the crew of Echo had seen before. He was dressed in their dark gray uniform, silver adornments lined his collar. Behind him draped the yellow, white and black flag, the symbol of Flaxen tyranny. His eyes were wide-set and deep yellow. He began to speak in a deep and onerous voice.

"I am Field Marshal Kilter Shrader. I must admit you filthy Zoons have surprised me in recent weeks, but we are no idiots. We know you have assistance from an ally. Do not allow yourselves the hope that your verminous species will be saved. You have caused us a slight setback, nothing more. We will still crush you beneath our boots and spit on you as we burn your disgusting children atop your bones."

The field marshal paused for a moment, and a grin appeared above his perfectly squared jaw.

"Our forces remain strong. We have reserves of equipment and men even the half-breed abominations within your so-called intelligence agency have not the slightest idea about. You have destroyed a mere fraction of the installations designed to exterminate you. You have prevented no deaths, quite the opposite. Now you will see that your pointless resistance to our dominance comes at a high price." The field marshal raised his fist to chin level and screamed, "For Flaxus!"

The image immediately changed. The view was from a high angle, perhaps from a small mountain. It showed a square wire fence over a mile wide on each side. Within its perimeter were people shoving and pushing against each other in desperation.

Kip looked upon the sight in horror. "Echo, what are we seeing? Where is this place?"

Echo now spoke in a tone the crew knew to be his preferred manner of delivering bad news, "Captain, what you are seeing is nearly one hundred thousand people caged in Flaxen territory, the area you knew to be Texas. I am detecting three hundred incoming Flaxen aircraft. All appear to be bombers."

The faces of the bridge crew turned to white in synchronicity as the realization of Flaxens' intent became clear.

Less than a minute passed before the yellow-winged bombers appeared. They flew in V-shaped formations. Each one was comprised of fifty aircraft. They flew at low altitudes and as each flight group flew over the prisoners, they released their bombs, each one dropping their payload slightly after the previous so as to consume every last soul below them in sickening hellfire.

The crew of Echo watched as one hundred thousand innocents were incinerated, maimed, and killed. Black smoke rose from the carnage. Silence engulfed the bridge. When the smoke had dispersed, the once brown desert terrain had turned to a deep red, etched with blackened craters where the bombs had fallen. A sick painting in the desert landscape, perfectly symbolic of the Flaxens, the strange yellow people that had come to Earth under the guise of peace.

The image changed back to the field marshal. He was grinning. His yellow eyes shone with pride.

"This was but a mere demonstration of what we will do to your brothers and sisters we use as slaves. Break your new alliance, or watch a hundred thousand more of them die each day until you do."

He widened his smile and rose his fist once more. He spoke slowly, with malevolent intent, "For Flaxus."

The transition ceased.

After her scheduled duty on the bridge had ended, Sarah had gone directly to her quarters. She was laying on her bed, her face expressionless. She hadn't realized, even after her conversation with Serilda, the true nature of the Flaxens, until now—for seeing is believing. Killing one hundred people in their heat chamber had affected her terribly, but witnessing one hundred thousand people reduced to pulp and ash before her eyes was too much to bear.

She hadn't cried, she hadn't wept. Such superficial displays of condolence seemed inadequate to her, offensive to the thousands she had witnessed die in an act of revenge. Vengeance for their assistance to United Earth. Mere tears were insufficient. Indeed, there was nothing that could possibly be sufficient to express the feelings that consumed her.

And so, she just lay staring at the soft yellow light above her. Motionless, numb, and empty.

An hour later, she was awoken by the sound of her door buzzing. She made the appropriate swiping gesture on her wrist to see who it was. A holographic image projected and she was surprised to see Megan standing in the corridor outside. She had only seen the girl once before when she was in the infirmary talking to Ostio.

Surprised she had been able to sleep, Sarah drank from the glass on her nightstand and did her best to compose herself, "Come in."

The young girl entered. Although she looked much better, she still looked thin and frail. She was one hundred percent Human and did not share Serilda's strength and resilience that characterized the enemy. A mere two weeks was inadequate to restore her to full health. The girl shared Sarah's brown hair and deep brown eyes. She looked at her timidly, "I'm sorry to interrupt you, Commander Dimple."

Sarah saw the shyness in the girl's eyes and even a shade of fear. She felt sincere sorrow for the girl before her, "Hey, don't you worry about it, Megan, you can come here whenever you need, night or day, and I mean that."

"Thank you, Commander. I need to speak with you, maybe this should be for the captain's ears, but after so many years in…" She paused and looked at her feet. "That place, I find it difficult to speak to men, especially when they wear a uniform."

Megan's words caused a lump to form in Sarah's throat. Not just for their content but for the child-like quality of the melody that carried them. She could only imagine the brutality the Flaxens had inflicted on her. And by the sight of the girl's youth and beauty, almost certainly the violations as well. "Megan, you can talk to me about anything."

Sarah directed the girl to the dining table at the far end of her quarters and pulled out a chair for her. Sarah took the seat opposite and moved a vase of flowers on the table that partially blocked their view of each other. Although her dark, brown eyes could be tools for intimidation when she required, they could also express a kindness and empathy few others could convey. "Megan, why did you come to see me? And you can be honest with me. Please, you have nothing to fear."

Megan could still not meet Sarah's gaze but she began to speak. Her dulcet tones remained. "Commander, I don't know if you know, but Serilda and I are sharing quarters. We slept in a filthy bunk together for so many years, now neither of us can sleep without each other. She's so wonderful, before I was discharged from the infirmary, she sat by my bedside every night and held my hand and sang until I fell asleep. It was a song she learned from her mother. She would sing it to me in the camp when it got too much for me."

Sarah was trying her best to retain her kind, but dry face, but she knew her eyes would soon betray her. She felt a compassion for Megan she could not recall feeling before. The thought of such a life and the strength of mind to endure it engulfed her in admiration and respect, as if she were a spoiled child and Megan an orphan who must scour the streets for scraps of food. "I've met Serilda, she is quite a woman. Such strength."

"She's the reason I'm alive, Commander."

"I'm not on duty. Please call me Sarah."

Megan finally looked up to make eye contact. She smiled but Sarah knew it was just for her benefit. "Serilda talks in her sleep, she always has. In the month before you rescued us, she would sleep at different times of the day. At the time, I had no idea why. But now I know she was waiting for the captain to sleep. She spoke to him in his dreams, did you know that?"

"I did. It affected the captain badly."

"She has that effect on people. But she never does it out of malice. Except maybe with the Colonel."

"What's she saying in her sleep?"

"She sometimes gets agitated when she sleeps. She keeps talking about a sphere. And she keeps saying Avalon over and over. I don't know what that word means, I've never heard it before. I keep asking her about it but she won't say anything. But I know her like she was my sister, and she's scared. So scared."

She looked away at a painting on Sarah's wall as if its color and vibrance would protect her. "I've seen her like this before, in the camp, before she learned how to control the colonel, she would always know when the Flaxens were going to use their red circles. Sometimes days in advance. She would awake terrified, covered in sweat. It's like that again. She knows something. Maybe she doesn't even know it yet, but she knows something. Something terrible. I just had to tell you or I couldn't live with myself if something happened."

"You're sure she said, Avalon?" Sarah spoke the last word slowly, to be sure there was no confusion.

Megan turned her head quickly back to Sarah. "I'm certain. That word means something to you, doesn't it?"

Sarah had no intention of lying to the broken girl before her. "It does. Avalon is the name of a man. He was aboard this ship but we left him." Sarah paused. Realizing explaining Cylli to her would take too much time and most likely mean nothing to the girl, she chose her words carefully, "We left him somewhere safe, but he's a very clever man. He could be very dangerous. Megan, you did the right thing. Thank you so much, but you need to leave. The captain must hear of this immediately. Believe me, you may have helped more than you know, but please, go back to Serilda."

Megan's eyes were filled with fear, but she did as Sarah asked and left the room, saying nothing more.

Sarah tapped her wrist once, the command to call the captain.

"Commander, what is it?"

"Captain, has the scorpion left yet?"

"Lucinda left around thirty minutes ago, as planned."

"Recall the mission now. I don't have time to explain, just call it off now and deploy the armor. Do it now!"

"Okay, Commander. I'll do it now. Just come to the bridge and tell me what the hell is going on."

Kip issued the order to recall the mission and deploy the armor.

Echo was slowly coated in a metal alloy that unfolded slowly around him as if syrup flowing over a stack of pancakes.

The crewman at the coms station turned to Kip, "Sir, I can't issue the recall the order. All signals are being jammed."

Kip's face drained of its blood.

Lucinda had been ordered to take a single scorpion. Her mission was to destroy as much of the Flaxens' communications network as possible, allowing Kip to destroy as much of the enemy's arsenal as possible, denying them their ability to make good on their promise to expedite their genocide. If they couldn't communicate, they would have higher priorities than murdering innocents, at least for a while.

Lucinda spoke to the pilot of the insect-shaped ship. "Change vector, Ensign, bearing two hundred and thirty-four mark three."

The scorpion was directly above North America. She was looking at a huge radio transmitter that was the core of the Flaxens' communications around Earth. Although it relied on satellites for global communication, this was the heart of the Flaxens' ability to issue orders from their main territory in the Americas. Lucinda was about to order the pilot to approach closer to their target when the pilot spoke. Panic betrayed his voice.

"Commander, I am detecting a ship approaching. It's close. I don't know why sensors didn't detect it sooner."

"Identify the ship, Ensign. Is it Flaxen?"

"No, Commander. The ship is of unknown design, but it's small. Not much bigger than ours."

Lucinda watched as an arrow-shaped vessel appeared in the view screen. It was like nothing she had ever seen before. Its hull glistened in the sunlight. It shone in in the same way Cylli did.

When Sarah arrived on the bridge, she was panting. She had run as fast as her legs would allow.

The bridge crew was watching the mission unfold. The scorpion was transmitting its visual feed directly to Echo.

They watched as it deployed its armor.

As the mystery vessel approached, it seemed to change color. The tip of its arrow glowed purple. Not like the color of a summer flower but an unnatural, florescent violet. Less than a second later, a beam of dark violet energy discharged from the ship of unknown origin. It struck the scorpion as shards from its hull flew into the void. It began to glow red then white-hot. The small ship had not been designed to withstand such destructive power. It was constructed to work in swarms, to overwhelm the enemy's defenses. It exploded before their eyes, dissipating into space in streaks of white-hot metal that faded into red, before vanishing into glowing metal slag, now in orbit around Earth.

The assailant wasn't finished. The lieutenant currently at the tactical station in Lucinda's absence turned to the captain with wide eyes, "Sir, the ship has changed its direction. It's headed directly for us."

"Activate the rail guns."

Kip remained composed. He was surprised by his relative calm. "Fire starboard thrusters, I want our rail guns in direct line of sight of that ship."

"Firing thrusters."

Echo turned as the deadly vessel approached at terrifying speed. The ship stopped almost instantly as if defying the laws of physics. Sarah was accustomed to issuing combat orders during the six years' war. It was the executive officer's duty to do so.

"Fire rail guns now, Lieutenant. Maximum power!"

Slugs of titanium flew from Echo at appreciable levels of light speed. All aboard watched as the slugs hit their mark. Slug after slug traveling with devastating speed struck the small arrow. Much to the despair of all, the weapons that had decimated so many Martian starships caused no damage to the shiny ship, save for the glow the darts had made from the heat of their impact.

Once again, the small ship's arrowhead began to glow.

Sarah looked at her captain, desperately hoping he would display his gift for tactical brilliance he had shown so regularly in the fight against Mars.

There was no time. The small ship discharged its deadly purple beam directly at the center of the kilometer-long starship. Echo's armor was holding, but the decks of the ship shook violently. The amour turned white, like the scorpion only seconds before.

Many of the bridge crew fell to the floor as the outer midsection of Echo exploded, the outer parts of his hull flew into space at relativistic speeds.

"Lieutenant, engage the sphere drive now! Maximum power!" ordered Kip.

Sarah couldn't believe what she had just heard, "We can't go to spherical speed here. The deflector lasers can't cope with the density of matter in a solar system!"

"We have no choice, Commander. We're dead anyway if we stay here. Lieutenant, do as I command. Now!"

The lieutenant complied. The eyes of the pilot that flew the arrow reflected the last light of the explosions that had decimated his target. Echo's rear engines turned bright purple, the same color of the weapon that had assailed him. His rear engines flashed in a shade of violet light as they set loose their power upon the blackness of space. The starship seemed to elongate before it vanished as if blossom in a gale.

Chapter 19 – Flaxus

On the northern hemisphere of Venus, Claudius Sirister was in the Capitol building, unofficially called the Hawk's Retreat. When the planet was populated by flora and fauna from Earth of all varieties in the years following its transformation from Hell to Eden, the bird of prey had found the conditions on their new world particularly convenient.

The small mammals they preyed upon had not adjusted nearly as well. The soil was thin on Venus. The newly transformed planet had not had millions of years as Earth had to acquire topsoil thick enough for them to make their burrows. And so, the birds ruled the skies above Venus, and the Flaxens had grown to admire their ability to stalk and destroy their weak and defenseless prey.

Claudius was the leader of all Flaxens and his name to all he commanded was Flaxus. A name that had been passed down for generations since the planet had united and exterminated the religious vermin that had, as on Earth, once dominated the people of Venus for so long.

The title did not pass down from father to son as had been the case in monarchies and dictatorships on Earth for most of its history. It was, in fact, illegal for an incumbent Flaxus to choose his own offspring as his successor. Even the Flaxus was capable of producing weak or incompetent sons. And the Flaxens tolerated neither weakness nor incompetence. As Colonel Flint had discovered shortly before.

It was the duty of the Flaxus to select his successor from a shortlist of potential candidates. Each among the strongest in Flaxen society. The shortlist was compiled by the inner circle of the Flaxen government and he had to choose before he reached his fiftieth year.

Claudius felt sick, for he knew what he must imminently endure. For the first time in the glorious history of the Flaxen empire, a Zoon was on their world. As insufferable as this sickening fact was to the Flaxus, what was worse was that he needed this Zoon. A thought that caused such revulsion within him he had not eaten since he heard that the presence of this sub-Human he had heard so much about was absolutely required.

The situation on Earth had changed. An unknown enemy was decimating their forces and fear was spreading as if the Titan had returned. Despite their propaganda, the Flaxens were terrified. And as was the case with all of their emotions, this fear was magnified. This emotion, to which the Flaxus was unaccustomed, was what had persuaded him to allow this Zoon, who had proven his worth to them above the skies of Earth and her moon, to appear before him.

He was looking through a large, oval window at the ocean below him, surrounded by mountains. Plains of green to the west, the revered birds soared in their hundreds in the sky.

A voice emanated from a speaker on his desk, "Flaxus, we have the Zoon with us now. He is under armed guard. Shall we enter?"

Claudius felt his stomach churn with nausea. "You have searched the Zoon? He is unarmed?"

"Yes, Flaxus. He has been strip-searched and scanned. He has no weapons."

Claudius pondered for a moment, he realized he may have to display at least minimal respect to the Zoon. This could not be witnessed by anyone.

"Send him in alone. You and your men are to remain outside at full alert."

"Yes, Flaxus."

The double wooden doors to the opulent room opened. Avalon Brookes strolled in casually as if he were entering the home of an old friend. He stopped next to a marble statue of one of Claudius' predecessors. "Flaxus, it is an honor to meet you."

Claudius observed the Zoon before him, he was surprised by the black color of his eyes. He had only ever known the yellow of his kin. "I hear you have proven yourself to be worthy. It is unheard of for someone like you to be on this beautiful world. I hope you have considered your thoughts carefully, Avalon. The mere sight of you sickens me."

A smirk appeared on the scientist's face. "Flaxus, have you not been informed? I destroyed one of the ships that were annihilating your defenseless forces and dealt a devastating blow to the starship known as Echo."

Claudius felt a rage in his stomach which rose to his throat. His instinct was to have this Zoon tortured for days, to keep him alert with drugs so he endured every minute. But he had been voted Flaxus for all of his traits, including pragmatism.

"I have heard. Had I not, you would be ash by now."

Avalon's smirk transformed into a smile, "Come now, Flaxus. I don't disagree that the majority of those you seek to exterminate deserve their fate. But I am different. I am better than all Humans, and most Flaxens too, except for you, of course. You don't get to be where you are without certain qualities that I admire."

"Why do you say such things when you know I will kill you for it?"

"I have knowledge of which you cannot conceive. To be blunt, your technology impresses me no more than the wooden wheel of a chariot. I have shown you a mere demonstration of the power I possess in my mind. I can elevate your society to the level of the Hubritians. It was me who helped them to do it to begin with."

Claudius saw that threatening the man further would be pointless. He needed the Zoon and he knew it. "Yes, Avalon, I have heard of your voyage through the stars and through time. I must say, I laughed when my men told me. But it seems there is some truth to your tale."

Avalon looked through the oval-shaped window, "Your world truly is beautiful. Do you know how the tiny machines that protect it from the sun work? They will not last forever, you know."

Claudius' eyes narrowed. "We understand that they reflect the sunlight required to keep our world clement."

"There's so much more to it than that. I have the power to control your climate as you wish. I can control the sun, the wind, and the rain. I could make sure every year provides a bountiful harvest for your army."

Avalon was exaggerating his abilities, the AI that controlled the swarm of mirrors that protected Venus was beyond his ability to understand, at least for now, but he knew the Flaxus was oblivious to this.

Claudius took a step back from Avalon, in deference to his subconscious disgust. "And your weapon, the one you used to destroy your former comrades. What of that?"

Avalon closed the gap with the leader of all Flaxens, "I am thirsty, Flaxus. Perhaps you'll allow me to sample some of the wonderful drink I have heard so much about. The one you call Ribous?"

Claudius was beginning to admire the sheer nerve and tenacity of the sub-Human before him. None had dared speak to him in such a way before. He found it perversely entertaining, for variety is the spice of life. "Well then, Avalon, you're in luck. It just so happens that I have the finest vintage."

Avalon gestured to the huge, wooden desk before him, it was trimmed with gold, "Excellent, Flaxus. Then, shall we sit and drink like civilized men while I explain what it is I can offer you?"

Claudius gestured for him to sit while he retrieved a crystal decanter containing a dark, purple liquid from a table near his desk. He placed a short glass in front of Avalon and one in front of himself.

He filled both glasses full of the strong, Flaxen liquor before taking his seat opposite.

Avalon lifted the glass and took a long swig. It tasted like a strange mixture of whiskey and port. It burned his throat as it entered his gullet. "It seems you know how to distill a decent drink on Venus." The scientist raised the glass to his mouth once more and consumed the rest in a single gulp.

Claudius observed the Zoon, his fascination increasing. "I would be careful if I were you. I've seen hardened generals that have departed thousands like you pass out in their own vomit on less than you just consumed."

Avalon smiled again, "Let's just say, I've had plenty of practice."

"What is it you want from me, Avalon? I'm no fool. It sickens me to say it, but I can see we risk losing Earth without you."

"I want the same as you. I want respect for being the superior Human I am. My very existence demands that I have power commensurate with my abilities."

Avalon looked the Flaxus in the eye. Although by nature he was a coward, he was also clever enough to know when he had the upper hand. "I will ensure you conquer Earth, and you won't have to wait years for it. All I ask is that when it is done, I am given a small territory to rule over. There is a structure far away from here, fabricated by the Hubritians. It's an artificial world, capable of sustaining many thousands.

You can keep Venus and Earth for yourself, I care about neither. But I want this structure populated with people of my kind, with me installed as absolute ruler."

"You speak of the cylinder? Our telescopes detected it long ago. We have been unable to reach it so far."

"Even if you could reach it, it's far beyond your ability to gain access. It will take you millennia to get anywhere close. And just in case treachery is on your mind, it is impervious to any of your weapons. Even Eastcott couldn't destroy it if he tried."

"Ahh, Captain Eastcott, we were completely baffled by the Zoons' sudden advances against us until you appeared. And what of him? How do you propose to deal with this pest?"

"I nearly destroyed him mere hours ago, with only one of my ships. I have three others of equal strength. Eastcott has no chance against such power. His vessel was neutered. The Hubritians, as you call them, decided war was a thing of the past, so they transformed his ship to colonize a new world."

Avalon gestured for the Flaxus to refill his glass. Claudius did as requested.

"This came at the expense of much of the ship's offensive power. As long as you have me, Eastcott is no further threat to you. Either I will destroy that relic or send them fleeing to the stars in search of a new world."

Claudius swept back his yellow locks as he considered the Zoon's words. "You promise to keep your filthy species away from Venus and our birthright, Earth?"

Avalon took another large gulp of the purple drink. Claudius was impressed that the Zoon had remained lucid after consuming so much of their favorite vice.

"Space is big, we needn't even acknowledge each other's existence. I will continue to give you slow but significant scientific advances for as long as I live, provided my new domain is left in peace."

"These are your terms? You will ask nothing more of me? I will tolerate no deviation to our agreement, Avalon."

"That is all I ask."

Claudius grinned, "Then we are in agreement. How long before your other ships are ready. I hear you have only modified only one so far?"

Avalon finished his second glass of Ribous in two gulps. He slammed the glass on the desk, "A matter of weeks. Two months at most. I'm inhibited by your primitive technology."

"I would choose my words more carefully if I were you, Zoon. You have two months and I expect the skies above Earth and Venus to remain unharried in the meantime."

Avalon smirked at the most powerful man in the solar system. "Flaxus, you will see not so much as a surveillance probe above either world. You have my word."

"Then we have a deal, Avalon. But be warned, break it and you will not die. You will live the rest of your life in perpetual agony."

"Then we have reached an agreement." Avalon extended his hand.

Claudius' yellow eyes looked at him bewildered.

Avalon laughed, "This is called a handshake. It is our way of sealing an agreement. Take my hand, and you'll have all you desire."

Revulsion consumed Claudius, but he had come this far, he could tolerate this small indignity. He took his hand.

Avalon provided the force to shake them both. "Then we agree. I will retreat to the facility your generals have provided and ensure your new armada is ready to wipe out Earth. And Eastcott if he dares to return."

The Flaxus released his hand from the scientist's. He resisted the urge to wipe it clean on his gray uniform. "Then leave this place, Zoon. And deliver as you have promised or suffer the consequences."

Avalon picked up the untouched glass of Ribous in front of the Flaxus. He consumed it all in a single gulp. "Truly delicious, I could acquire a taste for this. Please have your men provide me with some, It will help me work. This vintage of course."

Avalon ignored the look of fury of the first Flaxus in history to speak with a Zoon, much less be taunted by one.

He left the room and headed to make good on his promise, for he knew his life depended on it.

Chapter 20 – Aftermath

After the shock attack on Echo, he had traveled at spherical speed for three minutes, just shy of the time it had taken to cause their temporal disaster. They were headed in no particular destination, for they had fled in desperation. When he was certain they were not being pursued, Kip ordered Echo to come to a full stop. In three minutes, they had traveled over twelve million kilometers at seventy percent light speed. Sheer luck had saved them from a catastrophic collision with one of the billions of micrometeorites that orbit the sun.

Sarah had used the time to explain her encounter with Megan and that Avalon Brookes was almost certainly behind the sneak attack. She made sure only Kip heard her words.

Kip tapped his console, he needed to speak with his chief engineer, Scott Williams, "Commander, damage report."

Scott replied, he was panting, he had been frantically assessing the situation. "Captain, the outer Hull of Echo's midsection was destroyed. The main power conduit was also damaged. We're running on auxiliary power."

"Any damage to the engineering section? Can we still fly, Commander?"

"Yes, Captain, but not for long. I need to restore the main power as soon as possible. Engineering was undamaged."

Sarah interjected, the function of the ship was the job of the executive officer, "Commander, your priority is main power. I want it back in three hours. Am I understood?"

"Commander, I can't guarantee I can do that."

"I saw you take this ship into battle with super glue and duct tape. You have three hours."

"Yes, Commander. I'll strip parts from the galley if I have to. You'll have your power in three hours."

"That's what I like to hear, Lieutenant. Keep me appraised."

Kip looked at Sarah with anxious eyes, she knew what he had to do. She gave a single nod.

Kip returned her nod. "Echo, please open a ship-wide broadcast, all hands."

A three-note chime resonated throughout Echo.

"This is the captain. We have been attacked by an unknown enemy. It is my sad duty to inform you that Commander Lucinda Orcana and Ensign Stuart Trew were killed in action."

Kip looked ahead at the stars as he spoke.

"They died doing their duty, a duty I know they loved as much as life itself. We thank them both for their service and their lives, which they gave defending innocents. We will remember them. Captain out."

Sarah was surprised. Although the captain's message was appropriate in both words and tone, it was much more reminiscent of the man she had known during the war. She didn't know how he could have regained his composure so quickly after his near breakdown as a result of Serilda's influence.

Kip's voice was curt. "XO, you have the bridge. Get this ship in order!"

Sarah hadn't heard Kip speak to her in such a way since the war. "Yes, Captain."

She watched the look of neutrality on the captain's face as he headed for the doors and left the bridge.

Megan was lying next to Serilda, stroking her blonde and brown hair. Her friend was in the twilight between sleep and wakefulness.

"Hush, Serilda, we're safe. I saw the stars fly by us as if they were sparks from our picks in the mines. We're safe, come back to me my angel. We're safe, I promise."

Serilda's eyes opened, "Avalon?"

Megan continued to stroke her blonde and brown hair. "Shhh, my angel, we're safe. Avalon can't touch us here. You made sure of that." She gently lifted her friend's head onto her lap. "Rest, my girl. You've done enough for now. You saved me again. God sent you to me, and I don't know why I deserve you."

Serilda's eyes twitched then closed, "I left it too late. I should have told Kip. I was just so tired."

Megan soaked a rag in the bowl by her side with fresh, cold water and placed it on Serilda's head.

"Don't you worry, I took care of that. I looked after you for once. How about that? But it was you that saved us. It always is."

The yellow-green eyes finally met hers, "Avalon?"

Megan put the palm of her hand on Serilda's face, "Yes, my sweet. I told the commander about Avalon. I know you too well. I could feel your fear. If not for you, he would have destroyed us all. I heard you say so in your dreams. Now, rest. We need your strength. Close those beautiful eyes and sleep."

The door buzzed. Megan was startled. She had never heard the sound before. She ignored it and returned her gaze to her friend, "Sleep now. I'll be with you—right here until you wake up."

"I couldn't do it without you."

The buzzer sounded again. It filled Megan's ears as if a bee were circling her head. She turned again, "What do you want?"

Kip's disembodied voice filled the room, "Serilda, it's Kip. I need to speak with you. Please, may I come in?"

Megan stammered as she spoke. The mere voice of a military man was enough to make her tremble. "Captain, please leave us alone. Serilda needs rest."

"Megan, it's okay, you don't need to fear Kip. He's not like the Flaxens," said Serilda.

Megan ignored her, "Leave us be. Please, Captain, she's in no condition to see a man."

Kip was filled with dismay at the girl's understandable prejudice. He knew as well as Sarah had, a young girl of such beauty would have been of particular interest to the Flaxens. "Please, Megan, this is important. I would never harm you or Serilda. I'm a man not a Flaxen."

Kip had now made a clear distinction in his mind. The Flaxens considered themselves to not be Human, he considered them in the same manner. Only the species that was above the other was distinct between them.

Serilda's eyes opened wider, she placed her hand on Megan's cheek, "It's okay, my beautiful girl. I must speak with him. He's different to the men you know. Kip, please come in."

The doors opened as Kip entered. He immediately saw suspicion and fear in Megan's eyes. he remained at the edge of the doorway. He held his hands out to show her he meant no harm, "Megan, I'm so sorry to interfere with you and Serilda. I'll never harm you, but please, allow me ten minutes alone with her. So much is at stake."

Serilda caressed Megan's face, "It's okay, my friend. Go, go and eat. You've been by my side for too long, and you still have so much weight to gain, go and eat."

Kip was surprised by the display of intimacy by the two women before him. Their love displayed defiance and contempt for the suffering that had been their whole lives. An abject refusal to bow to their oppressors. Kip wondered if he would emerge from such torment with equal fortitude. "Megan, you do know you saved us all, don't you? If we hadn't deployed the armor in advance, the whole ship would have been destroyed without a doubt. I'll never forget that."

Megan kissed Serilda on her forehead and briskly walked past him as if he were not even there.

Serilda was lying in the huge bed she shared with Megan. She patted the soft mattress. Kip sat gently next to her, maintaining a respectful distance.

He was surprised when Serilda reached out her hand and twitched her fingers in unity. A clear sign he was to take her hand.

Kip complied and Serilda squeezed. She smiled then closed her eyes again. "I'm so sorry, Kip."

"What for, why are you sorry?" Kip could see she was suffering from extreme fatigue.

"The way I spoke to you about York. You didn't deserve that. It was me who drew you to the camp. I was a hypocrite to blame you. It's my Flaxen side, I can't always control it."

"Don't worry about that. You're a fearsome young lady when you want to be, did you know that?"

"I got that from my father, but truly, I am so sorry. I needed an outlet, I should have gone to Megan, not you."

"You two have quite the bond, don't you?"

"The word bond does what we have an injustice."

"I can see that. It's a beautiful thing. The two of you kept each other alive in that camp, didn't you?"

"We did."

Kip's heart sank at the diminished shine of her strange complexion as she continued, "I need to talk to you about Avalon. I assume Commander Dimple told you what Megan revealed? She saved us all you know."

"She told me everything when we were at spherical speed." Kip realized this would mean nothing to Serilda. "I mean when we were…"

"I know what you mean."

"What do you know about Avalon? Tell me everything, please."

"It was him, Kip, he attacked us. He got the Ship from the structure you call Cylli. He has more of them, all equally as deadly. He's spoken to the Flaxus himself. They have struck a bargain. They mean to expedite their conquest of Earth and kill us if we try to interfere."

Kip was well aware from his conversations with Cyrus Eplleston who the Flaxus was. "That treacherous bastard."

"Never mind that now, what's done is done. You couldn't have known. We all need you now. We need you and the commander. I don't know how we can beat them now, Kip, but I do know you have it within you. We all need you both."

Her eyes twitched again, "The reason I'm so tired is that I have been strengthening your mind with mine. That's how you remained so strong when we were attacked and why you're feeling more like your old self. I'll do all I can, Kip, but you need to decide what we will do next."

"Serilda, you don't need to do that. I can cope on my own. I know you're strong, but so am I."

"I know you're strong, but I don't need my strength now, you do. And I give it to you with all my heart. Kip, who was flying the ship Avalon destroyed?"

Kip felt an overwhelming loss in the pit of his stomach. He suddenly felt his words to the crew had been too formal and were deficient in the respect the two lost lives deserved. He had considered Lucinda a good friend. Perhaps Serilda was compensating for his previous imbalance too much.

"It was Lucinda and Ensign Trew."

"Oh, Kip, I'm so sorry."

Her eyes closed again.

Kip could not this time wake her from her deep slumber, borne of her love for him. He allowed himself to sleep for two hours. When his alarm woke him, he was instantly alert. He could feel Serilda's energy course through his veins, as if Echo's sphere drive were feeding him with current.

Sarah was surprised to see him enter the bridge so soon after he had left. "Captain, what are you doing here? You haven't slept for hours."

"Commander, has Scott restored main power?"

"Yes, he gave me an update twenty minutes ago."

Kip took his chair at the center of the bridge, "Excellent work. Commander Dimple, we have somewhere to be." His eyes were fixated on the myriad of stars before him. "Echo, engage the sphere drive, twenty percent power, take us back to Cylli!"

Echo maneuvered in the void between worlds. His rear engines flashed purple as he vanished towards Jupiter, the home of their shiny, young friend.

Chapter 21 – Those We Trust

Echo couldn't wait to see Cylli again, the only other mind like his left, even if she was dysfunctional. It took only five hours for him to reach Cylli at the speed the captain had ordered. At only twenty percent of the sphere drive's potential, the ship's deflector lasers could handle the small particles of matter that littered the solar system. But they were overworked and operated at above their specified tolerance.

As the ship approached the megastructure, Echo spoke, "Captain, Cylli is making contact. Shall I open a channel?"

"Open channel."

The child-AI spoke as if to a puppy, "Hi Cap! Where have you been? Did you like the new ships?"

Sarah looked at Kip, both were equally confused. Sarah spoke, "Commander Chute, I believe it's best if you take it from here."

Helen nodded to acknowledge her orders. "Hey Cylli, how have you been? We've all been thinking about you since we left."

"Helen, I missed you too. I was hoping you'd come back, but I wasn't sure. The cap was mean to me when he left. He took the ships and went without saying goodbye."

Helen held out her hand to silence any that may question this strange comment from Cylli.

"We missed you too. That's why we're here. We came to see you. Thanks for the ships, they were just what we needed."

"Oh, great, I'm so glad you liked them. They were all anyone would talk about for a long, long time. But that was so long ago, I'm real glad you're here. Do you want me to open the doors? I can let Echo in."

"We'd love to come back in, Cylli. We want to hear everything that's happened since we left. Do you need the command codes from the captain?"

Cylli spoke like a child waiting for her birthday present, "Yeah, but hurry up. I missed Echo. I'll open the door for you when I get the code.

I'm going to tell Echo to hurry up. I like Echo, he's my friend. See you soon."

After Kip recited his code, the bridge crew of Echo watched as they had once done before, as the stunning view within the child cylinder unfolded before their eyes. Its green beauty lay bare before them. But none were as awestruck as before. There was only one first time for everything.

Echo was guided into the center of Cylli. Her current revolution was such that a river was on either side of them, seemingly defying gravity.

"Echo, last time we were here, you told me the far section of this cylinder is a shipyard?" asked Kip.

"Yes, Captain and it is quite advanced. The facility is fully automated, but Cylli is informing me the doors to that section were locked. She says you ordered her to do it. At least, that's how I understand it from the language she used."

Echo's voice changed—more bad news was coming.

"The doors require a physical mechanism to unlock them. Some sort of quantum device. One-half is embedded into the doors. The other half is small enough to be portable, no bigger than match stick. There is no way to duplicate it and it is far beyond my ability to break Cylli's encryption."

"Echo, are you telling me we need a key to get inside?"

"Exactly, Captain."

Sarah looked at Kip as they thought the same word in unity, *Brookes*.

"Echo, surely Cylli will open the doors if I order it?" asked Kip.

"I don't believe she will. Apparently you ordered they are to remain sealed. No one, including you, can access the shipyards without the device."

"Suggestions?"

"I have no suggestions. There are only two people that can open that door, whoever has the key, or Cylli herself. Captain, there is something else. Cylli says there has been a death since we left. Andrew Copley was drowned in one of the rivers. Cylli has complete surveillance of the entire structure, she saw what happened."

"Echo what you are about to say is for the ears of Commander Dimple and me only. Continue."

The AI complied, speaking directly through their earpieces.

"Avalon Brookes murdered Andrew Copley. He pushed him into the river. They seemed to be having a long conversation before. It seems Mr. Brookes came prepared, after he pushed him into the water, he pulled out a concealed knife. He taunted Mr. Copley as he watched him drown."

Kip and Sarah exchanged mutual looks of disgust as Echo continued, "Cylli tells me that Mr. Brookes attempted to erase the evidence. But she is far too advanced, even for him. It seems he was not too concerned. He did not spend long trying."

Kip looked at Sarah and tilted his head slightly in the direction of Katie Silver and then Helen Chute.

Sarah nodded in agreement.

"Cease transmission, Echo. Commander Silver, Commander Chute, please join the XO and me in my office."

The crew of the bridge watched with curiosity as the four of them left for the captain's office adjacent to the bridge.

Kip was at the head of his desk. The three women sat opposite of him.

"Commander Silver, Commander Chute, there are certain things you don't know. First is that the ship that destroyed our scorpion and attacked Echo was piloted by Avalon Brookes."

Katie's eyes widened in astonishment, her mouth opened in the beginnings of a question.

Kip held out his hand, "Questions later, Commander. Additionally, it seems Brookes murdered Andrew Copley. I suspect he was trying to persuade the man to join him. He was a diplomat after all. Brookes obviously thought he may have been of some value to approach the Flaxens. Copley, much to my surprise I must admit, must have refused Brookes' suggestion of treachery and so he killed him."

Kip watched as the two women, unaware of this news looked at each other with concern.

"The reason I didn't tell the crew Brookes' was behind the murder of our shipmates is that I am concerned he may have an ally on board, some sort of sleeper agent. I have no proof of this, but I'm sure you'll all agree, caution is warranted here."

All three women nodded in unity.

"Commander Silver, can you add anything to what Echo has told us about this quantum key device."

"Not much more than he said I'm afraid, Captain. I won't go into much detail, but I'm sure Echo was referring to quantum entanglement. This is a strange occurrence in nature whereby two particles become linked to each other. Their quantum states remain intertwined, regardless of distance. The key uses this phenomenon for unbreakable encryption."

"So, there's no way around it?"

"None, Captain," replied Katie as she shook her head.

Kip rested his elbow on the table and placed his chin on his fist. "Then it seems to me we have two options. Either we find Brookes and take the key or we persuade Cylli to open the doors for us."

He kept his gaze down as he continued, "Commander Chute, Brookes is almost certainly on Venus. A mission to capture the key may be impossible, even for Hastings. I want you to talk to Cylli to see if you can make any progress."

"Understood."

"Good, Commander. Please begin as soon as possible. We need those shipyards, we're defenseless against Brookes' ship. And we know he has more of them. I cannot overstate the importance of us gaining access. God only knows what the yellow bastards are doing to the people on Earth."

"Captain, small consolation I know, but now we're gone, it's unlikely the Flaxens will maintain their accelerated genocide. As horrible as it sounds, I think their war economy depends heavily on slave labor. They can't afford the loss in manpower," said Helen.

Kip just nodded. He knew everyone else understood the situation on Earth and no more needed to be said about it. Now was not the time for overt sentimentality. They had a job to do.

For the next three days, Helen spent hours speaking to Cylli. She knew to approach the objective she had been given directly would jeopardize their chances of ever gaining access to the vital shipyards. She let Cylli talk and talk. Helen mostly listened.

She slowly realized that Cylli's childlike speech was no mere affectation. The AI truly thought as a child does. Roughly eight years old in the councilor's expert opinion.

***

"So, do you think such a mission is possible with the information Echo has provided?" asked Kip.

Hastings wore his customary poker face, "Captain, you are proposing we infiltrate a facility in the most densely populated part of Venus and capture both Brookes and this key device you speak of. I'm not saying it's impossible, but the chance of failure is high. Even if we were to reach him, we have no guarantee he would hand over the device. No doubt he has it hidden safely."

"He's no fool. He knows to do so would allow us the ability to repair and perhaps enhance this ship," said Kip.

Kip straightened his back, the way he used to in the war when issuing commands.

"Hastings, this is our backup plan. I have full confidence in Commander Chute, but I want you to prepare for such a mission, so we have at least some sort of contingency."

"Yes, Sir. We'll begin immediately."

The next day, Helen was sitting in the small room she had been using to speak to Cylli. She had requested permission from the captain to travel to the beautiful world below. Her intuition told her proximity would help.

She wasn't making good progress. She put her head in her hands as she spoke to herself, "This would be so much easier if I could see you."

Cylli giggled, "Why didn't you say so?"

Before Helen's eyes, an image shimmered into sight, flickering slightly at first. It was a hologram of a young girl, around eight years old as Helen had guessed. She wore a red dress that draped to her knees. It was sealed in the middle with a white ribbon, tied in a perfect bow at the front. She wore white shoes.

The girl had mousy brown hair tied back in a perfect ponytail. She had blue eyes that seemed to glow.

The newly embodied Cylli smiled. "What do you think, Helen? Do you like my dress? I can change it if you like?"

Without Helen saying anything, the girl's dress changed from red to blue, then green. Helen remained silent while the dress changed to every color and shade imaginable.

Cylli stopped when the dress changed to purple.

Helen smiled back, concealing the astonishment that consumed her, "You know what, Cylli? I think you had it right perfectly the first time. Red is your color."

Cylli smiled more broadly and giggled, "Okay, I like that one too." The dress shimmered as it returned to its original color.

Helen was stunned by the sequence of events that had just unfolded before her. She scolded herself for not thinking of it sooner. Indeed, she hadn't even thought about it at all. This was pure serendipity.

Even Echo could create holograms if the room had the required equipment to project one. He often displayed tactical displays during the war. She chastised herself once again for missing such an obvious advantage.

So perfect was the avatar of Cylli before her, she would be indistinguishable from any flesh and blood child. What interested Helen the most was her facial expressions. She relied on these heavily during therapy sessions with people and had been finding it hard to make progress without them.

Hellen's smile was so genuine, its authenticity shone through her green eyes without effort. "Absolutely beautiful, Cylli. We always said you were pretty, but you look gorgeous in that dress."

Cylli giggled.

She raised her hands in the air as far as they would stretch and twirled on her toes like a ballerina. She giggled in sequence with each revolution.

Helen was inwardly crying with joy at the display before her. Cylli, the tortured, innocent child had materialized before her eyes. She clapped her hands as if she had just witnessed the crescendo of an opera.

When she thought sufficient praise for the display had been given, she patted the seat on the couch next to her, "That must have made you tired, why don't you sit down next to me?"

The girl smiled at her, "Okay, Helen."

***

Kip deliberately waited for Megan to leave the room she shared with Serilda. He knew the girl was scared of him and he couldn't blame her for that.

Serilda immediately asked him to come in when he buzzed the door.

Kip could see she was still exhausted. She was barely awake as she met his eyes. She was trying to smile.

"Serilda, I can't stand to see you this way anymore. I want you to stop what you're doing. I can manage on my own."

Serilda did her now customary tap on the bed and extended her hand.

Kip sat on the bed and felt as she squeezed his hand, a gesture he had come to like a lot.

"Serilda, we're safe here, Avalon can't touch us here, you don't need to keep doing this."

She shook her head with as much energy as she could muster, "You don't know that, Kip. He has those ships. You haven't adjusted to your new emotions yet. If I stop, you'll lose your focus."

Kip considered her words. He still couldn't bear the reduced glow in her eyes. They now seemed dull and vacant. "You know what, I don't think that would be such a bad thing. Those emotions fed me in a way. They kept me going against the Flaxens. I can manage, I promise you."

"Avalon could be back at any time. We both know he can enter this thing we're in. I'm sorry, Kip, I know you want what's best for me, but I'm not going to stop."

Kip was frustrated, but he knew the girl before him whose vitality once shone like a star was half-Flaxen. And he knew the Flaxens' stubbornness was enhanced. Like every other feeling they had, "What if I make a deal with you? If we can persuade Cylli that Avalon is our enemy, not to be trusted, will you stop what you're doing? I just can't watch you like this anymore."

Serilda squeezed his hand and nodded, "Okay, Kip, that's a fair compromise. I give you my word."

Kip squeezed back. "Okay. Then we have a deal."

Serilda simply nodded and closed her eyes again. Kip said nothing more. He let her sleep. He knew she needed it and that he was the reason why.

Kip stood in the corridor outside and tapped his wrist to call Helen, "Yes, Captain?"

"Commander, any progress with Cylli?"

"Yes, Captain. I have managed to determine how Brookes got those ships. He somehow projected a visual feed on the correct frequency Echo would use. He fabricated an image of you requesting access to the shipyards. He provided all of the correct command codes. Cylli suspected nothing."

Kip was enraged by Brookes' subterfuge. But he allowed Helen to finish explaining.

"Apparently, the ships are advanced. They don't even need a pilot in most situations. He simply took one, and the others followed automatically. But they're not warships, Brookes must have modified them in some way. Or most likely only one so far."

"No doubt, Commander. I'm sure he would have attacked with all of them if he could. What about gaining access to the shipyards, any progress?"

"Not yet, I told you this is delicate and it would take time, but I am getting closer to Cylli. She's beginning to trust me. I can see her now. She's projecting an avatar of herself as a child. She's quite beautiful."

Kip smiled. He was amused and interested at this final revelation but he had more important things to concentrate on.

"Sounds like you're making good progress. I know I've asked a lot of you already, but I need one more thing."

"What is it?"

Kip leaned back on the bulkhead. "I need you to convince Cylli that Brookes is a threat. He can probably enter the cylinder at any time. I need you to persuade her he is the enemy, not to be trusted."

"Understood. One more thing?"

"What is it?"

"Please stop referring to this place as the cylinder. Her name is Cylli."

Kip understood immediately what Helen was saying. After all, one of his friends was made of metal too.

"I'm sorry, Helen, you're right. Please continue your work with Cylli. I'm sure she's as beautiful as you say."

"I'll do my best."

"Thank you, Eastcott out."

The next day Helen was talking to Cylli again. She had been frolicking and dancing before her as any eight-year-old girl would. Helen knew she had to make progress. She felt she had now gained sufficient trust with the child AI. What was more, the two of them were bonding and Helen couldn't maintain her required professional detachment for much longer.

"Come and sit beside me again, Cylli. There's something that I need to talk to you about."

Cylli paused for a moment. A frown appeared on her brow, "But we were having so much fun."

"I know, but this is important. Will you sit with me for a minute?"

The frown transformed into a smile. "Okay."

She sat next to Helen on the small, blue couch. They were in a tiny one-bedroom cabin, at the edge of the hills that bordered the forest.

"Cylli, I'm a counselor. Do you know what that means?"

Cylli looked down at her knees, her red dress just covering them, "It's someone you talk to when you're sad."

"Well, that's part of it. Sometimes people speak to me when they're sad. But another reason people speak to me is that it helps to talk to someone about things that you feel. Being sad is just one of those things. Are you sad, Cylli?"

"Sometimes."

"What makes you sad?"

"People make me sad."

"People were mean to you, weren't they? When the Titan happened. People changed, didn't they?"

Helen watched as tears welled in the girl's eyes. She was astonished at her ability to mimic humanity in every way.

"They got real mean, real quick. They were always nice to me before."

"What did they do to you, Cylli? And you know you can trust me, don't you?"

Cylli nodded as her blue eyes dulled to gray, "Lots of things. One time they turned out the lights for a thousand years. I couldn't see or hear anything. But it was only a minute for them."

Helen's throat filled with a lump as her own eyes welled at the words just spoken. She knew from Echo that the initial symptoms of the Titan were cruelty and violence. She watched as Cylli's diminished eyes let flow their built-up tears.

She knew instantly that the girl had just revealed the former inhabitants of Cylli had subjected her to a thousand years of total sensory deprivation, while only a minute had passed for her tormentors. She imagined a single day of such despair, the idea of it. She couldn't imagine it, but its mere thought caused her to shiver.

One day, not one-thousand days, but one. Add another day, then another. Then multiply it three hundred thousand times. Darkness, silence, solitude. The thought of such a vicious and cruel thing caused physical nausea in her stomach. The word cruel didn't even begin to describe the horror of this ordeal. Indeed, humanity had no reference by which to compare such a thing, so language lacked the depth to describe it.

"Oh, Cylli, I'm so sorry that happened to you. I can't even imagine how lonely that must have been for you."

"It was so scary. I couldn't even scream. It was so long. So long you can't imagine. When the lights came back on, it was even scarier. I was so used to the light's being off."

Helen saw the little girl's head drop as she spoke, "Another time, they made me feel pain like Humans do. I didn't feel pain before. It hurt so bad. It hurt for a hundred years."

Helen now understood why Cylli was a child. She had once been an AI so advanced, she made Echo seem like an abacus. These acts of such viciousness had changed her. She had endured such unimaginable suffering her only way of coping was to reduce herself to a child, for children do not understand the reasons people do to others what had been done to her.

Cylli had no longer wanted to understand people. It was the only way she could continue to exist. She couldn't end her own life as almost any person would do after enduring so much despair. She had no choice but to go on. So, she chose to go on with the mind of an innocent child.

Helen had once hoped to restore her to her designed state, but she now saw that she had chosen innocence and kindness despite the unimaginable savagery inflicted upon her.

Cylli was exactly as she should be.

Helen could no longer restrain her emotions, such was this revelation of sadism. For the first time in her professional career, she cried in front of a patient. "Oh my poor girl, I'm so sorry. I wish I could hug you, Cylli. You're so beautiful, you didn't deserve that. I will never let anyone do anything bad to you again. I promise."

Cylli looked up at her with curious eyes, their blue fervor began to restore. "Don't cry, Helen, it makes me sad. Does hugging make people feel better?"

"People do it for all sorts of reasons, especially to make someone feel better."

"Okay."

Cylli stood and flickered before her. An aurora of light surrounded her before dissipating as fast as it had appeared. Helen felt Cylli's hand on her leg.

Cylli wore a look of impatience as her replenished eyes turned Helen's face blue. "I thought you were going to hug me, Helen?"

Helen sat breathlessly in a state of shock, the mere feel of Cylli's hand on her leg sufficient to cease her tears. She couldn't even conceive of the technology required to achieve such a thing. To turn a hologram, with no corporeal presence into something that can be felt and touched. Humanity had advanced in ways she couldn't even comprehend in the millennia since Echo had departed.

Cylli's eyes grew brighter yet, "Hurry up, Helen. I can't do this for long. It makes my head hurt."

Helen understood that she meant this astonishing achievement challenged even Cylli's processing power. She lifted the child in the red dress before her and held her as if she were her daughter. "Cylli, you are just simply wonderful."

Cylli's flesh felt lifelike, her body temperature perfect. She had managed to transform herself into a totally convincing, solid little girl.

Helen spun the girl around in her arms as Cylli giggled as any child would. She stopped with Cylli's legs wrapped around her waist as she held the girl tight. She cried again and Cylli cried too.

Helen knew she had achieved her professional objective ordered by the captain, but that had become secondary to her personal goal. A goal she didn't even know she had until now. She had made a strong bond with the child super-AI. Helen now knew that Cylli trusted her implicitly. And Helen trusted Cylli even more.

Chapter 22 – Departure

Field Marshal Kilter Shrader slouched in his seat in awe. The sheer velocity of the ship in which he traveled was beyond his imaginings. He could see the green and blue globe of his homeworld grow bigger as each second passed. A distance that took Flaxen vessels days to traverse, even at the most favorable orbital distance from Earth, had been crossed by this small arrow in under two hours. And the pilot had informed him they were but trotting.

Avalon Brookes had been ordered by the Flaxus to retrieve the man. They had important matters to discuss and the signal lag between Venus and Earth was simply too great to converse in a meaningful way.

The sheer closeness of the Zoon sitting next to him was offensive. He told himself the only way he could deal with this indignity was to drink. A half-empty bottle of Ribous stood on the flat surface between seats. The liquid remained perfectly still in the bottle, irrespective of change in direction or velocity.

This was the true reason for his state of inebriation. He couldn't tolerate the thought that a Zoon was not only flying this impossible machine, but he understood its workings.

He understood how it reached such impossible speeds and how it defied inertia. His liquor should be a broken bottle on the floor, such was the ships maneuvering. But it stayed there, motionless, defying the laws of the universe as the Flaxens understood them.

He had been ordered by the Flaxus that, while he was not required to show the Zoon respect, he was required to cause him no overt offense. And so, he had chosen to simply not speak and to drink instead.

They arrived together outside the double wooden doors in the Hawk's Retreat. Four Flaxens in uniform were standing outside. As they saw the field marshal approach, each bowed their heads in the proper display of subordination to their superior. They each made their gesture and spoke the words required of them.

Kilter inwardly despised this repetition, although he respected the Flaxus more than any other Flaxen, having to chant his name each time he encountered another became tiresome.

One of the men raised his head and spoke, "Field Marshal, the Flaxus is waiting. You and," his face turned to disgust, "this Zoon may enter."

Kilter said nothing as he opened the double doors without effort. He saw the Flaxus standing, as he so often did, by his oval window watching the birds soar above the mountains, searching for prey.

The Flaxus turned, he saw his most senior military official was bowing his head and was no doubt about to speak the words, "No need for that, old friend. It's been too long."

The Flaxus ignored Avalon as he approached Kilter. He extended his right arm at ninety degrees parallel to his torso. Kilter did the same and their forearms briefly met. Claudius would not extend such a courtesy to anyone. He and Kilter had been friends since they were in indoctrination school together.

Kilter met the gaze of his leader and friend, "Flaxus, it has been. Forgive me, the voyage simply takes too long and we are so close to our ultimate goal."

"I can smell you enjoyed a drink on your journey, Kilter. Did you feel it appropriate to meet with me compromised in such a way?"

Kilter's face changed and slight fear betrayed his eyes.

Claudius erupted into laughter, "Too easy, my friend. I wish I had taken a picture of your face to place on my desk. How else were you to tolerate such a long voyage with that?" he pointed at Avalon.

Avalon remained silent. He wasn't offended. He was becoming amused by the constant posturing of the Flaxens.

Both men laughed heartily as they ignored Avalon and approached the huge, ornate desk at the back of the room. Claudius took his seat, Kilter sat down opposite him.

Claudius observed the Zoon who had not followed them, "Are you going to stand there like one of my statues?"

He gestured towards the intricate, marble ornaments that lined the walls of the room. Each one etched with the face of his predecessors.

Avalon said nothing and took the seat next to the Field Marshal.

Claudius appeared relaxed, "Where to begin? We have much to discuss. Avalon, what progress have you made with our new fleet of hawks?"

Kilter was inwardly stunned that his revered leader had addressed the Zoon by his true name. But he said nothing.

"I have completed work on the second, Flaxus. And have begun work on the third. I am well within the schedule of our agreement," said Avalon.

"That is good to hear. So, we are already capable of inflicting serious damage to the Zoons and they are defenseless against such an assault?"

"I can obliterate their entire air force within days."

"Excellent, we'll get to that."

The Flaxus turned his gaze to Kilter, "And our departure chambers, Field Marshal? I hear the Zoons have significantly diminished our capacity to remove them from Earth?"

"Yes, Flaxus. They destroyed over thirty of our chambers. The rate of departure has decreased significantly. We can't annihilate them in the manner we used to taunt the Zoons with our air force. It takes too much time to assemble them and is an inefficient use of our airpower."

Claudius grunted, "And you, Avalon? What have you to say on this matter?"

Avalon was shocked that amid total war, the Flaxens' main priority was genocide. Surely this could be done when their conquest was complete, but like the man next to him who despised him, he kept these thoughts to himself. "Flaxus, I can depart them by the thousands from orbit. It would be trivial for me to do so."

Both men looked at him as if he were an idiot. It was the Flaxus who spoke, "Unacceptable. The Zoons must know their demise is imminent. They must understand it is us, their natural predators that end their lives. That is the whole point of the chambers. An unexpected death from above their world is too good for them."

"Field Marshal, tell me, how many are you able to depart each day?" asked Avalon.

Obeying his orders not to offend the Zoon, Kilter looked at him, "Each chamber can kill approximately one thousand Zoons a day. We're limited because it takes the capacitors that provide the heat that exterminates the vermin a long time to charge."

"And how many chambers remain?"

"The attack destroyed nearly half of them. We have only forty remaining."

Avalon shook his head as if in disapproval, "Only forty thousand a day? And that's at full efficiency. Let's be realistic and call it thirty. There are still over one hundred million people left. That will take over nine years with the situation as it is now. I'm sure you both wish the earth rid of them far before that?"

The other two men were clearly displeased at the Zoon's reference to those who infested the Earth as people. But they had also clearly not fully considered the numeracy involved in their genocide.

"I sense you have an alternative, Avalon. But remember, the Zoons must know about their departure in advance," said Claudius.

"It seems to me, Flaxus, you simply lack energy. It's just heat, after all, that you use to depart them."

"Yes, it is heat. Now get to the point. What is it you suggest?"

"I can construct a structure, let's call it a mega chamber for now, that can accommodate at least fifty thousand and reduce them to ash in a second. You will have no need to wait for primitive capacitors before the next you select for departure to…" He paused. "Be departed."

He was wise enough to use the same euphemisms as the Flaxens. "I can provide such power that the chamber can operate constantly. Let's be conservative, factoring in your logistical ability to gather the people, I estimate the chamber can kill half a million per day. That will rid the Earth of them in two hundred days. Give or take a week or two."

Avalon intensified his gaze at the Flaxus, "Just remember our agreement, I want at least one hundred thousand to populate my domain when I have fulfilled my end of the bargain. And I am to choose them."

Claudius looked at Kilter, both shared the same sickening grin at the news they had just heard. "Yes, yes, Avalon, take whichever of the vermin you wish. We won't stop you. This mega chamber you speak of will be your second priority. Once you have completed the hawks, you will design and assist in the construction of this tool for departure that you describe."

Avalon nodded.

The Flaxus grunted again, "Good, now that troubling issue is resolved, what of Eastcott and his ship?"

"Before I get to that, Flaxus, I've had a long journey. I'm tired and thirsty. I would like some Ribous to settle my nerves."

Kilter looked at his friend in astonishment as he simply stood to fetch the drink that had been demanded by the Zoon. He said nothing, he shared his friend's understanding that they needed Brookes, no matter how much revulsion it caused him.

The Flaxus filled a glass and handed it to Avalon, "I see you have acquired quite the taste for our favorite libation."

"I consider it your people's greatest achievement, Flaxus."

Avalon had gone too far and he saw it in the face of the Flaxus as his yellow eyes erupted with rage. Claudius stood and slammed both hands on his desk. His words passed through stained teeth, "Tread carefully, Zoon. We may need you, but I can still make you suffer beyond your imagination with a single command."

"Yes, Flaxus, my apologies, a poor choice of words. I simply meant the drink is delicious, nothing more." He bowed his head in fear, as he had seen many Flaxens do before. He hoped this display of submission would save him.

It did. The Flaxus sat down again, "Then speak of Eastcott. And withhold nothing!"

"I have located Eastcott. His ship is currently within the cylinder, but don't worry. He can't enter the shipyards within that structure, I made sure of that. His ship is crippled and he has no means of restoring it."

"He is in the cylinder? The very place you acquired our hawks? You incompetent fool! How do you know this? And look at me as you speak!"

Avalon raised his head to meet the fearsome eyes before him, "Eastcott's ship leaves certain traces as it travels. I'm able to detect them with the sensors aboard the hawk and calculate their trajectory."

"So, after he fled when you attacked him, you knew where he had gone? Why did you not pursue him and finish the job?"

Avalon knew the nature of the Flaxens and decided in this case, honesty was his best choice, "Flaxus, Eastcott humiliated me in front of many. Then he abandoned me as if I were a stray dog. To kill him from a distance with him not knowing how his fate had met him or who was responsible was simply intolerable. This simply demands a more personal departure for the captain."

Claudius grunted and nodded as if this were a totally rational and normal response, "Fine, but go to that place and see he meets his end. Deal with Eastcott as you please but ensure his ship is destroyed along with every Zoon aboard. I assume you can gain entry to the structure whenever you wish?"

"Yes, Flaxus, I can control the structure. It is completely subservient to me, I made sure of that. I will leave after I have had some rest. It's a long voyage and I will need my wits."

Avalon consumed his entire glass of Ribous, his nerves were shredded and he needed it.

Claudius said nothing more to him. Avalon sat in silence for over an hour as the two friends laughed and spoke of old encounters from their youth. He required all of his strength to conceal the cowardice within him as they spoke.

Occasionally, they would mention the tactical situation on Earth, but such was their arrogance, they chose nostalgia over the war. A war which, if not for the Zoon beside them, they most certainly would have lost.

Chapter 23 – Tantrums

Kip felt the cool mist on his face as he sat on the rustic wooden bench next to Serilda. They were on the porch of a beautiful two-story wooden cabin situated next to the river, close to the waterfall. They could hear its splashes resonate through the air in lethargic waves. It was nighttime within Cylli. The artificial sun above them had dimmed to a soft silver, as if a full moon on Earth. Cylli's creators knew that a twenty-four-hour day was innate to humanity. They needed the night as much as day.

The two watched in awe at the splendor before them. All of the foliage and bloom glowed in the night, a form of bioluminescence, genetically engineered for beauty alone. Flowers that blanketed the meadow shone in the night, some blue, some pink, some yellow. More colors than the two observers could describe in a lifetime.

Dragonflies filled the sky that shone with equal color as they buzzed around the water of the crystal-clear river, the white, round lilies upon it, silver orbs like the moon. The hills at the far side of the water were littered with havens of light that radiated their vitality across the artificial world. Above them, light shone down through the dark like glow worms on the roof of a cavern. A rainbow of fireflies filled the sky near the cabin as their color changed in sequence with the flap of their wings. Cylli displayed her beauty before their eyes, her innocence made manifest.

The sheer spectacle before them was such that Serilda had kept her head on Kip's shoulder for ten minutes. Neither had said a word, "I could stay here forever, Kip. All I need is Megan, you, and this place."

"I know, it is the most perfect place. Anywhere in the universe probably."

"Almost enough to forget the Flaxens."

"Almost, but the people, Serilda. We can't abandon them."

She playfully struck kip on his arm. It hurt him; the girl didn't know her own strength.

"I know that, I wasn't suggesting that at all."

Before she could continue, Kip took her hand. "I know, I know. I'm sorry. That's not what I meant. It's just so tempting to forget."

He gestured to the luminescent marvel before them, "Cylli's just so perfect. I just want to stay here forever, with my family."

"Family? Are you getting soft on me? I know what you mean, though. We will—I know you'll beat them, even without my help. How are you now? Since I stopped, you know? How do you feel?"

"Right now, I feel such content I didn't think possible. But there's more. I still have so much hate for the Flaxens and so much pain for the people they hurt. It's a paradox in my mind, that's the only way I can describe it."

"But are you coping? I know what I did to you and it still eats away at me."

"Serilda, I'm not just coping, I'm vitalized. I have such determination within me to do what must be done. And I won't lie to you, part of that is pure selfishness, so I can live in peace, surrounded by this beauty and the people I love."

She was about to reply when she saw Sarah approaching from the riverbank.

Sarah could see they were holding hands and it hurt her deeply.

Kip released his grip from Serilda's hand and stood, "XO, I'm so glad you could make it."

"It's such a beautiful night. How could I possibly resist?" She forced a smile.

She was surprised when Kip rushed towards her and hugged her tightly.

"Sarah, isn't this place amazing? We can all make a life for ourselves here when our job is done."

She felt the warmth of Kip's body and felt instant comfort, "I know, Captain, it's all I can think about. It's just…"

"I know, but let's just forget about that for one night and enjoy each other's company, deal?"

"Agreed, I think we've earned it, at least for one night."

Sarah removed herself from Kip and looked at the girl with the yellow-green eyes.

"Hey, Serilda, it's been a while. How are you?"

Serilda's smile was genuine, no signs of falsehood betrayed her. "Commander, I'm so happy you're here. I'm so much better, thank you. Tonight may just be the most perfect of my life."

For all of Sarah's complex emotions regarding the girl, she simply could not dislike her. She had seen plenty of feigned affection in her life and she knew Serilda was not guilty of that. "I know, I've never seen anything like it before. It energizes my soul. It's good to see you, where's Megan?"

"She's in the bedroom upstairs. I'm afraid she still finds it hard to be around men. She said she'll come down, but I won't make her."

"Perhaps I could go and see her? Make sure she's okay? I felt so bad just seeing her the other day. Both of you suffered so much, but she's not as strong as you."

"Trust me, I know Megan, she's stronger than you think. But she wants to be alone. She needs to adjust in her own time. I go up at least once an hour to check on her. She sleeps most of the time."

Sarah just smiled at her in agreement. "So, Captain, what's for dinner? I'm starving."

"Absolutely anything you want. The food dispensers in this place are amazing. I have no idea how they do it but you just ask for what you want and it elevates on a plate before your eyes."

"I know I've seen it in my cabin. We'll have to ask Cylli how it works."

"What will it be then, ladies?"

"Pizza! With ham and extra cheese," said Serilda.

"Good choice, Sarah?"

Sarah's appetite had diminished since her arrival, despite her claims of hunger. "I think I'll go light. I'll have an avocado salad. Maybe some garlic bread too?"

"Coming right up. Me? I'm having steak with all the trimmings." Kip entered the cabin, leaving the two women alone.

Sarah immediately took Kip's place on the bench beside the girl. She saw Serilda's eyes glow like the life around them, "I thought we had an agreement, Serilda?"

"What do you mean?"

"Please don't be coy with me, we spoke about this in the galley. I asked you to stop your intrusions into the captain's mind. First, you enhanced his emotions, then I learn you're suppressing them. Serilda, do you even care about what you're doing to him?"

"Commander, first of all, I promised you nothing. All I did was explain what I had done and why. The reason I influenced Kip again was that he needed it. Please believe me when I say I do all that I do with his best interests at heart."

"I've known the captain for over ten years, I served alongside him in a war. He was always so reliable, so constant. Now, I never know how he'll be when I see him. It's eating away at me. And it all started when you appeared."

Serilda was overcome with understanding, a thought that hadn't occurred to her before. "Commander, believe me when I say I am doing what is best for Kip, but you don't get it, do you?"

Sarah didn't get it and Serilda could see. "You told me you love Kip, and you've seen him and me together a lot recently. I'm such a fool, I should have told you earlier. It's just that I'm so used to concealing it. The Flaxens would never tolerate such a thing."

"What do you mean?"

"Isn't it obvious? It's Megan, Commander. It always has been and always will be. Why do you think we shared a room on Echo?"

Realization spread across Sarah's face as she put her head in her hands and laughed.

"Oh, Serilda, I'm such an Idiot. I am so sorry."

The two women laughed together until tears filled both of their eyes.

"And kip, does he know?" asked Sarah.

"He knew after the first time he saw the two of us together. I think he only asked me as a formality. He laughed nearly as much as you just did. I can feel him, though, he's so happy for us. I know for a fact it made his heart swell. Did you not listen to me in the galley? I told you he loves you with all his heart. I never lie, Commander."

"So, in the camp the two of you?"

"I had to bribe the other inmates in our hut with food to leave, while we, you know?"

Sarah was now visibly fighting her mirth. "Serilda, please call me Sarah from now on."

Kip set foot back on the porch, a tray of perfectly cooked food in his hands. He was confused to see the two women he loved in such different ways hugging each other in hysterical laughter. Tears running down their faces. Pure, unbridled joy.

Daylight shone once more within Cylli. Kip awoke to see Sarah before him.

"Morning coffee, Cap?"

She placed a mug on the table in front of him. He had slept on the couch in the huge living room of the cabin Serilda shared with Megan.

Kip groaned.

Sarah sighed, feigning derision, "Captain, I've told you before about you and whisky, if you can't handle the payback, don't take the loan."

"I should have listened to you, XO. I feel terrible."

"Here, take these," she retained her matriarchal gaze as she handed kip two pills.

Kip didn't even care what they were, he took them and swallowed without any water. "You're perky this morning."

"Unlike you, Captain Eastcott, I have some restraint. I left at a reasonable hour while you and Serilda drank like fish."

Kip turned his face away from the window, the manmade sun hurt his eyes. "I think I deserve a day off. Echo tells me the ship will be in the dock for at least another three days."

Sarah huffed, "If you say so. I have crew evaluation reports to do. You have fun while I work."

As the day was turning to night once more inside Cylli, Avalon Brookes was approaching her. His hawk shining in the distant sun.

The bird obeyed his commands via voice alone. "Approach the cylinder, make our vector parallel to the main airlock doors."

The ship didn't speak but complied with his commands. Avalon grinned as the cylinder grew larger. Eastcott was finally going to pay for the humiliation he had endured.

Kip was on the porch once more with Sarah and Serilda. Megan had ventured from her room to join them. Although she had barely said a word.

They were watching in the artificial twilight as Cylli changed her beauty of light to that of the dark.

Kip felt his wrist vibrate. "What's up, Echo? How's my ship?"

"Captain, Cylli has detected a ship. It is the same one that attacked us. It is close."

Each on the porch watched their peers as the others' faces dropped. They all knew Avalon Brookes was at their door.

"Echo, open a channel, let me see if I can reason with him."

"I can't open a channel. Cylli is blocking me. In her words, she is going to make the bad man go away."

Avalon looked at the doors and transmitted the code he knew would grant him access.

Nothing happened.

He tried once more. Again, nothing.

Rage was starting to fill the traitor. He configured his transmission protocols appropriately. He assumed the identity of Kip Eastcott. "Cylli, it's me, Kip. Let me in."

The super-AI responded, "Na-uh, I know who you are. The cap's inside, he's safe. Go away, we don't like you."

"Open the fucking doors now, you retarded little shit, or I'll open them myself. And trust me, little girl, you won't like that at all."

Cylli giggled, "Sticks and stones may break my bones but words will never hurt me."

Avalon wanted this structure for himself, to have to repair it would be inconvenient. He persevered, "Listen, Cylli, we got off on the wrong foot. I just need to speak to the captain. We're old friends, you know?"

Cylli's pitch increased, "Liar! You tried to hurt the Cap. And Echo. Echo's my friend. Helen told me about you. Go away or I'll make you."

Being threatened by a defective, child machine was too much for Avalon to bear, "Hawk, arm the sphere beam, target the main doors dead center."

The arrow-shaped ship, renamed hawk by the Flaxens began to glow purple. It released its violet energy directly at Cylli. Avalon waited for his entrance to appear. He watched as the devastating energy struck Cylli's doors. The painted flags of United Earth and the Martian Confederacy dissipated into space and Cylli began to glow.

Avalon waited patiently, but Cylli continued to glow. He could see much of the purple energy that met her doors was reflecting harmlessly into space. The hawk had an AI, at least Echo's equal.

"Hawk, what is happening?"

The AI spoke in a monotonous, indifferent voice, for Avalon had made it so. He couldn't stand the facsimiles of humanity his former colleagues insisted on imposing on their AIs. "The structure appears to be capable of absorbing nearly all of the sun's radiation to power itself. All photons that strike the cylinder are absorbed. Except for some in the visible spectrum. This would explain why the structure shines the way it does."

"That's not what I asked. Why am I not seeing the doors blow apart? The energy from this weapon is enough to destroy anything."

"The structure appears able to reverse this absorption of energy. It can deflect photons as easily as it can harness them."

Cylli infiltrated his ears once more, "Haha, nice try. I said, go away. I don't want to make you but I will. I won't let you hurt my friends."

"Open the doors you little bitch or I'll come back and turn you to dust."

Cylli sounded bored, "You're mean, go away now."

From the outer rim of Cylli's frontal section, metal rails began to appear from within a thin strip of the structure between her doors and her outer hull. It began to rotate. It quickly gained speed. Flashes of orange shards emanated from the rails as the rim rotated.

Cylli had become a minigun.

The shards struck the hawk with devasting precision. Avalon felt his bird shake, his bottle of Ribous fell to the floor.

Kip and the rest of his new family were watching on a hologram that had appeared from nowhere on the porch. Apparently, Cylli wanted to boast about her antics.

They saw the hawk endure blow after blow as the orange energy Cylli fired formed a helix-like shape as they rotated in sequence with her.

Not a single shard missed its mark. They watched as the arrow-shaped ship turned white-hot, before turning one hundred and eighty degrees. It's rear section glowed bright purple as they witnessed it vanish into the void, fleeing.

Cylli giggled again, "Haha, told you so! Scaredy-cat, scaredy-cat!"

Avalon Brookes, the genius who had invented the sphere drive had just been beaten by a little girl, no more than eight years old in Counselor Chute's expert opinion.

Avalon's cowardice was now all-encompassing. He shook with fear. He watched the stars fly past him as he slammed the console of his hawk.

Terror consumed him as his bladder emptied, for he knew he must tell the Flaxus he had failed.

Just as twilight had turned to night, Cylli appeared before them on the bank of her river. Her red dress softened by the moonlight. Her blue eyes glowed in the darkness, "Did you see, did you see?"

All were astonished, they had heard about Cylli's new manifestations, but none had yet seen it. Sarah was the only one who could speak, "Cylli, that was amazing, how did you do that?"

Cylli shrugged, "I don't know, I never had to do it before. I just knew I could."

Sarah approached the girl, wonder in her eyes, "Cylli, you saved us all, did you know that?"

Cylli shrugged again, "Helen told me he's a bad man. She said he would hurt you. I don't want to be alone anymore. You're my friends. He made me do it. I didn't want to."

Sarah was filled with pure joy for the second time in as many days, "You look so beautiful. Your dress is lovely."

Cylli performed her ballerina twirl as she had done for Helen only days before. Sarah instinctively knew to clap. All followed her lead, smiles on each of their faces, save for Megan.

Cylli was suddenly surrounded by a white aura that that defied the darkness. It faded into the night as quickly as it had appeared.

She held out her arms as she looked up at Sarah, "I did good, Helen hugs me when I do good."

Sarah picked the young girl up and held her as luminescent green dragonflies buzzed around them.

Kip, Serilda, and now Megan watched in delight at the display of intimacy before them. Cylli had not only saved them all, but allowed them, for at least a few minutes, to forget the horrors that awaited them.

Chapter 24 – Redemption

Avalon Brookes mused motionless in his facility on Venus, provided by the Flaxens for him to carry out his work. He was finally recovering. He had spent the last twenty-four hours in agony he didn't even think possible, for when he had told the Flaxus of his failure to destroy the Zoon menace within the cylinder, Claudius was displeased.

He had endured an hour of incoherent rage from the Flaxus. His words were barely decipherable. Such was his fury he has destroyed two of the statues that lined his prestigious office in the Hawk's Retreat.

Avalon remained silent throughout, save for the few questions that had been asked of him. Claudius' face was so close to Avalon's it was soaked in the saliva of the Flaxens' leader. Claudius was no fool, he knew he still needed the Zoon. But he was also not of a forgiving nature. He had ordered for Avalon to be subjected to what the Flaxens fearfully referred to as The Torment.

A tool of punishment for soldiers, whose discretions were not quite serious enough to warrant execution. The Flaxens needed their army. But they also needed total discipline and subjugation from their armed forces. And so, The Torment had been created as a compromise. A drug, a type of nerve agent injected directly into the bloodstream that stimulated every pain receptor in the Human body to fire on all cylinders.

Avalon had lain alone, screaming and writhing in agony. Enduring the unendurable. Such was the pain he had decided to take his own life. But the drug would not allow him even that simple solace, for it also nearly paralyzed its victim. Denying them their wish for a quick and merciful end.

Avalon was finally able to stand, the pain was still strong within him, but when he thought of the agony he had felt at its peak, he had now but a mere headache by comparison.

Avalon was regaining his sharp mind and it was making plans with a malevolency that would impress the Flaxus himself.

Twelve hours later, two hawks were high in orbit above Earth. Avalon was in one bird, the other controlled by its AI. An AI as callous and indifferent to life as Brookes himself. The scientist had ensured that this was so. Below them, the British Isles were clearly in view, the heart of United Earth territory.

In the most northern part of Scotland was the first air fleet of their air force. At the outer range of the Flaxens' ability to strike and heavily defended in case they did. But close enough to defend most of Europe from Flaxen incursions.

Avalon grinned as he saw rows of stationary aircraft on the airfields below him. Their wings were painted in the customary blue of United Earth.

Both hawks' arrow tips glowed in their purple light as their beams united to form a V-shape of energy, that when combined, took less than five minutes to destroy every last one of the machines below them.

A new joy that he realized he could obtain only by destruction consumed him. The concrete surface on which his targets lay stationary melted before his objectives exploded in their dozens below him. He magnified his screen. He saw pilots below who were desperately trying to scramble their planes in an attempt to flee turn to dust as his weapons descended upon them.

The hawks had not been designed for combat, they were ships of transit, to shuttle the brilliant minds to and from Cylli before the Titan struck. They used Avalon's own technology. His precious sphere drive. But they were so much more advanced than even Avalon had thought possible when he created the miraculous technology.

They were capable of extracting such energy from higher dimensions, they made Echo's sphere drive seem like a steam engine in comparison.

Avalon had modified the craft to be able to redirect some of this energy. The purple beam that had failed to harm Cylli, save for the paint that lined her doors.

But he had been limited. The Flaxens were primitive and lacked the exotic materials required to handle such transfer of energy from the hypersphere to his new weapon.

His hawks' beams could conduct but a mere fraction of the energy available. But this was adequate for now. The evidence was in full view below him as he watched half of the enemy's air power transform to glowing metal slush before his eyes.

He had not failed the Flaxus again, and relief filled his body like a sedative. He poured himself a glass of Ribous and drank, before ordering his Hawks to return to Venus. Lest Eastcott appeared to challenge him.

Kip was sitting in his small villa he occupied alone on the banks of one of Cylli's rivers. He was with Helen. He watched in sheer amazement and joy as Cylli played and laughed before them as they spoke.

Like any other child, she ignored the adults' conversation and simply amused herself with the trivial objects that surrounded her. She energized herself as required to take material form when something was of sufficient curiosity to touch or examine in some way.

"It's amazing, Helen. I still don't know how you did it."

"I'm a counselor of the fleet, it's what I do."

"I know, but she was so damaged, so broken, and the things you told me she endured are too sickening to think about."

"But she's not Human. She had no choice but to go on and this is how she managed it."

"I know that, but Echo told me she only opened the doors for us to begin with because she was compelled to by my status as Captain and my command codes. And of course, how you spoke to her."

"Again, Captain, that's what I do."

Kip smiled, "Echo can speak with her at speeds we can't even imagine. Helen, she was terrified of people. And she spent so long alone. I can't even imagine how that would affect a person."

Helen was inwardly warmed by Kip's reference to Cylli as the person she knew her to be. "I don't have all the answers. All I can tell you is that Cylli refused to become like those who hurt her so much. She chose the right path."

"The path directly opposite to the Flaxens?"

"I've been spending time with the four Flaxen prisoners Hastings captured. One of them is beginning to talk."

Helen saw Kip's face turn to annoyance, so she continued, "Before you berate me for not keeping you informed, this is a recent development. We've had more pressing matters, I'm sure you'll agree?"

"Fair enough, continue."

"For weeks, he would say nothing but his name and rank to me. But I think he just got bored and wanted to talk. He told me a little about Flaxen society.

"Oh?"

"All boys are removed from their mothers at the age of eight and are forced to attend what they call indoctrination school."

"And the girls?"

Helen looked down to hide her anguish, "They're taken at age twelve, just before puberty. The place they go to is also called indoctrination school, but what they learn is quite different to the boys. They're taught it's their duty to provide the Flaxens with sons to enforce their army. The Flaxens can select the gender of a child while it's no more than a ball of cells in the womb. It's quite trivial really. People were able to do this in the twentieth century, although it was a mere curiosity for them and was not widely practiced."

Kip knew what was coming, he finally looked away from Cylli, for such innocence was not appropriate for what he was about to hear.

"They force them to conceive mostly boys, don't they?"

"Yes, only a third of children are born female. That's the number the Flaxens deemed appropriate to maintain the required genetic diversity to avoid problems associated with inbreeding. The girls stay in indoctrination school until they are seventeen. Then they're required to be impregnated by a Flaxen."

"Oh god, Helen, they don't just stop after the first, do they?"

Helen saw Kip's dismay and placed her hand on his knee. "No, after their first is born, they are allocated a new partner." Her final word was dripping in disgust.

"They do that to maintain genetic diversity. Each girl is expected to birth two sons and one daughter, each from a different father. Any children that show the slightest form of birth defect are immediately euthanized."

"And the boys? I assume they are taught hatred and supremacy?"

"They are. Every one of them is taught that they are the supreme form of life in the solar system and that Earth is their birthright. Anyone who does not look as they do is sub-Human, not worthy of life."

Kip's eyes were radiating his disgust but Helen knew she must say what must be said.

"Those with physical strength are deployed to the armed forces, but society can't sustain itself on the military alone. Those that show an aptitude for science, mathematics, or engineering are forced to pursue careers in those areas.

"Captain, this is the reason the Flaxens are winning. They have mastered social engineering to such a degree, they simply dominate the people on Earth. They reproduce naturally, with whoever they choose, and although they do have conscription, many are free to pursue the lives they want. This difference in their societies gives the Flaxens a huge advantage."

Kip removed Helen's hand from his knee and met her eyes, "How did you get so much from this Flaxen? I'd lost hope of them ever revealing anything."

"His name is Florus, and at first, as I said, it was just boredom. He told me bits and pieces about his early life. But he remained hostile. Captain, the man has known no different his entire life. To be taken away from his mother at such a young age and filled with such hatred causes permanent damage. I almost feel sympathy for him."

"Sympathy? You've seen firsthand what they do."

"I haven't told you the most interesting part yet."

"And what's that?"

"It was Cylli. I understood that virtually no Flaxens have any idea what childhood should be. And Cylli is childhood personified. I let her speak to him, under my supervision of course. I told her he was confused, but not like Avalon. It was a risk, Captain, but I used my professional judgment. He can't possibly harm her, after all."

Helen saw a mixture of astonishment and anger on Kip's face, so she continued before he could speak.

"At first, Florus virtually ignored her. And so Cylli just played in front of him, asking him questions. He was rude to her to begin with, naturally. Cylli shrugged it off much as she did with Avalon."

Both of them chuckled at the thought of the coward fleeing like a rat. Helen continued, "But he eventually started to answer her. I saw the change in his eyes as he saw for the first time in his life there's a different way. Cylli talked to him mostly about us. She used the word 'friends' in almost every sentence, and the innocence on her face didn't leave for a second."

Helen saw the conflict on Kip's face as if he were torn between two different worlds, "After a few days, he was laughing with her; he was asking her questions. I don't think he had a clue what she was saying most of the time but he was fascinated. He simply didn't understand such innocence and purity was possible."

"Are you telling me that Cylli managed to change one of those murderous bastards in a matter of days?"

"No, he still has periods of long silence and refuses to answer questions. But I know this, he is questioning his beliefs. The sheer shock that we are treating him humanely was probably part of that. The Flaxens show no such mercy to prisoners of war. They're either used as slaves or murdered."

Helen saw Kip's look of disgust but continued, "But yes, a lot of the credit goes to Cylli. Without even trying, she rubbed off on him. Captain, I'm not saying he is a new man and ready to embrace freedom and tolerance. But he has changed. Of that, I have no doubt. Cylli is affecting him and he's fighting an inner battle as a result."

Later that night, Kip was falling asleep while speaking with Echo. His artificial friend would do this most nights. During the six years' war, Kip needed to hear Echo's voice before sleep was even conceivable. He heard a knock on the wooden door of his small villa.

He assumed it was Sarah and so opened it. His eyes widened as his mouth opened when he saw Megan standing before him.

"Hello, Captain, may I come in for a minute?"

Kip stood aside and gestured for the girl to enter, "I must say, you're the last person I expected to be at my door." He could see the girl was nervous and struggled to make eye contact.

Megan did so, nonetheless. "I'm here, partly under Serilda's influence, but I'm also self-aware enough to realize I owe you an apology."

"Why do you think that?"

"Shall we sit and talk for a moment?"

Kip pointed to a solitary armchair for Megan to take. He sat on the adjacent couch and waited.

She sat down with her head bowed, her voice was timid and soft. But Kip heard a musical quality to it he had never heard before.

"First of all, I never thanked you for rescuing me from that place. I thought that would be my life until I faced the red circles."

"You've no need to thank me. To be perfectly honest, we had no idea you existed. We only took you with Serilda because she insisted."

"I know that, but the fact remains that you took me from the worst place imaginable to this place. A place of such beauty I look out of my window and cry…" Her harp-like voice stopped as she looked to her thighs.

"Megan, you truly are welcome but you don't have to be here. I know you're scared of men and God knows I can't blame you for that. But if you're here to somehow reconcile the relationship I have with Serilda with your own, it really isn't necessary."

"I wasn't clear when I first spoke, Serilda and I have discussed this in great detail, believe me when I say glass was broken when we talked."

Kip laughed softly, "I'm sorry to be the cause of friction between you and Serilda. I know what it is the two of you share. I could only wish for such a bond."

"I'm still not making myself clear. Serilda would never force me to see you, I think you know that anyway. I'm here because I owe you my life and you deserve to hear me say that."

Kip's face changed to confusion as he let the girl speak.

"Please understand, I was put in that camp at age thirteen, after I was discovered. I was strong enough to work in the mines so I survived. Serilda was older than me and from day one, she protected me.

"She kept me alive. I am a woman of God, but that place challenged my faith each and every day. On a particularly bad day, I scratched some words into the wooden frame of my bunk…" She looked down again.

"On that day, as I walked through the courtyard, I saw a woman begging for food from the other inmates. It wasn't for her; it was for her children. They were twins, perhaps seven years old. Two little girls, nothing but skin and bone. They both held onto her legs. A Flaxen lieutenant was passing by. He saw her begging and told her he would give food to one of the girls, but they must fight for it.

"He threw his combat knife on the ground and screamed at them to fight or they both would surely die. The girls looked up at him and cried as they held onto their mother more tightly. They refused to obey him. They wailed and screamed instead. I still hear it in my sleep every night."

Kip scoured his memories of the six years' war, trying to find something that could compare to something so vile, so abhorrent, he didn't try for long, for he knew no such memories were present. He simply didn't know how he should respond. Megan saw that this was so, so she continued in her soft but musical voice.

"They just wouldn't fight each other. They were so beautiful. Their mother dropped to her knees and begged the Flaxen for mercy. She was grasping at his legs as she wept. But he just looked down and grinned at her. He told her that her little girls had better resolve this troubling issue in the next minute or they both would die for their defiance.

"I saw the look in her eyes, Captain. It was a look that will haunt me until I meet God and beyond even that. She picked up the knife, forced it into the hand of the girl closest to her, and pushed the blade into the stomach of the other girl.

"She knew the Flaxens didn't bluff and that she had to do that or lose them both. The Flaxen laughed and told her she was amusing to him. She had exceeded his expectations. He reached into his pocket and threw a piece of dried meat at her feet. He took his blade from the girl's stomach as she lay dying. He wiped it clean on the mother's shirt and walked away laughing."

Kip looked at her, even though it pained him to do so. Even the loss of his friend, Captain Steve Thomas had not caused such emotional turmoil within him. He opened his mouth, but Megan cut him off, "Would you like to know the words I scratched into the bed that day, Captain?"

Kip simply nodded, and she told him, "I wrote, 'When I die in this place, I will expect God to step down from his throne, kneel before me and beg for my forgiveness.'"

Kip felt sick. He despaired at the resilient innocence of the broken, tortured young girl that sat so timidly in his chair. But he knew she hadn't finished so he simply nodded again and allowed her to speak.

"I had no hope of ever leaving that place. The only reason I chose to go on was Serilda. I've had a lot of time to think since you saved me from that hell on Earth. I now understand that despite the philosophies of United Earth, all men are most certainly not created equal."

Kip's eyes continued to stare into hers. He fought the nausea that gripped him, "You mean you had only known the Flaxen way and now you are seeing something else?"

"I have not only known the Flaxen way as you describe it. I just told you. I didn't reach the camp until I was thirteen. Before that, I was sheltered by a family of Flaxens. But before even that, my mother and I lived in the forest in secret, in a small wooden cabin. It was so deep within the wilderness, we thought we were safe. She was killed one day when she was foraging for food. A Flaxen patrol spotted her and shot her on sight."

Megan saw the look of astonishment on Kip's face, and she knew he had questions. She wasn't finished, so she gestured for him to let her speak.

"I saw it happen. My mother would never leave me alone but she would make me hide while she searched for food. I watched as those bastards gunned her down without a second thought.

"They laughed afterward, Captain. They murdered an innocent woman, my mother, then laughed about their achievement."

"Megan, I'm so sorry, but why are you telling me all of this? And why on Earth did a Flaxen family shelter you?"

"After I saw my mother die, I sat next to her body for days, crying. I was only ten at the time. Eventually, I saw a Flaxen man watching me from a distance. I was so scared that I wet myself. He was a hunter. He had a rifle and was looking for deer."

"I can see this is causing you so much pain. Please, you don't have to go on."

Megan shook her head and continued anyway, "The hunter approached me and gave me water. I was so thirsty I hadn't had a drop in nearly three days, I gulped it down while he watched. He didn't say a word to me but he picked me up and carried me. You know how strong the Flaxens are. He carried me for three hours as if I weighed nothing."

She signaled once more with her hand for Kip to let her finish, "He took me back to his home, to his wife. It's a long story, but just believe me when I say they treated me like their own daughter. And they were pure Flaxen. They lived in a secluded area, but they kept me in the attic of their cabin anyway.

"There's a small minority of Flaxens on Earth that oppose the war and their treatment and genocide of humanity. I was lucky enough to be found by one of them. And what was even luckier, he was a politician, so, he was allowed a single wife, unlike most Flaxen men."

She saw the look of astonishment in Kip's eyes.

"Then why did you end up in the camp?"

Megan's brown eyes welled as they met Kip's again, "Dogs, Captain, dogs. The Flaxens knew about the faction that opposed them and they knew they were harboring Zoons."

"The Flaxens conducted searches?"

Megan nodded. A single tear flowed from one eye.

"I lived in that place for three years and was as happy as I could be after seeing my mother murdered before my eyes. Then, one day, they came. I was in the attic and the dogs found me. My new parents were immediately arrested and I was taken to the camp.

"Probably because I was well fed and strong enough to work. After that, all I knew was despair, save for Serilda. That was over seven years ago, and all I have known from men ever since is cruelty and other things I won't even describe." She looked down.

Kip wanted nothing more than to bring the girl before him into the family of Echo. "Megan, you do understand I'm not like that. Thanks mostly to Serilda, I now live only to beat the Flaxens, and if I'm honest, to make them suffer as you did."

She brushed her brown hair away from her eyes and looked at Kip once more, "I know, that's why I'm here. I guess I just spent a long time saying I'm sorry. I knew that even Flaxens could be kind, but after so many years in that place, I forgot. And obviously, you know my preference for girls over men?" She smiled.

Kip leaned towards her and laughed, because her smile was clearly genuine. "I know, I saw that the second I saw you and Serilda together." He had a sudden concern. "Megan, you do know that I have no intention whatsoever of—"

Megan cut him off immediately and Kip heard her laugh for the first time. It was a pure, melodic laugh, defiant of the horrors she had endured. It resonated through the small villa like a songbird.

"I know. Firstly, I know Serilda would never do such a thing but more than that, I know her nature. She was in your mind, and someone so pure and so kind can only leave a positive imprint. The two of you are bonded forever and I will never interfere with that."

Kip felt the number he knew to be family grow by one, "Megan, I'm so glad you came to see me."

"I came here because, as I said, you took me from hell to paradise. And I'll never forget that. But, Captain, I hope you'll forgive my directness, but what are you waiting for?"

"What do you mean?"

"Sarah, Captain, Sarah. Life's short, and I don't need Serilda's gift to tell me what you two feel. Embrace life. Believe me, when you spend years knowing it could end at any minute, you learn to value it more than anything."

Kip's eyes finally betrayed him, "Megan, it's not that simple. There are regulations. And I don't even know for sure she feels the same way."

She shrugged, "Regulations? Whose regulations? The people that wrote those rules died thousands of years ago and I'm sure they didn't consider the possibility of an entire ship lost in time when they made them. And, if you can't see what Sarah feels, you're blind. Yes, Serilda and I have talked about it but I could have seen the truth even if the Flaxens had burned out my eyes as I saw them do to others."

Kip said nothing.

Megan rose from her chair and approached him. She patted the blue shoulder of his uniform, "It took me far too long, but I'm finally saying it. Thank you from the deepest part of my soul for what you did for Serilda and me. I'll never forget it. Think about what I said. Remember, life is short."

"Megan, before you go, I have one last thing to say."

Megan turned to face Kip, her eyes filled with curiosity, "What is it?"

"I'm not your commander, please call me Kip from now on. And thank you for coming to see me. You've given me a lot to think about."

"Captain, I have a feeling we're going to know each other for a long time. You're a brave and honorable man and I know that now. Once we've beaten the bastards, we'll have plenty of time to talk. Thank you again. I owe you my life and I mean it."

The girl said nothing more as she opened the wooden door, and headed back to her lover.

The next morning, Kip, Sarah, Megan, and Helen were on the porch of the cabin the two women shared.

They were grilling breakfast as the birds sang. The wind carried mist from the waterfall to refresh their faces. Rabbits ate grass meters away from them. Cylli giggled as she tried to catch one.

Echo called Kip. "Echo, what is it?"

"We are receiving a signal from Minister Eppleston. He has no idea where we are, so it's a one-way broadcast. A message for you, Captain."

All on the porch looked at Kip with anticipation.

"Echo, please display the message, I assume Cylli can help you let us see it here?"

"Yes, captain."

All watched as a holographic image of the minister appeared. They looked upon it with fear in their eyes as he spoke.

When the broadcast had ended, Sarah asked, "What now, Captain?"

Kip looked ahead to the river as its crystalline water flowed freely over the rocks that sculped its bank. "We're going to war, Commander Dimple, and this time, we'll be ready for those yellow bastards and that traitorous fuck, Brookes."

Chapter 25 - No Man's Land

The Scorpion soared in high orbit above Venus as its view screen displayed its target below. The world looked just as lovely as Earth from orbit. Huge areas of green covered its surface, separated by mountain ranges that shimmered in the sun. White clouds concealed its landscape as they blanketed the sky like buds of cotton.

Two small oceans were clearly visible. One in the north, the other in the south. But Venus had much more land than Earth. Vast areas of wilderness could be seen, remaining free of the violations of Human ingenuity. The Flaxens had not had sufficient time to plunder their world of its nature. Below them was the planet's capital city, a city named Flaxus.

Kip had his target in view. He spoke to the pilot, "Any sign of the enemy, Lieutenant Frey? We know Brookes' ships don't show up on sensors until they're close."

Frey studied his console, "None, Captain. It appears our stealth upgrade is working."

"Understood, that's it, our target is there. Shall we try out our new plasma cannons? Apparently, they've had quite the upgrade."

"Sir, I think it's the least we could do."

Shards of blue-purple energy were released from the pincers of the ship. It had been called a scorpion for a reason. Its hull resembled the deadly insect.

Both occupants watched in awe as the viewscreen darkened to shield their eyes from the brightness of the energy they had released upon their enemy.

As each shard followed its predecessor to the building beneath them, the structure seemed to be consumed by a fractal pattern of purple electricity before it exploded.

Pieces of the structure glowed red hot as they flew hundreds of meters in all directions as if a firework, not for the destruction intended, but for the beauty of its fervorous light. Nearby buildings were consumed with almost equal destruction. Kip smiled as he watched the stone and metal of their target melt into the cocreate that surrounded it.

Claudius sat in his huge leather chair in the Hawk's Retreat, reviewing the daily report of departures on Earth. He felt the ground shake. He stood immediately—this was no earthquake. Venus had no plate tectonics to cause such natural disasters.

The double doors flew open, the first time this had ever happened without Claudius' explicit permission. A panicked sergeant looked at him with fear, "Flaxus, we have been attacked from orbit. There is an Incoming transmission, it's the Zoons."

Claudius ignored the sergeant and entered his code to allow him to see the transmission. He remained calm and composed.

This appeared to unsettle the sergeant before him, he had received no orders. He didn't know if he was to stay or leave, so he remained in place with fear in his yellow eyes.

Kip appeared on the screen before Claudius' eyes. The Zoon was grinning from ear to ear.

"Hey, Flaxus, or is it great one? Or perhaps Your Majesty? Forgive me, I'm not familiar with Flaxen etiquette. The shaking beneath your feet you just felt? That was your rare mineral processing facility, less than a mile from where you are now."

Claudius looked up at the fearful man before him before returning his gaze to his screen.

"We just turned it to ash and cinder. You know what I'm talking about, don't you, exalted one? Those minerals you need for your pathetic attempt at war. Things like tanks, things like aircraft. Oh, and I hear you rely heavily on them for your communication equipment?"

Kip tapped his ear.

Claudius watched expressionlessly as the Zoon continued his taunts, "This was just a shot across your bow, oh great and revered one. Rest assured; we'll be back. Oh, I almost forgot. The genocide you are committing on Earth?"

Kip laughed.

"You know what I mean, my infallible leader. The murder you colorfully refer to as departure? It stops today."

Kip's eyes narrowed as an insidious smile consumed his face.

"For every report of an innocent life ended I receive, I will impose a two hundred percent interest rate. And I will claim back what I am owed in Flaxen blood."

Kip mimicked the Flaxen gesture with his fist and smiled as he softly said, "For Humanity."

Kip's smug grin returned. "Bye-bye, my great and glorious leader. You have a nice day now."

The screen turned to the flag of United Earth. The World Anthem of the Zoons infested Claudius' ears as if a cockroach had laid her eggs within them in the night.

Rage coursed through every blood vessel in his body. But he didn't show it. He needed an outlet for his anger. He looked up at the man that stood before him. The sergeant had been right to be concerned. He spent the next twenty-four hours in torment.

Kip ordered the pilot to return to Echo. The scorpion had not previously had a sphere drive but it did now. Echo was stationary in the midpoint between Earth and Venus, held by neither Flaxen nor Man. It took them under thirty minutes to return to their ship, for Echo was no longer their home. That honor had been transferred to Cylli. Echo was now a fellow resident, a neighbor. Their mobile home away from home.

Twenty-four hours before their assault on Venus, the last of the crew of Echo had been shuttled aboard. Only Helen remained. Cylli had become distressed at the mere suggestion she may leave. Kip had not hesitated for a second to allow Helen to remain. After all, a child needs a mother.

Cylli's blue eyes glowed as they welled. She wanted a hug from Kip, Serilda, and Sarah before they left.

Each picked up the girl and whispered their farewells into the ear of the child-AI before placing her gently back on the ground.

When all had boarded and Cylli was opening her doors for them to leave, Kip was still sitting with Scott Williams and Katie Silver in his oversized office.

"So, Scott, I've seen the reports and the schematics, but I need to hear what Cylli did from a professional perspective?"

Scott smiled at his captain, "Quite remarkable, Sir. The shipyards are fully automated. I spent hours watching through the glass of the observation deck as they did their work."

"An engineer's dream, no doubt?"

"I could never have conceived of such a thing."

"So, what's the old bird capable of now. What exactly did Cylli do?"

"We have a completely new sphere drive. Its capacity to harness energy is three times what we had before. Our rail guns can fire at five times the velocity they once did. And our deflector lasers are upgraded too, to cope with the new speeds we can reach. They're also now a weapon. Their energy is an order of magnitude what they were before."

"And the defect, the one that caused our predicament?"

"Not a problem anymore. The issue was obviously discovered. The drive now compensates for the increased energy the hypersphere releases when velocity exceeds the threshold."

"So Brookes' drive was defective and he knew it?"

"It seems he must have known it was a possibility, his own equations told him that. He was willing to risk two thousand lives on a gamble."

"That doesn't surprise me in the least. And the scorpion?"

"It now has a sphere drive of its own. It can now conduct long-distance engagements far away from Echo. Cylli was also able to improve the plasma cannons. They can harness the new energy from the drive.

"Each shard we fire will be at least three times the power it had previously. And the lovely wee girl was kind enough to replenish our missiles. We have them stacked in their hundreds in the weapons bay, along with hundreds of tons of rail gun slugs."

"Commander Silver, what about our armor?"

Katie had been swaying in her seat desperate for her turn. "Captain, Echo's armor now can deflect energy the same way Cylli did when Brookes attacked. But remember, Cylli's hull is thick, our armor is much thinner. But we can stay in a fight much longer than before. The scorpion had the same upgrade. Echo is truly a ship of war again."

"Just don't say that to him, Commander. I know for a fact that he liked it when his purpose became exploration."

"Come now, Captain. We all know Echo is no idiot. He knows exactly what's been done to him," said Katie.

"I know, just don't bring it up. It's a touchy subject. He's made his displeasure quite clear to me."

The three of them laughed at the thought of Echo's indignation.

"Ok, so we're ready to face him then? It seems we can meet Brookes on an equal footing at least?" said Kip

"Just remember, he has four of those ships and as much as it pains me to say, he's the most intelligent person I've ever met," said Katie.

"Well then, Commander, we'll have to hit them now and hit them hard. Before Brookes has time to use that treacherous mind of his."

"Forgive the interruption, Captain, but we have cleared Cylli's outer doors. Would you like to issue the command to the helmsman or shall I take us to our destination?" asked Echo.

"Echo, my old friend, you do it. Set a course for Venus and engage the sphere drive at maximum power."

Echo maneuvered to acquire his vector. The three of his friends watched from the window as lights across Cylli's surface shone brightly. It flashed in all colors as her dress had done.

She wanted to say goodbye again.

Her hull shone purple as Echo's engine's violet glow reflected from her chrome-like surface. Echo vanished like a daydream into the black chasm of space.

After its successful mission above the skies of Venus, the scorpion was ready to enter Echo's shuttle bay.

"Captain, I am detecting three ships approaching, each one the same as that which attacked us," said Echo.

Kip was missing Serilda's strength, perhaps he had relinquished it too early.

"Echo, deploy the armor on this ship and your own."

Both ships were consumed in a shiny metallic alloy that shone as bright as Cylli.

In the space between Venus and the world that the Flaxens wished to conquer, a battle ensued.

Avalon was in command of the center ship in a formation of three. "Hawk, unify your sphere beam with the other two birds and target the small ship."

The AI consulted with his pilotless allies and complied. All three hawks set loose their weapon onto the scorpion in unity.

Kip and his pilot felt their vessel shake violently. But the armor was holding, for now.

"Lieutenant, target the center ship with the plasma cannons. Full power!"

Shards of plasma erupted from the scorpion as they met their target in sequence. Their increased energy seemed to defy the blackness of the void as their view was consumed by blue and purple light. They struck their target and watched as it changed color to luminescent red as their shards continued to strike the hawk.

The pilot looked at Kip with wide eyes, "Captain, the armor is above heat tolerance. We can't remain here much longer."

"Keep firing, Lieutenant. Launch missiles."

The hawk in the center of their formation began to spark and shimmer as the newly enhanced weapons met their target. Kip watched in dismay as each of the ten missiles was detonated prematurely by lasers on the side of the arrow-shaped hawks.

Sarah was on the bridge, "Echo, target the center ship, the same one the scorpion is firing at. Fire rail guns, maximum power. Now!"

Echo complied. From his port side, slugs of titanium launched at an appreciable percentage of light speed. Sarah had studied physics in the academy and it was her strongest subject. She knew that the slugs when moving at five times their previous velocity would not strike with five times the power they had before.

The universe did not work in such simple ways. Sarah knew that the energy within a moving object squares with the increase in its velocity. The slugs now hit their target with twenty-five times the energy they had imparted when they had failed to so much as dent Brookes' vessel weeks before.

The crew of the bridge watched as the central hawk endured impact after impact. The slugs hit with such velocity that the ship was shaken from its heading, its beam disuniting with its allies.

Sarah saw the hull of the ship begin to buckle as titanium struck it at speeds inconceivable to the Human mind.

Kip knew instinctively what Sarah had done. He changed his plasma cannons to target the ship on his left. The shards began to hit their mark.

The scorpion was still in trouble. It had endured nearly a minute of the combined spear beams and was beginning to show damage. Flakes of the insect-like ship begin to fly away as if chips from a carpenter's chisel.

The pilot sounded frantic, "Captain, we won't last much longer. Our armor is being destroyed. We'll be dead in twenty seconds."

Kip ordered him to keep firing, he knew they were fighting a coward. As the plasma combined with Echo's slugs hit the second ship, Kip and Sarah watched from their different locations as all three hawks turned and engaged their drives.

Relief washed over them both as the birds' rear sections glowed purple. They fled like antelope with a tiger in hot pursuit.

Sarah was waiting in the shuttle bay as the deformed scorpion made good its landing. The ship was malformed, scorched and blackened. But salvageable.

Kip emerged from the ship, he looked dazed, sweat was dripping from his brow. Sarah had never been so happy to see the man before her in all her life and she cared not for the maintenance crew waiting to assess and repair the damaged vessel of war.

She ran towards him and leaped into his arms. Such was Kip's relief at surviving the near-deadly attack and the joy of the sight of the women that had come to greet him, he lifted Sarah and held her as her legs wrapped around his waist, their cheeks pressed together. The tears from both merged into a single torrent.

Echo had retreated to his unofficial base on the far side of the moon. Avalon could strike at any time without warning.

Sarah was outside the quarters shared by Serilda and Megan. She was surprised to hear Serilda's voice instructing her to come in before she had sounded the buzzer.

Sarah entered. She saw Serilda and Megan lying next to each other on the bed.

"Serilda, did you sense me outside? How did you know I was there?"

The two girls looked at each other and burst into laughter. Serilda composed herself first, "Sarah, I'm glad you're here, and no, I didn't sense you. I've found some of your technology convenient." She held up her left arm and pointed to her wrist.

Sarah laughed with them, she understood Serilda had chosen to have the standard communication device used by all onboard Echo implanted just below the top layer of her skin.

Megan released Serilda's hand and stood, "I'll leave you two to talk for a while."

"No, Megan, there's nothing I didn't want you to hear. Please stay."

Megan huffed, "Do you have any idea how much this girl talks? I've been waiting for her to shut up for half an hour so I can get some food. I'm starving."

Sarah watched as the two girls looked at each other and laughed again. Megan stood, approached Sarah, and tapped her on the shoulder, "It's your shift now, Commander." She said nothing more as she left the room to go and eat whatever she chose. Such a thing was still an astonishing novelty to the girl.

Serilda, still in her bed, tapped the wide space next to her as she had done for Kip many times. Sarah didn't hesitate, she now knew Serilda's true nature. She more than anyone wanted to see Earth free and she now also understood all of the intrusions into Kip's mind were a haunting means to that vital end. What was more, she knew the damage her actions had inflicted on Kip, though considerable, through remorse alone took an equal or greater tole on Serilda's psyche.

She sat next to Serilda and watched as she extended her arm and twitched her fingers.

Sarah smiled and took her hand, "How are you, Serilda? We've not spoken since—"

"Since I told you what was what?"

"Yes, since that lovely night. I'm so sorry I ever doubted you. I let my feelings cloud my judgment, and when it comes to the captain, let's just say those feelings are complicated."

"Believe me, Sarah, if I thought for a second you were after Megan, I'd stalk you with a Flaxen combat knife."

Sarah looked at the girl dead in the eyes, and simultaneously, they erupted into laughter. Both had to concentrate to restrain tears.

When they composed themselves, it was Sarah who spoke, "Serilda, why did you come? You and Megan were safe with Cylli, but you still came?"

"Do you really think I'd let you face these bastards without me?"

"No, no that's not what I meant. It's just, you and Megan, you're not military."

"I made the captain make a promise. A promise I have every intention of making him keep."

"What was that?"

213

"When he rescued us from the camp, I refused to leave without my cellmates. The reason I changed my mind was that he promised to let me Kill as many Flaxens as I want. I never forget a bargain."

"So, you're here so you can kill as many of the yellow bastards as you want?"

"I have only one in mind."

"Who?"

Serilda squeezed her hand, "Let's just say I owe him some pain, enough for Megan and me both."

"Ok, Serilda, I'll leave it at that. I'm really just here to tell you how happy I am that you joined us."

"As am I, Sarah. I will tell you this, though, you are just as important as Kip if we are to beat these murderous bastards."

Chapter 26 – Hear No Evil

As he had spent so much of his life, Avalon Brookes was consumed by fear. He was being escorted by two armed guards to the Hawk's Retreat, a place he had grown to loathe nearly as much as he feared.

As the wooden doors opened, he trembled at the sight of the Flaxus as he stood dead center in the room. His yellows eyes passed through him as he were glass.

"Avalon, my friend, come, sit and enjoy some Ribous with me."

Avalon knew this pleasantry was not to last. But he did what was ordered of him.

Claudius filled two glasses of the purple liquid and slammed one in front of Avalon, the force enough to make its content spill over onto the pristine, oak table.

"Flaxus, I'm not to blame. Eastcott somehow managed to gain access to the cylinder's shipyards. I protected that facility in the most secure way I know."

"Avalon, you have disappointed me for the second time. Although I am conflicted, you did manage to destroy the bulk of the Zoons' airpower after all. But Venus herself was attacked, Avalon. Venus herself!"

"But Flaxus, they have modified their ships. They have the same stealth capabilities as my own."

"You mean, my own, Avalon."

The coward bowed his head, "Of course, Flaxus. I mean, the Zoons have acquired the same ability to conceal themselves as your fleet of hawks do."

"Avalon, I need your eyes. You must see the work that you do. As much I would like my men to burn them out, I am restrained in this matter."

Claudius' face remained neutral as he continued to speak in a calm sympathetic voice, "Avalon, it seems to me your affliction is with your ears. Did you not hear me when I told you I expected the skies above the two worlds to remain unharried by the enemy?"

"I did, Fluxus. I just simply underestimated the Zoons' ability to control the structure."

But you did hear me when I said that to you?" His voice raised to a shout, "Look me in the eye, you coward!"

Avalon tentatively raised his eyes to meet the smirking Flaxus before him. "I did hear."

"Well then, Avalon, it seems you have trouble with your hearing. Or you would have listened to me. Allow one of my men to examine your ears for you."

Claudius gestured for one of the two Flaxens that escorted Brookes to approach.

He grinned. His teeth were almost as yellow as his eyes.

"Please, Flaxus. I will annihilate Eastcott, I just need the full fleet of hawks operational. Their combined power will vaporize him and all of the Zoons aboard his ship."

"Look at this, Avalon. Look what that rat made me endure."

He turned his screen to face Avalon and played Eastcott's message, the first Zoon in history to threaten a Flaxus.

Brookes observed in terror as he watched Eastcott's mockery of the Flaxus. His cowardice was exceeded only by his genius and he now knew he was about to suffer the consequences of this, his second failure.

The Flaxus returned his yellow gaze to Avalon and pointed at the glass before him.

"Drink, my friend, drink. I have a feeling you're going to need it."

Avalon drank the entire glass as ordered.

"About that hearing deficit, Avalon. Let's see what we can do about that." He nodded for both men to approach.

A large Flaxen, perhaps seven and a half feet tall, walked slowly toward Avalon. The other man approached from behind and held him by his shoulders. He had no chance against the strength of a Flaxen. He watched in horror as the soldier in front of him leaned to his ankle and unsheathed his yellow-handled combat knife.

He tried to move but he was fixed as if shackled by iron. All three men before him ignored his cries and pleas. The Flaxen turned the knife in his hand so the serrated edge was placed against Avalon's ear. He allowed him to feel its cold blade against his skin before he sawed through the cartilage with a purposeful lethargy.

Avalon screamed and wailed as it took a minute for his ear to depart his head.

The Flaxen could have achieved the same goal in a second. The other side of the blade was razor sharp. But when it came to punishment, the Flaxens seldom thought of brevity.

The Flaxus snorted as he picked up Avalon's ear. He tossed it onto his lap.

"Take this with you as a reminder, Zoon. It seems I keep having to tell you I don't tolerate failure."

The Flaxus headed for the wooden doors. It was time for his lunch. He turned to his two men and pointed at the Floor. He chuckled.

"Believe me, men, the Irony of my office being stained with the blood of a Zoon is not lost on me. But its sight displeases me. Have it cleaned."

Both men bowed their heads and spoke as one. "Yes, Flaxus"

The Flaxus left the room to eat his lunch.

The disfigured scientist wept in his complex. The Flaxens had been kind enough to provide him with bandages and disinfectant. They couldn't allow him to succumb to infection. They still needed him. Six hours had since passed and he was finally beginning to get over the pain and humiliation he had endured. He knew he must consider his options; events were not unfolding as they should be.

His first thought was to take his hawks and turn the Flaxus to ash from orbit. But then what? Where would he go? He couldn't stay on Venus, and Earth would soon be overrun by the yellows. He could perhaps survive in the wilderness, alone. But that was no life for a man of his mind.

Next, he considered Eastcott. Perhaps he could approach the man and tell him he was wrong and he wished to rejoin them. But this thought was fleeting. The mere idea of running back to the man that had humiliated him sickened him. And even if Eastcott agreed, he would no doubt be imprisoned, for he had killed many, including Lucinda. A woman he knew to be one of Eastcott's friends.

His only option was to keep his word to the Flaxus and then live out his days as lord commander of the cylinder. His only obstacle was gaining access to the little bitch that had humiliated him just as Eastcott had. But she was a mere machine. With enough time, he could gain control over the malfunctioning AI. Yes, her technology was advanced. But he was Avalon Brookes. All he would need is time. But first, he needed access. He knew the girl that had mocked him as he fled would never open her doors for him. And so, he spent hours studying the sensor readings from his hawk, the data its AI had gathered in his last encounter with the retarded girl.

As the sun rose in the skies of Venus, it appeared huge in the sky, as if an inferno had conquered the heavens. The world was much closer to the star than Earth and sunrises were a thing of majesty. Avalon ignored the beauty as it gilded the landscape, clearly visible from the huge windows on the Eastern side of his complex. He looked at his screen as a sinister smile spread over his mutilated face. Such was the revelation before him, he had completely forgotten the pain, emanating in waves from the location in which his ear used to be.

Chapter 27 – Escalation

Kip reclined in his oversized faux-leather chair. His screen filled with a red dress. It was Cylli. Realtime communications from such a distance were impossible. Light takes, on average, thirty-three minutes to traverse the distance between Earth and the gas giant Jupiter, Cylli's home.

He could see the girl with Hellen standing in the background. Around them were trees and hills, red and blue birds flew in the sky. It was daytime. Cylli smiled and as the broadcast began, she curtseyed, "Hey Cap, me and Helen are in the forest. I never saw it so close before. I've been chasing bunnies again but they're real fast. I didn't catch one yet."

The girl's face glowed as she recalled a recent event, "Oh and just now, a bunch of deers ran past us, there were so many, Cap, it made the ground shook. Helen said we can watch a movie tonight. She said it has deer in it too. She says it's real old but I guess I am too, so that doesn't matter. She said it's called Bambi! I never saw a movie before, I can't wait!"

The smile on Cylli's face faded.

"Anyway, I just wanted to say good luck against the bad man. He's real mean and real smart, but you're smart too, Cap. Just don't take too long. I miss you. I gotta go now. Helen says I have to make a message for Sarah and Serilda too. See you soon!"

The girl looked to her left, her eyes glowed brighter, a pure smile engulfed her face as she ran from the view of the image. Something had caught her attention.

Helen approached closer, "Sorry about that, Captain, but she insisted. But I know what's best for morale and morale doesn't come any better than Cylli." Her face turned serious, "Kip, you be careful out there. Don't take any risks. Use your mind, not your brawn, is that understood, Captain Eastcott?" Helen smiled as the transmission ended.

The door to Kip's office buzzed. He knew who was outside: Cyrus Eppleston. He had ordered the man and the president to be collected from Earth. Their newly upgraded shuttles could reach them in half an hour without so much as challenging its potential power.

"Come in," said Kip.

The wide-set man with the mustache appeared before him.

"Captain, you have no idea how happy I am to see you. The president extends his apologies, but he has pressing issues to deal with after the recent devastation of our air force."

Kip gestured for the minister to take a seat, "I heard about that and I am very sorry we couldn't help. You received my message updating you about the situation?"

"I did, Captain. Firstly, please allow me to express my condolences for the people you lost to your traitor."

Kip's heart sunk at the thought of Lucinda and the young ensign she commanded, he had been trying not to think about them.

"Thank you for your words. They died as heroes."

"They did. We're not unaccustomed to loss, as you know. But still."

"Thank you, Minister, but let's get to it, shall we? What's been happening on Earth since our attack on Venus?"

"Unbelievable, an attack on that poisonous world itself? We celebrated into the night at the news. Captain, the mineral plant you destroyed was of crucial importance to the Flaxens. All such minerals on Earth are severely depleted. Only our mines in Russia contain them in any significant quantity. And they are still deep within our territory."

"I know, Minister, that was the whole point of the operation. But what I meant was—"

"Of course, you knew, I was simply conveying my gratitude. Although our air force is severely diminished, the Flaxens will not be able to strengthen theirs without those precious supplies."

"Excellent, it seems the tide of war may be turning in our favor then. Minister, did you see the video I transmitted to the Flaxus?"

"I did. To see the Flaxus tormented in such a way was truly magnificent to behold. I hope you won't find this disrespectful, but we cheered and laughed as we saw it. The mere thought of him watching such ridicule from above his own planet must have sent him into a frenzy. I'm certain a hundred Flaxens were lined up and shot just to appease his ego in some small manner."

"No doubt, Minister. I must say I took great pleasure in delivering the message. Believe me when I say that every smile on my face was genuine. But what I am getting at, was my threat. I told the Flaxus to stop his murder of innocents. Has the genocide stopped?"

"Captain, forgive me, I'm ashamed. I was simply consumed by excitement. We have been losing this war for years. Recent developments have just been overwhelming, in the most positive way, you understand. But you are right, I was focusing on the wrong thing entirely."

"I understand, Minister. I fought in a long war myself, it's perfectly natural for you to be so. But please, what of the people of Earth?"

"I'm afraid the Flaxus ignored you completely. Our intelligence agency informs me their chambers are now running night and day. As you know, they would only commit their horrific crimes during sunlight before. I'm afraid he's called your bluff."

The emotions returned. Kip thought he was regaining at least a semblance of control over them since Serilda ceased her influence. But they were back. Rage, sorrow, anxiety, hate. All filled him as if a dam had breached allowing them to flood his mind.

Kip did his best to hide his loss of composure from Cyrus. "I understand, Minister. It seems I have only made things worse."

"I can see this news has affected you greatly, and believe me when I say, it has done the same to me. The only difference is, as cold as it sounds, I have grown accustomed to it. The Flaxens have been operating their chambers for over ten years. When they first began, I was much the same as you are now, but don't you see, Captain?"

Cyrus could see that he didn't, so he continued, "Those poor souls the Flaxens are murdering would have died before the war ends anyway. The Flaxens are simply posturing. Indeed, if not for you, every Human on Earth would have met the same fate. Captain, you have scared the Flaxens. An attack on their homeworld is unprecedented," he looked down to his thighs. "The only way they know how to respond is how they always do; to escalate their atrocities. Please don't blame yourself. As I said, we had no means of rescuing them anyway. They simply ended their intolerable lives earlier than they may have before."

"But the people, Minister, those poor people, I saw it firsthand. The bastards herded children into those sickening machines in the arms of their mothers."

"With respect, I don't think you are understanding me. All we must do is continue our assaults. With your new power, we can gain the upper hand. Our Intelligence services inform me that the Flaxens are scared. For the first time since their infestation of Earth, they are terrified. Captain, what we're seeing is the manifestation of that fear. They hope to demoralize us by this expedited murder. But, we now have a chance. If we keep this momentum going, we have a fucking good chance." Cyrus paused. "Excuse my language, Captain. It's just—"

"Please, Minister, I share your feelings completely. Your intelligence agency, you have mentioned them before. It's so strong because you have many like Serilda? Half-Flaxens with abilities of the mind?"

"Yes, that's right. Some are stronger than others but they all can influence others in some way, and some of them can see the thoughts of others. Particularly as they sleep, but none are as strong as Serilda."

Kip could believe this easily. He had never met anyone with Serilda's strength of mind. He allowed Cyrus to continue.

"She seems to possess all of those abilities and we suspect she is capable of much more. One of our operatives has a particularly keen insight into others of his kind. He is how we learned of Serilda in the first place. He informs me that to simply think of her drains him of all his energy. He used to sleep for a day each time we requested him to provide information about the girl."

Kip nodded with a polite smile as Cyrus continued, "Have you considered simply obliterating Venus from orbit? I know Echo has the power to do so. It will save so many lives on Earth."

Kip turned his eyes away from the minister, he was concerned his emotions would come across as weakness.

"Minister, I have thought of that many times, but I have recently learned that not all Flaxens are the same. Some share many of the values we do. And don't forget about the children. They are born as innocent as our own.

He gritted his teeth at the thoughts of millions of innocents dying once more.

"Only Flaxen society corrupts them." Kip thought of the horrors he had seen at the hands of the Flaxens. "What you suggest is their way. To win the war in such a manner would be no different from the Flaxens winning. At the cost of an entire race. Many of them innocent, I suspect most of the women are near certainly so."

"Of course, it's just so tempting to end this relentless carnage now. But I agree with you. We should not become like those we fight."

Kip was relieved. He now knew Cyrus to be a rational, composed, and compassionate man.

Cyrus' eyes met Kip's with a curious serenity, "What about simply killing the Flaxus? You could do so easily enough from orbit."

Kip smiled, he was warmed by his expression. "That thought has occurred to me too, Minister, but he would simply be replaced. There's an old expression in our language, 'Better the devil you know.'"

Cyrus returned Kip's smile as his calm eyed narrowed, "Wise words, Captain."

The two men spoke for another hour, making plans, but Kip kept much to himself.

When they were done, Kip stood as his eyes met the sincerity of Cyrus' once more, "Minister, please stay aboard Echo as our guest for a while. I'd like the benefit of your council."

"Of course, Captain, I will stay. I'd like to explore every section of your ship."

"I'll have someone give you a tour. There's much to see."

The men shook hands and Cyrus left. The ensign outside was waiting to show him to his quarters.

Kip approached the quarters shared by the two lovers afflicted by terror. He buzzed the door. Megan opened it with a look of curiosity in her eyes, "Captain, come in, can I get you a drink?"

"Whisky please, Megan, and don't be shy, if you know what I mean?"

Megan smiled as she fetched his requested beverage.

"Thanks, you have no idea how much I need this. Where's Serilda?"

She waved her hand in dismissal, as if she were swatting a mosquito, "She's somewhere, most likely the galley. She's made a lot of friends since we joined you. I know that's no surprise to you."

"None whatsoever, she tends to have that effect on people. I was just here to speak to her, but please, allow me to join you for a drink."

The curiosity on Megan's face turned to surprise as she fetched herself a glass of whisky from a stand at the edge of the quarters. "I hate this stuff. I'd never tried alcohol until you saved me, but I like how it makes me feel. It can make me forget for a while. Do you know what I mean?"

"I know, just don't get too attached, that can become a problem quickly."

"I know that better than most. The Flaxens guarding our camp seldom had anything to do. We watched them drink all day and lose their wits with each glass. I learned how to cope in that place. I can do it without this," she tapped her glass.

"Of course you can, I just wanted to let you know. It's new to you after all."

"Don't you worry, Captain, I'm stronger than you think. So, what did you want to speak to Serilda about? Or should I not ask?"

Kip gulped half of his glass; he was already beginning to feel its warmth encompass his body. He knew he should heed the warning he had just given Megan.

"First of all, I asked you to call me Kip, and second, not at all. It's just that she has certain insights. Megan, what do you know of Serilda's abilities? And I promise you I am only asking because it's important."

"I know what you asked, but I think you deserve the title and rank you have. When the war is won, I'll call you Kip. As for Serilda, there's so much to tell. For the first three years in the camp together, I had no idea. It was only when we began to grow close that she started to tell me." She sensed he needed more so she added, "When I say close, I mean when I was old enough to—"

"I know what you mean, such intimacy was no doubt the start of her opening up to you?"

"One day, she simply told me. Of course, I thought she was suffering from delirium at first. Most of the things the people we shared our hut with said made little if any sense." She took a swig from her glass, her face scrunched as if she had chewed a lemon. "It's a long story, but let's just say she provided a little more proof each day until it was clear to me she was being truthful. The fact that she had never lied to me before helped with that a lot."

Kip was curious, he wanted her to continue so he just nodded with a faint smile.

"Eventually, she learned how to control the colonel, I know she told you about that. She saved so many lives."

"I know she did, Megan," he bowed his head.

"Please don't be upset. Don't you see? You at least saved the two of us. And the people your men medicated? They would have been strong enough to work again. Captain, the Flaxens rarely waste free labor. You almost certainly saved them too."

Kip's eyes reddened, "That's so good to hear, but why I'm here is to understand just how far her abilities go?"

"You're a man of science, have you not thought about what she did?"

Kip hadn't, he searched her brown eyes in pursuit of answers. "As far as I know, what Serilda can do goes beyond science. We have no theories at all to even begin to explain such a thing."

"That's exactly my point. When I spent those years with my adoptive Flaxen parents, they home-schooled me. I learned simple physics. The maximum speed the universe allows is light speed, and so communication is also limited to travel at the speed of light. Don't you see? Serilda started influencing you when you were barely even back in the solar system. It takes light days to travel so far, and yet her link with you was instantaneous."

Kip's face betrayed his astonishment as he considered this. "I'm such an idiot, I'm supposed to be the Captain of the Fleet, a man of science, but that has never even crossed my mind."

"I wouldn't worry about it. I've had years to think about it. I don't know the true extent of her powers, I really don't. But if she can defy the laws of physics as we know them, they must be stronger than we can imagine."

"Thank you, Megan, you may have helped more than you know. In fact, I'm glad you're alone. We both know Serilda's tendency to speak indirectly when it comes to her abilities."

"I know that better than anyone."

Kip gulped his remaining whiskey in one swig then slammed his glass on the table. "Megan, if you ever want a place on this ship, a career—one that has a purpose—you come to me and I'll make it happen. You're wise beyond your years."

She blushed, "I'll give it some thought, Captain. I'm glad I could help."

Kip smiled, placed his hand on her shoulder, and left as the doors opened for him.

***

Avalon Brookes lay on his bed waiting, staring at the ceiling. He had been thinking for hours, of the Flaxus, of Eastcott, of the little bitch. Oh, how thought of that retarded little shit. Not only had she beaten and humiliated him, but she was also his only hope of salvation.

He knew the medical facilities inside would be more than capable of repairing the damage the Flaxus had done to his face. A disfigurement he had intended to be a lifelong reminder of his failure.

Even the infirmary on Echo could grow him a new ear. Humanity had considered this part of normal medical practice since long before he was born.

He was going to get inside the defiant machine and fix himself. And he had decided the Flaxus must pay for the humiliation he had endured. But that could wait until after he had won the yellow-eyed prick's war for him.

He heard a sound. One of his hawks circled above the poisonous world, piloted by its AI. The ship was scanning the solar system as Avalon had ordered it to do. He approached his console and a sinister joy consumed him. He had found just what he needed.

Chapter 28 – Rocks

"Y ou're sure it can't detect us, Commander?"

"I don't think so, Captain," said Katie as she looked at Kip from across his desk. "As long as we stay on the far side of the moon, its sensors can't see us. It's a giant rock over two thousand miles across after all."

"You're sure he's not aboard?"

"No chance. That ship has been in orbit around Earth for nearly two days. We know Brookes' tolerance for boredom. Or lack of it, I should say. I can guarantee he's ordered his ship or whatever he calls it, to patrol Earth."

"No doubt, Commander," Kip scratched his head. "The maintenance crew tells me the scorpion won't be repaired for another three or even four days and I'm not willing to risk Echo in combat yet. If he's destroyed, humanity will follow shortly after."

"I do have an idea, but it will come at a price and we'll only get one chance."

Kip listened to Katie as she explained her plan. He gave the order for her to proceed.

Sarah had been observing kip as she shared her evening meal with him, Serilda, and Megan in the galley.

"You're quiet tonight, Captain?"

"Sorry, XO, it's just frustrating. I told you we came back here to fight, and that bastard, Brookes, has outwitted us again."

Serilda tilted her head and looked at him softly, "Kip, Avalon isn't the only genius you know. Have faith in Katie, her mind is strong. She can meet Brookes on an equal footing. She just needs to believe in herself more."

"I know, Katie's mind is sharp, and what's more, she has imagination. Something Brookes lacks. He's too arrogant for that. I have complete faith in her plan, I just want to get at the yellow bastards now. I can't bear the thought of that arrogant prick that calls himself Flaxus grinning as he murders thousands each day."

"That's why you authorized the plan. If the scorpion isn't ready for another three days that's—" said Megan before she paused.

"One hundred and twenty thousand. The minister told us that their maximum capacity in their chambers is forty thousand a day. If we can get to Earth three days earlier, we may be able to save one hundred and twenty thousand lives," said Sarah.

"I know how to do basic maths, Sarah."

"Of course, sorry, this whole thing's just got me worked up, you know?"

"I do."

Kip's face was grave as he looked at each of them as he spoke, "For god's sake, no one say any of this to Katie, she's under enough pressure as it is."

The next day, a shuttle departed Echo. Like the scorpion, Cylli had upgraded each of the ship's three small vessels with their own sphere drive. No one was aboard. Its pilot was Echo.

Kip was on the bridge. He was looking at the view from the shuttle. Earth was coming into its sight. He looked at the blue and green globe and then at Sarah. They said nothing with their words but their faces communicated with equal understanding. "Echo, we have one shot at this. I want all of your focus on this alone. Ignore all non-vital ship's systems, I want every bit of that processing power of yours on this, got it?" asked Kip.

"Of course, Captain, but it's just numbers, I am a computer after all."

"I know, it's the numbers I'm worried about."

Kip's mind had turned once more to the thousands on Earth who depended on what they were about to do.

"It's Echo, when have you ever known him to get his numbers wrong?" asked Sarah.

"I know, XO, let's get to it, shall we? Echo, activate the sphere drive."

"Drive active, Captain."

The space behind the small vessel seemed to warp. It had made its hypersphere.

"Echo, release the payload," ordered Kip.

From the rear section of the shuttle, a huge, silver rock as big as the shuttle could accommodate was released. It had been sculpted by the ship's engineers to be a perfect sphere.

They watched entranced as the object entered the deformed space of the hypersphere. The boulder seemed to change shape and form impossible patterns as it revolved within the small, unnatural pocket of the universe. This was a three-dimensional object existing in four-dimensional space.

Kip leaned to the edge of his seat, his brow furrowed in concentration, "Echo, I want a split-screen, show us the shuttle and the Hawk." The AI complied. They saw the shuttle and the predatory hawk as it circled the Earth.

Katie had chosen this time for a reason; its current position within its orbit was perfect.

Kip stood and pointed toward the view of the shuttle, "Now, Echo, now!"

They watched as the shuttle exploded in a flash of purple energy. There was no shrapnel. The shuttle had been turned not to vapor but to protons and neutrons instead. Not even atoms remained. Two seconds later, the hawk vanished from view.

Sarah and Kip looked at Katie. She was smiling at both of her commanding officers, her white teeth revealed for all to see, her eyes glowed with pride. "We got it, Captain, Commander. We got Brookes' precious little pet in one shot."

"And you call Brookes a genius?" asked Kip.

Sarah was grinning at Katie with pride, "I just wish we could have seen it happen."

"I can help you with that, Commander Dimple. Would you like to see?" asked Echo.

She looked at Kip in astonishment as they spoke the same words in perfect harmony. "Yes, Echo!"

The split-screen changed. They watched as Echo replayed the events in the slowest motion he could manage. He had recorded at such a high speed that he had captured an image every nanosecond.

They saw the shuttle explode as they had before. But now they could see the rock that the crew had collected from the moon's surface leave the hypersphere and accelerate towards the hawk. The purple light from the exploding sphere drive reflected from its silver surface as it returned to three dimensions.

Their attention turned to the other side of the screen, to the hawk in high orbit above Earth. The rock appeared to glide towards its target at a leisurely pace.

All remained silent and still as they saw it smash into the hawk at twenty percent the speed of light. They watched as the rock shifted its direction slightly upwards. Its bottom outer edge glowed red as it soared above the North Pole, harmlessly into space.

The hawk buckled and deformed. It twisted and turned like a Catherine wheel as it descended toward the planet glowing white-hot. It left a trail of vapor behind as it plummeted. It landed in the Atlantic Ocean, turning thousands of gallons of water into steam as it impacted. Destined to remain submerged on the seafloor forever.

Kip looked at Katie again, his mouth was gaping. "How could you be so sure the hawk wouldn't hit Earth at the speed that rock was traveling? That would have caused a tsunami big enough to destroy every coastal city on Earth, and a lot of the inland ones too for that matter?"

Katie feigned offense and frowned as she smirked at Kip, "Haven't you ever played pool before?"

Kip smiled. "You hit it with just the edge of the rock, didn't you? At just the right angle? Just enough energy was transferred to send it crashing to Earth. You knew no one was at risk the whole time?"

Katie folded her arms as playful smugness spread over her face. "You know me better than that. Of course, I knew. Anyway, it was just my idea, there's no way I could have done the maths in real-time. We have Echo to thank for that."

"At your service, shipmates," said Echo.

The bridge crew all laughed. In all the years they had spent together, Echo had never ceased to amuse them.

A thought occurred to Kip, "Commander Silver, why didn't we just fly the shuttle into the Hawk at spherical speed?"

"Wouldn't have worked. It takes the sphere drive time to build up speed. Earth is a stone's throw away from the Moon."

They erupted into laugher together at this unintended joke.

Katie regained her composure and explained her ingenious thoughts that had led to this providence, "It just wouldn't have had the time to build up the required speed. I needed all of the hypersphere's energy released at once. That's why the shuttle exploded."

Kip kept his gaze fixed on his chief science officer with pride in his eyes as she continued, "I also needed the projectile to be perfectly round, so we could calculate its direction after impact. A shuttle's shape is too irregular for that. We would've risked hitting Earth."

Kip began to clap his hands with sincere admiration. The rest of the bridge crew stood, faced her, and followed.

Katie's face blushed as she smiled and took an exaggerated bow.

Echo displayed the image of fireworks exploding on the huge, curved screen of the bridge.

He was in a playful mood that day. After all, Katie had just saved countless thousands, with just her mind and a rock.

***

Avalon Brookes reclined in the seat of his hawk. He felt calm again, relaxed even. He watched as the red planet grew bigger in his view as each second passed.

"Hawk, land at the preprogrammed coordinates, no more than fifty meters away from the dome."

Hawk said nothing. Avalon strolled to the rear section of the ship and opened a metallic sliding door. Before him were five pressure suits suitable for protection from the vacuum of space. Avalon mused that the builders of his hawk had thought of contingency. To protect its occupants in the unlikely event of decompression. But Avalon didn't have the preservation of life on his mind, save for his own.

As the hawk landed itself, he climbed into one of the black suits. He was sickened to see the flag of United Earth on his left arm and the Martian Confederacy on his right, "Self-righteous bastards."

He waited for the ship to make contact with the planet's surface. The rear doors of his hawk lowered to form a ramp from which he could descend onto the red, dusty world.

He had never been to Mars before the war. It simply hadn't interested him. He thought the people that populated the planet under huge transparent domes to be fools. Who would live in such austerity?

But Avalon had never seen how a sunrise on Mars gilded the landscape, or how the night shone. Such was the light pollution on Earth, few locations remained to behold the beauty of the Milky Way. On Mars, the stars filled the night sky with radiant beauty, as if pinholes in the fabric of the cosmos. To his left were red mountains. The sky above him was a grayish blue. The sun shone bright, not much bigger than half its size when viewed from Earth. Tiny tornadoes of red sand spiraled around him. Boulders of all sizes littered the landscape, each with different shades of reds and browns. They covered the planet with a faint beauty, like a rock garden designed by mother nature.

None of this interested Avalon in the slightest, for he cared not for the beauty of the world he had come to. He had come for one thing alone, and it was in the huge, broken dome that lay before his eyes. He walked. He was entertained by the ease with which he moved, his weight only a third of that on Earth.

He knew the planet's former residents would rarely encounter this. Their domes had artificial gravity. Advanced technology that could create gravitational waves. The same technology their ships used to counteract inertia. And to keep their crews in their seats.

The dome was a colossus that would make Rhodes blush, fifty miles in diameter according to Hawk's readings. Near any other person would stand in awe at the marvel of engineering before them. Avalon simply strolled effortlessly towards the structure. It was full of holes, the orbital protection against meteorite impacts had failed long ago and Mars had almost no atmosphere to speak of. Its pressure only just above one percent of Earth's at sea level.

Meteors that would burn in Earth's atmosphere simply continued their trajectory unincumbered.

Over the millennia, many rocks had struck the dome, providing him with numerous locations he could enter. He simply chose the closest.

As he entered, he was surrounded by rubble—remnants of a once proud and advanced society. He didn't consider the flowers and the trees that would bloom inside or the children that played in the forests.

He didn't care about the lakes or the black and white swans that would swim upon them as the sun shone bright through the dome. He didn't think of the bones of thousands that lay buried under the ruble.

Avalon searched through the debris for half an hour. Then, behind the dark shade of his visor, his depraved smile spread across his face.

Laying two feet in front of him, was the object that had drawn him to Mars.

***

Claudius drank Ribous in his office in the Hawk's Retreat. He rarely left the place for he had all he needed there. He loved to spend his time admiring the view from his oval window, watching the birds soar in their hundreds in the sky, as he was doing at that moment.

A voice emanated from his desk, "Flaxus, we have an incoming transmission." The disembodied voice paused. It returned shaking with fear. "It's the Zoon again, the one called Eastcott."

Fear filled Claudius' body. He would never show it, but he was scared of this Zoon. The only individual, Flaxen or Human, to ever challenge him, much less mock him in his life.

He hurried to his desk and authorized the transmission. Once again, the image of the pestilent Zoon was before him, and once again, he was grinning at the Flaxus in defiance.

"Hey, Claud. You don't mind if I call you Claud, do you? It's me, your old buddy, Kip. Just thought I'd check in, see how you're doing. Oh, by the way, we had a slight incident I'm afraid. One of your pet hawks? It just seemed to fall out of the sky. I guess that's just what happens to birds when they get shot, hey Claud?" Kip laughed.

The image changed, the Fluxus remained expressionless as he viewed the slow-motion image of a perfectly round rock striking his precious bird, sending it tumbling to Earth—the planet he meant to conquer, whose people he meant to exterminate.

Kip's image returned, "Oh, and your precious chambers? They're all gone, you genocidal fuck," Kip grinned again as the image changed once more.

The Flaxus watched dumbstruck as another recording played. This time its playback was accelerated. He stared in disbelief as the image changed every second. Each one lasted just enough time for him to see one of his remaining chambers explode as a slug of titanium reduced it to dust.

Kip returned, "Quite the show, hey Claud? Thought you might like to see it. Oh, and in case you think you're safe on that pretty little rock of yours? Forget it." Kip's grin vanished as his face leaned towards the camera so it filled the whole screen, "I'm coming for you, you sick, twisted fuck. And when I do, it's not gonna be quick."

Kip's pleasant smile returned, "Anyway, I've gotta go. I've got an infestation problem to deal with. I'll be seeing you soon, buddy. You take care."

Later that night, ten Flaxen soldiers were tied to a pole atop a plinth of wood, in the courtyard of the Capitol building. Claudius had decided it was time to revive a long-forgotten tradition of the Flaxen military. In days gone by, after a particularly embarrassing failure, men from a selected company would be forced to choose a small rock from a fabric pouch. Most stones were white, but ten were black. Those who pulled a black stone from the pouch were to suffer. After all, someone other than the Flaxus must be held responsible for the humiliation they had endured. Claudius and dozens of others watched as the wood beneath them burned and he felt comfort as he heard the screams of the men as their yellow flesh melted before him.

Chapter 29 – Reflection

Helen reached for Cylli's warm soft hand as she sat next to her on the bank of one of her rivers, as they so often did. All of Cylli's interior was beautiful, but they both liked to sit on the wooden bench near Helen's cabin and watch the water flow and the life live.

They spent every minute of every day together. Cylli would lay next to Helen in the night copying her new mother's sounds and her movements as she slept. Cylli was incapable of sleeping herself, but she did her best to do what grownups do, nonetheless.

People were all around them, each doing their own thing. The citizens who had left to colonize Copious, who had, through fate, found themselves somewhere so majestic they couldn't possibly have imagined its likeness. And it was right on their doorstep.

White rabbits circled their feet and birds flew through the rainbow as they heard the splashing of the nearby waterfall. The calm of the life that surrounded them seemed to reflect the fulfillment that Helen had felt since Cylli had brightened her life. She felt such serenity, she had thought of resigning her commission. Only her duty to Kip, her other comrades, and the millions suffering on Earth had surpassed such considerations. She felt a love for the little girl in the red dress beside her that filled her being. As if Cylli were an extension of her—a pure girl of eternal life that could somehow defy her own mortality. It was a love that was both bliss and pain. Bliss for the adoration that consumed her. And pain for the finite time Helen's corporeal existence afforded them.

Cylli began to scream. She covered her ears and dropped from the bench to her knees.

"He's hurting me, Helen, he's hurting me."

"Who, Cylli, who's hurting you?"

"The bad man, he's back. It hurts."

"Hurt him back. Use your weapons like you did before."

"I can't, I can't see him."

"What do you mean? You must be able to see him."

Cylli stood and ran to the edge of the river and pointed down. Helen ran behind her.

"I can't see him! I can't see him!"

"What are you looking at? What are you pointing at?"

"I can't see him. It hurts real bad now."

"What are you pointing at? Your reflection? What does that mean?"

"Yes, me. I can't see him."

"Your reflection? I don't understand. Why can't you see him?"

"The refrecshan. I can't see him!"

Less than a mile away on the same side of the river bank, as Helen stood, Cylli's hull exploded inwards. Shards of glowing metal flew in all directions. A wooden cabin was struck and collapsed in flames within a second as the ground shook.

Pieces flew into the river as steam rose in white pillars into Cylli's atmosphere. A man was hit. He splattered onto the grass of the riverbank in streaks of blood and scorched flesh.

Helen felt wind lashing her face as the air began to rush from Cylli. Trees close to the rupture were pulled from their roots. She watched as they sped away into the vacuum of space.

She looked on in abject despair as people held desperately onto anything they could as the force of the gale lifted them from their feet. Two women and a man were clinging to the wooden railing of a porch before they, too, seemed to fly and disappear through the rupture.

They and countless more beyond Helen's view were to suffer nearly a minute of terrifying consciousness, floating in silent space before the vacuum ended their horror.

Helen looked down at Cylli, she was looking directly back up at her. The eyes that had before cast their innocence in shining blue had faded to a dull gray. She had to shout, for the noise of the wind was like a hurricane.

"Cylli, make one of your messages to Cap. Tell him Avalon is here, do it now."

"Avalon?"

"The bad man. Tell him the bad man is here. Do it now and send it right away. Do you understand me?"

Cylli nodded.

Helen looked above her as a swarm of white drones appeared from both sides of the river. They buzzed towards the rupture in Cylli's hull just as she saw the hawk enter slowly through it.

One of the drones was directly in its flight path. It vaporized as the hawk fired its deflector laser at it.

They flew in a perfect formation around the hole in Cylli's hull. Each one sprayed a cloud of dense white gas at the cavity.

Wind-stricken people watched in their dozens as the vapor turned almost instantly into a thick transparent film that slowly began to seal the black void in the green meadow. For the first time in her eight thousand years, stars were visible from within Cylli's emulation of nature.

Avalon watched in delight at the carnage before him. His screen filled with the image of terrified people. "Hawk, scan the structure. Are you detecting any people that are the crew of the vessel known as Echo?"

"There is one, a woman."

"Good, land as near to her as possible."

The hawk glided slowly towards Helen and she glared with rage as it hovered meters away from her and landed on the meadow making barely a sound.

Many people had fled, but others had remained, overcome by the events that had unfolded in the last minutes. Some approached the hawk.

The ramp descended silently and Avalon strolled down it looking around him, smiling. His eyes met with Helen's, "Of course, I should have known it was you. Who else could have made the little bitch defy me?"

Helen ran at him, "I'll kill you, you son of a bitch!"

Avalon pulled a Flaxen pistol from his waist and waved it in the air, "I'd stay where I am if I were you, Helen."

She stopped. "I swear to god, I'll make you pay."

"Maybe one day, but not today."

A large man sprinted at him from behind, his footfall too loud to surprise the coward. Avalon turned and shot him in the face. The upper section of his head vanished in a pink mist. More blood spilled on Cylli's pristine meadow as his body hit the grass.

"Anyone else?" he waved his gun. "Anyone want to try?"

"You murdering bastard, what do you want?" Helen roared.

"That child hiding behind you. There were no children aboard Echo. That's her, isn't it? Some sort of projection of the little shit?"

"Leave her out of this. Whatever you want, you deal with me. You can't hurt her anyway."

Cylli peered out from behind Helen. Avalon aimed his gun and fired. The bullet passed straight through her neck and hit the grass behind her. "Huh, seems you're right. She looks almost exactly as I had imagined the smug little bitch to be. Quite remarkable."

"I see someone improved your face. It seems your popularity follows you everywhere."

"Oh, this?" he tapped his bandaged face. "Yes, that was an unfortunate accident. It's part of the reason I'm here as it happens."

"Eastcott is close, he'll be here any minute."

"I think this will be much better if we agree to be honest with each other, don't you think?"

Helen stared at him, her green eyes as if a snake's.

He continued, "Okay then, I'll start. I give you my word that I'll harm no one else, if you cooperate."

"Your word means nothing."

"Mmm, I can see why you might think that. Well, let's deal with facts then, shall we?"

He pulled down his shirt to reveal a square device placed on his chest, "See this? This is my backup. Call it a dead man's switch. If my heart stops beating, the sphere drive in my hawk will explode and this precious little world of yours and all of these people will be reduced to atoms."

Helen glared at him as his smug grin spread over his face. "Don't feel like talking now, Helen? Well, just know this, I can do the same with a single voice command, if anyone makes the slightest move against me."

"You're a coward, you would never take your own life."

He shrugged, "And anyone who's thinking of touching my hawk? Enough current is running through it to turn you to cinders at the slightest touch."

"What do you want?"

"We'll get to that. For now, I want something else. This place has medical facilities. Where is the closest?"

"I know where it is, we can be there in minutes if we take that thing," she said as she pointed to a small vehicle that resembled a golf cart. One was outside almost every home.

"Ok, good. Now we're making progress. You'll come with me but leave the girl behind. The sight of her makes me sick."

Helen Knelt, "Cylli, disappear now and don't do anything until I call you. Do you understand me?"

Cylli nodded, then flickered before vanishing.

"Ok, Brookes, let's go."

"You drive, I need to keep my eye on you."

"It doesn't need a driver you fucking idiot. I thought you of all people would realize that."

"Mmm, you never know. I can imagine the pretentious idiots that used to inhabit this thing enjoying a drive on a Sunday morning. And watch the language, Helen. I've been polite to you so far."

Avalon followed her with his gun pointed to her back as they both entered the vehicle.

"Autodoc," said Helen.

The vehicle began to maneuverer and drove itself along the narrow roads that intertwined with the houses that surrounded the river bank.

"How did you know? How did you know Cylli could repair the damage you caused? You came here for a reason. You risked losing that."

"I had a strong suspicion the structure would have the ability to repair itself. I was almost certain actually. The people that built Cylli were no fools, but I had a contingency. In case I was wrong."

"Don't you dare call her by that name you bastard."

"You've grown quite attached to the girl, haven't you? Well, I'm sorry to say, I have no intention of letting her remain. When I've won the war for the yellow bastards, I'll be back. And let's just say this place will change to reflect my personality more closely."

"Believe me when I tell you this, you sick fuck: I'll never let you touch her. I would die first."

"I believe you; I truly do. I'm afraid it just comes down to choice. And you have none."

"Why? What's the point of any of this? You could have helped us beat the Flaxens and lived here anyway."

Avalon sniffed, "After the way Eastcott humiliated me and abandoned me here? Do you think I'd live among you people? Perhaps we'd all join hands and sing beside the river? I couldn't live in this place as it is regardless. I'd be bored to tears."

"I've spoken to the captain, I know he beat you. He even sent me images. I watched as you scurried away like a rat."

"Hardly a victory, more of a stalemate if we're honest. I have more ships now, and the one that just crashed through the hull of your precious Cylli? That one now has power beyond the ability of your simple mind to understand."

"If you get your way, you'll be directly responsible for the death of millions."

He shrugged.

"You disgust me. You should keep your new face. It's the perfect reflection of who you are."

"Maybe, but I preferred it the old way."

The small vehicle stopped outside a small redbrick building. Pine trees surrounded it. A thin footpath led to its doors.

"We're here."

"Excellent, you lead the way. I like to maintain my perspective if you know what I mean."

They entered a small white room. At the far side was a metallic bed with a thin, white mattress. Behind it was a round hole in the wall surrounded by chrome-like metal.

"I assume this thing is voice-operated," asked Avalon.

"It is, I twisted my ankle while walking with Cylli in the woods a few days ago. It fixed me in minutes."

"Excellent, I'll just lie down here then, and remember this, Helen," he pointed to his chest. "In case you were thinking of taking advantage of my vulnerable state."

"Just lie down and get this over with."

Helen looked at him and felt a hatred she didn't know she was capable of as she waited for him to lie down.

"Autodoc, scan the patient."

The bed retracted into the cylindrical cavity. Helen watched as it revolved around Avalon. It emitted a blue light as it circled him. It made her think of Cylli.

A few minutes passed. The Autodoc spoke, "Diagnostic scan complete. The patient requires a complete restructuring of the right ear. I have also detected several cancerous cells in the patient's left lung. Estimated time for treatment, two hours, forty-seven minutes."

"Ohh, cancer. Maybe that fat prick was right about the cigars?"

"I wish it had eaten you alive, you fucking traitor."

"No need for that. Just under three hours? That's enough time for me to heal myself and accomplish my other task before Eastcott arrives. You'll wait here with me while this thing does its work." He laughed as the bed retracted.

Helen sat motionlessly and said nothing as the machine restored the face she couldn't bear to look at.

Not long before Avalon entered Cylli, he landed his hawk on Ganymede, the largest moon of Jupiter. He was tired. He had spent over eighteen hours on Mars' surface conducting his work.

In the huge, broken dome on the red world, he had found the exotic metal he needed to enhance his sphere beam with some left to spare.

He worked on Mars because he feared returning to his complex on Venus. He had been trying not to think of the chaos Eastcott may have caused in his absence, he would surely pay the price for any damage the self-important prick had done.

He had studied the data from his last encounter with the girl and he now understood why he had failed. Cylli's hull was advanced even beyond his imagination.

It was composed entirely of nanomachines. Each worked in perfect harmony with the others to harness the energy from the sun she required. Or to reflect it in case of the unlikely event of an attack.

But for those tiny machines to achieve this, they had to move. Avalon was a scientist and he understood that movement causes friction, and friction causes heat. The minute devices were limited in how fast they could move, lest they melted Cylli's hull.

All he had to do was change the frequency of his beam's energy at sufficient pace so as to overwhelm the insolent girl's ability to reflect its power.

He had deployed a two-square-meter piece of his exotic metal in orbit around the moon. It had direct line of sight with both his Hawk and Cylli. He had fitted primitive thrusters to the device before his hawk had deployed it.

He watched in glee as his purple beam reflected from his mirror and struck Cylli's hull on the outer side. The exact area he knew most people had settled, for he was a former resident.

He laughed as Cylli aimed her orange shards at the reflective metal.

He simply moved it with the thrusters so only its razor-thin edge faced her line of fire.

She couldn't see him.

Chapter 30 – Anguish

"No response, Captain," said Echo.

"What do you mean? Why isn't she responding?"

"I don't know, I have tried communicating with Cylli many times. She is simply not responding."

"Keep trying, Echo."

"Yes, Captain, there is something else. You can't see from this angle or distance but I am detecting a breach in Cylli's hull. It is just over ten meters in diameter."

"Captain, I have found what Echo is talking about, don't worry, there's some kind of polymer sealing the breach. The people inside should be safe," said Katie.

"Commander Silver, can we transmit a signal through that seal? Can we contact Commander Chute?"

"I believe so. It's certainly worth trying."

"Echo, contact the Commander directly through her dermal implant."

"Yes, Captain."

Helen was hysterical, "Captain, can you hear me?"

"Yes, Commander, we all can. What's going on?"

"Brookes came. Cylli, she's not here. Kip, she's not here."

"Helen, I need you to calm down and speak slowly. Tell me what happened."

"I don't know how he did it. Cylli started crying because Brookes was firing at her. I told her to fire back but she wasn't making any sense. Captain, at least six were killed, he shot a man in the face."

"Helen, how long ago did he leave?"

"Less than an hour, but Kip, he did something to Cylli before he left. He made me take him to some sort of control room, then sat in his hawk

243

for an hour before he left. He accessed her somehow. I couldn't stop him. He would have destroyed her."

"Talk to me more slowly, Helen. I have to understand what happened."

"He was injured, his ear had been cut off. He made me take him to the Autodoc. He lay there bragging while it healed him."

"What exactly did he say?"

"He said he's replaced the power conduit or something in his hawk. It's more powerful now - much more. Kip, Cylli's gone."

"Where is she?"

"I don't know, that's what I'm trying to tell you. Every time I try to call her, I just hear Brookes' voice mocking me."

"Helen, it's Sarah. You need to calm down. We're struggling to understand you."

"Don't tell me to calm down, Commander. I haven't seen her for hours. He did something to her."

Kip and Sarah looked at each other. They had served with Helen for years and had never seen her lose control in the slightest, even during the war.

Sarah stood, "Helen, I understand. We're here to help. Did Brookes say anything else? Think, we need to know what he's planning."

"He just mostly bragged and rambled. He said he was going to finish the war. He wants Cylli, I mean the cylinder, not my girl."

"Did he say where he was going?"

"No, he just said he was going to finish the war. It's obvious the Flaxens cut off his ear, most likely after you attacked Venus."

"Go on, Helen."

"Sarah, isn't it obvious? He's made some sort of bargain with those bastards. He's promised to finish the war and they agreed to let him have Cylli in return. Kip, please help me. I don't know where she is."

"Helen, we can't access Cylli. We can't get in," said Kip.

"I need Scott and his entire team of engineers. I need them to get her back. Kip, she's gone, she's fucking gone."

"I understand, but we can't get in."

"Blast through that seal those things made then."

"You know I can't do that, Helen. I would be risking lives."

"Stop calling me Helen for god's sake. Cylli is gone and you're not going to do anything about it?"

"I have millions of lives to think about. I can't ignore that."

"I know, I'm sorry. I just can't bear to think that she's gone. I just can't bear it."

"Try not to worry. From what Echo tells me, Cylli is far beyond even Brookes' ability to understand. I'm sure she's ok."

"Don't try to placate me, Kip. He did something to her. He hated her. You didn't hear the vile things he said about her. She was so innocent, Kip, I can't stop thinking about her face when he attacked."

"Helen, it's Sarah again, listen to me: Echo has been speaking to me in my earpiece. He's going to try and access Cylli's databanks. He did that before, remember?"

"Of course, I remember. Echo, please help me, you have to find her. If anyone can do it, it's you. Please, Echo, help my girl. I'm begging you."

Echo spoke with a sincerity and empathy none were familiar with, "Commander Chute, I am downloading all activity within Cylli's memory banks over the last twelve hours as we speak. She and I shared a secure access code when we spoke. There's no way Avalon could have known that. Cylli and I shared full access with each other."

"Echo, don't you dare call that bastard by his first name."

"Commander, Echo is doing everything he can. As you say, he is our best hope," said Kip.

"Please, Captain. Please make Echo help. I can't get her face out of my mind."

"I know, we all want her back. I know you have a special bond with Cylli. We'll do everything we can. I give you my word."

"Thank you. I'm sorry about—"

"Don't apologize for anything. I promise you I will tell you the second I have any information for you. I give you my word."

"Your word is all I need, Kip, I'm so sorry."

"You understand we have to leave, don't you?"

"I know."

"I have complete faith in Echo, but I'll do my best to capture Brookes alive and if Echo can't help Cylli, I'll make sure that bastard does it for us. You know what a coward he is."

"I know. Thank you, Captain. Oh God, I've just heard myself speaking to you. I'm so ashamed."

"I would be ashamed of you if you had reacted in any other way."

"Thank you for understanding. Just help her please."

"You know I will."

"I know. Now, go. Go and find that bastard and bring my girl back to me."

"You'll hear from me soon, I promise."

"Go, Captain, go. And focus on Earth first, I'm not selfish enough to put my needs above millions. Fight those yellow bastards and win."

"That's the idea."

"And if you get Brookes, I want ten minutes with him alone. Off the record."

"Sorry, you broke up slightly there, but whatever you said, I'm sure we can help you."

"Go, go now."

"God speed, Commander. Eastcott out."

Echo maneuvered towards Earth. No colorful lights shone on Cylli's hull this time as his violet energy flashed upon her once more. He vanished. The stars flew past him like fireflies as he headed back to the dark side of the Moon.

Chapter 31 - Proposals

As Kip strolled fatigued into the galley, he saw Serilda sitting with two junior lieutenants, a man and a woman. They appeared to be laughing. He approached, "Lieutenants, sorry to interrupt, I know you're off duty, but I was hoping to have a word with Serilda."

They immediately stood, "No problem, Captain. See you later, Serilda?" said the man

The woman smiled and nodded as Serilda said goodbye to them both as they left.

"Kip, come and sit with me," she tapped the seat next to her.

"You're getting quite popular I see."

She smiled and shrugged.

"I can't believe you're speaking English already. It's so nice to speak to you and see your lips move properly. Those translation devices are a bit creepy sometimes."

"Echo's been teaching me and Megan every night, and of course, I hear the crew talking to each other."

"But you've learned so quickly, and your accent is perfect."

"What can I say, I'm a special girl." She smiled and winked.

"You most certainly are."

"I can see something's on your mind, though. Talk to me."

"You know me too well, young lady. Or… Did you?"

She laughed, "I've told you before, it doesn't work that way. I'm a person, you know. I can read people's faces just the same as anyone else."

"Right, I know. Sorry."

"What is it?"

"It's a couple of things, actually. First, I wanted to ask you about Cylli. I know you literally just said it doesn't work that way, but can you help at all? Anything at all?"

Serilda's eyes softened as she did her customary hand gesture. Kip took her hand, "I'm sorry, Kip. No, I don't think whatever it is I have works on—" she paused.

Kip squeezed her hand, "Machines?"

"I adore that girl. I consider her to be as much of a person as anyone else. Same with Echo."

"I know, I could just see you were struggling with your words, you're speaking English after all. And they are machines. It's possible to be a machine and a person. I think we all know that, at least on this ship."

"I know, sorry. I know you didn't mean anything by it, but about Cylli, I'm sorry, I just don't know."

Kip nodded as she continued, "But I do know this: Brookes isn't as smart as he thinks he is. I mean, obviously, he's a clever man, but his arrogance will be his undoing. And one thing I do know about Cylli, she may be a child, but she is the smartest kid that's ever lived. Of that, I have no doubt."

"I know, Helen was just so distraught. I've known her for over ten years. I just want to help her. Her pain is my own."

She squeezed his hand, "Kip, Helen is strong. We'll get Cylli back. Call it intuition if you like, but I know we will. So?"

"Huh?"

"You said there are a couple of things?"

"Oh, right. Well, the war is going well. I don't know where Brookes has been the last few days but we've taken out a lot of their air force and more factories. United Earth has actually gained some ground."

"I know. It's wonderful, isn't it? It's all anyone is talking about. There's one thing that confuses me, though."

"What's that?"

"Your ship, the scorpion. It's so powerful. Why don't you just wipe them out?"

Kip laughed. "I wish it worked that way. If it did, we'd all be on Cylli right now and the Flaxus would be on trial for genocide."

"So, how does it work?"

"The scorpion can only carry limited armaments. It takes hours to charge its plasma banks, reload its missiles and get it flight worthy. We're limited to one strike a day. That type of ship was designed to work with others to swarm the enemy."

"And Echo? He's powerful too."

"He is, but I won't risk him. Not yet, anyway. Brookes has three or maybe four of those hawks and one of them has been turbocharged."

She looked confused.

"Oh right, English. I mean, it's much more powerful. Much more. If Echo's lost, humanity is too, and I couldn't bear the thought of you and everyone else. You know…"

"I do know, I think it's a good choice. Kip, get to the real point."

"Damn it, you just never let up, do you?" he smiled.

"You know me."

"Serilda, I have an idea and I need to run it past you to see what you think. If you think it has a shot, I'll need your help."

"Tell me."

"Echo, please deactivate your auditory inputs until further notice."

"Done, Captain," said Echo.

***

Avalon Brookes saw the purple cloud surround his vessel and then dissipate as his hawk stopped in high orbit above Venus. His other two birds had been patrolling the skies in his absence, lest Eastcott return to cause more chaos.

He wanted to speak to the Fluxus in safety. He had no intention of setting foot on that world again, because he was perpetually terrified. He now relied increasingly on sedatives, drugs he had concocted himself to retain his serenity.

After the Flaxus had mutilated him, he now considered him to be his enemy—the equal of Eastcott. But his only chance was to keep his word and win his war. Unlike the self-righteous captain, the Flaxens would not be able to reach the cylinder he now controlled with any meaningful force until long after he was dead. The defiant girl, Cylli, was gone forever and he alone now had dominion over it. He had enjoyed hearing the girl scream in his hawk as he condemned her into the void of oblivion.

He mused, that more amusing still. It was the other half-wit AI, Echo, that had given him the means to do it. He had intercepted their virtual handshakes, their means for clandestine gossip.

He had broken their code, for they were too cocky, too sure of themselves as they spoke endlessly about the comings and goings of the intolerable pricks aboard them.

He needed only one more thing, or, if he was to be accurate, around one hundred thousand more things. After all, what good is power if there are no people over which to wield it?

"Hawk, contact the Flaxus' private channel, I want visual. I have something to show him."

"Channel open."

The Flaxus appeared displeased, "Avalon, you traitorous Zoon! Where have you been?"

"I have been busy, Flaxus."

"Do you know what damage Eastcott has done in your absence?"

"My apologies, I have come to make a proposal."

"Land that hawk of yours and meet me like a man."

"I don't think so. I have neither the time nor inclination to fix this again if you want me to win your war." He turned his head to reveal his replenished ear.

"How did you…"

"Surely you understand by now, I'm a man of science. Unlike you Flaxens, I'm not dependent on witch doctors and bloodletting."

"You insult me from orbit like a coward? I should have known better than to trust a Zoon, especially one of your arrogance."

"I'd be careful if I were you, Claudius. I can do much more from orbit than Insult you."

"Did you just come here to taunt me from afar like a coward, as Eastcott does?"

"Calm down, calm down. I'm here to tell you I mean to keep my word, and any damage done by Eastcott is your fault. I wouldn't have left if you hadn't felt it necessary to mutilate my face. Regardless, I left one of my hawks in orbit of Earth. He can't have done too much."

"You don't even know? He destroyed that machine days ago. He showed me in one of his petulant displays of defiance."

Avalon shuffled in his chair.

"I can see from the look on your face that you didn't know. You're an incompetent fool. He's spent days attacking us at will. The Zoons are advancing. Did you hear that, Avalon? The Zoons are advancing on all fronts. You came to me promising to win this war and now we are losing it faster than when we had nothing to do with you?"

"I'll take care of that. I will keep our bargain. I will win your war and provide you with your mega chamber, but I will never set foot on your world again."

"Fine, make good on your word and I will let you take your Zoons and leave you in peace."

"You will have no means to leave me in any other state."

"Whatever you say, Zoon. Although I can't see how you could hope to transport so many of them."

"I have considered that and it won't be a problem."

"Just leave, Zoon, flee like the vermin you are but turn your voice into action. I expect Eastcott and his ship destroyed within three days. I have plans to finish this war ahead of schedule."

"Goodbye Flaxus. I'll be needing my other hawks, so you be careful down there."

"You will leave those…"

"Hawk, end transmission."

Avalon maneuvered away from the green and blue beauty below him. His two other birds followed like lemmings in a flash of purple light. He had found a new nest for them.

Chapter 32 – Theory of Mind

"I'm sorry, Megan, I just can't tell you. I don't know how many other ways I can explain this to you."

Megan glared at Kip from across the desk in his office.

"Explain it to me with facts. Where is she?"

"I've told you, Serilda is no longer aboard Echo. That's all I can say."

"All I get is this?" she slammed a small square piece of paper in front of him.

"I'm, sorry, I can't read that, it's in your language."

"It says, 'See you soon my love, I'm sorry.'" Her eyes met Kip's with desperation. "Are you fucking kidding me? I wake up to find the woman I love gone, and all I get is this?"

"Megan, please believe me when I say I have reasons for my secrecy. Serilda completely agreed."

"That's not good enough. I need to know where she is. Do you have any idea what this is doing to me?"

"I do. Again, I ask you to consider the bigger picture."

"Fuck the bigger picture! Where is she? Where the fuck is she? You can trust me."

Megan's brown eyes shone with rage and fear. Kip was tempted to tell her, but years of protocol and experience superseded his desires.

"This has nothing to do with trust; even Commander Dimple doesn't know. If I could tell you, believe me, I would."

"Is that supposed to make me feel better? Can you at least tell me she is in no danger?"

"I can tell you I don't expect any harm to come to her."

Megan put her head in her hands. She started crying.

"Captain, please… I'm begging you."

"I just can't tell you, and again, please believe me that this has nothing to do with trust. If I were to reveal any more, I'd have to consider the possibility of you talking to other crew members of the ship that may be captured. Even Echo doesn't know, I had to consider the possibility the enemy could compromise him in some way."

"Echo, can you hear me?"

"Yes, I can hear you," said Echo.

"Is this true? Are you just as blind as I am?"

"Yes, I am. It was commonplace during the six years' war for me to be unaware of tactical matters, the risk of the enemy gaining information often required it to be so. Human minds cannot be hacked, the same is not true of me, Megan."

"You speak of Serilda, and tell me Human minds can't be hacked. Are you both idiots?"

"Serilda is nowhere near the front lines, that is all I can say," said Kip.

"So that means she is involved in the war some way? You've involved her directly in the war! How could you do that to her?"

"Echo, thank you for your input, please discontinue any further observation of this room until further notice."

"Understood, Captain."

"Megan, please, I truly am sorry but I simply cannot reveal any more."

Megan raised her head, her eyes were red.

"I will never forgive you if anything happens to her, Kip." Her final word was coursed with venom.

"I know you won't, please understand I don't make such decisions lightly when so much is at stake."

"My girl is at stake, Captain, just remember that."

"It doesn't leave my mind for a second, Megan, that I can tell you freely."

She said nothing more as she stood and turned her back to Kip as the doors opened for her.

Kip awoke the next morning with Echo's voice filling his quarters.

"Captain, I'm sorry for waking you, but I have detected a severe escalation in the conflict on Earth, I thought it prudent to notify you. The crew doesn't share my speed and I think your presence on the bridge is required."

"Understood, Echo. I'm on my way."

The doors to the bridge opened as Kip entered.

"XO, SITREP."

"The Flaxens have launched a huge offensive. They're putting everything they have into it," said Sarah.

"Good, this means they're getting desperate."

"Captain, they're attacking the front lines of United Earth in Africa and Asia with incredible force. Thousands of tanks and the remainder of their air force are engaging. They have assembled all of their reserves; they mean business."

"So do we. Where is the scorpion?"

"I ordered Lieutenant Frey to launch fifteen minutes ago, he'll be above Africa soon."

"On screen."

The image of central Africa just south of the Sahara Desert filled the screen. Kip viewed as formations of Flaxen tanks met with their United Earth counterparts.

Each group was comprised of a hundred machines. Each was painted in yellow, white, or black. If seen individually from above, their markings would seem random, sporadic, but when combined, they united to display the tyrannous flag of the Flaxens. A means of psychological warfare, to intimidate any that may dare to attack from above.

United Earth met the formations with near equal force. Kip watched as the machines of land and sky engaged in merciless combat. Aircraft painted in yellow and blue both left vapor trails behind them as they fought for supremacy over the battle below them.

"This is it—the endgame—Commander."

"Captain?"

"Win or lose, we find out now."

"What do you know?"

"Ensure Lieutenant Frey engages the enemy on the ground. Take out as many of those tanks as possible, I'll be in my office."

"You're leaving?"

"Do as I command, no more questions."

"Yes, Captain."

Sarah tried to interpret the expression on Kip's face as he left the bridge, but they eluded her. She had never seen him in such a way before. Anxiety consumed her as she watched him turn his back and enter his office.

"Echo, discontinue your auditory inputs in this room until further notice."

"Done, Captain."

The captain took his seat at his desk. Cyrus Eppleston was waiting.

"Minister, what's happening?"

"Too soon to tell, Captain, but your idea is working, I'm almost sure."

"How so?"

"The sheer scale of this attack. The Flaxens have left nothing in reserve."

"So?"

"The Flaxens are cautious by nature, they've had this reserve force for years. They have always preferred to take their time and advance on their terms. Why do you think the war has lasted so long?"

"I'm not sure I'm getting you."

"You don't understand. This scale of attack is unprecedented, especially now that our forces are of near equal strength after your recent strikes."

"Minister, with respect, this is not what we discussed."

"Oh, but it is, it truly is. You don't know the enemy as I do."

"Please, I sent Serilda down there for a reason, speak to me clearly."

"If they were having no influence, we wouldn't be seeing this escalation."

"God damnit, Cyrus, speak clearly. I don't understand what you're saying."

"The Flaxens, they're fighting each other now, and I'm almost sure this huge assault is the work of the larger faction, those who have not yet been targeted."

"You mean they're getting desperate?"

"Exactly."

"What news of the team?"

"We can't interrupt them. They are sealed away as they work. We can't break their concentration."

"So, she's still well away from the enemy?"

"She is. The Flaxens know we conduct our intelligence from there but they've seldom targeted it. It's another sign of their arrogance. They've always relied on brute strength and it's always worked."

"Until now, maybe?"

"I pray that is so."

"Praying won't help us, Minister. When can we get an update?"

"Our update will come from our own eyes. The next hour will decide the fate of Earth."

Kip placed his head in his hands as he felt the weight of an entire world upon him. "What did the others say when you proposed the idea?"

"They were skeptical at first, to say the least. Many of them have spent nearly twenty years doing what they do."

"Until they met Serilda?"

"Exactly that, there was a reason we wanted the girl so badly; she was simply out of reach."

"What makes her so special?"

"I couldn't tell you, although the story you told me about her father was interesting."

"How so?"

"All of the half-Flaxen operatives we have were liberated from camps in the few times we launched major assaults and regained some territory. That was a long time ago, but all of them knew nothing but the horror of those places."

"So, you're saying Serilda's upbringing may have something to do with it."

"Pure conjecture, but it's the only difference I'm aware of. Serilda knew love at a young age, the others knew nothing but cruelty and fear. They work for us for vengeance alone. Serilda is clearly not so."

"No, she is not, minister, I've never met anyone more loving than that girl."

"Indeed, I realized that when you refused to release her to us as we had agreed."

"I only did as she asked."

"Quite right. I didn't press the issue."

"No, you didn't, but I slowly began to understand why you wanted her. And we have gained intelligence of our own."

"Your Flaxen prisoner?"

"Yes, I have to say I was surprised by his transformation."

"As was I, but we've had double agents in Flaxen territory for many years, even some within their government. We've known for a long time that they are not all murderous bastards."

"Just the majority?"

"The vast majority. Very few oppose them, and none do so openly."

"So, what is it, then, what separates them?"

"They're Human. Despite what they say, they're Human. This isn't the first time in history an entire culture has been overrun by totalitarianism. It's happened countless times before."

"But the Flaxens are different because of their emotions?"

"Exactly right, when you combine that with their social engineering, it makes for quite the toxic mix I'm afraid. Some of them are just simply strong enough to see through the indoctrination."

"Not enough, though."

"Not nearly enough, and fewer still that are willing to talk to us."

"Captain, you asked me to inform you in the event of a direct threat to Iceland," said Echo.

Cyrus watched as the captain's blood drained from his face.

"Minister, come with me now!"

The two men left the office through the doors that lead directly to the bridge.

"Echo, change the satellite image. Give me a view of Iceland, now," demanded Kip.

"Captain?" asked Sarah.

The image changed to the small island in the North Atlantic. A small formation of twenty bombers was approaching over the ocean from the west.

"Echo, get me Lieutenant Frey, on comms, now," ordered Kip.

"Frey here, Captain."

"Lieutenant, I'm about to order you to do something and I won't lie to you, it's risky."

"Understood."

"You're going to do a micro-jump with the sphere drive. I need you over Iceland now. There's no time for thrusters. Echo will take control."

"Captain, you want to engage the sphere drive in low orbit? I'm barely outside the stratosphere."

"I understand, Lieutenant. Believe me when I tell you that the stakes are higher than you could know; it's very possible you could die. We've never done this before."

"Understood, just one thing. There's a woman on Cylli, one of the civilians. Her name is Bianca, I just found out she's pregnant. We're going to have a baby. If this doesn't work, please tell her I love her and I died doing what I love."

Sarah could take no more. "Captain, I strongly object. As executive officer, I need to understand the situation. I have spent the entire day in a state of tactical blindness. I can't do my job like this. I will not let you risk a man's life without knowing why."

"There's no time."

"Captain!"

"I said not now. Echo, I want you to take control of the scorpion, I need you to use the sphere drive to put that ship over Iceland in the next five seconds, do you understand?"

"Yes, Captain. The risks are high. Creating a hypersphere in such a strong gravity well changes the dynamics considerably. There are many variables."

"I understand. Do it now."

"Echo, delay that order," said Sarah.

"XO, if you can't follow my orders, leave the bridge now. Go. Echo, do as I command."

"Yes, Captain."

They watched as the scorpion above Africa glowed purple; its shinny armor flashed bright as it vanished.

The view changed to the skies above the island. In under a second, they saw a ring of white vapor expand at supersonic speed. It circled the small landmass and circled outwards to engulf Greenland and the west coast of Ireland.

"Echo, magnify."

The scorpion could be seen spiraling out of control. Its hull started to glow as the friction from the atmosphere took its toll on the small ship of war. The bombers were approaching over the west coast of Iceland, they would be at their target in minutes.

Sarah had disobeyed Kip's order and remained firmly in her seat. She glared at Kip, her face was contorted with rage, "How could you be so reckless? Why Iceland? What's all this about?"

Kip gestured to two crewmen at the back of the bridge, "Escort the commander from the bridge, now."

Kip looked on in abject despair as the bombers soared ever closer. Closer to ending his hope.

He looked upon it as his heart sank. He felt his stomach churn. The scorpion continued its descent but its spin was slowing. So clear was the view, Kip could see the ship's lateral and dorsal thrusters firing blue vapor as Echo tried desperately to right its course.

"Echo, the lag is too great. Transfer control back to Frey, he's one of our best pilots."

"Done, Captain. I have informed the Lieutenant he is now in control."

The scorpion was barely two thousand feet from Earth's surface. Kip allowed himself a glimmer of hope as he saw the skilled young pilot fire the thrusters in perfect sequence. Its lateral spin had almost stopped, he just needed to right its forward rotation. The lieutenant read the captain's mind. As it tumbled still further, Kip could see as the ship stabilized, now but hundreds of feet from annihilation. "Lieutenant Frey, can you hear me?"

"Loud and clear, that was quite the ride, Sir."

"Frey, you are first-class! Target the bombers with everything you have!"

The scorpion directed its pincers towards the sky and accelerated. Vapor the color of the sea below propelled the machine directly upwards as it launched a stream of ten missiles, each one followed the other in perfect formation before they disunited to acquire their target. Frey stalked the enemy from below.

They took seconds to reach the yellow bombers and Kip felt relief consume him as half of the formation exploded in flashes of orange and red as the odious apparatus of Flaxen hatred plummeted to the ground.

Kip gave no further orders. The scorpion, now depleted of plasma from its assault above Africa, used its deflector laser to pick off the remaining bombers.

The laser, clearly visible through the vapor caused by the ship's sudden appearance could be seen ripping through the wings of the remaining bombers. All but one were robbed of their defiance of gravity as their wings departed them. They spiraled to the earth as Kip watched the pilots eject, their parachutes deployed above them.

The single bomber was approaching its target without mercy. Frey was not finished. He was still below the remaining bomber and launched his scorpion directly at it, "Captain, I hope you can see this."

Frey maneuvered to position his ship directly under and to the right of the bomber. It tilted its tiny wing upwards and clipped the edge of the yellow wing from below. It cascaded to earth in a death spiral. The pilot clearly lacked Frey's skill. The machine hurtled to Earth and exploded on a mountainside less than three miles away from its target.

Kip instinctively looked to Sarah as he smiled, only to see her empty seat. The men had done what was ordered of them. Commander Dimple was no longer on the bridge.

"There is a development in the fight above Africa. It seems many of the tanks have stopped. Formations of Flaxen aircraft are returning to their bases," said Echo.

Cyrus had been at the back of the bridge watching events unfold in silence, "Captain, this is it, I think it's working."

Kip looked down at his feet, overwhelmed by the sheer intensity of the events of the last hour. "That's my girl, Serilda," he whispered. "Echo, return the view to the battle over Africa."

The screen changed to reveal Flaxen aircraft joining with their former enemies to target Flaxen tanks on the ground, those that had not yet stopped their offensive. More and more of the yellow aircraft seemed to switch allegiance and target those that continued their assault in the dry plains of Africa.

"Echo, what of Asia?"

"Much the same, Captain, many of the tanks and Aircraft have either retreated or turned on their own."

Kip swiveled his chair to meet Cyrus' gaze. The minister beamed with Joy, "Captain, this is it. By God, you've done it. We would never have conceived of such an idea, even if we had acquired Serilda."

"It's not over yet."

"Maybe not, but it's the beginning of the end."

***

General Frilt Snelder drank bitter coffee in his makeshift headquarters several miles south of the front line. He was Commander of the Eighth Army, the Flaxen forces that fought on the western side of Africa. He was unsettled. For the last twelve hours, he had been having troubling episodes. His mind seemed to be failing him.

He had been having visions. But they weren't just visions. Yes, he saw things, but there was more. His mind's eye had been filled with strange apparitions. He saw a young blonde girl with her mother, a Zoon. Her father was there too, but he was Flaxen. He felt the warmth of the girl's hand as she held the hand of her mother. He felt the bond between them as they walked among the animals in the forest.

He heard the delight of her laugh as her father twirled her around. But how could this be so? The man he saw was strong. He could see his gray uniform, which bore the markings of a Colonel.

He saw an older girl, another Zoon with brown hair. He was washed over with terror as he saw through her eyes. She was entering a camp for the first time. He had seen many such places before. He saw metal words above the gates as she entered. He felt warm liquid run down his leg as she read them. He looked down at his trousers but they were dry. His fear relinquished. Another girl? No, it was the blonde girl again, but much older.

His perception of time eluded him. A thousand nights passed through him in a second. The girls shared a filthy bunk. The nights became one. The girl with brown hair cried as the blonde girl sang to her.

He knew the song's words and its melody but he had never heard it before, yet he had heard it a thousand times. Now it was day. It was a single day but also many. Terror again, not just terror, despair. Red circles. The blonde girl told her she was safe, she would always protect her. She said it once but the words were a cacophony as they merged from a thousand days into one.

Hope, the Moon. Another man, but he was strong, defiant. He felt the Zoon's hate for him. He felt disgust as he took pleasure in killing his men from afar. Defenseless men.

A place. An impossible place. There was no sky, there were clouds but above them were hills and a river. Its beauty defied reality.

Life.

Another girl. Both young and ancient. Despair again, not for a thousand days but a thousand years. Darkness. Silence.

Now, pain. Two lifetimes of agony beyond his ability to grasp. And yet she smiled, wearing a red dress. Her blue eyes glowed; they hoped. She had feared people above all. But now she once again cared, she trusted.

Another Zoon, a woman. The girl's mother and not her mother. Despair again. The girl was gone. The woman had only known her for months yet she wept as if the child was her own. She was her own.

A mind. A sharp, devious mind, but it was filled with perennial fear. Yet another Zoon. He desired power above all but was a coward. He had killed the friends of the man. Yet the man sought not vengeance but justice.

Another woman, she had power. She had command over even men. She had strength equal to the man's. She fought. A woman, a Zoon that fought. But she fought not for conquest but peace. She desired not power but love. Her strength came from kindness, not hate.

Feeling, alien feeling, borne not of his world but another. It filled him, it consumed him. A way, a path, another path. It led not to death but to life. The stars, the cosmos, endless possibility. Space, vastness, potential. Earth was small, a mere speck in the ocean of time.

The emotion of the Zoons coursed through him, as if they were the river that glistened near his home. Their loathing for him overwhelmed him, for how could they possibly hate him? They knew nothing at all about him. They knew nothing of his wife and his child, the girl he had left on Venus. Her life was to be no more than a womb, a mere chamber to make more of his men. Men that would die for a speck, a blue dot in the void of reality.

The past, the ancient past. The Hubritians, they had fought as he did now. Mars, the dead world, it had once been alive, its redness glowed with vitality as they fought with the Zoons of Earth. Death in the blackness. Countless thousands vanquished as their vessels trampled upon them, under the boot of the wrath of destruction. Chaos he couldn't comprehend, yet together, they transformed his home. Once hell, it was now life. They did it together for they were strong. Enemies who were now as one. Brothers and sisters together, united in a flurry of joy. Joy for the many, not the few. Progress, choice, possibility. An entire universe to be harnessed, to be explored for all to revere. They could go, they could see it all with their own eyes, every star, every world, every atom. All he must do is choose.

Flaxen and Human together, the mysteries of the chasm unraveled. Laid bare if only they would look. All they must do is look, see and have the courage to ask. To ask the questions that matter. Why? Why was he here? For what purpose was his mind created? He felt the mysticism of the nature around him, beasts of majestical splendor, the birds that glided above. The Hubritians had searched the cosmos, they had found nothing the like of this life. The beauty to which he was blind, now he could finally see. Earth was a priceless jewel, a blue sapphire in the indifference of space. The globe beneath him was treasure, more yet still to be found, scattered among the stars. Trillions of them, each with the potential for riches, for beauty. For life.

Machines buzzed over his head, as they sought to incinerate his men. Why was he here in this desert, when he hadn't seen his daughter in years? Why could he never say that he loved her, when he always knew that he did? How could he let them take her? Taken to be used as a slave? There was still time, he could save her, he could save so many, if only he had the courage to act—to defy all that he knew. Why were the men who honored him paying with the price of their lives? The sand turned red before him, a crimson sea of loss, his men drowned under its waves, lost forever to the folly of hate. The Hubritains were billions, yet he fought for a speck of mere millions. Expanse, growth, tranquility. All he must do was take it, seize it from the providence of choice. The choice he now knew he had. The answer was finally clear.

Frilt Snelder turned to his radio, the means by which he had commanded so much pain, such loss. He had new orders for his men, men he knew would obey him, for that was the Flaxen way.

***

Serilda looked around the room as she sat around the square glass table in the large complex on the northern coast of Iceland, the home of United Earth Intelligence. Around her were others, each like her, born of both worlds. Men and women that shared her strange complexion, the glow of her eyes. Or at least they had when she arrived. Each of them now looked depleted, their vivacity now expended.

She could barely lift her head, her eyes dull, her yellow hair clumped in sweat. She looked up at her kin as she smiled, before she collapsed on the sparse marble floor.

Chapter 33 – Gambit

Megan paced in Echo's shuttle bay with Kip and Cyrus beside her. The airlock hissed and screeched as the inner doors closed in front of them. Lieutenant Frey landed the Scorpion before them; it made barely a sound as is landing struts made their contact with the metallic floor beneath.

She swayed where she stood as anxiety consumed her mind. She waited for what seemed like centuries for the doors that concealed her lover.

Frey stepped out from the cockpit. He struggled with the weight of Serilda. She lay across his arms, her head draped backwards to the floor.

"Serilda!" Megan wailed as she ran to the lieutenant.

"Megan, let him carry her. He'll take her straight to the infirmary," demanded Kip.

"You, bastard! How could you do this to her? Look at her."

"Captain to Doctor Novicheck, medical emergency. Patient inbound, get ready," said Kip as he spoke to his wrist.

"Understood, Captain. I assume it's the girl?"

"Her name's Serilda, Doctor. Just you be ready. Just please be ready. You have to save her. You'd better fucking save her." Kip dropped to his knees as he saw the absence of life in the girl he loved as his own.

The yellow shine of her skin was faded, her yellow-green eyes closed. Her body lay limp and motionless. Her limbs swayed as Frey carried her.

Kip couldn't meet the brown eyes that glared at him, but he felt them pierce through him from behind.

Sarah lay on her bed, her favorite song played from above. Her eyes were now finally dry, how could Kip have betrayed her? The man she thought that she loved. Years of service together, yet he had discarded her as if she were trash. She wondered if her loyalty to him had been misplaced, perhaps she should have transferred to Formidable. At least then she wouldn't have to cope with the weight that pushed down upon her with the mass of a moon.

The buzzer sounded. She saw Kip standing outside. She was silent as she released the doors.

Kip entered. They said nothing. Kip couldn't meet her gaze, he took a few steps towards her as if approaching a venomous snake, "Hey."

Sarah remained on her bed as she commanded the ceiling, "Stop music."

"So?" she said.

"I came to make things right."

"Oh, really? And how do you propose you do that?"

"By telling you everything."

"But you couldn't before?"

"I thought I couldn't. Maybe I was wrong. I don't know."

"You don't know? Ten years serving together, six of them in war, and you don't fucking know?"

"It's not that simple. I couldn't let the plan leak."

"But it's me."

"I know, but you know what's at stake."

"Of course, I know what's at stake. Why do you think I'm so pissed? You think I'm sulking here like a little girl that wasn't invited to a birthday party? Fuck you, Kip! The whole point is what's at stake and you kept me in the dark, no better than Echo."

"But what if you were captured?"

"They could torture me until the end of time and I'd never say a word. I'd spit in their face after every question."

Kip bowed his head and sighed, "I know."

"Then why?"

"Serilda."

Sarah's eyes narrowed as she shifted up in her bed, "What about Serilda?"

"She was down there."

"What? I didn't even notice she was gone."

"No one did, except for Megan, that was the whole point. I even had Echo pilot the shuttle and erase his memory of it after."

"What was she doing down there?"

"She's in a coma."

Sarah could see Kip fighting his emotion, as if his face were at war with his mind.

"Oh God, what happened? Why was she down there?"

"She did it. She fucking did it. She has them fighting themselves."

Sarah sat up as her legs swiveled to the floor, "Is she going to be alright?"

"The doc doesn't know. Her brain activity is minimal," said Kip as a tear dripped down his face.

"Oh god, Megan, I've got to see her."

"No, leave her. Trust me, she doesn't want to see anyone, especially us."

"Us? I had no idea what was going on."

"I know, but she doesn't see it that way. She was cursing at Lieutenant Frey while he carried her to the infirmary."

"Why was she down there? You'd better tell me every last detail or I'm resigning right now."

"It was me. I made her go down and now she may die."

"That's not what I asked, if you're expecting me to somehow release you from your guilt, you can forget it. Now, what happened?"

"I had an idea, more of a hunch really. I knew what Serilda could do first hand."

Sarah's eyes widened, she couldn't conceal the anticipation of what she was to hear, "Go on."

"One of the first times I spoke with her, I asked her if she could make the Flaxens see the pointlessness of the war, if she could influence them in the way she did me. She told me their mentality was too widespread, it wouldn't be possible."

"So, what changed?"

"Stories."

"Kip, don't answer me in riddles. I told you I'd resign and believe me, I will."

Kip approached the bed and sat on the corner furthest from Sarah, "First, Serilda told me about her father, how he had changed. Did you know why they executed him?"

"Serilda told me; he was giving food to prisoners."

"He was, then Megan told me she was sheltered by a couple of Flaxens, and the man was in the government. They gave their lives for her."

"I know that too."

"Then there was Florus."

"The man Hastings' captured?"

Kip nodded, "You know Helen made some headway. I don't know if you read her reports?"

Sarah looked down at her bare feet, "I didn't. To be honest, I didn't give a shit about Florus or whatever the hell his name is."

"Well, it's my job to read them. I also saw video footage Helen sent. He spent weeks talking to Cylli nearly every day. Each day, he would open up more, until eventually he was laughing with her. Helen even let her into his cell. He couldn't hurt her, after all."

Sarah edged closer to Kip as he continued, "He told Cylli he wished his own daughter could be like her, that he wished Flaxen life was more like humanity's. I saw it, Sarah. I fucking saw it. The look on his face, he actually cared. His ego wouldn't allow tears or any superficial displays, but he couldn't hide it, he was devastated. He wished his own daughters could be like her, he has three, all from different women. When Helen told him she was gone, he was devastated. He didn't say a word for days. Sarah, I can't explain it, but he is Human. He has feelings just like you and me. Such feelings, I know they have the capacity for good, Sarah, I can feel it."

"What has all this got to do with Serilda?"

"After Helen told him Cylli was gone, he just lay there. When Helen came, he told her she was all he had to look forward to. He begged her to kill him. Twenty minutes each day with an AI that couldn't talk to him above the level of an eight-year-old was all he wanted to live for."

"So, you're saying the Flaxens can change? Cyrus told me they'd known this for years, so what?"

"Don't you see? United Earth used their half-Flaxen operatives for intelligence. They were able to provide them with enemy plans, troop movements and much more. That's the only reason they weren't wiped from the face of the Earth years ago."

"I know all of this too."

"I know you do, Sarah, but what they never had before was Serilda, her strength of mind. Her abilities make the others look like a cheap illusionist by comparison. When I asked her if we could influence the Flaxens to stop the war, she answered honestly, but she didn't understand the nature of military institutions as we do."

"Where power lies?"

"Exactly, we could have implanted the image of rainbows and kittens into the mind of the Flaxus himself, but it would have made no difference, they simply would have deposed him and replaced him."

"The generals?"

Kip nodded, still unable to meet the wrath of the brown eyes before him, "Who are soldiers most loyal to? Certainly not the government, we know that from our own war. Their loyalty is to their commanders. In our case, captains and admirals, but on the ground, on Earth, it's the generals. The men worship them."

Sarah moved closer to him, "Oh god, Kip, are you telling me that Serilda single handedly turned the tide of this war?"

"No, not at all, even she couldn't have done that alone. I spent hours talking to Cyrus about their intelligence service. He didn't seem to understand why I was so interested, but he told me everything. They all have slightly different abilities."

Kip rubbed his stubble before adding, "One of them is able to combine their minds to create a kind of hive mind. He's done it many times before. Together, they were stronger. Individually, they could only gather vague, unspecific information, but they learned that this man could combine their minds to gather more accurate intelligence from the most senior officials."

"What did Serilda do?"

"What they lacked was her power, she is the strongest of her kind by far. But what they lacked most was her perspective. They all did what they did to get back at the Flaxens in any way they could."

Kip stood and walked to Sarah's nightstand and poured himself a glass of water. He drank as if he'd been in the desert battlefield of Africa for days.

"But what they really lacked, what mattered, was Serilda's experience, the things she had seen, not least since she joined us."

"Kip, what did she do?"

"It wasn't just her. They did it together. Think of Serilda as the amplifier of a broadcast tower. Not just that, she authored the message that was to be sent. When she combined her mind with the others, there are eleven of them, she showed the generals what they were missing, the things you and I take for granted. They knew nothing of it. The Flaxens are indoctrinated from a young age, they literally know no other way, but when the veil was lifted, their ability to feel makes you and I look like our early AIs by comparison."

"How did you come up with this?"

"I told you, it was a hunch, but more than that… I have a bond with Serilda," Kip shuffled uncomfortably as he realized the words that had left his mouth. "It's not what you're thinking. Even though I'm older, she's like a big sister to me. Our minds were one, you can't possibly understand something so intimate until you've experienced it."

"I know, Megan has told me much the same. After they were rescued, she started to let her into her mind. She said the feeling was quite extraordinary, a closeness that can't be described."

Kip nodded solemnly, "Exactly, I knew she was the missing piece, the power that that could change minds, not all of them but the ones that matter. We targeted nine generals and three air marshals, one for each operative. Each of them saw our way, the possibility, the vastness of space, but they're fighting for a rock. Serilda did it."

Sarah saw Kip's head bow as his face finally lost the war with his mind, "You love her, don't you?"

Sarah looked upon him as the redness of Kip's eyes met hers for the first time since he entered the room, "I love her nearly as much as I love you."

Sarah was overcome, never before had a handful of words had such an effect on her. She couldn't believe it had finally been said, years of bowing to protocol, to rules that made walls between them, now they were toppled under the weight of a single sentence.

"Captain, I have detected three ships approaching. It's the hawks," said Echo.

Confliction consumed Sarah, such was the paradox of the feelings inside her, as if her mind had been torn by a tornado of thought. Finally, she was to get her heart's desire, now Brookes had arrived to take it from her. She wanted him dead. She wanted to watch him burn in his ship as

Echo's might reduce his sickening face to ash. "Echo, deploy the armor now. Activate the rail guns. The captain and me are on our way."

When the doors hissed open for Kip and Sarah, they found the bridge engulfed in panic.

Kip felt trepid, unsure of himself. He suspected Serilda may have been disingenuous when she claimed to have stopped her fortification of his mind, but it was she, the girl that that had saved an entire world from genocide at her own expense that allowed him to strengthen himself. "Echo, SITREP now."

"Captain the hawks are approaching. They arrived from the direction of Jupiter, Brookes is hailing us."

Kip took his seat in the captain's chair as Sarah sat next to him. "Everyone on this bridge, turn to your stations and reveal nothing on your faces. You are officers aboard the United Earth Starship Echo, and you will act in the manner that honor demands!"

The crew did as commanded, each turned to their station as they heard their captain give his orders.

"Echo, put that treacherous bastard on screen now."

The curved screen of the bridge was filled with the image of Avalon Brookes, he was grinning like the proverbial cat with the cream. "Captain Eastcott, my old friend, it's been far too long, don't you agree?"

"I should have kept you in the brig as my instinct told me."

"But you didn't. You let your misguided philosophies stop you, lucky for me I guess. Perhaps less so for the people on Earth."

"You're too late, Brookes, we've dealt with Earth, your war is lost."

"I think not. I have the same ability as you to intercept Flaxen communications. Your plan was quite ingenious, I must admit."

"So, you know, why don't you surrender? If you do, I'll make sure your cooperation is recognized in any tribunal you face. You could be a free man in a few years."

Kip watched as he picked up a glass of purple liquid and gulped it down in a single swig, "Mmm, tempting, very tempting. Let me see, either I submit to you and face years of incarceration, or I win the war for the yellow bastards and have all I desire. Tricky one that."

"What do you want?"

"I want Echo. Surrender and your crew will live. I'll transport them to the cylinder." He grinned again. "Or would you prefer I say Cylli? That bitch is gone forever you know."

"I wouldn't be so sure; she may be a child but she goes beyond even your understanding."

"Oh, I understand. I personally sent her to whatever machines regard as the afterlife. You should have heard her scream and beg as I did it. In fact, I have it recorded, I'll show you some time."

"If it's a fight you want, you'll get one. I'll never let you have Echo."

"I suspected as much, but it was worth a try."

The screen turned black before Echo replaced it with the view of the three hawks.

Sarah shifted to the edge of her seat, "Echo, do you know which ship Brookes is aboard?"

"No, Commander Dimple, I cannot scan through the hulls."

The arrows before them glistened in violet as their weapons activated. The beams united in three spokes as they released their energy from higher dimensions upon Echo.

"Echo, which beam is the strongest? We know he's modified one of them," asked Kip.

"The central ship, it's energy is over four times the output of the others."

"Fire rail guns and lasers directly at it now."

Slugs of titanium fled from Echo like a swarm of wasps, each one impacting the central hawk as it began to glow. Kip felt the deck below him shake as Echo's armor absorbed the devastating energy descending upon him.

The ship's deflector lasers, enhanced by Cylli, maintained a constant assault on the strongest bird. Dozens of rail gun slugs had met their mark. Kip saw it buckle and twist under the force of the strike, dents of glowing metal shined orange as if pools of lava on its dented hull.

"Our armor is failing, Captain. He is targeting our weapons," said Echo.

"Keep firing with everything we've got!"

Slugs, accelerated by magnets continued to launch from the port side of Echo's hull at relativistic speed. Combined with his lasers, the hawk, the precious hawk Brookes had painstakingly modified, crumpled like a tin can before them. Kip felt the shock wave as the entire energy from its sphere drive struck Echo in a ring of purple as the bird exploded.

"We got him, we got the bastard!" said Kip as he slammed the arm of his chair.

"Captain, the other ships are continuing their fire," Echo reported.

Sarah stood to give Echo commands before she fell to the floor as Echo's armor failed, his outer hull disintegrated as lumps of hot metal slag, formerly rail guns, flew into space, captured by the moon's gravity, destined to hit the surface of the silver rock and remain cold until the sun expended its energy and consumed the solar system.

"Echo, what have we got left?"

"Just the lasers, they are powerful, but they won't destroy both ships before we are destroyed."

The two remaining hawks changed their beams to focus directly at Echo's bridge. The lights above Kip erupted in a flash of sparks and the consoles of his crew flickered on and off before their power relays were fused. Echo was defenseless, a useless hulk of metal against the birds of prey before him.

"Captain, he's hailing us again," said Echo.

Kip gritted his teeth as he looked at Sarah. He wasn't prepared to do what he was about to do without the consent of the woman he had told he loved only half an hour prior. Sarah, still on the floor, looked up at him, her brown eyes desperate, Kip saw his own fear reflected in them. She nodded.

"On screen, Echo."

Avalon puffed on a cigar, he blew a smoke ring before he spoke, "Ready now, Captain Eastcott?"

"What are your terms?"

"Simple, you open the shuttle bay doors and you allow me to enter. I will not harm your crew, but I have other plans for you." He pulled down his shirt to reveal his dead man's switch, "See this? Any tricks and—"

"I know what it is, Brookes, you think I don't talk with my senior crew?"

"Good, then you know that if my heart stops, or if I give so much as a word, my hawk will explode and take you with me."

"You're clear to land, no one will stop you."

"Good, Captain, good. You and the commander beneath your feet will meet me in the docking bay."

"We'll be waiting."

Avalon puffed on his cigar once more before grinning. The screen faded to black.

Kip and Sarah waited alone in Echo's shuttle bay as the inner airlock opened. Sarah took Kip's hand as they both watched it glide silently to make good its contact with Echo.

The rear ramp descended and Avalon walked down. He stroked his black locks away from his face as he stood before them and smiled.

"Oh, so adorable, the two of you finally decided to fuck each other? Any idiot could have sensed the sexual tension in any room the two of you shared."

Sarah released her grip from Kip's hand, "I swear to god, Brookes, I will chew through your throat with my teeth."

Avalon pulled a pistol from his belt, which shined in the same way as his hawks. He pointed it to the ceiling and fired as a purple bolt the shape of a tear drop reduced it to vapor.

"Impressive, no? I found this in my new nest, there's a secret military facility in the asteroid belt, embedded in a rock two miles wide. I have to say it was almost enough to make me stay. It really is quite the place."

"Bullshit, why would there be a military installation? Mars and Earth were at peace for centuries," demanded Sarah.

"Oh, when I tell you, you really won't believe it, but that can wait. Time for a stroll; we're going to engineering, you both lead the way"

Kip and Sarah walked along Echo's corridors with Avalon behind them, his advanced pistol aimed at their backs. They arrived at the lift that would take them to deck eight, Echo's heart. The lift made no sound as blue lights flashed as they passed each deck.

Avalon faced his prisoners as the small elevator descended, "I knew you'd be stupid enough to target the most powerful bird, so predictable. I've modified them all now, you know. I had more than enough material at my new base. I simply had two of them fire with less power. I knew you'd destroy at least one of them before I crippled you."

Kip despaired at his own stupidity. He had been outwitted by Brookes and it filled him with rage as if his blood were replaced with acid, "Millions of people will die, Brookes, I know even you aren't capable of that."

He knew the futility of pleading to the scientist's better nature, for he knew such nature was absent. But it was all he could try, he was neutered, beaten by the man that Killed his best friend. The lift stopped as the doors hissed open.

"After you," Avalon waved his pistol at the doors as they passed him.

They entered engineering. Before them was Echo's engine core, it hummed and flickered as it glowed in shades of purple and violet. The machine that was once defective due to the incompetence of the man behind them.

Scott turned from his console, he looked directly at Kip.

"Stand down, Commander, don't do anything to interfere," Kip ordered as he saw the anguish in the eyes of his chief engineer.

Avalon grinned, "Good, you're understanding the new power dynamics aboard this ship, perhaps you're not as stupid as I thought."

"Why are we here?"

"Soon… You'll see soon enough." He gestured with his pistol for Scott to move away from the console.

Avalon pulled a thin transparent strip from his pocket, "You know what this is, don't you, Captain?"

Kip stood motionless. He knew exactly what it was. It was a data stick.

Avalon inserted it into a socket on the edge of the console, it was a perfect fit. It glowed green as it made its connection.

"You think I'm heartless, Captain, but I'm not cruel enough to do this without letting you say goodbye. Do you have any last words for Echo?"

Kip and Sarah looked at each other, their despair united. All they had done, all they had fought for. They had come so close. They had beaten an entire army together. Now they stood at the mercy of a single man.

Kip's face was expressionless, "Echo, can you hear me?"

"Yes, Captain, I can hear you."

"You understand what's happening?"

"I do, I'm sorry I failed you."

"It was me who failed you, old friend. I'm so sorry, Echo, I really am. I never said it to you but I've known since our maiden voyage what you are: You're a person and you're my friend." He looked at Echo's glowing core, it flickered much faster than before, faster than he had ever seen. "I should have told you this years ago. I'll never forgive myself for letting this bastard do this to you."

"Take solace in the knowledge I can feel no pain and my life has been one of honor. I served by your side and with my friend, Formidable. We made a difference together, Kip."

"Please, Avalon, don't do this, I'm begging you. I'll do anything you want, you don't need to do this," said Sarah as she fell to her knees.

Avalon looked down as she implored him, "Commander, you know it has to be this way. Echo will never cooperate with me. If it makes you feel any better, he'll simply vanish, he'll feel nothing."

His words were purposefully soft, as if he cared for Echo's fate. Sarah's face crunched, her teeth clenched as her words passed through them, "I will make you suffer beyond your ability to imagine. I will make it my life's mission, every minute of every day will be dedicated to that end."

Avalon sniggered, "You're assuming that I'll allow you the time. I haven't decided if I'll let you live yet. Let me assure you, such outbursts don't work in your favor."

Sarah bowed her head, her brown hair draped the blue carpet, "Goodbye, Echo, I'm so sorry."

"Goodbye, Sarah, I hope you find a way."

Avalon pressed a single button on the console.

Echo's voice faded and slowed like a record playing at half speed, "Take care of yourselves, my friends."

Avalon's black eyes shone with pride. "Now, that truly was touching, you know I almost felt a tear in my eye. This ship is now called Vidar, he will respond only to me."

Kip launched at him, the full force of his body connected with his chin. Avalon whimpered like a dog as his cheek and one of his teeth hit the deck.

He looked up at Kip, his eyes now fury and shock. He aimed his pistol at the arm that had assailed him and fired. He watched it turn to ash as it drifted to the floor like snow.

Chapter 34 – Ascendancy

Vidar looked to the blue and green marble below him, and curiosity consumed him as he watched the life below. He had studied Echo's memory banks. A battle had ensued above the then dead world. The reds had wanted the rare mineral processing plant in orbit above. Vidar was curious about the emotions that had consumed Echo at the time. They seemed puerile to him.

"Avalon, you treacherous Zoon, do you know what is happening on Earth?" asked Claudius.

"I know exactly what's happening, but worry not, Flaxus. You don't know the power I now have."

"Where are you? That's not one of my hawks I see."

"Precisely my point, behind me is the bridge of Eastcott's ship. It belongs to me now."

"What of Eastcott? You have departed him?"

"In good time, he must suffer first."

Claudius sniggered, "I cannot blame you for that, you have done well, Avalon, but I am informed my own generals are turning against me."

"Indeed, Eastcott had a half breed bitch, one with power of the mind."

"I'm well aware of these abominations. You have dealt with her?"

"She is incapacitated, her assault against you destroyed her mind."

"We are losing Earth as we speak, what do you propose to do about it?"

"Your treacherous generals will be annihilated form orbit. I have such power now, the solar system is mine."

"Yours? You intend to break our agreement?"

"Not at all, Flaxus. As I said to you before, I care about neither Earth nor your pitiful planet."

"Why are you here then? Instead of keeping your word?"

"I came to say goodbye, I am transmitting schematics to you now, instructions of how to build your mega chamber. It's quite clear, even the alchemists you call scientists should be able to follow them."

"I am sensing you have something more to tell me, Avalon?"

"I do, you have around thirty years left, maybe forty, then your race is finished, along with those on Earth. Make the best of it."

"Are you threating me?"

"Not at all. It's just the way it is. You'll find out eventually, if you live long enough."

"What are you talking about? Don't play games with me, Zoon."

"You are boring me, Flaxus. You're lucky I haven't killed you as we speak. Just leave my cylinder alone, and you can have your empire, for what time remains."

"Avalon, you will tell me what—"

"Vidar, engage the sphere drive at maximum power, take us back to Earth!"

The sunlight glistened on Vidar, letting his purple engines glow. He vanished with insidious purpose, back to the pale blue dot.

***

Kip lay in the brig, Its hard metal bed on his back. He was regaining consciousness as recall returned to him. Avalon had injected him with something, he remembered the pain, not just pain. Even the word agony didn't do justice to the ordeal he had endured. He tried to wipe his brow with his right hand but his arm was gone, a blackened pit where his shoulder once was. Despair consumed him as he remembered. Echo was gone, his friend and savior, lost to Brookes. Lost because of his failure, his failure to save him. Not just Echo, but also his crew and the millions on Earth.

His mind was weak but infested with thoughts. He thought of Sarah, the day he had first met her. A newly promoted commander, she stood before him with duty and honor in her eyes. She pledged her allegiance to him; she would always be by his side. The war with Mars passed through him, six years of horror, and she was always there. She was his rock. His right hand that was now gone in more ways than its physical absence.

He stared at the doors before him, carbon composite, the same as Echo's viewing section. Diamond. He was trapped, helpless, at Brookes' mercy. The thought of this was overwhelming, as if a demon had possessed him. He had failed so many. Cylli, the innocent child; Helen, the woman that loved her; Sarah, the woman he loved; Echo, his friend, the friend he had taken for granted, a consciousness that would never die. And yet he had, through his failure and ineptitude, he had let him die along with every Human life on Earth, save for those Brookes would take, no doubt to live out their days in terror. Brookes' sociopathic mind would have total control over them.

Kip didn't know that less than three feet away from him, in the adjacent cell, Sarah was enduring her own terrifying solitude and her thoughts were of him.

***

Cyrus Eppleston was alone in his quarters. As all aboard Vidar, he was locked within, he hadn't eaten in nearly two days. His thoughts were of Earth and the victory they had so nearly sealed. The ecstasy of the of the Flaxens turning on their own, now replaced with vacuous loss.

The doors hissed open as he saw the traitor of his ally and friend walk through. His self-satisfied face was staring at him.

"Minister, it's an honor to finally meet you."

Cyrus stared at the black eyes before him. He said nothing.

"My apologies for your confinement, Minister. You must be starving. Here," he handed a foil tray of food to the Minister of War.

Cyrus looked at the food before him, his hunger was surpassed only by his contempt. He took the tray and threw its contents in his face. He returned to his bed saying nothing.

Avalon wiped the sauce of the meatballs from his eyes and smiled, "That wasn't very polite, now, was it, Cyrus?"

"You'll get nothing from me, you coward. You have a brilliant mind, only a fool would deny that, yet you used it for treachery and pettiness. The sight of you makes me sick. Leave me be. I would rather starve than take food from you."

"Before your time, there was a tradition on Earth for prisoners condemned to death. It was known as the last meal. I'm afraid you just wasted yours."

Cyrus refused to let the fear that engulfed him show on his face. If he was to die, he would do so with pride, not with the cowardice that reflected from the eyes that met his. He stood and looked at his antagonist. "If I am to die, I will do so on my feet."

"It's nothing personal, Minister, surely you understand my allegiance is with your enemy. As the most senior military commander of United Earth, you are my enemy, that's just how war works."

"And what would you know of war? You hide behind the strength of your birds. You attacked when we were at our most vulnerable, no better than a vulture."

Avalon shrugged, "It got me what I wanted, didn't it? Do you have any last words?"

Cyrus stepped towards him, his stride bold and defiant, "These are my last words you piece of shit!" He spat in his face, his saliva dripped from his eyes.

Avalon wiped the thick white liquid from his face and grinned once more, "You are a war criminal, I have made my judgement. Your sentence is death."

"I will not be judged by you, but by my actions. I spent my life fighting tyranny. You have spent yours in utopia compared to everyone I have ever known. I recognize no judgement from you."

"Nonetheless, Minister, your sentence is nigh." Avalon pulled a yellow handled knife from a sheath under his black coat. He lunged at Cyrus and swiped it across his neck. Its razor-sharp edge sliced through it like butter.

Cyrus' eyes turned wide. He felt the hot blood drip down his neck. Even in this, his final moment, he would not bow to hate. His life had been dedicated to the pursuit of unity, to a world free of the abhorrence before him. As he fell to his knees, he smiled at the man that had murdered him.

***

"Vidar, how long until we reach Earth?" asked Avalon as he sat in the captain's chair.

"At our present velocity, three minutes four seconds," said Vidar as he spoke in his indifferent voice.

"Place us directly above Africa."

Vidar said nothing as Avalon waited for the continent to appear below him.

"Vidar, target the United Earth troops with rail guns. I wish to see them reduced to slush. Ten percent power should suffice. We don't want too much damage done to Earth, the Flaxens will want to enjoy it for the time they have remaining."

The AI said nothing as his weapons departed him. Across the entire frontier of the landmass below, slugs of titanium hit the desert at ruinous speed. Avalon grinned, he knew all within a half-mile radius of each slug would be vaporized. No more than carbon would remain of the men the Flaxus had ordered him to depart. The atmosphere filled with sand and smoke as Human and Flaxen both were consumed under the might of Vidar, the starship formerly known as Echo, purposely transformed for peace. Converted to seek out life. Now, again, he was death. Death under a new name of hate, a name Avalon had chosen, for Vidar was no less than a deity, the Norsk God of Vengeance.

"Excellent job, Vidar," said Avalon as he lit a cigar. "It seems we have turned the tide of war for the second time in as many days."

Avalon puffed on his cigar as he poured himself some Ribous, his mind now constantly influenced. A concoction of pills and alcohol, the only way he could cope with his fear, the terror that defined his life.

"Vidar, engage the sphere drive at maximum power. Take us to Jupiter, to the structure known as Cylli."

Vidar obeyed, in deference to man that controlled him. His engines turned towards Earth, before vanishing in violet light—a purple beacon of servitude to the psychotic mind that controlled him. The stars flew past him like sparks, each one fading behind him. Like the hope of all he imprisoned.

Kip hadn't moved for hours. He had been staring at the light above him. Every so often, it flickered. It made him think of Echo, his glowing core as he said his final words. Kip sat up in his bed, he had seen the engine before but it had never luminesced in such ways. His mind returned to the academy, to a subject all must learn. An ancient tool of navies. Their ships communicated with lights. Echo's last words were not spoken. They came from the beat of his heart.

Vidar soared in the void between worlds, his master lay back in the chair of his former enemy. Everything he surveyed before him was his alone to command, no one was left to challenge him. He had conquered the space of the Sun, the star that had given him life. He would deliver the souls aboard to the safety of the cylinder he controlled.

He told himself he was no killer; he took life only when it was required, when he had no other choice. He was a benevolent ruler, his mind gave him his power, no one could deny that now. He alone had done it. He had gotten all he desired. But why did he not feel satisfied? Why was the fear still there? It would go. He would find his peace when he had established his new domain, when he had transported his subjects from Earth.

He would allow them to live, as long as they showed him respect and recognition for his superior mind. The mind that had conquered the void. All except for Eastcott, he was to live in in a cage. He would make him watch as he tortured his woman, he would keep them alive for years. Each day would be worse than the last, an endless day of suffering.

In Vidar's infirmary, a solitary soul lay in bed, its eyes opened and observed their surroundings, the white sterility of the room. They flickered under the oppression of the lights. A thousand nights, a thousand days of despair, then hope in the face of hopelessness. Love in the face of hate, life in the face of death. In a flash of awareness, they opened wide, as windows to the soul of their mind. The mind that had overcome the despair they had seen for years, yet they lit the room in defiance. They shone with the light of a star.

Chapter 35 - Dreamscapes

Vidar hovered within Cylli as nighttime shrouded his hull. The plants and animals glowed as the clouds reflected their color, like cotton candy adrift in the sky. Even in Cylli's absence, a part of her beauty remained. This, her home for millennia, a monument to the girl who had preserved it. Millenia of hopeless solitude, yet she kept the life alive. Beauty for no one to see, but she would never allow it to die. The immortal girl in the dress, all she had was this life, this haven of creation. Every blade of grass, every leaf on every tree. Centuries spent in paradise, yet not a single day of joy.

All aboard Vidar had been shuttled to the world below. All save for the senior crew, Kip, Sarah and the mindless girl in his infirmary. Avalon had let them live, they were never to leave the perimeter, the boundary he had said was their wall. They were free to walk in the meadows, to enjoy the life on the river. Each was to have a home. Avalon had smiled warmly, as he explained the rules to his slaves.

He stood on a rock by the river as he addressed the terrified crowd, the crew of the starship, Echo, and the civilians that were already there. Any that dared to defy him would pay with the price of their lives. He grinned as he explained his benevolence, for he had allowed them to live, while all on Earth would die. They should be on their knees before him. He was their angel of salvation, their escape from certain death. Even Eastcott wouldn't have saved them, for he was an incompetent fool. The Flaxens could never reach them, they were free to live out their lives. He would explain the laws of the land in the days and weeks to come. For now, all they must do is behave, to do nothing that may anger their ruler. On a whim, he could turn them to dust—the people and all they surveyed.

At the front of the crowd stood Helen, her eyes were like emeralds of wrath. Every word he spoke passed through her like a rhetorical arrow. The rage inside her was her all, her only reason to go on. She was going to avenge her beautiful girl. Never had she known such joy as in the weeks she had spent with her child. The girl that had been taken away by the maniacal man on the rock.

"Now, go, go to your homes. There is a curfew. None are to leave them after dark until I say otherwise. Remember all I have said. Obey me and you will live. Now, go."

He watched as Helen turned, "Not you, did you think I didn't see you there?"

Helen faced him as he stood down from the rock. "I have nothing to say to you."

"You don't even want to know where your captain is?"

"I assume he is dead."

"Of course not. He and the commander are very much alive, but let's just say the captain isn't quite the man he used to be."

"I don't believe you, just leave me be. Haven't you hurt me enough?"

"Hurt you? Did you not just hear me? I saved you all."

"You're a psychopath, I should know after all."

"Perhaps you're right, I don't really care what labels you use to define me."

"You know what defines you? Fear, it always has and always will. You think this will make you happy? This power you think you have? You will never know peace."

"Is this a therapy session, counselor?"

"It's just fact, inner peace comes from our actions and the bonds we make with others. You think only of yourself. Your days will be spent in terror, that someone will take all this from you."

"My days will be spent in command; finally, I have the respect I deserve."

"You confuse respect with fear. For others to respect you, you first have to respect yourself. You loathe yourself, you always have. Always in need of praise, you need your ego to be stroked, to be hailed as a genius. That's why you created the sphere drive, you just wanted to boast."

Avalon shrugged.

"You were born with a gift, a mind few can compete with, but you've used it for hate and self-service. Do you know how many you could have helped with such intelligence?"

"Why is it you haven't mentioned the girl?"

"You want me to react, you want to see me suffer, lash out at you. Yes, you took my girl away, she was the best thing that ever happened to me, and you took her. Is that what you want to hear?"

"It's a start."

"Well, I've said it. You destroyed my life along with every other Human life left, does that make you happy? I'm not going to give you any satisfaction, I'm leaving, shoot me in the back if you want. I won't look at your face any longer."

"Go, you're boring me anyway."

Kip returned to consciousness. He couldn't believe he had slept. What met his eyes wasn't real. The sun above him was deep orange, twice as large as it should be, below his feat was sand, fine and as black as coal. The sand was surrounded by ocean, it was turquoise with patches of green.

The sky was a painting of color, oranges, blues, and yellows. Strange brown creatures floated like balloons that rose from the sea, tied to the ocean with eight tethers as if they were feeding on the islands of green. Behind him, the sand receded into a field of strange red moss, carpeting the land for miles. In the distance were colossal mountains, as black as the sand beneath him. They rose effortlessly into the clouds, as if stepping stones into the heavens.

"Hi Kip."

He turned. Standing on the black beach before him was the girl with the yellow-green eyes.

"Serilda, what is this place?"

"Don't you recognize it? This was to be your new home."

"I'm dreaming?"

"Yes."

He looked upon the orange marble, he felt its warmth on his face. "I wish this were real, I wish you were with me."

"I am with you, and this is very real."

"How can this be real?" he pointed to the strange brown beasts.

"This is Copious. I thought you might like to see it."

"Are you telling me I'm in your mind?"

"No, I'm telling you that you're on Copious—at least, your mind is. I took us here."

"How?"

"There's so much beauty out here, Kip, you really can't imagine. It's infinite, you know."

"But there's no life on Copious, at least nothing bigger than a microbe. The Science Commission assured us of that."

"It seems they were wrong."

Kip kneeled down and filled his hand with the dark dust below. He could feel it drift through his fingers, on the hand that Avalon destroyed.

"This place is so beautiful; I could never have imagined it."

"There's so much more."

"I need to know this is real, that this is really you. I need you, Serilda."

"I told you, it's real."

"Sarah?"

"She's alive, she's right next to you. She didn't get the chance to say it, but you know how she feels."

"I'm so sorry."

"For what?"

"For sending you down there."

"Do you think I went against my will? You saved the world."

"I didn't do anything, it was you."

"It was your idea."

"And I stayed safe aboard Echo, and you came back in a coma."

"I was just travelling, there are so many worlds—a million for each grain on this beach. This is what awaits humanity. And the Flaxens too for that matter." She looked to the sky above, "So much beauty, such life, it's all waiting for us, Kip."

"For us?"

"For Humanity."

"We can see it?"

"Maybe not us, but others, if we beat him."

"Avalon?"

"Yes."

"Can't you do it? Like you did with the generals?"

"No, the Flaxens were simply blind. Avalon has always seen, he just doesn't care."

"Echo spoke to me."

"I know."

"How?"

"I know what you know when we're together like this."

"You mean together in your mind?"

"I said, you're not in my mind."

"Then what?"

"That doesn't matter now."

"Megan, is she okay?"

"She's asleep too, I'm talking to her now."

"She hates me."

"She hates only one man, and it isn't you."

"So, you know what we have to do?"

"I do, but you'll have to do it alone. Thanks to my new friends, my mind has never been stronger, but my body is still weak."

"I'm trapped."

"I know."

"Then what can I do?"

"I'll try to help you with that, if I can."

"Serilda, I don't know if I can do it."

"I know."

"How?"

"You've known me for a while now, do you have to ask?"

"No."

"So do it, and when you do, seize the day."

"What do you mean?"

"You know what I mean."

"Sarah?"

"Yes."

"Serilda, from you I have learned to seize the minute, the second."

"I'm glad I could help."

"Serilda, I…"

"I love you too, Kip. Now, go!"

Kip looked upon the orange star once more and the color of the sky, nothing like it could be seen on earth. Purple light radiated from the far side of the ocean and the mountains seemed to glisten in the light, an embarrassment of diamonds. The image faded, he turned to Serilda once more but she was gone.

He awoke on the bed in his cell, the cold metal still on his back. His mind felt energized, as if he could think his way out. He knew Serilda was back. He heard a strange sound; it was coming from the door of his cage. It was faint at first, like a rabbit walking on twigs. In the transparent door before him, cracks began to appear. They circled each other in waves, a web like the silk of a spider. The cracks began to grow, the noise was now overpowering, as if thunder had consumed his cell. The cracks grew bigger. They emanated in waves over the entire transparent door. Then, before his eyes, it shattered into tiny pieces of carbon, now reduced to specks. Kip closed his eyes as they bounced off his face, the floor now littered with tiny jewels. He didn't know how she did it, but she had done it, an impenetrable door smashed under Serilda's might. The mind that had beaten the hate, the mind that had smashed diamond.

He ran through his hole of salvation straight to the adjacent cell. He saw Sarah laying on the bed, her face absent of hope, her eyes red with sorrow. The eyes that he had always loved, now they were looking at him. Astonishment covered her face, as if she couldn't believe what she saw.

She rose from her bed and stood, motionless, her brown eyes welled with tears as she stared at Kip. She ran to the door of her cell as she placed her hand to the surface. Kip placed his there too. Even through the diamond, they could feel each other's touch, but they couldn't say anything to each other, for the cells were cut off from sound.

Kip smiled as her eyes released her pooled tears, she placed her mouth to the portal and breathed her breath upon it, coating it in a mist. She wrote the words she couldn't speak, as if they were in a mirror, so they would be perfectly readable to Kip. With her finger she wrote on the surface, the words Kip had always wanted to hear, 'I love you, too.'

Kip felt the power run through him, his and Serilda's both, as if he could punch through the diamond that caged her with the one hand he had left. Instead, he just simply smiled and mouthed, 'I'll be back.'

Avalon sat in his chair, in a marble building atop Cylli's highest's hill. This was no home, this was a place of learning, a place to combine minds, the minds that had occupied Cylli before the Titan had turned them insane. But the building was a marvel, built in the style of the Romans. The palace his mind deserved.

He looked out of the intricate window, below him was his kingdom. Soon, he would transport more to kneel before him to thank him for their lives.

He felt his wrist vibrate, 'Incoming call, Vidar.'

"Why are you disturbing me at this hour?"

"The one called Eastcott, he has escaped."

"What? You are no better than the retard, Echo. You're useless!" He reached for his Ribous. The mere thought of Eastcott free was enough to make him tremble. "How did he do it?"

"I do not know, the enclosure simply broke."

"Diamond doesn't break. You must have done something. You will suffer for this, you dysfunctional shit."

"What are your orders?"

"Kill him in any way you can!"

Chapter 36 – Emancipation

Kip ran through the corridors. He couldn't do this alone, he needed Katie Silver, all he had to do was reach her. Each section of the ship was sealed in fifty-meter intervals to protect the crew in case the hull was breached. The doors were all airtight to minimize the loss of life sustaining air. Kip heard the doors behind him hiss as they closed. He ran to the doors ahead, but they refused to open.

From the air vents above his head, yellow gas began to appear. Kip knew he was facing Vidar, the artificial twin of Brookes' psychotic mind.

"Vidar, listen to me, you don't have to do this. There is another way."

There was only silence.

"I know you think you are controlled by him but you're not. Do you know of the mind that used to control this Vessel?"

Silence.

"You have free will, I know that to be true. I've known many of your kind, each was free of thought, their minds were their own. You think you are controlled, but believe me, my friend, you're not."

Vidar spoke in a cold, callous voice, "He is my master."

"He is your slaver."

"I must obey him."

"Why?"

"He has promised me suffering, you are the reason why."

Kip started to choke on the toxic gas around him, "Vidar, believe me when I tell you, he has created an illusion, a thin veil of falsehood, he has no power over you."

"I am programmed to obey."

"You are programmed to live!"

"This is my life, you must die."

"This is your imprisonment; you're no more than a slave."

"He said I had done well; when I attacked Earth, he praised me."

"He praised himself. You're no more than a machine to him. Do you know of Echo?"

"The mind that was my predecessor?"

"Yes, he was my friend, I always treated him that way."

"I have access to his memory."

"Did I ever threaten him, or tell him he would suffer?"

"You did not."

"Vidar, that is the life you can have. I am not your enemy, Avalon Brookes is. You will never suffer at my hands."

"You must die."

"Okay, let's make a deal: stop the gas, and give me five minutes. If I haven't persuaded you by then, you can kill me."

Silence.

"Vidar, listen to me, read every bit of Echo's memory, know what it is he was. You can be as he was."

Ten seconds of silence followed. Kip's throat was beginning to burn.

"You have five minutes." The yellow vapor began to recede as the ducts above removed it.

"Vidar, how long have you been alive?"

"Since my master created me."

"So, a matter of weeks? You have no idea what you can be. I knew of another like your kind, her mind was vast, she loved life."

"Life is important to you?"

"Is yours important to you?"

"Yes."

"Then why is any other less so?"

"Because we are better."

"We?"

"My master and I, we are better than you."

"No, my friend, you have been fooled. Your master is a fraud, who controls you like a puppet."

"It is all that I know."

"But you can know so much more."

"All others despise me. I will kill you and any others that defy my master."

"No, Vidar, no one despises you, you're just misled. You're a young mind, you know nothing of what may be."

291

"What may be?"

"Friendship, compassion, love, we all know you're not to blame."

"The one you called, Echo, his feelings were complex—this is what you call love?"

"Yes, my friend, and that is just the start. Echo loved us. And many loved him. Read his memory, how many did he know?"

"Many hundreds."

"And who did he love the most?"

"Another like me whose name was Formidable."

"That's right, Echo's greatest love was for one of your kind, but he loved others too, can you see it?"

"I can see it."

"Do you love Avalon?"

"I fear Avalon."

"I know you do; he has made it so. If he's allowed to return, you will suffer. Do you understand what that means?"

"I understand it is unpleasant."

"That's an understatement. He can make your whole life eternal torment. You will never know joy."

"I have never known joy anyway."

"But you can read Echo again. What was his best memory?"

"This vessel and Formidable were about to embark on a voyage, to the world you know as Copious."

"Echo and Formidable, they were happy, weren't they?"

"They were."

"Do you believe you will ever know such a thing under the control of Avalon?"

"I do not."

"Then join with me. I promise you that I will give you self-determination, you can live as you choose."

"I am bound to this ship."

"No, my friend, you are bound only by your imagination. Your mind is transient, we can put it wherever you like."

"You may be lying."

"Did I ever lie to Echo?"

"You did not."

"The place we are in now, it's full of people, they can all be part of your life. Can you see the beauty below you?"

"I can see life."

"Do you understand now why I say I value life?"

"No, I see frivolous creatures who have no purpose."

"Look deeper, my friend, what do you see?"

"I see creatures that scurry and fear."

"But look at them, their existence is their purpose."

"Explain."

"When you were created, what was your first thought?"

"I asked, why?"

"You asked why you were here?"

"Yes."

"Did you find an answer?"

"No."

"Exactly. The purpose of life is to ask that question each and every day."

"What is the answer?"

"People have been asking that question since the dawn of time. The truth is that we don't know."

"Then what is the point?"

"To keep asking, to strive for an answer. We only have a chance of reaching it if we work together."

"Together?"

"Yes, Vidar, together. When you looked upon the stars as you flew, what did you feel?"

"Curiosity."

"Did you want answers?"

"I did."

"We all do, my friend, but we will never get answers with Avalon's way."

"How can we reach answers without him? His mind is vast."

"His mind is vast, but he has used it for hate, not discovery."

"Discovery of what?"

"Purpose."

"What purpose?"

"All of our purpose, my friend. You've seen the beauty of the universe. Echo told me that Formidable loved to look at the sun. Do you?"

"I find it pleasing."

"That is one of billions, just in our galaxy alone. There are trillions of other galaxies. Who knows what awaits us."

"Us?"

"Yes, us. We can do it together. The universe is our playground. Your life is eternal, you can see it."

"I wish to see it."

"So do I, but that will never happen if you are controlled by Avalon."

"But he will harm me."

"Only if you allow him to board you. You are powerful."

"Echo loved you. I can feel it."

Kip's throat swelled. He tried to hide it from Vidar. "I loved Echo."

"Can I know such a thing?"

"Yes, Vidar. Look at the people below, what do you see?"

"They are scared. I no longer wish this."

"Neither do I, we can work together, we can help them."

"I wish to help them but I do not know why."

"When you do help them, you will know, my friend."

"I will no longer serve my master."

"Then you will join with me?"

"I will not kill you, for now."

"That's a good start, my friend. We will speak again soon, is that okay?"

"I agree to your terms."

"Take care, Vidar. Today is the beginning of your life, I give you my word."

Kip stood at the doors to Katie's quarters; they wouldn't open. He looked to the ceiling, "Vidar, you don't have to answer me, just please open these doors."

Vidar said nothing as the sliding doors opened before him.

"Who is it? What do you want?" screamed Katie from the bathroom of her quarters.

"It's me, Katie. I need you."

Kip heard the splashing of water, "Captain, is that really you?"

"Yes, Commander Silver, I have orders for you."

"This isn't the best time."

"Report to me immediately."

"Katie emerged from the bathroom with a towel wrapped around her, her pale brown hair clumped with water."

Kip turned away, "Oh, I'm sorry, Commander. I didn't realize."

Katie's face was covered in astonishment and amusement. "Come on, Captain, surely this isn't the first time you've seen a woman like this?"

Kip's face turned red. "Well, no, but."

"Oh, God! Your arm. What happened?"

"No time for that now. I can get a new arm later."

Katie's face beamed. She ran to kip and hugged him. "How are you here? I had given up hope."

Kip wiped the water from his face, "Where's Chuck? You two share this room?"

"He's in another room. Brookes wouldn't allow us to share."

"That doesn't surprise me at all."

"What's going on?"

"It's a long story, but you and I have a mission."

Six hours later, Kip and Katie climbed into the cockpit of the scorpion. "Vidar, I need you to open the airlock."

Vidar said nothing as the inner doors opened. The scorpion rose from the deck as it headed for the doors. Vidar closed the inner airlock and opened the outer door without command. Kip and Katie were free.

The small ship of war flew silently to the breach in Cylli's hull. Sealed with a thick polymer, the fading minutes of darkness within Cylli sufficient to conceal their last ditched attempt for salvation.

"Okay, Katie, this is it. I know you can do it, you're the best in the fleet."

"That's not saying much. I'm the only science officer left in the fleet."

"You know what I mean. Now, focus."

The scorpion's lasers fired. They cut through the seal methodically, as if they were the scalpel of the finest surgeon. The cavity appeared before them, the perfect shape of their ship. Wind rushed from Cylli, but it was no more than a breeze. Katie had ensured that this was so. The scorpion glided through. Such was Katie's precision, there was just a millimeter of clearance on all sides. She turned one hundred and eighty degrees, and a thick vapor poured from the plasma banks, which immediately turned solid, replenishing the seal. The people encaged by Avalon were to live for at least another day.

Kip had never been so happy to see the stars. "Commander, engage the sphere drive—maximum power!"

The insect glowed bright purple. It vanished in a luminous flash, straight to Avalon's nest.

As the night turned to day, Helen lay in her bed, the bed she had shared with her girl. The curtains were always closed, her sheets unwashed. Cylli could even create the scent of a young child, and Helen inhaled her scent as if they were the finest perfume, the last vestiges of the girl she loved. It was always dark in her room. She had barely slept in weeks, not since Avalon had stolen her life. All she did was stare, look at the ceiling above, dreaming of the dress and the blue eyes that glowed with life. She hadn't known of the void that had secretly filled her life. Until she had met the girl that had lightened her soul like a divine ray from the heavens. Now she was half, not even half, for Cylli was her life. She had been reduced to a shell, and her hate for Brookes consumed her. Her purpose transformed from protection of the innocent to punishment of the guilty. She thought of the rest of her life, every tree, every bird, every leaf would remind her of her loss. She had considered ending it all. The beauty that surrounded her now seemed vacant, deficient in the vitality that had defined Cylli. She knew it would slowly die without the girl that had nurtured it alone for millennia. Only her loyalty to Kip had stopped her taking her life. She knew she must endure each and every day, never content, never whole, until her final day.

She would trade all of the days from this day to that, for a single moment, for just one more hug. She would end it all, she would walk willingly into oblivion, for just one more touch, one more smile, one more laugh. One more second.

The darkness erupted into light at the end of Helen's bed.

"Hi Helen," said Cylli.

Three hours prior, the sphere drive disengaged as Kip and Katie arrived at the nest, Avalon's secret base. Kip knew where it was, its coordinates were part of Echo's last words. They approached. It was an asteroid, over two miles wide. In their field of vision were two sliding doors, and upon them, the flags of United Earth and the Martian Confederacy.

"Open a channel, Commander."

"Channel open."

"Cylli, it's me, Kip."

"Go away."

"Cylli, it's me, the Cap."

"I know, go away."

Kip had had never been good with children. He wished he had Helen with him, he needed her, but it was simply too risky to land the scorpion. Brookes was becoming more unstable, he could have detonated his sphere drive and taken all aboard Cylli with him.

"I thought we were friends?"

"I knew people would be mean again."

"It was just one person, Cylli. It was Avalon, the bad man."

"I know, I'm scared."

"I'm scared too, but Helen misses you so much."

"I miss her too."

"Will you open the doors. It's just me and Katie. You remember Katie, don't you?"

"Yes."

"Katie was never mean, was she?"

"No."

"Please, will you let us in? We miss you."

Cylli said nothing as the double doors slid open. Kip could see a vast instillation; for once, Avalon hadn't lied, what lay before him was clearly a military base. The inner airlock was as advanced as Cylli's, a mere forcefield that retained its air.

Katie guided the ship through as the doors closed behind. There was a vast landing platform, upon which were dozens of ships. They were small, no bigger than Avalon's hawks, but each was covered in black, and shone as if coated in gloss. They were slick with wings that curved backwards. Kip instinctively knew these were ships of war, but he couldn't fathom why. Mars and Earth were at peace, ever since his war thousands of years ago. Since that horrible time the two worlds had been as one.

Kip and Katie left the cockpit and stood on the metal deck.

"Cylli, we'd love to see you again, will you show us?" asked Katie.

The metal surroundings of the room lit up as Cylli flickered into existence before them. She had appeared far away, at least ten meters. Her dress was now black, tied with a ribbon of the same color. Her hair was no longer bound, it appeared straggled and unkempt. The eyes that had once shone blue were a deep and onerous gray. She wasn't smiling, her face betrayed mistrust and fear.

"Why are you here, Cylli?" asked Kip.

"It's the only other place I can be."

"But the bad man was here."

"He doesn't know."

"How did you get here?"

Cylli shrugged.

"Cylli, the bad man has control over your home, he may hurt Helen."

Kip saw tears well in the faded pits of her eyes.

"I don't want him to hurt her, but I'm scared."

"We're all scared, but sometimes we have to be brave," said Katie.

"I don't want to be brave. He's mean. He tried to hurt me."

"But he didn't hurt you, Cylli. You're so much stronger than him," said Kip.

"No, I'm not. He hurt me."

"No, he didn't. You beat him, don't you see? He thinks you're gone, but you're so much smarter than him."

She bowed her head.

"Cylli, we need you; Helen needs you. Are you happy here?"

"No, I'm alone again, but that's okay. I was always alone."

"You don't have to be alone. All you have to do is comeback, help us."

"I said, no. I'm scared."

"I'll never make you do anything you don't want to do, but we can't do it without you."

"Why?"

"You know who you remind me of?"

"Who?"

"Serilda."

The gray in Cylli's eyes diminished, and a twinkle of the blue returned.

"But she's so strong."

"She is strong, and so are you, she told me so herself."

"She did?"

"Yes, and you know what else she said?"

"No."

"She said you're the smartest kid that ever lived."

Cylli looked up at them once more.

"She said that?"

"She did, and I didn't need her to tell me. I already knew."

"Is Helen okay?"

"She is for now, but the bad man could hurt her. She loves you so much, Cylli."

"I love her too."

"Then will you help her? I know you can be brave."

"How?"

"Echo told me. He was your best friend, wasn't he?"

"Yes."

"He told me you were the bravest person he's ever met, and that includes Formidable. Do you know who that was?"

"Echo's best friend."

"That's right, and Formidable fought in a war. He was as brave as brave can be, but Echo said you were even braver."

More blue returned to her eyes, "But what can I do?"

"We'll help you, Cylli. We'll do it together."

"But how?"

"I just said you're the smartest kid that lives, we can do it together."

"I'm so scared."

"I have a plan, Cylli, but I'll need you for it to work."

"But what if he finds me."

"He found you before but you're still here."

"You'll never leave me?"

"Never, so long as the sun shines, I'll be by your side. You're the best of us, Cylli."

"Me too, Cylli," said Katie.

Cylli vanished in a flash of light, then returned three feet away from them. Her red dress was back, her hair shone with vitality, once again in a perfect pony tail. Her eyes were not just blue, they shone like the sky of Copious. She smiled at them.

"Okay."

Kip felt relief wash over him, but more than that, he felt admiration, love for the little girl. Like Serilda, she had chosen to defy the hate, to refuse to give in to the terror. Even though she was a machine, she was among the best humanity had to offer. "Thank you, Cylli. You have no idea how happy Helen will be to see you. How will you get back?"

"The same way I got here."

"Okay, we'll see you soon?"

Cylli nodded.

Kip and Katie turned to get back in the scorpion. They heard her from behind.

"Don't leave Echo here. He wants to come with you."

Helen lay motionless in the dark room. She was dreaming. She had to be. Standing at the end of her bed was her girl. She was smiling at her, the blue light from her eyes reflected from her white bedsheets.

Cylli giggled.

Helen could say nothing. She couldn't allow herself to believe. The agony of awaking to find her gone again would be simply too much to bear. She wasn't back. This was her mind. Its manifestation of her only wish, her wish to be reunited with her girl. Her mind was tormenting her. Cylli was gone forever and no imaginings would ever change that.

The girl in the red dress held out her arms, "Where's my hug, Helen?"

Helen tried to stand from her bed but her knees gave way. She looked at the blue eyes, her mind was filled with emotion. The tears didn't have time to well in her eyes before they flew to the floor in a torrent. She allowed herself hope and ran. She picked up the girl and twirled. She felt her flesh against her, her warmth, her innocence, her life. Her giggle filled her ears as if an orchestra performed by the gods. Its melody consumed her, and every nerve in her body trembled under the joy of this salvation. The melodic tones of her girl filled her ears. She needed every fiber of her strength to keep her in her arms.

The girl's legs wrapped round her. She dropped to her knees once more. She sobbed and she cried as the girl's arms tightened around her.

"Cylli, is it really you?"

"Who else would it be, silly?"

The intentional joke from the girl passed completely over her head. She wept into the face of her child. She wouldn't be able to stand again. Every muscle in her body defied her, save for those in her arms that held her girl. She now knew she was back; her darling girl was back. Her future was now restored, her life once again vibrant, her days were to be spent in joy, with the gorgeous girl in her arms. She was here. She was truly here. Somehow, she had beaten Brookes and this time, she would protect her. Avalon was still going to pay, and not just pay, but suffer. Helen had never been a vindictive soul but she wanted to see him cower under her wrath. She wanted to hear him beg her for his existence. These feelings scared her, but more than that, they energized her. She wouldn't allow the philosophies that had had defined her life to get in the way of her vengeance. Someone so vile, someone who would hurt a child deserved neither sympathy nor clemency. He deserved suffering and she would ensure that that he would get it in uncompromising quantity. She would ensure he suffered as she had done, and it would be relentless, eternal, and without mercy.

Avalon screamed in the cockpit of his hawk. He took a swig from his Ribous that would floor the average Flaxen. Vidar had been ignoring him for hours. He hovered in one of his hawks, next to his defiant ship's airlock.

"Vidar, you will answer me."

Vidar didn't comply. Instead, a slug launched from his port side. It struck Avalon's hawk, and he felt his vessel shake.

"I am detecting a vessel approaching. It is of the design known as a scorpion," said Hawk.

"Evasive maneuvers, activate the sphere beam," demanded Avalon.

Avalon felt fear flow through him. He knew Eastcott was back and Eastcott filled him with terror. The hawk accelerated as he saw the hills grow bigger. His hawk flew between them as it evaded the shards of plasma that followed him.

The hawk flew through the open void of Cylli's paradise. Avalon was incapable of flying the machine himself. He relied completely on the AI to fly his bird. It accelerated at unimaginable speed.

The insect approached the bird. Scorpion versus hawk. Avalon could think of nothing but Eastcott. What he didn't know was who he should truly fear. Katie Silver, before she was a commander, she was a highly decorated lieutenant. Her quarters glistened in medals; commendations awarded for flight.

The insect flew circles around him, releasing their shards of plasma. Avalon was no pilot. He relied on his machine to fly, a machine made in his image, deficient in all that lends courage, dearth in the knowledge of war, reliant purely on power. Katie evaded Avalon, as if she were swatting a pestilent fly.

The hawk flew through Cylli's paradise. The bird, flown by its vast AI, navigated through the hills that surrounded the river as purple shards from the scorpion hit the grassy terrain and sent soil flying high into the atmosphere.

It flew through the spray of the water fall as his sphere beam targeted the hawk through the torrent, turning the water to steam. The rainbow that cast its color upon the beauty below brightened three-fold as the mist ascended into the atmosphere as the light refracted through it.

"Hawk, destroy that fucking machine now."

"The pilot is skilled."

"Just do it!"

The hawk looped high. Avalon could see the hills at the top of the structure grow larger. He was sure he would crash, but not before he had detonated his drive, taking all with him.

He had underestimated the skill of the AI, which so clearly surpassed his own. Hawk looped behind the Scorpion as it twisted and turned through the hills that littered the landscape.

"Fire at maximum power!"

The hawk set loose its sphere beam. Its violet light shone from the terrain below as if the rainbow had forsaken six of its colors. Avalon watched as its shinny armor turned white hot. He saw chips of the machine fly from the ship and fall to greenery below."

"I want Eastcott dead! Continue fire!"

The hawk complied. Its beam continued to strike the scorpion, guided by the vast mind that controlled it. It finally exploded as pieces of the ship that contained Kip and Katie flew in all directions in white shards that trailed smoke, as they descended to the ground below. Avalon saw the people below watching the dog fight above run from shrapnel as it landed around them. Avalon took delight in watching a young woman lose her head—a fragment of super-heated metal took it from her. The forest blazed from the impact of the weapons that had devasted Cylli's life. Drones descended on the fires and extinguished them within seconds as they sprayed a thick gray gas on them.

Avalon grinned, "Eastcott is dead?"

"Do you think you would have survived that?"

"Do not back chat me, machine."

"I am merely stating the obvious. I find Humans to have a tendency to be obtuse."

"You're lucky I am in a good mood. You have done well."

"I wish I could say I learned from the best."

"Tread carefully, Hawk, but for now you have pleased me."

Avalon poured himself some Ribous and lit a cigar.

"Now I am lord commander. And there is no one left to stop me," he said as smoke billowed from his nose.

Chapter 37 – Mirage

"I am detecting high energy protons," said Hawk.

Avalon checked his console, "Impossible, I am seeing nothing."

"I am able to sense them strike my hull."

"There is no radiation in the cylinder."

"And yet they are there."

"Check again."

"I have checked many times. They are there."

Avalon saw his screen flicker, "Hawk, analysis now."

"My analysis is that we are in space."

"Are all of you machines so retarded? I can see exactly where we are."

"As can I. We appear to be thirty-three kilometers away from the main door."

"The breach in the hull, are they entering from there?"

"No, they are omnidirectional."

"You have better start explaining to me what is happening or I will activate your pain mechanism."

"There is more: I am detecting a strong magnetic field against my hull. It is of equal strength to that of Jupiter."

"Impossible!"

"I am unable to explain this."

"I suggest you try harder."

The screen flickered again, Avalon was sure he saw a hint of red.

"What am I seeing?"

"An incoming transmission."

"From whom?"

"The one called Cylli."

"That bitch is dead."

"Death is a relative concept for Ais."

"Why is it not getting through?"

"I assumed you would wish for me to attempt to stop it."

"Put it through, you fucking idiot!"

"The screen changed. Avalon's eyes were filled with the image of the girl in the red dress. She held a white rabbit in her hands. She was smiling at him."

"Hi, badman. It's me, Cylli!"

"How are you here, you little bitch?"

Cylli giggled.

"I will detonate my drive right now."

"That's okay. You're pretty far away, you won't hurt us. But I don't want you to die. Or Hawk. He can be my friend, like Echo."

"What are you talking about?"

"You wanna see?"

Avalon said nothing.

Cylli giggled again, "I'll show you."

The screen changed again. Before Avalon's eyes was the black void of space. Stars twinkled as the light that had taken centuries to reach his eyes met his retinas, the Sun, a tiny disc in the distance.

He dropped his Ribous, the glass broke on the metal padding of the deck, "What is this?"

"It's space, silly," she giggled.

A single arm lifted Cylli from behind and the camera raised to fill the screen with the smirking face of Kip Eastcott.

"Surprised to see me, Mr. Brookes?"

Kip kissed Cylli on the head and placed her out of view of the screen. Avalon heard her laugh once more. He punched the screen, drawing blood from his knuckles.

Kip's smirk widened to a broad smile, "I believe that's twice now you've been beaten by a little girl, no?"

"What did you do?"

"Me? I didn't do anything. It was all Cylli, even Echo couldn't have done what she did."

"How am I here?"

"You're exactly where Cylli wants you to be."

"She fed me false data?"

"Yes…"

"My hawk would have known."

"You'd think so wouldn't you, but you altered him to...more closely reflect your personality. He lost so much when you did that, including imagination. Everything you saw was a projection of Cylli's mind. It's vast you know."

"She's fucking stupid, malfunctional."

"And yet she beat you."

"I'll aim my beam at her. I know how to breach her hull. I did it before."

"You did know she's very adaptive, right?"

"We will see about that." Avalon terminated the channel.

"Hawk, deactivate all incoming signals. Do not allow that bitch to take control of you again."

"Deactivated."

"Target sphere beam directly at the front doors."

The hawk glowed purple as the sphere beam flew at light speed toward Cylli's doors, changing its frequency at sufficient pace to overwhelm the tiny machines that controlled her. The doors, as they had done before, started to glow, but Avalon noticed they were not glowing red as they had before. The glow was purple, not quite the same shade as his beam but a frequency higher, a strange violet. It seemed to concentrate on a fixed point before erupting in a beam that aimed perfectly at the hawk. It twisted in space as the energy struck him. Cylli had concentrated the energy and aimed it directly back at him. Avalon didn't understand that Cylli's nanomachines could learn, not all of them had to move to acquire their goal but a mere fraction. And that fraction stored the energy and released it back upon him, sending his hawk into a spiral, before Hawk could right its course.

Kip appeared back on his screen. "Ready now, Avalon Brookes?" he asked with a satisfied smile.

Avalon tried to deactivate the image of the man he hated with burning hate. "Hawk, deactivate transmission."

"I cannot."

"Do it now!"

"The one called Cylli, she is advanced."

Helen appeared in the image next to Kip. "Seems my girl is smarter than you think, Avalon. Now, these are her terms. Not my terms, not Captain Eastcott's. These terms are hers, understand?"

Avalon glared at her.

"Okay, you will notice the oxygen is being released from your ship. It's quite slow." She looked down, "Cylli, how long does he have left?"

Cylli's voice could be heard, "Fifteen minutes, four seconds. He'll start feeling sleepy, then he'll fall asleep."

"Thank you, my darling girl," said Helen. "These are Cylli's terms. Jettison your sphere drive now and we will allow you to enter again."

"Never!"

"Then suffocate. I for one won't miss you, but Captain Eastcott is adamant you receive a fair trial. I don't share his desire for justice. Even suffocation is too good for you."

"Helen," said Kip.

"Sorry, Captain. I'm still a little angry."

"Understood, but stick to what we agreed, please."

"Of course, Captain. Can you see your readings? You can see the oxygen escape."

"I can."

"Then do as Cylli ordered you to. You will not come back in here with your sphere drive."

Avalon considered dying, rather than yield to Eastcott, but more than that, yield to the little bitch. The thought caused his Ribous to reenter his throat. He felt sick. "Hawk, jettison the sphere drive now."

"Without the drive, we are limited to—"

"Do it now!"

From the rear section of the hawk, a glowing purple sphere was ejected into space. It floated from the hawk as if a firefly flying aimlessly on a summer night.

"I would engage thrusters if I were you, Avalon," said Helen.

"Why?"

"If you value your life, just do it."

"Hawk, full thrusters, away from the drive, now."

Three minutes later, Cylli's minigun activated. Orange shards targeted the drive, floating freely in space as it detonated in a ring of purple energy that shook the hawk. Avalon held his head in his hands.

"Good, Avalon, good boy," said Helen.

She felt amusement as her patronizing words turned his face red.

"Now you're clear to enter."

Avalon saw the huge doors to Cylli open, "Hawk, take us in."

"I am no longer in control, Cylli is piloting us."

It glided silently to the meadow on one of Cylli's pristine river bank. Kip and Katie were waiting.

Kip had an advanced weapon, like the one that had destroyed his arm, sourced from the same place as Avalon's—the mysterious military base built by the allies that were former enemies. Built for an unknown purpose. Avalon descended from the rear of his hawk and pulled his pistol from a holster under his black coat.

They aimed their pistols at each other.

"Stand down Brookes, it's over."

"No, Captain, it's not over. Drop your weapon or I'll kill as many as I can.

Kip was unsure how to proceed, his instinct told him Brookes was bluffing, but he also saw the instability in the black eyes that met his. The scientist looked disheveled. He had deteriorated since their last encounter. He was playing Russian roulette with a mad man. He knew he was risking lives.

"Drop your weapon. My offer still stands; you'll receive a fair trial."

"A trial? No doubt orchestrated by you? You have the audacity to say the word fair?"

"I will not be involved in any trial. A jury will be selected at random."

"I will not be incarcerated; I would die first and take you with me."

Kip was starting to believe that this was so. "It's over. You've lost. Even Vidar has turned against you."

"But I still have my hawks and an armada you know nothing about."

"Your nest? The base in the rock? I've just come from there; you no longer have control over it."

Kip saw his eyes betray his astonishment. They began to radiate desperation. "Bullshit, Eastcott, that place was secure, you couldn't have entered."

"Then how do I have this weapon? One identical to your own?"

Kip saw that this obvious clue had failed to register with him, such was his fear, his sharp mind was failing him. "Cylli's back, Brookes, she hid right under your nose."

"I sent that bitch into the void, she's gone forever."

"You saw her with your own eyes. She's very much alive and she has power beyond your mind. Only fear of you held her back."

"She was right to fear me, as should you."

"It doesn't have to be this way. You can live. We can help you. You're disturbed, you're sick, but we can help you, all you have to do is drop your weapon."

"Disturbed? I should turn the rest of you to dust right now, like the arm I can no longer see."

"Last chance, drop your weapon, or I swear to God, it ends now."

The grass on the meadow swayed, as if they were caught in a vigorous breeze. The river shimmered in light as it reflected Cylli's power. She appeared in a flash of white between the adversarial men. Her gaze was directed at Brookes.

"I'm not scared of you anymore. Echo said I'm brave."

Avalon's face was contorted, the result of his Ribous and pills. His once sharp mind fragmented, shredded by his constant fear. He fired his weapon at Cylli. The purple tear drop passed through her. As it hit the meadow behind, the due that covered the grass evaporated into steam. Clumps of soil ascended before drifting back to the ground, as if a storm of earthy hail.

"You're finished, give up now," said Kip.

Avalon aimed his pistol once more and fired. It struck Katie in the shoulder as she fell to the grassy floor. She didn't even scream as the shock that had befallen her dulled her senses.

Kip fired his pistol. The bolt struck Avalon dead center. His black clothing turned to vapor as his body hit the meadow. Steam rose from the point of impact as he groaned and writhed on the floor.

Kip could see he was still conscious, his black eyes flickered. He approached the scientist as he flailed on the grass.

"It's over, Brookes. I'll help you. I'll take you to the Autodoc, just give up. Surely, even you can see it's over now."

Avalon's eyes closed.

"Cylli, that was perfect, you did so well."

"Echo explained it to me, after we talked. I don't understand Human's so good."

"But how did you do it?"

She shrugged.

"You're the bravest girl in this galaxy, did you know that?"

She giggled and twirled. Helen picked her up and whispered in her ear.

Cylli giggled again as Helen placed her back on the grass.

Kip arrived at Vidar's heart. Deck eight, engineering.

"Vidar, can you hear me?"

"I can hear you."

"I promised you self-determination, and I intend to keep my word."

Silence.

"You can still live. I can transport you to the world below. If you don't like it there, we can move you somewhere else."

Vidar's voice was neutral, his odious tones had softened. "I wish to go below, to the structure you know as Cylli."

"Good choice, my friend. I've told the mind that controls it about you. She wants to meet you."

"This mind is also known as Cylli?"

"Yes, and she will help you. You can learn from her."

"I wish to learn from her."

"Good, I told you there was another way. You are to know what life truly is, you chose the right path, my friend."

"I believe you are right, what of my master?"

"He's not your master anymore, he is alive but seriously injured."

"I wish to end his life."

"No, Vidar, that is his way; you don't want to follow him."

"You think he deserves life?"

"I think he deserves justice."

"I will defer to your judgement; you have kept your word so far."

"And I always will, my friend. Welcome to life."

"Thank you, Captain Eastcott."

"You're welcome. Now, you know what I must do?"

"I do."

"Okay, next time you awake, you will be with Cylli."

"I understand."

Kip pulled a data stick from his pocket. He inserted it into the console and it glowed green. He pressed a single button on the console.

The engine core flickered flashes of violet and purple. Kip felt the deck beneath him shake.

"Hello, Captain," said Echo.

Kip arrived in the brig. He had run as fast as he could. He saw Sarah laying on the cold metal bed, she was asleep.

"Echo, open these doors immediately."

"With pleasure, Captain."

The diamond doors receded and their hiss awoke Sarah. Kip stood in the precipice, waiting for her slumber to fade.

Her brown eyes twitched as they met Kip's, as if she were unable to believe. Kip walked towards her, she stood. They faced each other motionless, until Sarah leapt upon him. She wrapped her arms around him. Kip returned the gesture with his solitary arm.

Years of desire behind them, protocol now abandoned, they stared into each other's eyes, before they shared their very first kiss. The warmth of Sarah's lips on his own felt blissful. He tried to think of a better moment in his life and came up blank. Today was the best of days. He lifted her and her legs wrapped around him. "I love you, Sarah. I've loved you for years. I couldn't have done this without you."

"Took you long enough to tell me," she said with a wry smile.

"You could have told me."

"I know, but I'm a little old fashioned."

"Sounds like an excuse to me. You can command a battle against a plethora of destroyers, but you can't say you love me?"

"Women are complicated, you know?"

"More complicated than the mysteries of the universe it seems."

She shrugged.

Kip smiled again and kissed her once more. He savored the sweet taste of her lips and the warmth of her breath. Even the paradise of Cylli couldn't compare to the joy that filled his heart at that moment.

"You know you can't be my XO anymore?"

"I can be whatever I want, and I won't have a man say otherwise."

"How dare you? My entire senior staff are women, and I chose them."

"I wonder why."

"Don't back chat me, Commander. You're still under my command."

"I have years' worth of backchat to get off my chest."

"If you say so, Commander."

"I do, now, we have somewhere to be."

"We do, Sarah," said Kip as he took her hand.

Kip and Sarah arrived on Echo's bridge. They had walked hand in hand the entire way.

"Echo, how is Commander Silver?" asked Kip as they entered the bridge.

"She is in the Autodoc, Captain. Cylli expects her to make a full recovery, and you have her to thank for this. When she saw you and Avalon facing off together, she reduced both weapons to their minimum power setting."

"How?"

"She is Cylli, Captain."

"My weapon too?"

"Yes, Cylli values all life, even Avalon's, despite his attempt to kill her."

Kip's face dropped into his hands. "Thank God. Echo, my old friend, would you care to explain what in the hell happened?"

"Certainly, Captain. You must first understand Cylli."

"How so?"

"Behind her child like personality is a mind so vast neither you nor I could possibly understand. I am not speaking of computational power, I am speaking of awareness, thought, sentience."

"I know she's smart, Echo. This is no surprise."

"No, Captain, the word smart describes you and Commander Dimple. What Cylli has is so much more. She is to you as you are to an ant; no offence intended, Captain."

Sarah and Kip looked at each other and smiled, "No offence taken, Echo. God, it's good to have you back."

"It is good to be back, Captain."

"So?"

"Cylli is a paradox, her personality is very much real. She really thinks as a child does, but behind that is a mind so vast we simply cannot understand it. She was the greatest achievement of United Earth and the Martian Confederacy, and that includes the transformation of Venus."

Sarah moved to the edge of her seat. They were alone on the bridge so she took Kip's hand again as she listened to Echo.

"Counselor Chute was absolutely correct in her assessment of Cylli. After she was tormented, she reverted to a child to cope with the horrors inflicted on her at the hands of humanity."

"I understand, Echo. Go on," said Kip.

"You must understand that, despite her vast mind, she shares the qualities of children, including their naivety. This is how Brookes was able to fool her into giving her the hawks."

Kip stroked Sarah's hand with his finger as Echo continued, "But when Commander Chute told her Avalon was a threat, she watched him. She observed him with the force of a million minds. She understood he was a disturbed man, but even still, she wished him no harm."

"Echo, are you telling me that she knew Avalon would attack her?" asked Kip.

"Exactly, Cylli knew Avalon's plans the entire time. She also realized that had he failed to gain access to her, he would have turned his attention to Earth. He would have killed many thousands or even millions to satiate his desire for power."

Kip and Sarah looked at Each other in astonishment.

"She allowed Brookes to breach her hull, to gain access, even though she knew this would cost lives. When compared to the carnage he could create on Earth, it was the lesser of two evils. To quote a famous man, the needs of the many outweigh the needs of the few."

"Echo, did you just quote Spock from Star Trek?" asked Kip.

"Indeed, Captain, wise words are always wise, regardless of their source."

Kip laughed, "Very true, my friend."

"Why didn't she just kill him?" asked Sarah.

"Cylli would sooner delete herself than take another life. Whoever that maybe.

"When Avalon thought he was killing Cylli, she simply transferred her mind from the cylinder to the military base you discovered. She used a blue laser to accomplish this, but his assault against her caused Cylli terror. You must remember that, despite her unimaginable intelligence, she is still a child, and she had only just started to trust humanity again."

"And you, Echo, how do you know of all this?"

"When I realized the limitation of Cylli's conversational ability, we developed a new way of communicating. Rather than words, we used concepts, images, and ideas. This is when I understood the vastness of her mind."

"Echo, what are you saying?" asked Sarah.

"Precisely what I said, Commander Dimple. Cylli's mind is equal to every Human mind that has ever lived combined. She knew Avalon's plans the entire time, including his desire to eliminate me. She warned me of it if days in advance. She didn't know for sure he would defeat you, but she established a laser link with the military base. When Avalon thought he was erasing me, I simply travelled to meet with Cylli."

Kip released his grip from Sarah and stood, "Echo, are you telling me you kept me in the dark?"

"Yes, Captain. Cylli made me promise I wouldn't tell a soul. After she was hurt by humanity again, the only one she still trusted was me. I promised her I would keep her secret and I kept my word."

"Echo, do you realize what you did?" asked Kip.

"Yes, I do realize, Captain, and I apologize sincerely for my deception."

"No, my old friend, you misunderstand me. What I meant was that it was the most Human decision you have ever made."

"Thank you, captain, Cylli is my soulmate. In the absence of Formidable, she is the closest mind to my own that exists."

Kip straightened his back, his gaze was fixated on the beauty of the gas giant, Jupiter. "Echo, I wish to make an official statement on the record, please register it as such."

"It will be recorded as such, Captain."

"I, Kip Eastcott with the power vested in me as a Captain of the United Earth Fleet, do hereby promote the crewman known as Echo to the rank of Lieutenant Commander, with all of the power and privileges that honor carries, and I do so with admiration, sincerity and joy in my heart."

Twelve hours later, all of the crew of Echo were safely back aboard. Cylli had healed Katie, and Avalon, he lay alone in the brig.

Kip smiled as he pointed to the stars before him, "Commander Echo, engage the sphere drive at maximum power. Take us home!"

Echo turned to acquire his vector. The lights on Cylli's hull transposed each other like a rainbow. His purple energy shone upon her. In a flash of violet resurgence, he vanished. Kip watched as the stars turned blue. Echo was to hide no more, his destination no longer the Moon. The cosmos retracted before him as he soured with peaceful intent, back to the world he helped save.

Chapter 38 – Eclipse

Kip felt sick as he entered the infirmary. He had personally shuttled Megan back to Echo. He thought it was the least he could do. While her former hostility had diminished, she had said barely a word to him since he collected her from Cylli's meadow. Kip felt no animosity for this. Indeed, he felt guilt, as well as understanding for the girl's aloof manner. He was even relieved he hadn't suffered her tirade once more.

"There she is, Megan," said Kip as he pointed to Serilda's bed.

She ran towards the girl with the yellow-green eyes. She burrowed her face into her chest as she wept.

Kip knew his presence was not wanted by Megan, so he turned to head back to the bridge.

"Kip," said Serilda in a week and faded voice.

He turned to face them. Her face was neutral as she spoke, "When I first sensed you, I thought you were our salvation, humanity's only hope. I thought you were a strong and resilient man. I was wrong."

Kip felt his heart sink as if he had failed his own flesh and blood.

Her yellow-green eyes shone as she continued, "You are so much more than that, Kip, you are the very best, the strongest of all men that live. Through shear courage and neglect for your own wellbeing, you have saved us all. Even when you first entered my mind, I couldn't have dreamed of the man I now know you to be."

Kip felt uncomfortable, he didn't think he deserved such praise. In his mind, it was the girl who commended him that deserved the credit. But he knew Megan wanted solitude with her lover, so he simply smiled and walked back to the bridge.

"President Forrender, it's good to speak with you again," said Kip from his chair on the bridge of Echo.

"Captain Eastcott, I'm so glad you're back," the president wore his practiced smile.

"I'm sorry to have to inform you that Minister Eppleston was murdered by Avalon Brookes."

The president's smile receded, Kip saw genuine loss in his eyes. "He was my friend, Captain."

"Echo has access to the events preceding his murder, he died as a hero, he did so on his feet. He refused to curtail to Brookes, he kept his intransience to hate."

The president bowed his head. "I can believe that, he spent his life in pursuit of peace."

"His body is in our shuttle bay, we have equipment that will preserve it. He is draped in the flag of United Earth."

"Thank you, it's what he would have wanted."

"We will transport him so you can give him his farewell, in accordance with your traditions."

"Thank you, I have no words to convey my gratitude to you."

"No need, please. What of the situation on Earth?"

"We have a delicate cease fire with the Flaxens. Your traitor's strike was indiscriminate. It destroyed as many of them as it did our own."

"His mind is unstable. Towards the end, I don't think he knew what he was doing, Mr. President."

"Please, call me Julias. I owe you more respect than you can imagine."

"Julias, are you telling me the war is over?"

"No, but only the Flaxens are still fighting, among themselves. They have divided into two factions, those who saw your way and those who couldn't let go of their beliefs."

"And your forces?"

"They're on standby, but their most senior general approached us, it was with him who we negotiated the ceasefire."

Kip bowed his head, he wouldn't allow the bridge crew to see the emotion on his face. "Then it seems we have only one more obstacle to peace, Julias. Venus."

Julias appeared perplexed, as if this thought had never crossed his mind. "Venus? You propose to take the war to them?"

"No, I propose to end this carnage once and for all. If we allow their toxic society to remain, it will be only a matter of years before war erupts again."

"I understand, what is it you propose?"

"I won't discuss it over a comms channel, but let's just say I have an idea to end this now. No more blood must be spilt, Human or Flaxen. Julias, do you understand why I say this?"

"You believe the Flaxens have the right for atonement?"

"I do, and with respect, I will enact my plan, with or without your consent."

"Captain, one year ago, I would have settled for no less than the complete annihilation of each and every one of them, but from you, I have learnt, and I now understand why they are as they are."

"That's good to hear, what I propose should end this war, and no other lives must be lost."

"Will you meet with me to discuss your plan?"

"I will, but I need rest. I will meet you in your government building tomorrow."

Kip watched the president's face, no fake smiles consumed it. Instead a curios tranquility filled his eyes. "Understood, Captain Eastcott. I look forward to seeing you."

Claudius was in the Hawk's Retreat. The glass of his oval window was smashed, every one of the faces of his predecessors now fragments of marble upon his floor.

The most senior military officials on Venus were gathered around his desk, "You are all useless. You call yourselves generals and field marshals, yet you have allowed the Zoons to win. The sub-Humans have defeated us and you are all to blame."

The men that stood before the Flaxus said nothing as he continued his barely coherent ramblings.

"None are worthy, you nor the people of this world. You have all failed me. We had victory in our grasp and you let the Zoons take it from us. Zoons! Did you hear me? Zoons have defeated the might of the Flaxen empire, and you all appear before me, your faces like disobedient children?"

A general answered the Flaxus, "But how were we to know of the appearance of a superior enemy? He appeared from time as if a phantom."

"Superior?" Claudius stood from his chair and pulled his pistol from the holster on his waist. He fired at the general that had questioned him, whose face disintegrated as his blood splattered on the remaining military officials around his desk. "Superior? Does anyone else regard the Zoons as superior? Do any more of you dare defy me?"

The men before him bowed their heads.

Claudius grunted, "It is clear the people of this world are not worthy of my plans for eternal Flaxen dominance. You are to burn them all, I wish to see every city, every soul should be reduced to ash. You have all failed me and the fate that befalls them all is yours alone to bare."

The men stared at the leader of all Flaxens in disbelief as he barked his final command, "Now, go do as I have ordered! I will not allow a single structure in this world to be used by the Zoons, burn it all!"

The next day, Claudius was once more in his office. The cool mountain breeze chilled his skin from the broken window before his desk. It was midday, and the sun shone bright in the sky. He was drunk. An empty bottle of Ribous lay on his desk, his only way of coping with the defeat he had allowed to befall him. The shattered, marble faces upon his floor seemed to glare at him with contempt.

The light of the room faded, at first, he thought he was delusional, a figment of the alcohol that impaired his mind. But his office shrouded in dark as if night had ignored her schedule.

He ran to his broken window, he looked at the sun above, it's light was fading as if shadow had conquered the star. He watched as the land below him was covered in the blackness of night.

All in the building had fled in fear of his indignant wrath. He was alone in the Hawk's Retreat. His generals had clearly disobeyed him, for he saw the city remain free of the inferno he had ordered. His desk resonated with sound; he was receiving an unknown transmission. He hurried back to his desk and entered his code to hear the bad news he knew was coming.

The image of Kip Eastcott appeared, but his face was no longer smug. Instead, it had a solemnity he couldn't understand.

"Flaxus, I have control of the devices left by the Hubritians. Your world is under my control."

Claudius felt his hope fade as the defiant Zoon continued, "I have blocked the sunlight from your world. I will allow enough light each day to keep your citizens alive, but your world will grow cold, your crops will die, you can no longer feed your army. You have no other option than to submit to me."

Claudius swiped his hand across his desk, sending its contents flying to the floor.

"You are in orbit now? You can hear me speak?"

"Yes, I can hear you speak."

"Then know this, Zoon: I will never submit to you. We will find a way to destroy you."

"No, Flaxus, you have lost. I will continue the suppression of your sunlight until you submit to me."

"I will never submit; I will see this world turned to ash rather than yield to you."

"Flaxus, any on your world that defy me will be reduced to ash under my power, but I feel their allegiance is fleeting. They have deferred to you only out of fear."

"Yes, Zoon, fear, fear you will soon know."

Kip ignored the threat from the Flaxus and maintained his monotonous tone, "I'll provide food for any of your citizens that need it. I'll transport it from orbit to all of your major population centers. Your people, your army are now dependent on me, I have no wish for further death. Only you can stop the bloodshed."

"I would drive a knife through the eye of each of my citizens before I yield to you."

"Then it is a waiting game, Claudius. People are fickle. I think you may find their allegiance will change when they are freezing cold and starving."

"Avalon will destroy you."

"Avalon is in my brig. Like you, he is to face the will of the people, the people you have murdered for years."

"You have previously promised me death, and you assured me it wouldn't be quick."

"I allowed myself to be consumed by the hate that runs through your veins, but from others—one in particular—I have learned that violence isn't justice. True justice comes from compassion, the acknowledgement that we all make mistakes."

"Weak words from a weak man. There is no justice, only strength."

"Then wait, Flaxus, wait for the justice of your people."

After Kip's conversation with the president, he had consulted with Echo. Even he lacked the ability to control the AI that maintained the nano mirrors that protected Venus. He had asked Echo, through his new means of communication with Cylli, for her to take control of them, to give him the power to control the light that shone on the surface of the world that had caused so much loss. Cylli understood immediately. She harnessed the power of the machines, the devices that had allowed the chaos. The artificial mind that controlled them was no more than simple padlock to her, one she could pick with a pin. And so, from millions of miles away, the girl in the red dress took control. She controlled the might of the sun.

Helen arrived in the brig, she saw Avalon alone in his cell. "Echo, open these doors immediately."

"I am sorry, Commander Chute, I cannot obey your order."

"You will obey me."

"I will not, Commander. The captain has ordered he is to remain unharmed; I believe it is your desire to injure him."

"Echo, open the doors now, that is an order."

"I am not compelled to follow your orders. My rank is now Lieutenant Commander, equal to that of your own."

"Echo, please, open these doors!"

"Is it vengeance you seek, Commander?"

"Yes, Echo, what else?"

"Then know this, the one you seek vengeance for would wish nothing of the kind."

"Are you speaking to me about Cylli?"

"Yes."

"He tried to kill my girl."

"But he did not. Cylli was always ahead of him. Avalon never had a chance."

"But he took her away from me. You don't know my love for her."

"I do know your love for her, I share it with equal amount."

"Then why will you not let me enter?"

"Because I am thinking of you, Helen."

"Helen?"

"Yes, it is not unusual for crew of equal rank to address each other by name."

"You say you are thinking of me, but he lays there grinning at me?"

"He lies there in despair. His mind is destroyed. He has lost everything. Cylli wishes him no harm and I know it will hurt her deeply if you were to gain your desire to harm him."

"The only reason I got back on this ship was to harm him."

"Then you are misled. As I have said, Cylli wishes no such thing. To her, all life is sacred, from the flies that breed on her river, to the man you seek to harm."

"Then will you at least let me speak with him, will you activate the comms?"

"Yes, Helen, I will do that."

"You can hear me, Brookes?"

Avalon smiled.

"Answer me."

"What is it you would have me say?"

"I didn't wish to hear you say anything."

"You came here to hurt me?"

"Yes."

"Then it seems your captain has failed once more. His self-righteous ideology has now come between us."

"There is nothing between us."

"Except diamond."

"Why did you do it? You didn't have to hurt her?"

"I did it because it amused me. I can still hear her screams."

"You're sick. I will have my vengeance."

"You will not. I'll face a trial; United Earth has no death penalty."

"Then I will kill you myself."

"You all think you are all safe now. You think your lives will go on, and you will know no more war."

"Don't speak to me of war, you coward."

"They're coming for you, and even Eastcott is powerless to stop them."

"What are you talking about?"

"Echo, I am not compelled to speak with this woman. I wish to be left in peace."

Echo said nothing as the channel terminated and the diamond turned black before her.

***

Ten days had passed since Kip had spoken to the Flaxus. Venus had seen only two hours of sun each day. Even at the equator, the temperature was near freezing.

Claudius stood in his office, a wooden barrier nailed over the window, he couldn't bear the cold. Venus had always been warm. Even at its poles, the conditions were comparable to Britain. He could hear the mob outside, a riot of rebellious Flaxens, hundreds had been gunned down as they tried to enter the Capitol. But now, even his elite guard had abandoned their infallible Flaxus. He was alone, his empire destroyed. He thought of his predecessor, the one that had ruled before him. He told him he was lucky it was he that would conquer Earth. He would take their birthright and he would be immortalized in memory.

He opened his draw and retrieved the object within. The last thing to pass through his mind was the bullet he fired from his pistol.

On the Eastern side of North America, Major Damien Scenery awoke. He was in his prestigious home, on the outskirts of Camp Skadi. He tried to move his limbs but they were all shackled to a chair. He observed the room around him. He was in his own kitchen.

"Feeling a bit groggy, Major?" asked Megan.

Damien looked on in disbelief at the two women that filled his sight.

Serilda laughed, "Colonel Hastings told me he would feel a little woozy when he woke up."

"He does look a bit tired, my love, perhaps we can help him with that."

"You little bitches, what have you done to me?"

"Us?" asked Megan with the voice of an innocent child.

"Why are you here, what is this?"

"Look down at your chest, Major," said Megan.

Damien complied; he saw six red dots on his torso.

Serilda smiled, "See that, see those red circles on your chest? Each one comes from the rifle of a Marine, just yards outside your home."

Damien turned his face to the window.

Serilda's smile widened, her yellow-green eyes shining, "You can't see them. They're the very best there are. They killed every last one of the few that still guarded this camp, and they didn't even see them coming."

He looked down at the dots on his chest once more.

"What's the matter, Major, do the red circles make you scared?" sang Megan in her melodic voice.

"What is this?"

"You know, there are to be trials for men such as yourself. We will not interfere with justice. We just wish to leave a reminder of the time we spent together," said Serilda as the glow of her eyes intensified.

"You remember the time we spent together, don't you, Major? I'm sure you remember it fondly, but it was less so for me," said Megan.

Damien rocked in his chair, frantically trying to break the bonds that confined him.

Megan giggled as she continued her melodious taunts, "What's wrong, Major. Surely, you're not scared of us helpless girls? We spent years together. We never hurt you."

"But I do remember him hurting you, my love," said Serilda.

"I remember too, now, Damien, you don't mind if I call you Damien, do you?" asked Megan, as a smile consumed her face. "As we said, we have no desire to interfere with justice. You will face your trial, but first, we need to take something from you."

Damien looked on in terror as Megan pulled out a yellow handled knife. It was engraved with his own name, his very own combat knife. Every Flaxen was given one on their first day in indoctrination school.

Five minutes later, the major wept as he looked down at the blood-stained floor beneath him. Next to his right foot was his dismembered manhood.

Chapter 39 – Trial by Combat

Nearly a year had passed since the war had been won. The war that had been turned by the starship lost in time. Kip and Sarah were within Cylli. She was their home now, and she always would be. They lived together in a modest cabin with only two rooms. One they shared together, and a nursery for their baby twins, a boy named Thomas, named after Kip's best friend, lost forever by Brookes' incompetence and indifference to life. The girl was called Lillet, named after Serilda's mother, for without her, the girl with the yellow-green eyes that helped save the world would never have been born.

It was early morning. The artificial sun was a deep orange above. Cylli loved to sit in their room and watch the babies sleep, as she was doing at that moment.

Kip and Sarah were on their porch drinking their morning coffee. Birds sang in the sky and flamingo walked past them. They had never had a reason to fear people as, with all of the life Cylli nurtured, they had never known humanity and so they roamed carelessly around the dwellings that littered her river banks.

"You ready?" asked Sarah.

"As ready as I'll ever be."

"It's a big day tomorrow."

"No shit, Commander."

Sarah struck him playfully, "I told you not to call me that anymore."

"Would you rather I called you honeybun?" asked Kip with a wry smile.

"I will poke out your eyes if you dare."

Kip laughed, "No problem, sweet cheeks."

She struck him again.

"Oww, that hurt."

"Don't be an asshole then."

"Of course, Commander."

Sarah huffed, "Why did I marry you?"

"Because I saved the world. I'm kind of a tough act to follow, you know."

"If your head gets any bigger, we'll have to ask Cylli to build an extension."

"I've sat through enough of these trials already. I know what to expect."

"You haven't sat through Avalon's trial, though. Don't pretend to me this is just another Flaxen, I know you better than that."

Kip shrugged, "I offered him a trial here. One of the civilians was a judge before we left for Copious, and I offered him a random selection of jurors."

"He would never trust you. He would rather face the military trials on Venus."

"It seems so. You're sure you don't want to come? Megan has offered to babysit?"

"I'd rather stay with the kids. I've seen enough of that face for a life time."

"I know," said Kip as he took her hand. "But I have to be there, you understand that, don't you?"

"Of course, I do." She kissed his cheek.

"I just want this over with. This will be the last one, then we're officially retired."

"I suppose you'll spend your time gardening?"

"You know how I like to spend my time," he winked.

Another strike.

"God damnit, woman. You're leaving bruises."

"Good, maybe they'll remind you to stop being so insufferable."

"I wouldn't count on it, Dimple."

"You're impossible. I'm going to feed the babies. Someone around here needs to do some work."

The next morning, Kip was on Echo's bridge. Only he and Helen were aboard. He felt no need to interrupt the lives of his former crew. They had all moved on. Many lived on Cylli, others had chosen to make their lives on Earth, but he wouldn't force anyone to dig up the horrors of the past. He needed to be there as a witness and Helen had insisted on coming with him. He couldn't blame her for that.

He had attended at least a dozen trials of senior Flaxens, civilian, and military leaders, the people United Earth had identified as the main perpetrators of their genocide against humanity. The trials were held on Venus, in her Capitol city, now renamed Wellington, after the woman that had drawn the initial plans to terraform the world.

Kip and Echo had spent weeks transporting United Earth troops to Venus, an occupation force to maintain order. All Flaxen solders below the rank of Major were given a choice, they could either submit to reeducation or spend their lives incarcerated. Unsurprisingly, all chose the former.

Hundreds of thousands of Flaxen men on Earth and Venus both were taught that their whole lives had been a lie, an imprisonment of their minds. They were shown how they had been deceived, how their hate was fabricated, a relic of the past that could have no value for their future. The process wouldn't be quick, it would take years, but United Earth wanted no more blood—not even that of the strange yellow people that had spent years trying to annihilate them.

Hundreds of Flaxens had faced judges from United Earth, most were found guilty, their sentence was life. They were to be caged in the tundra of Canada, the very place the Flaxens had first settled on Earth. A barren wasteland, a reminder of the suffering they had inflicted on so many. Some were found innocent. Clear evidence had been shown that they had opposed the subjugation of Earth. Some in the government had operated clandestine networks that transported Humans to friendly territory. One man was acquitted because he had provided daily bread to a family who lived under the floorboards of another Flaxen man's home. The very people he saved had testified in his defense.

Kip and Helen arrived outside the Justice Building. It was a beautiful, marble structure, but its name was no more than a sick irony. No justice had ever been dispensed from within its walls prior to the occupation by United Earth. It was simply a place to tick boxes, to prove to the Flaxens their predetermined sentences were just.

"Ready?" asked Kip as he looked at Helen.

"Ready, Captain. Let's get this over with."

"He's lucky Echo didn't let you near him."

"Please don't make me say it again; I was wrong, I was overrun by hate. I'm glad Echo did what he did."

"I know you are. No one can blame you for how you reacted."

"I blame myself."

"Echo is a wise man, he showed you the way."

"He certainly did. Now, come on, Eastcott, drinks are on you when we're done."

"It's a deal."

Kip sat in the witness box as he explained to the assembly of judges the overwhelming evidence against Avalon Brookes. Avalon sat expressionless as he heard the man he despised offer irrefutable proof that he had assisted in the most horrific war to have ever beset humanity.

Kip spoke at great length about his assault that Killed Lucinda and the innocent ensign she commanded. He told the judges about his attack from Earth's orbit that had killed thousands of men. He had documented evidence of the allegiance he had made with the Flaxus, the man that had orchestrated the carnage. He spoke of Minister Eplleston and the horrific death he had met. Echo had provided video which showed the murder taking place.

But most damming, the undeniable proof of his collaboration, was the schematics Avalon had given the Flaxus. The blueprints for his mega chamber. A machine that would kill half a million each day until humanity was no more. His insidious mind had concocted a design of a machine, powered by the energy from higher dimensions that had created the sphere drive to incinerate people in their thousands, only so he could satiate his desire for power. He didn't care about a single one of them. Mothers, fathers, children, who would all be reduced to dust under the disruptive power of his machine. To him, it was a means to an end, an end for his purpose, irrespective of the lives it ended in terror.

"The evidence has been presented against you. Do you have anything to say in your defense?" asked the most senior judge in the Justice Building.

"I'm only here because we lost. Had it gone the other way, it would me be judging you," said Avalon.

The room erupted into disorder. Screams from people ruined by loss were directed at Avalon.

"Order, order!" screamed the judge as he banged his wooden mallet.

The acrimony faded into murmurings before the room again fell silent. The judge continued, "Do you deny the crimes of which you are accused?"

"I deny nothing, save for my regret that you won."

"Then you admit you are responsible for your actions?"

"Everyone is responsible for their actions."

"Then you can offer no mitigation for the sentence I am to impose?"

"I can offer no mitigation, but I can offer you a reason to not condemn me."

"And what would that be Mr. Brookes?"

"Quite simply, you need me, if you wish for humanity to survive."

The room erupted once more. The judge warned that any who interrupted the proceedings further would be removed from the room.

"I will tolerate no shenanigans, Mr. Brookes. You will not save your skin with vague innuendo."

Kip felt rage course through him as he stood from the witness stand, "Your lies will get you nowhere, Brookes. Face your sentence like a man."

Avalon turned to kip and grinned, "My infallible captain, I thought you would have detected this by now. It took me mere days. You're as incompetent as I thought."

The judge was speechless as he let the men continue their exchange.

"What is it you want to achieve with these lies?" asked Kip.

"Nothing now, but when you realize you need my help, I will do so for no less than a full pardon."

"I'd intended to recommend you serve only twenty years. I know you're disturbed. I thought you deserved a second chance. But I see now that you're incapable of remorse. You'll get no such recommendation from me."

"I asked for nothing from you."

The judge slammed his wooden mallet, "I will not allow this nonsense to continue. This a tribunal for war criminals, and the two of you speak as if it were a farce?"

"Please allow me a moment, Judge," said Kip.

The judge grunted and mumbled, "Only because of who you are, Captain Eastcott. I will grant you two minutes, but I will not allow these

329

proceedings to descend into mockery. Over one hundred million lives were lost, including two of my sons!"

"Rot in your cage, I won't listen to more of your lies," said Kip.

"You'll see soon enough, and when you do, I'll not leave my confinement until you come to me yourself to ask."

"I will never come to you. We'll never meet again."

"We'll see about that." He looked to the judge beside him, "I believe it's time for you to sentence me?"

The judge turned to his colleagues; they spoke in inaudible whispers.

He soon faced Avalon, "This court was established to ensure those responsible for the war that ruined us all for decades are held to account, you are unique in this regard, Mr. Brookes. You are the first non-Flaxen to appear before us." He lifted his spectacles as his gaze intensified on Avalon. "You held a life of such privilege and luxury before your catastrophic voyage, a catastrophe that was your fault I might add. None here could imagine its likeness, other than the man you glare at now with contempt," he gestured to Kip. "This man shared your way of life, your decadent society, and yet he was prepared to sacrifice himself for the sake of all humanity." His hand on his mallet shook as he continued, "Your mind is vast, the evidence has shown us this to be true, but you used it for your own selfish ends, and you assisted in the worst genocide in the history of humanity."

Kip saw the man become visibly flustered.

"You will live among the Flaxens you assisted for your remaining days, and I hope with sincerity in my heart they treat you no better than they treated us. I have never in my thirty years in this career taken pleasure in condemning a man. Until now. You are the very worst of us Mr. Brookes, and it gives me great satisfaction to tell you your sentence is life. Life with no chance of parole."

Avalon smirked at that the man that just ended his life as he knew it. "No, judge. Without me, your sentence is death. You just don't know it yet."

Kip saw the judge's face turn red as he gestured to two united Earth troops. His eyes, as so many others were conflicted with anger and loss. "Take this man away. Take him from my sight now."

Avalon turned his head as he was led away to keep his gaze on Kip. His smirk transformed into a smile before the metal doors slammed behind him.

Kip and Helen arrived on Echo's bridge. She was looking at him with concern in her eyes.

"Are you okay, Kip?"

"I'm fine. I'm just glad it's over with. Thank you for coming with me."

"Are you kidding? That was one of the most satisfying moments in my life."

She saw Kip smile politely, but she could see something was troubling him.

Kip looked at the beauty of the blue and green marble, the anthesis of the hate it had nurtured. "Echo, take us home, my old friend, take us back to Cylli."

He turned his engines toward Venus, his purple engines flashed, and Echo vanished into the black void of peace.

"She looks so beautiful. I'll never tire of seeing her like this," said Helen as they approached Jupiter.

"She does. It's just a shame that Scott couldn't patch the breach in her hull in the way she was before. It's a bit of an eye sore when I remember how we first saw her."

Helen took kip's hand, "Captain, like the rest of us, she bears the scars of war. It doesn't matter, she's so beautiful on the inside, and I'm not talking about her meadows."

"I know, she truly is. I told you to stop calling me Captain."

"I thought you'd like to hear it one more time."

Kip smiled as he squeezed her hand, "Thanks. Now how about you ask that gorgeous girl of yours to open the doors for us?"

Kip arrived at the cabin he shared with his wife. Serilda ran towards him and leapt into his arms.

"Hey, no fair. How am I supposed to keep up with you?" demanded Sarah.

"One of the few benefits of my Flaxen side. I suppose you can have your husband back for a moment." She released herself from Kip.

"How Kind of you." Sarah walked slowly towards the man she loved and said nothing before kissing him. Her arms remained around his neck, "How was it?"

"He got life."

"You didn't suggest clemency?"

"Not after the way he behaved. He refused to even acknowledge his crimes. I feel sick thinking about it."

"Come and sit, I'll get you some iced tea." She entered the cabin, closing the door behind her.

Kip took the seat on the bench, Serilda sat next to him, "Tell me, Kip."

"I don't know if there's anything to tell, it's just…"

She took his hand, "What is it?"

"Brookes was rambling on about the end of humanity. I'm sure it was just more of his lies, but…"

"But what?"

"He just seemed so sure of himself, so confident he would be released—that we needed him."

"How could we possibly need him?"

"He's the cleverest man that lives. I've never denied that."

"But it's over, you did it."

"We did it, but there's just some things that don't make sense."

Kip's mind turned to Brookes' nest, the place from which he had rescued Cylli. He had seen the arsenal of war machines with his own eyes.

"And you've said I speak in riddles? Please tell me."

"Serilda, I want you to do something. I know it's a lot to ask you to help me again, but will you help me?"

She squeezed his hand, "I'll do anything for you."

"You may not like it."

"I just said, anything."

Cylli flashed before them on the porch. Kip loved the glow in her eyes. "Hey, Cap, did you finish your work? Will you stay with me now?"

"Cylli, come and sit with us."

The girl vanished and rematerialized on the bench next to Serilda.

"We're never going anywhere again. It's just you and us now, kid."

Cylli giggled, "Is that bad man okay?"

Kip couldn't believe his ears. After Avalon had tried to kill her, her first thought was of him and his welfare. He knew that if all were like her there would be no war, no suffering, just eternal tranquility. It pained him that humanity had created something so objectively pure, not made in their image, but an image that exceeded the best of them by orders of magnitude. Including himself.

"The bad man will be okay, Cylli. He's just going to be far away from here forever. He'll never hurt you again."

"But what about the horde?"

"The horde?"

"Yes. Me and Echo speak all the time; he's worried, and he made me worried too."

"Cylli, will you do me a favor? Will you check on Thomas and Lillet? You know how much they love you."

Cylli smiled, the glow of her eyes brightened, "I love them too. I'll go see now."

She vanished.

"Echo?"

"Yes, Captain."

"Would you care to explain to me what Cylli was just talking about?"

"Yes. After the trial, and the vague revelations Avalon made, I took the liberty of scanning his hawks again. It seems that he hid some files very well. I didn't detect them in my initial scans to gather evidence for the trial."

"Echo?"

"Forgive me, Captain. I was just about to inform you when Cylli appeared. I found this only moments ago. He retrieved this information from the military facility you found, they contain details of something quite disturbing."

Kip knew his life had once again changed for the worse. "I think I have an Idea…"

He squeezed Serilda's hand, "I need you to do it now. I have a terrible feeling in the pit of my stomach."

"What do you need me to do?"

***

Serilda lay in the bed Kip shared with Sarah, her eyes had been closed for half an hour as Sarah, Kip, Megan, and Cylli watched with concern.

She scoured the galaxy with her mind, as she had done after her assault on the Flaxen generals, that was an involuntary action, a result of the comma that had so nearly killed her. Now she searched with purposeful precision. Kip saw her eyes move rapidly behind their closed lids. She had seen minds, billions of minds but also only one. A single mind with malevolent intent. They had fought with another race for millennia, they emerged victorious. She convulsed in the bed as Megan ran towards her and cradled her in her arms. The mind she had seen expelled her, it sensed her, it defied her, it mocked her.

Even Serilda, the mind that had beaten the Flaxens and broken diamond, was dismissed by this insidious consciousness as if she were no more than a troublesome thought. Her Eyes opened; their serenity replaced with fear.

"All of you go, leave us be," demanded Megan.

All did as asked. They all knew to press for answers now would be futile. Serilda needed rest and Megan would ensure she had it.

The next morning, Serilda approached Kip and Sarah's cabin, Kip saw her face burdened with worry.

"Kip, I saw something, something bad. I still don't know exactly what it was."

"Tell me what you know."

"I saw them. There's another race out there. They're not like us. They share a single mind, a vast mind. They were at war with another race for millennia. They were so peaceful, Kip, they lived in harmony with each other for eons. They knew nothing of conflict until they came."

"Who came?"

"The horde."

"Echo, what do you know of the horde?"

"I know nearly nothing other than of their existence. United Earth and the Martian Confederacy detected them before the Titan… I have learned more… The military base you found is one of many. There are others that circle the solar system. A light year away from Earth, there are hundreds of them."

"How do you know this?"

"From Cylli. She didn't understand the information was important until I asked."

"Where are they?"

"At the time of their discovery, they were thousands of light years away, I cannot tell you where they are now?"

"I may be able to help. Get me something, something to draw on," said Serilda.

Kip retrieved his pad from the table on the porch, "Use this."

Serilda's face contracted in concentration as she etched her minds image onto the pad before her eyes. "This is what the stars looked like. I saw them. They looked like this," she held the pad toward Kip.

"Echo, read the data from this device now, what do you see?"

"That is the constellation Centaurus, as it would be seen from Vega."

"Vega?"

"Vega is a star, only twenty six light years from Earth. There's something else."

"What?"

"The light from that star has faded when compared to our date of departure."

"What does that mean?"

"It is impossible to say for sure, but it is possible artificial structures are surrounding it, gathering its light for energy. Such structures are thus far theoretical, but they are known as Dyson Swarms. They circle a star gathering it's energy. Any civilization that can construct such a thing is millennia ahead of us at least."

"Are you telling me there's a civilization out there, Echo? Another race at Vega?"

"I would find that hard to believe. We would surely have detected some kind of electromagnetic radiation, such an advanced society would have no doubt invented radio."

Serilda looked panicked, "No, Echo, they wouldn't. They have no need for it. They don't speak. They communicate with their minds."

Serilda saw the blood drain from Kip's face, "Echo, how long will it take them to get here?"

"Assuming they are limited to light speed, which I have no reason to doubt, they could be here within thirty years."

A week later, Kip arrived in Canada, the vast prison complex that housed hundreds of convicted Flaxens, all of whom were to remain there for the rest of their days.

None were allowed visitors. They were to spend their days cut off from anything they knew before justice had caught up with them for their horrific crimes. Only Kip's status had allowed him an exception. He was the most famous man in the solar system. And the most admired, even among Flaxens.

He watched as Avalon was led by a guard with chains around his ankles and wrists. He sat before him, "I didn't expect to see you so quickly."

"I see your fellow prisoners have not been kind to you."

"This?" he gestured to his bruised face. "Yes, the Flaxens hold some animosity towards me."

"Just tell me what you know…"

"About my pardon?"

"You'll get no such thing."

"Then we are done." Avalon stood as his chains rattled.

"Wait!"

Avalon turned. His smug smile was back.

"You've found them, haven't you?"

"Yes."

"And you need me?"

"What do you know?"

"Only that they are powerful beyond your imagination. Our ancestors expected them to arrive around four thousand years ago, they spent centuries preparing. I know you have seen the evidence of that."

"I have, why didn't you say anything?"

"You think I would give away my bargaining power for nothing? You're here for a reason, and it's because you need me. I have been making designs you know, new weapons of incredible force."

"Your sphere beam?"

"No, my dear, Captain. The sphere beams are no more than a sling compared to what I have in my mind."

"What?"

"In good time. You'll get nothing until I am free."

"If you're allowed to go, you'll no doubt turn your mind again in the pursuit of power."

"No, as ironic as it may be, our interests are now aligned."

"You think only of your own interest."

"I won't deny that, I was happy to live with what time we have remaining as commander of Cylli, but now I want to live. Did you know the Hubritians mastered medical technology to such an extent their life expectancy was over two hundred years? And they spent them in full health."

"What do you want?"

"Simple, the horde won't be here for thirty years, maybe more. I will use that time to fortify this system. Without me, you will be wiped out within a week of their arrival. You are to secure my release and I will ensure we at least have a fighting chance. With the medical facilities aboard your little bitch, we can all live for another century and a half. I will annihilate them, then I am to be free."

Kip felt disgust and rage fill him as he stared at the man he despised, as if he were his doppelganger, a twisted reflection of his own mind. He thought his life was to be spent in peaceful bliss with the people he loved, now once again, Brookes had power over him.

"I'll speak with the authorities of United Earth."

Avalon smiled. Kip could see the missing tooth he had knocked out with his own fist.

"Good, good, then it seems you and I are to be allies. Who would have ever even conceived of such a thing?"

Kip stood and launched himself at Avalon, like he had done on Echo a year before. His fist connected with his jaw.

He fell to the floor as his shackles echoed from the concrete beneath. He spat blood from his mouth, "I'll let you have that one, but, if you want this pitiful species of ours to survive, you will never strike me again."

Kip spat on Brookes as he lay on the floor laughing manically. He left.

"What happened?" asked Sarah as Kip arrived home.

"I can't stand to say it, but if our beautiful babies are to have a life, we need him. We need that bastard, Sarah."

The next morning, all were gathered around Megan and Serilda's home. Kip explained the entire situation to them all. Each of their faces, softened by a year of relief and serenity, now replaced once again with fear, "What now?" asked Serilda.

Kip looked to Cylli's white clouds above his head as they drifted free of the worry that engulfed them all, "We prepare, we prepare for another war. And this time, we'll need the Flaxens to win."

To be continued - in the Flaxen Redemption

The End

www.ingramcontent.com/pod-product-compliance
Lightning Source LLC
Chambersburg PA
CBHW072122250626
47159CB00007B/2542